MOONDOG
FOREVER FREE

A novel by

Thomas Trock

Thanks to:

Special thanks to the Lord Jesus Christ for saving my soul.

~~~

My beloved wife Jenny, whose love and patience are beyond amazing.

~~~

Rebecca Coursen for her insight and editing skills, and for making me a better writer.

~~~

The students at Victory Christian School, whose input proved both valuable and entertaining.

~~~

And for all the wonderful dogs the Lord has given me through the years. My life is richer because of them.

Chapter 1

"Is he the one?" asked Tysius. "The one hiding under that pile of leaves?"

"Yes, he's the one," replied Fleytius.

"Hmm…"

"You were expecting someone else then?"

"Oh no, it's not that. He's – he's just so young."

"He is that," agreed Fleytius. "At least in earth time. But in many ways, he's a bit older than he looks. I've seen him before in my coming and going. You'll understand what I mean when you meet him, which I think you may do shortly. You've seen his companion as well?"

"Indeed. Yes indeed." Then Tysius turned to his friend. "Sometimes I don't know exactly what's coming next, and that is certainly the case now, isn't it?"

Fleytius nodded as he put his powerful hand on the golden hilt of his sword. He drew the heavy weapon skyward, the sound of the blade reverberating from its sheath. "I must be off now. There are battles on many fronts."

The smaller yet burly angel drew his weapon and held his blade up against Fleytius' sword. "For the King!" cried Tysius.

"For the King!" echoed Fleytius, a shower of multicolored sparks encircling them as it cascaded from their swords.

In an instant Fleytius was gone.

Chapter 2

Joseph and his companion watched in silence as five of the deer – three does and two fawns – disappeared into the yellow and orange brush toward the northeast. From under the leaves atop the small knoll, Joseph felt the reassuring warmth of his buddy on his left as they lay side by side on their stomachs. The aroma of damp earth mixed with the autumn leaves just under his nose. Joseph filled his lungs with the evening air and closed his eyes for a moment. *Remember, remember.*

From their vantage point Joseph and his friend now gazed at a large buck several yards behind the other deer. The buck lifted his big head and pointed his wet, black nose high to scent the air. Joseph noted that the buck spent more time doing this than the other deer, and that he looked about with an air of guarded confidence. Even so, Joseph saw that the buck took smaller steps than the does, keeping his feet under him, ready to dart off in any direction at a moment's notice.

A small piece of dried velvet suspended from the buck's antlers caught Joseph's eye as it hung down and swayed slightly in the cool evening air. The buck walked close enough that both Joseph and his companion saw his chest expand as he took in a deep breath. As the deer crossed the creek below them, Joseph strained his ears to hear his hooves on the rocks, the clatter almost obscured by the rush of water sliding past the black stones. Neither Joseph nor his friend moved as the buck slipped up the hill and into the brush toward the fading light. Joseph kept his head on his hands and took in another deep breath of the fragrant air. *Maybe, just maybe, we'll get to see him this time.*

Next to Joseph lay Moondog. His right shoulder rested against Joseph's left, his golden-colored head down on both front paws, eyes alert and bright, and ears up beneath the pile of leaves. Suddenly, Moon saw movement toward the southeast and let out a quiet breath. "Hafoof."

Joseph saw the gigantic buck a moment later and softly breathed his command to be still, barely audible to Moon lying only inches away. Even with Joseph's finely honed observation skills, the massive buck seemed to materialize out of nowhere.

Joseph sucked in his breath. *This deer is even more magnificent than I thought!* Joseph squinted and willed his sight to cut through the fading light of the autumn evening as he tried to count the tines on the antlers. *Seven or eight points on one side and at least that many on the other, perhaps more. The tips of those tines look as white as ivory.* Joseph deliberately blinked to help clear his thinking. *The beams of those antlers look thicker than my wrist, and there are drop-tines at the end of each beam that make them look almost like stars. This animal is enormous. He looks like he's from another planet!*

The two camouflaged spectators watched the buck amble downhill toward the creek in front of them. Joseph observed how the tremendous animal continued to look back over his shoulder and from side to side as he came. *This guy knows things are safe in front of him,* thought Joseph. *The smaller buck and other deer are out in front and will warn him of any danger from that direction. That's why he let them go first. The breeze is behind him, so he can smell any danger from that direction long before the threat ever reaches him. He's in no hurry. You don't get to be the biggest deer in the woods by being careless.*

Joseph and Moon watched in astonishment as the big animal seemed to float across the ground in front of them. Although much heavier than the previous buck, Joseph never heard the sound of his hooves on the rocks as he crossed the creek. The buck stopped and turned to his left. He then looked directly at Joseph and Moon as he studied the landscape. The massive deer stood only ten yards from them now.

Joseph could feel his own heart thumping in his chest so loudly that he feared everything in the woods could hear it. As the buck stared at them, Joseph tried hard not to breathe. The young man and the magnificent animal seemed to have locked eyes, and Joseph didn't want to be the first to blink. Little did Joseph know the dilemma brewing only a few inches from his left ear.

Joseph's efforts in his meticulous arrangement of the leaves upon Moon and himself to make them all but invisible to the deer had, thus far, worked well. However, sometime while the gigantic buck moved down to the creek, Moondog had snorted a small piece of a dried leaf into his left nostril. The leaf now tickled the inside of his nose unbearably. Moon could breathe in without any problem, but as soon as he tried to exhale, the tickling became worse. In the past few moments, Moon had filled his lungs with the cool autumn air. Now his sides looked so swollen that if Joseph had seen them, he would have thought his dog to be ill. As the huge buck stood staring at them, Moon could wait no longer.

"Wwwwssssssnnnnnfffffcccchhhhhh." Moon let out a sneeze so massive that his head whipped around from side to side and his front paws lifted off the ground. In an instant he scattered the pile of leaves as if a small grenade had gone off.

The giant buck almost tripped over himself as he jumped ten feet away from Joseph and Moon in a single leap.

"Aaaayyyyyeeeaaaa!" Joseph jumped to his feet and flailed his arms wildly as he screamed, his left ear ringing from the sound of Moon's explosive sneeze going off a few inches away.

In a flash the huge buck vanished.

"Whoa, whoa, whoa," Joseph puffed as he put his right hand on his chest while his heart pounded. He looked bug-eyed to where the buck had stood only seconds ago and then back to Moon. Moon lay down as his ears and tail drooped, a whimper coming from the golden dog's chest.

Joseph watched a large orange maple leaf, airborne a moment ago, settle on top of Moon's head. Then his dog began to crawl toward him while the sound of the crunching leaves mixed with an occasional grunt as Moon's stomach bumped into a protruding root.

As his heart began to slow a little, Joseph let out a shaky sigh. He looked to where the buck had stood and then back to his dog inching toward him, the reality of what had just taken place slowly sinking in. Joseph began to smile, and then to laugh out loud.

At the sound of Joseph's laughter, Moon stopped crawling, cocked his ears up, and tilted his head to the side. The maple leaf balanced for just a moment on top of Moon's ears, and then slid off toward the front of his face. Joseph watched Moon raise his eyebrows as he caught a glimpse of the stem of the leaf. Then Moon arched his eyebrows straight up as he rolled his eyes to see the edge of the leaf less than an inch from his eyes.

Joseph started to laugh so hard that he felt his knees buckle. He doubled over and collapsed on the pile of leaves. Then he rolled on his back and looked up at the fading crimson sky through the trees. Moon stood up and shook the leaves off his body, then walked over and stared down into Joseph's face.

The silhouette of Moon's golden head filled the sky above Joseph as the big dog's dark eyes sparkled at the sound of his master's laughter. Joseph ruffled the fur behind Moon's ears as he continued to replay the buck's reaction to Moon's enormous sneeze. Joseph laughed so hard his eyes started to water and blur his vision. Finally he took a few deep breaths and composed himself as he wiped the tears from his eyes.

"Oh my Moondog, what am I going to do with you?" said Joseph softly as he kneaded Moon's thick yellow mane. He could feel Moon's tail swinging from side to side at the sound of his voice and touch of his hand.

Chapter 3

As the sun set, Joseph felt chill bumps on his arms from the crispness of the autumn air. He stretched out his hand to Moon and felt his companion's cold, wet snoot. Joseph sat up while Moon lay underneath his left arm, a soft sigh of contentment emerging from his dog. Then a stark remembrance of what the coming cool weather meant sent a chill of its own through Joseph.

"What do *you* want?" Joseph could still hear a classmate he'd thought was his friend say mockingly as a group walked past him outside of school. "You know you don't belong with us guys," added a second. "Yeah, why don't you go and play in the woods some more with that squirrelly dog of yours and leave us alone?" chimed in another. Joseph's sharp observation skills betrayed him as he replayed the details of the event in his mind.

Moon looked up at his master as Joseph let out a deep sigh. *What is wrong with me? Why can't I fit in? If they want to do things I know are wrong, that's up to them. But I'm not going to give in to them. Why can't people at school just leave me alone?* Joseph began to recall other times he'd been bullied much more severely and when he'd felt the peer pressure to cave in to do something he knew was wrong. And he remembered the vivid details of the flak that he'd caught because he wouldn't give in to the pressure. Joseph clenched his teeth. Then he closed his eyes and shook his head as he tried to scatter the thoughts into the leaves around them. Scatter them off and away where they couldn't bother him and steal away the current peace which surrounded him and Moon. *Enough of that, enough already! Focus, focus on what is here right now. Bend your mind to it – Focus.*

Joseph looked down and noticed the stark contrast of the golden fur of Moon's thick mane and the dark bronze color of his arm. *So many days in the sun with Moondog this summer,* Joseph forced himself to smile. *This has to be the very best time in the very best place with the very best dog in the whole universe. Now keep focusing.*

As the light of day faded, Joseph watched a red-tailed hawk circling toward the north, searching a field beyond the forest for an unwary mouse or rabbit. At the same time he forced himself to concentrate on the high-pitched chorus of crickets and tree frogs all around them. He once again took in a deep breath and noticed the sweet smell of maple leaves under his feet.

Joseph closed his eyes as thoughts of a bully at school tried to crowd in. *Not again, not this time,* Joseph determined.

A big grin spread over Joseph's face as he studied the creek and remembered how he and Moon had tracked a raccoon through this area a few weeks ago. Joseph recalled the warm weather on that day and the direction of the wind as they followed the animal up the edge of the stream. He remembered how Moon's remarkable sense of smell led them away from the creek as they tracked the unsuspecting critter right to the base of a huge oak tree. From there Joseph saw the raccoon asleep in the crotch of the tree about thirty feet up. Then Joseph backed up and called Moon to him with a hand signal. He sat down and lined up his head next to Moon's and pointed. Joseph studied his companion's face as Moon concentrated on the tree. He knew the moment Moon saw their target. Moon's cheeks puffed out and Joseph heard Moon's quiet "hafoof." Then Moon grinned at Joseph and buried his head in Joseph's chest, tail swinging so hard that his whole body rocked from side to side.

Then it happened.

A shrill cry from the red-tailed hawk pierced Joseph's memories and shattered his daydream, shaking him back to the present. He knew the meanings of many bird and animal sounds and instantly recognized the bird's distress call. The echo from the scream had not yet faded when Joseph and Moon felt a blast of cold wind slap them from behind. They jumped up and whirled around to see dark purple clouds rolling toward them along the horizon with incredible speed. Suddenly the air was filled with hundreds of yellow and red leaves whipping past as if shot out of a jet engine.

Squirrels, surprised by the fast approaching storm, bolted back to their hollow trees for shelter. Joseph and Moon caught glimpses of birds zipping in close as they rushed to settle near the trunks of the large maples and oaks. Joseph jumped as he felt the brush of a bird's wings on his face. Large trees began to sway wildly around them in the swirling wind. Joseph knew that animals are always the best of weathermen, but he was stunned that he and Moon, and all the other critters, never sensed the approach of this storm.

"Come on, Moon," Joseph urged as they began jogging toward the southwest and home. Before going twenty yards he felt the chill of cold rain coming down in sheets against them, driven from right to left as they headed for shelter.

Suddenly a tremendous cracking noise split the air behind them. They spun around in time to see a huge beech tree, one of the largest trees in the area, uprooted and crash to the ground across the creek. Joseph turned and stumbled a few more steps before hail began to pelt them, driving them further from home.

The hail stung Joseph's eyes as he struggled to see Moon through blurred vision even though they were only a few feet apart. "Moon, heel!" Joseph cupped his hands and shouted to his dog, then staggered several more steps toward the south as the hail and wind stung the right side of his face and side. Joseph's mind raced. *If we're separated, we'll never find each other until this storm is over. We're in big trouble if we don't find shelter soon. This hail is getting bigger by the second.* He felt his heel catch Moon under the snoot as he took another step, and knew that Moon understood the need to stay close.

If I can somehow locate that big, hollow maple tree, it might be big enough for both of us to get inside. Joseph thought of the huge beech tree that had toppled in the wind only moments before and knew it would be a risk getting inside a hollow tree in this kind of wind. But the hail continued to get bigger and large branches now began to snap off trees all around them. Thousands of multicolored leaves flew past, many sticking to Joseph and Moon's right sides as the two struggled to keep moving.

The hollow tree abruptly appeared a few feet in front of them. A moment later, to the right of where they stood, the wind sheared off the top of a red-oak twenty inches in diameter. With tremendous force the entire tree top hurled down directly toward them. Joseph instinctively put his hand up at the sound of the tree tearing apart. An instant before it crushed Joseph and Moon to the ground, the treetop struck something unseen and stopped only inches above Joseph's hand, splintering into thousands of pieces. Joseph quickly dropped to all fours and crawled inside the hollow maple, feeling his cold, wet Moondog burrow his way up against him.

Drenched and covered with leaves and ice, Joseph breathed a cautious sigh of relief. He stood up slowly and tried to shake off some of the water and leaves. Moon shook off in a far more efficient manner and looked up at his master in the dimming light.

"You've got to teach me how to do that someday, buddy," Joseph managed to pant while trying to mask his fear. He knelt down and held his dog close so they could get some warmth from each other. "This tree is barely big enough for us to fit inside," Joseph tried to reassure his companion, "but it's enough to keep us out of the brunt of the storm for now."

Looking out the entrance they could see leaves and hail whipping past, along with water running down the side of the tree trunk. The hail beating on the trunk and the wind swirling across the hollow treetop sounded like a freight train roaring over their heads.

"I've never seen anything like this before, Moon buddy," shouted Joseph as he brushed hail from Moon's ears. "I'm grateful we're both still here, the way the top of that tree came flying down on us."

Moon started trembling under Joseph's arms. Joseph couldn't tell if Moon was cold or if he somehow understood how close they had come to being killed by the falling tree. In the past Moon had never shown any major distress from the cold or heat. Then Joseph noticed Moon's fur start to stand on end.

"It's okay, Moon, don't be afraid, we're alright..." Joseph's shouting trailed off as he began to realize that what Moon felt wasn't fear. His own eyes grew large as he noticed the hair on his arms stand up as the truth of their dire situation dawned on him. With all the strength Joseph could muster, he grabbed Moon up in his arms and dove out of the tree back into the teeth of the storm, holding Moon close to his chest.

Lightning ripped through the tree just as Joseph and Moon passed through the opening of the hollow trunk. They flew high in the air and completely flipped over, the concussion of the lightning strike knocking them both unconscious. Joseph landed on his back with the front half of Moon's body lying on his chest. Joseph's left arm lay under Moon's front legs, and his right arm wrapped over Moon's back, hands joined, forming a complete circle.

The heavy rain, which had turned to hail only moments ago, began changing to snow.

<h1 align="center">Chapter 4</h1>

"Sorry I'm late," Joseph's father said as he pulled his chair up to the table. "Ran into some downed fence in the far pasture and fixing it took a bit longer than I thought it would."

Joseph's mother smiled. "And our son?" she asked as she placed a warmed-up plate of chicken and potatoes before her husband.

"He's not back yet?"

She shook her head as she sat down across from him.

"Well, you know, he's been helping me out around here quite a bit lately. Plus we know how school can weigh on him, especially when he first starts back. So I let him and Moon have a couple of hours off this afternoon. I'm pretty sure they went to look for that phantom buck they've been tracking for months now.

"He's put a lot of time into that one, hasn't he?" she replied. "Of course, if not the big buck it'd be something else."

"No doubt. I have to admit it is pretty amazing what Joseph and Moon pulled off this past weekend."

"And which exploring feat would that be?"

"Oh," recalled Joseph's father, "you know that little buck they found sleeping in the brush. Remember how Joseph explained it, how he watched Moon picking up a scent near the creek, and doing his usual Z-pattern, walking upwind, and going side to side like he does?

"Ah, yes. I've seen Moon do that pattern a few times myself when I've been out in the garden. I've watched him zero in on a ripe strawberry from fifty feet away, walking this way and that into the wind until he found it. Then he scarfed it down and looked at me with that big grin of his."

"Yup, I've seen it too," agreed her husband. "Remember Joseph telling us how they crept through the brush that day until he could barely make out something lying on the ground in front of them? And, how he's trained Moon to stay put so he can go on ahead? I think that's pretty remarkable in itself, I have to admit."

"Well, Joseph did say Moon can hardly stand it when it comes to that point in their game," replied Joseph's mother. "But apparently he did manage it this time. How did Joseph put it? 'Moon stood there quivering but never moved an inch', or something like that.'"

Her husband nodded. "And how Joseph saw the little buck curled up asleep in a ball with his head facing in the other direction. As he said, the damp leaves helped to mask his movements; he could have never gotten so close on a day like today. But for Joseph to be able to reach through the brush and lay the tips of his fingers on that deer without it ever waking up had to be a real thrill. Joseph's eyes just lit up when he told us, remember?"

"Oh I remember. He kept looking at his right hand with his face just glowing. 'A wild deer, I could feel him breathing. This is so cool.'"

Joseph's father grinned. "Yup, that's my boy alright," he stated proudly.

"Our boy," she corrected. "I think you telling him not to mention the story to too many people was wise advice. I doubt they'd believe him."

"Knowing how much grief Joseph has caught at school for mentioning far less remarkable experiences, I doubt he'll be telling anyone else. Maybe he should write a book or something."

"Who would believe him? You know, now that we have Moon, he doesn't seem to be interested in anything else but being outside with him.

"Did Joseph tell you about Moon and Cap chasing each other yesterday after he got done painting the barn?"

She shook her head.

"Joseph said that when he finished, he went to the pasture and saw both horse and dog romping around like two big kids. They'd run side by side for a while until one pretended he needed a rest. Then the other would come up and nip at his heels. The tired one would whirl around and chase the other across the field as fast as they could run. When Joseph first noticed them, Cap, with his ears back, was taking off after Moondog. Joseph thought he was going to see his dog stomped into the ground and was about to start screaming at the two. But as they approached the far corner of the pasture, Moon made a quick move to his left and sidestepped the big horse, then proceeded to chase Cap back across the field to where Joseph stood. Then Moon and Cap stood puffing and looking at each other, Cap throwing his head back and 'stretching out his lips,' as Joseph calls it when he sounds like he's blowing a raspberry. Joseph figured this little game they've got might help keep our dog and horse in shape, but wondered if his own heart could take much more of it.

"Well, I know he tells his science teacher more about what is going on out there than what he's learning in the books. I wish he'd spend a little more time on other subjects like math or something. But we both know there are things someone his age could get into that would be terrible for him. I think we're pretty fortunate right now, and besides, he'll outgrow it all soon enough, don't you think?"

Joseph's father shook his head. "I don't know about that. I've never seen anything like it to tell you the truth. You know I've been around animals all my life, and I'm not half bad as a tracker myself. But yesterday Joseph had me look at some tracks. He showed me how the track changed by what the animal did at a certain moment. Like if the animal stopped and turned its head this way or that. Joseph said he could see it in how the track registered in the dirt, how the animal's weight shifted to the inside or outside of the track, and so forth. He went on and on about the most minute details. I asked him how he could know all this. He told me that he and Moon would often watch a deer or fox wander through an area, then he'd go over and carefully study the tracks. He said they'd repeated this so many times he felt pretty confident in what he saw.

"Of course, you know Joseph. He's quite humble about all of it, saying he couldn't be sure what was going on by just a track. Yet every detail he explained to me made a lot of sense and he really seemed to understand what took place out there. Whatever it is with him, it's special when it comes to the outdoors. Maybe he *should* take the time to write some notes or something. Then one day he could write a book and become famous and take care of his parents in their old age."

The windows of the old farmhouse rattled violently. Both of Joseph's parents looked outside the kitchen window toward the south and saw a clear sky in the fading evening light. They gave each other a puzzled look.

"You finish your dinner, I'll go look out front," said Joseph's mother as she stood. "I wish Joseph had come back with you."

"Now dear, you know he can take better care of himself than most of the animals out there. I'm sure he'll be along. It'll be getting dark soon. Besides, he's got Moon with him, remember? They'll be all right."

In a few seconds he heard her urgent call. "Hun, you'd better come out here."

Joseph's father jumped up and hurried to the front porch to join his wife. From there they watched in dismay as dark purple and black clouds churned low to the ground at incredible speed, rolling straight at them from the northwest. The storm, which had seemed a good distance from her when she first looked out the front window, now filled half the sky. Huge trees in the front yard began to bow under the fury of the wind.

"Keep an eye out for Joseph and close the shutters. I'll try to get some of the stock into the barn before this thing hits," he called to her as he spun around and grabbed his coat.

"Got it." The petite woman moved valiantly about the outside of the house as she struggled with all her strength to secure the shutters against the whipping wind.

Joseph's father felt the sting of icy raindrops against his back and legs before he even reached the barn door. He fought through the anxious cows and horses that were nervously pacing about. As he pressed through the animals, he could see large raindrops ricocheting off the fresh red paint of the barn. He rolled open the big front doors and quickly stepped aside as the animals pushed in. After they passed he tipped his cap low over his eyes and held it in place with his right hand. He looked into the wind, toward the pasture. From there he could see the rest of the stock running in his direction. He had often left the pasture gate open, allowing the animals to come and go as they pleased. Many of them had weathered storms in the field without incident, seeming to prefer the cleansing rain on their backs to the warm shelter of the barn. But not this time.

Joseph's father squinted his eyes against the wind and rain as he tried to shield them with his hat. He could barely make out the figures of horses and cattle against the dark purple clouds churning behind them. "Come on Joseph; where are you, son?" he said quietly as he bit his lip.

He got behind the shelter of the door and turned on the lights inside the barn as the big animals came skidding in. Hail now raged down as the last of the stock scrambled inside. Joseph's father leaned his full weight into the massive wooden doors to get them to close against the gale. He turned to see the animals instinctively go into their respective stalls and anxiously stamp about as the howling wind and hail beat against the barn walls and roof.

"You'll be alright as long as the roof stays on," he said softly as he turned back and looked out a small opening between the doors. He took a deep breath, cupped his hands, and shouted as loud as he could into the wind, "Joseph, Moon!" In only a few feet, the wind caught his words and sent them spinning into the barn behind him. The sound of a thousand hammers beating on the old building echoed around him as the wind and hail unleashed their fury.

"Joseph, Joseph, I hope you and Moondog have made it back to the house in the last couple of minutes," Joseph's father whispered to himself. He slipped out between the doors and barely managed to pull them closed. He then looked toward where the house stood, but he couldn't see it. He bent his body forward into the driving wind and hail until he saw the porch light only a few yards away.

As Joseph's father reached the farmhouse he saw a tremendous bolt of lightning cut across the sky toward the northeast. The light over his head flickered and went out as they lost power and phone line. A moment later he heard a deafening roll of thunder that again rattled the windows and reverberated deep in his chest. As the final light of day faded, he looked up at the sky and saw snow beginning to fall.

Chapter 5

"Joseph. Joseph, wake up. Come on now; it's time for you two to get moving." A hand gently shook Joseph's shoulder.

Joseph opened his eyes and blinked hard to try to clear his vision. Moon's head lay on his chest, with Joseph's arms still holding his dog close. Joseph saw a man standing over him and sat up with a start, waking Moon in the process.

"Who are you? Where did you come from?" Joseph shot a quick glance around and realized he had never seen this place before.

"Do not be afraid. My name is Tysius. Come, there is much for you to see." The man turned to go.

Moon got up and shook himself. He looked at Joseph and began to wag his tail.

Joseph jumped to his feet and looked around. He could see a few trees, but most everything looked various shades of brown, nothing at all like where they'd just been.

The man stopped and turned around. "Are you coming, Joseph? There is much for you to see."

Moon pranced about and seemed anxious to follow. For some reason that Joseph could not figure out, neither he nor Moon felt afraid of this fellow. In fact, Joseph had a strong desire to walk with the man, yet he didn't know anything about him.

Joseph studied the stranger looking back at them. He wore a white robe with a silver belt around his waist. Simple clothes but strange. His face appeared handsome but not striking. His eyes seemed to sparkle in the sun, and his voice sounded like none Joseph had heard before. Pleasant to hear, but strange, so strange.

"Are you afraid, Joseph?" the man asked.

"No, I'm not. And I don't know why. I have no idea who you are or where I am. Who are you?"

"I already told you, my name is Tysius. And this time, you are right not to be afraid. You have nothing to fear."

"I've never heard of that name before, at least not that I can remember. But I don't seem to be able to remember anything right now. Where are we and how did we get here?"

"Follow me and I will show you where you are. And be sure to bring your Moondog with you. You will need him."

"How did you know his name? And how do you know my name? I've never seen you before."

"I know you've not seen me before, but I have seen you. Moreover, and far more important, Someone else has taken notice of you. That is why I'm here. Come now. Follow me." The strange man turned and walked off.

Joseph looked around and then down at Moondog. He could not remember where they had been before.

Moon's tail swirled as he looked up at Joseph, and then at the man walking away. Moondog let out a barely audible hum and started toward the man, then looked back at Joseph.

Joseph faintly remembered that on occasions when he couldn't find any animals to stalk or fresh tracks to follow, he would turn Moon loose and tell him to lead. Joseph had learned that every time he did this, Moon's instincts proved correct. He knew Moon could see, smell, and sense where to go when he, Joseph, could not. Moon somehow knew what Joseph wanted, and would lead him to where he wanted to go. Now Joseph called Moon back to him, knelt down, and got eye to eye with his big dog.

Moon's bronze-colored ears, slightly darker than the rest of his head, tipped forward as he studied his master. The dog's nearly white front feet stopped inches from Joseph's knees.

Joseph looked into Moon's brown eyes as Moon gazed back into his. The same deep trust, the same total confidence they had in each other had not been altered with the change of their surroundings. "Okay, we'll follow for now," stated Joseph softly as he glanced at Tysius walking away, and then back at Moon. "But let's be careful. And stay by me."

Moon's tail wagged in agreement as they set off after the strange man dressed in white.

"How do you know my name? Have we met somewhere before?" asked Joseph as he and Moon caught up with Tysius.

Tysius expressed his amusement with a resounding, pleasant laugh that made Joseph's heart sing with joy. "Fleytius told me that you would ask many questions, but I did not think I would be inundated by them from the first moment with you. No, we have never met before; at least you have never met *me*. I know your name and your dog as well. He is a fine dog. He is for you, you realize. You helped establish that back when you first asked for him. It is because of the way you asked, the faith that you had. Do you remember the peace you felt when you asked God to work things out? The faith you had that He would, even though it did not look possible for you to get this dog of yours?"

Joseph's thoughts swirled around in his brain. *Who is this man and what is he talking about?* For the moment, Joseph struggled to remember the time right before he got Moon. He felt like he was running through dense fog in his mind, trying to see something out of sight, just on the other side of the fog. Like, driving through heavy, dark mist, and trying to see beyond the headlights.

"I – I – can't seem to remember," Joseph started. "I know it's there, but I can't quite get the details. I remember going somewhere to look for a dog, and how my Mom didn't like dogs at all, so I thought I had no chance. And I remember someone else wanting Moon as well, and them, not me, having first choice at him. So then I went out to the woods and asked God to help. I didn't know if God even cared about me or a dog."

Joseph looked at Tysius. "But when I tried talking to God, I saw no one else around. Nobody else heard me. How do you know about that?"

Tysius stopped and looked at Joseph. "What do you mean nobody else heard you? You weren't praying to the trees were you?"

"No, I'd never do that. That would be crazy."

Tysius let out another laugh that filled the air with joy. "I know you wouldn't, and more important, God knows it too. You know better than to worship what the Father has created. Yet you have more respect for it than most. You understand, and strive to understand, what He has created, yet you do not worship it. For there is only One who is worthy of praise and worship, and honor and glory. Only One, and holy, holy, holy is His Name."

Tysius sang now, a strange, beautiful song of worship and praise. The beauty of the singing stunned and deeply moved Joseph.

Moon sat, tilted his head, and actually seemed to smile as he stared up at Tysius.

"There are many reasons for your being here," Tysius began, "but this is one you may be able to understand, at least in part. Because you determined in your heart to believe and live the truth, and not allow the criticism of others to sway you, you have been chosen," stated Tysius. "I know you have struggled, but listen carefully. It is essential, absolutely vital, that you be who God created you to be, and for you not to be moved by another's critical remarks and opinions. You must now follow the One Who is the truth. Some live their entire lives on earth and never realize how critical this is."

Tysius then led them to a ridge top overlooking a large valley and pointed across it. "Look at this."

On the other side, Joseph could see a stream of people walking north. He saw hundreds of them, some moving more swiftly than others, but most headed in the same direction. From where they stood, the mass of people looked like a slow-moving train across the distant side of the valley, curving its way to a small town several miles away.

"What do you see, Joseph?"

Joseph studied the scene. "I see a big group of people moving along a ridge and down the mountain toward that small village. And there's this big desert-looking valley down below, separating us from them."

Tysius turned to Joseph, a hint of disappointment in his voice. "You have spent almost all of your short life observing and analyzing what you see and hear and sense. Look again."

For some reason Joseph felt the sting of letting this man down and had a strong desire to do his best for him. Joseph studied the scene before him. What else could he notice? He scrutinized the strange-looking land, the contours, and the color. He felt the warm sunshine on his arms and smelled the slightly sweet fragrance of the desert shrubs. Joseph again looked at the people across the valley, making their way slowly down the trail. He started to look elsewhere, and then abruptly looked back to them. He shaded his eyes from the bright sunshine and stared.

"It looks like there are some important people over in the group near the second big ridge. Some people who are special, but I don't know why. I can't see any details about them, it's too far. Who are they?" Joseph did not take his eyes off the two individuals across the valley.

"Excellent, Joseph, excellent. From now on, you can observe what is taking place, but you must in no way interfere. You must not. You may observe only. Observe and learn. The language barrier is taken away. But you cannot interfere, do you understand?"

"No, I don't understand what on earth you're talking about," replied Joseph, still shading his eyes and looking at those moving toward the village.

"What on earth indeed, Joseph. You are about to witness something you have heard of, yet you will not know what is about to happen until it takes place in its own time," replied Tysius. "May your heart be filled with joy as you see the things that are before you, for you are granted this by His grace. Now you must follow those people to the village. Although I cannot promise it, I may meet you there later."

Joseph continued cupping his hands around his eyes to help see across the sunny valley, trying to understand why something looked familiar about those two people. "I still don't understand what you're talking about."

"You will, in due time. But remember, you must not interfere in any way."

"Okay, okay, I won't interfere with anything. But what do you mean you'll maybe meet us…" Joseph's voice stopped as he looked back toward

Tysius but couldn't find him. Joseph turned a complete circle and didn't see Tysius. He looked down at Moon. Moon gazed upward, but not at Joseph. Joseph looked up for a moment, but he didn't see anything.

"Where'd ya go? Hey, Tasus or whatever your name is, where'd you go? And who is this Fleetus fellow who told you I'd ask a lot of questions? Hey!" Joseph looked down at Tysius' tracks. They stopped next to him and Moon.

Chapter 6

"Moon, will you slow down?" panted Joseph, half out of breath. "Just because what's-his-name disappeared doesn't mean you can take off on me. Now, heel, Moon."

Joseph watched Moon turn around and look at him, a big grin on his dog's face as he urged his master on. Joseph jutted his jaw. "Moon," said Joseph sharply as they reached the valley floor. "Come here. We don't know where we're going or even where we are. Come here."

Moondog lowered his tail and came back as Joseph knelt down so they could see eye to eye.

"Look Moon, stay by me, okay? We don't know what's happening here, and we don't need to get separated. This is sort of crazy, and I don't need you acting like an idiot. Just relax buddy, just relax."

Moon glanced at the horizon where the sun had already set. He looked back at Joseph and started nervously prancing about.

Joseph took a deep breath. "Relax Moon, we'll be all right." He stood up and looked around. Joseph could see very little shelter and he didn't wish to spend the night in this nearly barren land if he could help it.

Moon gave a nervous snort and kept prancing about.

They could still see the line of people moving toward the small village. Joseph saw the two individuals whom he vaguely recognized pass over a rise and out of sight. The village appeared some distance beyond them.

Joseph looked back the way they had come and tried to remember where they'd been before they had met Tysius. No matter how hard he tried, at the moment he couldn't remember anything before that. Yet for whatever reason, he felt no anxiety about it.

"Okay Moon, we'll go after those two, but we've got to stay together. There are some animals walking along with that big crowd, and you don't need to get tangled up with any of them. You've got to stay by me. Let's go."

Moondog reared up and pawed at the air with his front feet when Joseph said go. He capered in a quick circle around Joseph and then fell in obediently at his side as they made fast strides toward the main trail. As they neared the road that led to the village, Joseph got in Moon's face yet

21

again and told him directly to heel. Joseph sensed that Moon's excitement could override his desire to obey.

Joseph and Moon neared the road, climbed up a small embankment, and merged in with the other travelers. No one seemed to take notice of Joseph's unusual clothing. Moon stepped in close to Joseph's left side as they walked. Joseph saw that many people walked along either barefoot or wearing sandals. He immediately perceived that almost all the travelers looked weary from what appeared to be a long journey.

The two walked slowly at first with the same group of people. No one said anything directly to them, which suited Joseph. As he looked down at Moon, he could see his dog was antsy to catch up to the people ahead. *How could he know who is up there? How could I know who is up there? This is really weird.*

As they walked, Joseph saw that the road widened enough in areas so that he and Moon could pass some of the people. Joseph hoped they wouldn't draw much attention to themselves while they speeded up their pace. As he and his dog weaved their way along the road past the people, Joseph couldn't help hearing their grumbling.

"Sorry leader he is," stated one weary man. "Just wants more money from us, that's all. That's all he ever wants. Someone should take him out, that's what I think."

"Hush now, dear, you hush," came the words from someone Joseph guessed to be the man's wife. "You know what can happen to you if the wrong people hear you talking like that. Let it go."

"Let it go? Look at us, we just got things going at home and look at us. You know this is all about money just as well as I do. Money and power. I don't care who hears me, everyone knows what all this is about. Sorry leaders we've got."

Joseph welcomed the chill of the evening on his arms and face as they continued to speed up their gait. He knew the cool air had to feel good in Moon's lungs and on his wet nose. Their rapid trek had warmed them both. But as Joseph cooled quickly, Moon's thick mane was designed to hold in the heat, and now the cooler air was a real blessing to his faithful dog.

As they walked over the final rise, they could see the village below them. The dirt streets were jammed full with people. Joseph called Moon to the side to get out of the way of the crush of travelers. He wanted to observe all he could before they made their descent into the crowded town. They both could see several oil lamps burning, yet the edges of the streets seemed barely lit up.

Moon lifted his snoot high as he sniffed the air. Joseph watched him twitch his nose like a big rabbit, and he knew the scent of livestock had to be strong. From the looks of Moon, Joseph could tell he didn't sense danger from any animals. But both Joseph and Moon could easily hear men arguing and fighting with each other down in the village. *If we find trouble, that's where it'll come from,* thought Joseph.

From the rise where Joseph and Moon stood taking in the scene, Joseph finally located the couple he had somehow recognized on the road. They were many streets over and appeared to be in some sort of dispute with a large man. Joseph could see that the big man had his hands planted on his hips. The male traveler gestured, his hands in front of him with palms upheld toward the dim sky. Joseph caught a glimpse of the woman, rocking slowly while she sat doubled over.

Joseph squatted down next to his companion and lined his head up with Moon's. "We've got to see if we can get through all these people and over to them," he said as he pointed to the couple. Moon's gaze followed his master's hand as the big dog searched the village below.

A few worn-out travelers saw Joseph kneeling next to his dog, pointing toward the village. Tired and irritated, and a long way from home, they couldn't resist. "What's the matter with your stupid dog? Can't he see the town from here?" one jeered. "Yeah, is he blind or something?" another added. "If he is, this walking stick will do the trick on him, and then he won't be no more bother to you."

Joseph nearly responded but wisely decided against it. As Moon looked where Joseph directed, he too saw the couple over the sea of people. "Hafoof."

"Good dog, Moon. Stay next to me." Joseph smiled and ruffled Moon's mane. "There are people all over the place down there. From the sounds of it, some may be pretty cranky. You watch out for me and I'll do the same for you, buddy."

Joseph straightened up as he determined the best route to take through the throng below. *Man, I hate crowds,* he thought. Then he gave his beloved dog a command as they stepped back into the line of travelers. "Heel Moon, heel."

Joseph felt Moon bumping up against his left leg as his dog obediently stuck close to him in the crowd. Once in town they felt the mob shoving and pushing against them as people moved in various directions searching for a place to spend the night.

"Moon, Moon!" Joseph called anxiously above the clamor of the people as he lost sight of his dog. Joseph felt a cold sweat break out as he turned around searching for his companion in the press of the crowd.

Moon heard Joseph call, put his head down, and simply burrowed his way through the sea of feet and legs surrounding him until he ran into Joseph.

Joseph felt the sharp pain from the top of Moon's head against his shins, but he sensed a surge of relief nonetheless. "Good dog, buddy," Joseph called to his dog as he quickly ruffled Moon's mane. "Good dog."

After several more anxious minutes of straining against the crowd, Joseph and Moon arrived at the place where they had seen the two special travelers. Joseph knocked on the door of the building, and a rather angry man popped out from behind the door.

"Ah – excuse me," said Joseph, "did a man and woman just come by here?"

"What are you, some kind of wise guy or something?" growled the big man as he towered over Joseph. "Listen kid, people have been coming by here all week looking for a room. I ain't got any more rooms, you hear? Now get lost."

"You mean you didn't let them stay here? You turned them away?"

"Are you deaf or something, kid? No, they're not here. I haven't had an empty room in quite a while. And I don't have room for you either, and if that's your dog there, you can take him when you leave." He pointed a meaty hand toward Moon.

"But you don't understand," pleaded Joseph, "those people are really important; you can't turn them away…" Joseph sought for the right words.

"Yeah, yeah," sighed the manager, "everybody's important, everybody's special, everybody wants a room."

Joseph watched the big man put his hands on his hips, apparently his standard position of defiance when dealing with the crowds. Now he continued his argument. "Well who are they, anyway? They didn't say they were anyone special."

Joseph thought hard. "I don't remember who they are, but they're important, really important people."

The manager put his hands on his knees and brought his face so close Joseph could hear him whisper.

Moon put his hackles up and stepped beside Joseph. He crouched slightly as he saw the man get close to his master.

"Listen kid," the manager hissed, "We're full, completely and totally full. If Augustus himself came here asking for a room I would send him away. Understand?"

The man's breath nearly knocked Joseph over. Joseph had heard that name before but couldn't place it. He figured it must be someone in the government. Joseph looked him straight in the eye. "I don't believe you," he said quietly.

The man stood and felt his back crack as he straightened up. He sighed as he studied the young man, and then looked at the golden dog with his hackles up standing alongside him. The man straightened up even more. A few of Moon's teeth shone in the dim light as the big dog crouched and trembled slightly. The man moved a step to the other side of Joseph as he cut his eyes back to him. He squinted his eyes as he looked up and down at Joseph's clothes. Then he sighed again as he looked around as if to be sure no one else could hear.

"Look kid, you're right, I wouldn't send Caesar away. But if he stayed here right now, I'd have to kick out the people who already paid for rooms just to make a place for him and all his soldiers. Now that wouldn't be right, now would it?"

Joseph thought about it for a moment. He didn't understand who he was talking about, but he knew that kicking a lot more people out into these already crowded streets didn't sound like a good idea.

"No, I guess not."

The manager's face softened a little. "Hey, I don't like sending people away. If I could have put them up, I would have, especially those two. The guy looked desperate." The manager ran both his hands through his hair. Then he gazed over the top of Joseph's head at the crowded streets behind him.

"I think I believe you now," Joseph said, barely audible.

The manager came back from his thoughts. "You believe me about what?" he snapped.

"I believe you don't like sending people away who need your help," Joseph smiled faintly at the man.

The innkeeper studied the boy once again. "How come you haven't asked me for anything for yourself?" Then he slipped inside the door and quickly returned with something hidden in his coat. He looked about once again to make sure no one saw him.

Moon looked on as he stood next to Joseph. His hackles remained up as the man stepped close to Joseph.

"Here," the manager opened his coat. "Here's a blanket for you. You'll need it tonight; it's going to be cold. I ain't never seen clothes like you're wearing before, but they don't look too warm to me. Just don't tell anyone where you got this, you hear?" The innkeeper tried to sound gruff.

"And don't worry about those other two; at least they got a roof over their heads, of sorts, anyway. I seen to that I did, though it ain't much for 'em." The innkeeper looked off toward a hillside. "There are some caves over there, stables for the animals. I'll send someone around later to check on them."

Joseph could sense his concern. He held the warm cover to his chest. "Thanks for the blanket. I'll return it tomorrow,"

Moon's hackles came down a little.

"I won't have any room for you tomorrow either, and we won't be getting any warm weather for a while. Just keep the blanket, kid. Besides, if someone sees you bringing it back and finds out I gave it to you, it'll ruin my image." The innkeeper looked up at the black sky for a moment. "Stay out of the wind and you'll be all right. I'll tell those two in the morning that you're asking about them if you want. What's your name?"

"Um," Joseph suddenly remembered giving Tysius his word about not interfering in any way and wondered if he'd already done too much. "It's not important, really – and I'll see them tomorrow anyway. Thanks again for the blanket." Joseph and Moon retreated into the darkness and the crowded street.

"Okay kid, just keep yourself warm." The innkeeper shook his head and smiled as he walked back into his hotel. "Lydia," he called to one of his workers as he stepped back into his inn. The poor woman jumped at his voice and almost dropped the armful of towels she carried.

"Yes?"

"Oh – sorry I scared you – and ah – sorry I've been so on-edge lately too – sorry about that." The man tried to smile and apologize at the same time. "Anyway, in the morning, please see that you check on a young couple in the stables. I sent them there a while ago and the girl is in a bad way."

"Ah – why – yes sir," said Lydia as her boss walked past. She shot a quick glance up toward heaven and shook her head as she hurried back to her work, a hint of a smile on her face.

Joseph looked around at the edge of the crowded street. He took a deep breath to battle the tightness growing once again in his chest; Moondog raised his hackles, and they both stepped back into the crowd.

They had gone only a short distance when an argument broke out between two men close by. Joseph and Moon got caught up in an ocean wave of humanity as people pushed and shoved to get away from the scuffle. Joseph felt the roughness of a large tree trunk against his right hand. He quickly grabbed Moon by the scruff of the neck, and the two swung around to the other side of the tree. There they took shelter behind the trunk like a couple of fish behind a boulder in a roaring stream. Joseph hunkered down with his back planted firmly against the tree and held Moon as close as he could while scores of people crowded past. They heard angry shouts and cursing of men, along with women screaming and children crying.

"It's okay, Moon, it's okay," said Joseph as calmly as he could. "I don't know where we are or what's going on here, but just as soon as we can we're getting out of this town. I remember a field right before we started dropping into the village. It looked deserted to me. I'll take us there just as soon as I can. I promise you. We don't even know who's in the stable, and it'd be better to meet them in the daylight than now."

Moon let out a low grunt and pressed in even closer to Joseph as someone else stepped on his toes. Then a small break appeared in the crowd. Joseph jumped to his feet with Moon sticking close to his side. They didn't stop again until reaching the edge of the vacant field.

Chapter 7

Joseph felt his teeth tingle as he drew a deep breath of the cold night air. "Whew, whew, whew, Moondoggie. I am sorry about that, buddy. I hope I never put us through anything like that again. I'd rather be out in this field with just you and me in the pouring rain than down in that crowd in the sunshine."

Moon looked up at Joseph and looped his tail in big circles.

Joseph gazed into the sea of stars and marveled at how clear everything looked. Although at the time Joseph couldn't remember where he'd learned it, he knew how to spend the night in the outdoors without fear. His father had taught him how to use the bark of a birch tree to keep warm on cold nights. He would gather a good amount of the dried bark and twist it into a tight ball. Then he'd find a good observation spot near a deer trail and clear a small place on the ground down to bare soil. He'd place the bark on the soil and light it. After some initial burning, the coals remained virtually smokeless. Joseph would sit over the fragile glowing coals and wrap himself in the blanket with his Moondog curled up next to him. The coals would keep them warm for hours, and often he would peer out of his blanket in the morning only to see that a covering of snow had fallen in the night. Yet both he and Moon would be warm the night through.

Now Joseph looked around. The rising moon gave enough light for them to see and avoid stepping into holes. Joseph felt a breeze blowing in from the west, and it sent a chill through him. "That man told us right, buddy," said Joseph as he wrapped the blanket around himself. "From the look of it, things will get cold tonight. Let's see if I can find what we need."

The two walked slowly across the big field and up a slope to an outcropping of rock. Moon showed Joseph a few gopher holes that he'd sniffed out along the way, along with an old bone of some kind.

At the far end of the grassy field, against some of the large rocks, Joseph found a place out of the wind. They turned around and saw some of the dim lights from the town below the far edge of the field. Although Joseph did not know where they were, he sensed peace returning to him with every breath of the cool evening air; he felt no fear in the solitude.

Moon stood facing west, nose up, and inhaled great amounts of air. Joseph could tell his companion smelled something unusual, but he saw only calmness in Moon. He knew they were in no immediate danger.

In a few minutes Joseph pulled enough tall grass to make a soft bed. "Moon, come here buddy."

Moon took one last sniff, and then trotted over to his master.

Joseph knelt down and stroked Moon behind his ears. "Well buddy, as clear as it is, we shouldn't get any rain," said Joseph as Moon swung his tail back and forth. "And this is a great blanket the man gave us. I think it's stuffed with wool. It should be just big enough to cover us and still small enough that I can use it sort of as a coat to wrap around me tomorrow. Then we can find out where we are and who those two are down in the stables. And maybe find Tysius again, wherever in the world he went off to. For now, we ought to be okay. At least we'll have some peace and quiet up here."

Moon swished his tail. Joseph intended to sit a while under the blanket and give some thought to the entire situation. However, as soon as he and Moondog curled up on top of the soft grass and he put the blanket over them, Moon began to snore lightly. The carefree sound of his dog snoozing touched something deep within Joseph and, in a moment, he too fell fast asleep.

"Hafoof."

Joseph wearily cranked one eye open underneath the blanket.

"Hafoof."

Okay, Okay, something significant is going on... Joseph fought to clear his mind but it took him a while. *I wonder if Moon is dreaming. I wonder if I'm dreaming.*

"Hafoof."

Okay, Joseph, start close by and go out from there, he thought as he struggled to clear his mind. *Where is Moon?* Joseph opened both eyes to see Moondog lying at his feet with his head and ears up, peering out from under their cover. Joseph followed Moon's gaze out into the field. The light from the moon cast dim shadows across the grass. Joseph sensed a slight breeze coming from behind their shelter and rolling gently over the large meadow. The light wind softly swayed the tall grass in countless waves washing away from them. The rustling sound of the grass reminded Joseph of water flowing smoothly over polished rocks in a stream.

Joseph squinted to see the silhouette of three people, one standing and the other two lying down, about 150 yards away and off toward the right. In front of them grazed several dozen sheep in the tall grass. Joseph wondered how they could have moved to the meadow and settled in for the night so near to Joseph and Moon without either of them hearing. It appeared to him that the three men and their sheep wouldn't move much more this night. He patted Moon's head.

"Good boy, Moon, good dog," Joseph said softly. "Nothing to worry about, buddy. Good dog. We must have been sleeping well for them to have gotten this close without us hearing them before now."

"Well, I see you're awake then." The voice came from behind them.

Both Joseph and Moon jumped up and whirled around at the same time, the blanket flying high into the air. Joseph grabbed the back of Moon's neck out of reflex.

The hairs on Moon's back stood straight up as he bared his teeth while stepping in front of Joseph.

"Oops, sorry to scare you, but it is good you're up." Tysius leaned against some rocks with what appeared to Joseph as a slight grin on his face. His white clothes glowed and eliminated any possible doubts as to his identity.

"Great day, man!" exclaimed Joseph, still panting from shock. "You about scared us half to death. Where did you come from, and how did you get so close without us hearing you? And where did you go earlier today? I never saw you leave. And how'd you know where to find us?"

Moon's hackles quickly went down as Joseph released his grip on his mane. Moon began to twirl his tail around as he recognized Tysius.

"So many questions, Joseph," replied Tysius. "You will understand in due time. As for now, I should say you two chose the perfect spot to spend the night. Just perfect. I see you have already seen the shepherds?"

Joseph looked back at the field. No one out there seemed to have noticed Joseph, Moon, or especially Tysius.

"Yeah, Moon saw them and woke me. He's good about that." Joseph turned back to Tysius. "But he never saw or heard or smelled you coming. I didn't think it possible for anyone or anything to get that close without him noticing. How did you do that?"

Tysius chuckled. "My dear Joseph, for now, let me ask the questions." The sound of laughter coming from Tysius made Joseph relax. He couldn't quite explain how he felt so safe, so at peace with someone he'd just met, and who seemed so odd to boot. However, Joseph knew he did not need to fear anything from Tysius.

"Do you notice anything peculiar about what you see out there?" continued Tysius.

Joseph collected the warm blanket and wrapped it around himself. He turned back to the field and looked at the scene before him as Moon walked over and put his head under Tysius' hand.

Tysius scratched his ears playfully.

Moon's fur lifted up and tiny white and blue sparks crackled at Tysius' fingertips. Moon wagged his tail with abandon and then walked back to Joseph's side.

"Well, it looks like three men, one watching their flock and the other two sleeping," began Joseph. "I'm kind of surprised the one standing hasn't seen us yet. It looks like he could see us from there. Actually, he probably couldn't see me and Moon since I'm dressed in fairly dark clothes and Moon is pretty low to the ground against these dark rocks. But he should be able to see you easily enough. You stick out like a white flare."

"That's pretty observant, but it's not exactly what I'm talking about. For one thing, they can't see me, only you and your dog can. I don't have time to explain that right now. Look again, and use all your senses this time. Tell me what is there. And remember, only observe, Joseph; do nothing to interfere with what's going on."

"What do you mean they can't see you? You look like a lighthouse in this dark field..." Joseph looked over and saw Tysius give him the 'quit asking so many questions' look again. Joseph had seen the apparent static electricity when Tysius touched Moon, and he had seen his dog's acceptance of the man. He knew Tysius didn't pose a threat to them.

"Okay, I'll look again." Joseph smiled, now fully awake and slightly amused at the riddles of this strange man dressed in white. Joseph turned and studied the men, the sheep, and the field. He could see nothing unusual. Then he looked up to the heavens and to the stars blanketing the entire scene. The stars looked especially brilliant tonight, clear and crisp, and more numerous than Joseph could remember. They dazzled beyond words, almost bursting with life itself. "The stars..." began Joseph, but the sound of his own voice seemed like an intrusion on the remarkable beauty of the scene. *The stars themselves look alive,* he thought. *How can this be?*

Joseph became aware of something else, but he didn't know what. He couldn't tell if the awareness came gradually or not. He felt like he was hovering a few inches above the ground, dreamlike. He watched intently for something to develop in front of him, something new, completely and totally new and clear and clean and perfect. Yet he sensed he had seen or imagined some of it before.

The air was humming with activity. There was an electrical charge in their surroundings, and Joseph's skin as well as every other part of his being became alive and alert. The wind seemed to whip around them at 100 miles an hour, yet Joseph remained calm, and peace pervaded him. Joseph was aware that he and Moon need not fear anything. His heart rate increased and he breathed quickly as he sensed the excitement in the air, and still his eyes saw none of this.

Abruptly, from straight overhead, a streak of nearly blinding light descended next to a shepherd. Joseph watched as the man continued to stand as if he had been turned to stone. The two shepherds who had been sleeping jumped up and stood staring at the white figure standing in front of them. All around them shone an incredible light; it was a light more beautiful and dazzling and colorful than any Joseph had ever seen. Then Joseph heard a voice – a perfect, beautiful voice come from the one standing in the light.

"Do not be afraid, for behold, I bring you good tidings of great joy which will be to all people. For there is born to you this day in the city of David a Savior, who is Christ the Lord. And this will be the sign to you; you will find the Babe wrapped in swaddling clothes, lying in a manger." And suddenly, there was with the angel a multitude of the heavenly host praising God and saying: "Glory to God in the highest, and on earth peace, good will toward men!"[1]

Joseph's eyes reflected tens of thousands of angels around them. The sky could not hold them all, yet thousands upon thousands more added their voices. Joseph had never heard such beautiful singing. The heartbeat of vibrant, sparkling life throbbed in time with Joseph's own pulse. He stood astonished by the dazzling beauty and brilliance that surrounded them. As fast as his mind raced, Joseph could not take it all in. He felt every fiber of his being become immersed to the utmost, like a dry, porous rock thrown into and engulfed by the entire ocean.

Joseph took a step back and sat down at the same time, never taking his eyes off the scene. He saw so many angels singing that he could never have counted them all if he had had days to do it. He felt the earth rumble beneath him as their voices resonated in the clear night air.

Although Joseph's eyes saw the event, his mind struggled to catch up to it. Even after the angels left, Joseph sat for a long time staring at the heavens, the shepherds, and back to the heavens. With all of Joseph's finely honed skills of observation, he had taken in as much as anyone could. He felt overwhelmed and rocked to the core of his being with this awesome sensory overload. He could feel his heart pounding in his chest, and he suddenly realized that he should breathe again.

Joseph lost track of time. He jumped a bit as he felt Moon's snoot nudging his arm. Joseph looked at Moon and back to the field. He wanted to say something, but words seemed so inappropriate, so inadequate. The shepherds had moved out of the field, leaving their sheep for the time being. Joseph turned to look back at Tysius, but he was no longer there.

Joseph wobbled as he stood. He tried to sense anything else going on around him. He could hear his own breathing and an occasional bleat from one of the sheep. The air smelled sweet to him, like the faint smell of honey near a beehive. He looked at Moon in the faint light, and the golden dog returned his glance with a big grin and swirl of his tail. Joseph started to feel the chill of the night air again and wrapped himself in the blanket. He looked up to the heavens. "Glory to God, glory to God, glory to God," he whispered.

Joseph and Moon slowly walked side by side over to the edge of the field and up to the top of the next little rise. As they walked, it felt to Joseph like his feet were barely touching the ground. From the top of the rise they could clearly see the now quiet village below. In addition, they saw a brilliant star shining brightly in the cold night.

Chapter 8

Joseph and Moon walked down the same path they had used to escape the town only hours before. Once at the edge of the village, they weaved their way through small shacks and buildings, walking in the shadows whenever possible. Once in a while they could hear people stirring or the sound of a farm animal inside one of the shelters. Then they reached the place directly beneath the star.

The star looked like none that they'd seen before, and its tail pointed straight down at them. The entrance to a small cave stood in front of Joseph and Moon. It looked to Joseph like a rough cloth covered the entrance; an old oil lamp lit the inside. He crouched in the shadows beside a shed and could feel his Moondog tremble as Joseph wrapped his arms around him. Or maybe he himself trembled, or maybe both of them did. Joseph couldn't tell. From their location they could hear voices coming from inside.

"Then they vanished, just as quickly as they appeared. I stood like a stone, afraid to move or even breathe. I heard my boys here come to my side. They saw the same thing I did, so we came here right away."

When the man finished speaking, Joseph and Moon heard the soft cooing of a young Baby. A surge of excitement pulsed through Joseph from head to toe.

Moon's ears went up and he tilted his head to one side. Then he started wagging his tail with reckless abandon. Moon couldn't keep his feet still as he snorted and pranced about.

Joseph felt the sound from the Baby go through Moon like an electrical charge. He knew his dog wanted to start frolicking all over the place, and Moon would have too, had Joseph not whispered a stern command for him to settle down and held him in a firm grip. Even at that, Joseph had major trouble controlling his dog.

The cloth draped across the cave entrance swung open and three people walked out. From where Joseph hid in the shadows he could see inside the cave for just a moment before the makeshift curtain closed. He managed to catch a glimpse of a woman lying on a bed of straw with a young Child wrapped in a blanket beside her. A man stood next to her,

35

watching the three people as they left, the last one securing the curtain behind him. A few farm animals stood inside the cave as well.

As the three emerged from the dim light of the cave, Moondog squirmed free from Joseph's grasp. He ran up to the three and started spinning and jumping off the ground, wagging his tail and snorting the whole time.

Joseph quickly stepped out of the shadows. "Moon, come here, you idiot," Joseph hissed at his dog. Then he looked up at the older man. "I'm sorry about that. He's usually a lot better behaved. I hope he didn't scare you." Joseph spoke in as soft a voice as he could for fear of disturbing the others inside. Meanwhile Moon kept up his prancing as everything behind his nose seemed to be wagging at the same time.

Startled, the three took a nervous step backward. Then the older man replied kindly, "No, don't worry. He surprised us a little, but after tonight, I don't know if any of us will be frightened much anymore. We've got to tell you what just happened to us. Come, we'll talk while we walk. We need to get back to our flock, and we shouldn't disturb these people any more tonight. They've had a rough journey and need to get some rest."

Joseph studied the three under the starlight. Though he couldn't be certain, they looked like the same ones he had seen in the field earlier in the evening. They all seemed to be beaming from within. Joseph glanced at the cloth hanging over the cave entrance behind them. Some peace and quiet *would* be good for those folks inside. "Alright, let's walk back to your flock for now. I'd like to hear what you have to say," Joseph replied, "especially about what you saw inside this cave. Come on, Moon."

Moondog looked at the cave door and back at his master. Then he stood staring at the cave door.

"Moon!" Joseph's sharp command to follow jolted the big dog. Reluctantly he turned and trotted beside Joseph and the three shepherds, glancing back at the hillside for as long as he could see it.

The small group made their way out of the village and toward the field where Joseph and Moon first saw the shepherds. As they walked, Joseph noticed that the youngest limped on his right leg. No one else seemed to take note of it as the older man began explaining what had happened to them.

"The wind became too strong for us to stay up on the slopes all night as we had planned, so we came down to a protected field near the village. After our flock had settled in for the night, I took first watch as my two sons here got some sleep. We hadn't been there very long when all of a sudden a great flash came across the sky. Then this man, or angel, or someone, stood right there in front of me – I mean right there." The man spread out his hands toward the ground in front of him to show how close this angel had been to him, his eyes wide with excitement as he continued.

"He was all full of light, and light seemed to shine from him all around me and the boys. Incredible – I've never seen anything like it. I just let out a yell and stood there, scared to death I'm not ashamed to tell you. All the wind went right out of me and I couldn't speak to warn my boys or anything. I just stood there with my mouth open and my heart about to jump out of me."

"That's when we woke up," interrupted the youngest, "when that big old angel came zooming in right on top of us. I almost took off running but I saw Father standing there between us and the angel, and my feet just froze to the ground, so I didn't take off. I guess I just kind of jumped up and stood staring at the angel. I thought I must have been dreaming, except I've never been so scared at any dream before."

"We were all scared. I could hardly breathe I felt so scared," added the older son. "I almost started swinging my staff around to hit the man. I didn't know what was happening."

"Then," the father quickly interrupted his boys, "this here angel starts to speak to us." The man let out a roaring laugh, like what he had just said had struck him as about the craziest thing he'd ever heard.

"Can you believe that?" the father asked Joseph. "Can you believe this angel sent from God Himself came all the way down here to talk to me and my boys?"

The man continued before Joseph could respond. "And that's not the half of it I tell you. This angel starts to tell us not to be afraid, because he's come to tell us some good news, incredible news, the greatest news this world has ever known." The man became so excited he started moving his feet and waving his arms around. Even in the dim light, Joseph could see that his eyes were as wide as saucers.

"The angel tells us that tonight there is born the Savior, the Christ, in a stable in the village, and that we should go see all this for ourselves. Then the sky just filled up with angels. I mean *filled* up. There were so many that it looked like there were more than the very sky itself could hold, yet they seemed to go on forever. And they all sang 'Glory to God in the highest.' We heard all these voices all singing together just perfectly. I've never heard such singing in my life. Amazing, just amazing. The whole sky lit up with these angels..."

The man stopped for the first time and paused to see if he could still hear them while he gazed up into the sky. Joseph and the man's sons stopped and looked at the heavens. Moon followed their gaze. All they could hear now was the strained breathing of the man as he caught his breath from all the excitement. After a long pause the father turned to Joseph as if coming back from some faraway place.

"And then they left, just gone. The whole thing, at the time, seemed to be lasting quite a while, yet when they left it seemed like they stayed here for only a moment. My head couldn't seem to understand all that I had just seen. I thought I must have been imagining it all."

"That's when I ran up and grabbed Father by the arm," chimed in the youngest boy. "I wasn't scared any more, but I didn't know what was going on. I'm still not sure if I know what's going on."

"Then we all started talking at once," said the oldest son. "Did you see that? Did you just hear that? What was that? Did you see it?"

"That's when I knew I didn't imagine anything," said the man, turning toward Joseph. "It was too real. I knew that already. But when the boys started talking, I truly knew it. We decided to leave the flock and head straight to town.

"I'm still shaking on the inside. We didn't know what to expect, but we went together. That's when we found it just as the angel had said to us. A young couple with a Child, a Child just born a few moments before all this started. Staying in a cave, kind of a stable, the Child lying in a manger, like what animals eat out of! They looked like ordinary people, those two, just tired young people who looked a little scared themselves. But that Baby, that Child, what a precious Child..." the man's voice trailed off and his face reflected the starlight. Joseph could see tears in the man's eyes.

"The Child – yes, the Child," said the oldest boy, just barely audible.

The four had now walked back to the field where the sheep slept or grazed contentedly. Joseph's mind raced. He had felt the passion of the man as he told the story. What Joseph and Moon had seen, these three had seen also. Three poor shepherds of little value to the world around them. The ones God chose to announce the arrival of the Christ, the Savior. Not to royalty, but to these people.

Joseph considered telling the three about what he'd seen, but he remembered Tysius' admonition not to interfere with things. The man's voice interrupted his thoughts.

"Where are you staying?" His question startled Joseph for a moment.

"Ah, well... we're just sort of sleeping outside tonight. Too many people in town for our liking. We don't much like crowds."

"Won't you please stay here with us?"

"Yes, please stay," asked the youngest boy. "It's been a long time since I've had anyone close to my age to talk to. And half the night is gone already. Please stay."

Joseph looked down at Moon, who seemed to have gotten over his disappointment in leaving the cave. His big dog again wagged his tail excitedly. "Well, okay, if it won't be any bother to you folks."

"It won't be any bother at all," said the oldest son. "Forgive our manners. We're so excited about what happened tonight we never introduced ourselves. I'm Simon," said the older son as he extended his right hand to Joseph. "My father's name is Ruben, and my little brother is Daniel."

Joseph shook hands with each of them and introduced himself. Then he looked at his companion. "This fellow with me is called Moon, except when he wears me out. Then I call him all kinds of names."

Moondog wagged his tail as he went from Ruben to Simon and then over to Daniel for a pat on the head. He then returned to Joseph's side.

"Well, I see you've got a good wrap to use as a blanket," said Simon as he motioned to Joseph's blanket. "Find you a soft place and sleep if you want. I'm not going to be able to sleep tonight anyway, so I'll take the next watch."

"I'll stay up with you," added Ruben. "I can't sleep either. Besides, I don't want to miss anything else that might happen. You two young fellas try to get some sleep if you can. We'll wake you if anything else happens."

The two older men moved some distance away and conversed well into the night. Joseph and Daniel found some soft grass and lay down about five feet from each other. Moon took his place next to Joseph, lying with his head up and eyes and ears attentive to the sights and sounds of the night.

"Joseph," Daniel whispered. "You do believe us, don't you? We really did see everything that my father told you. I am still so tied up inside that I don't know if I'll ever be the same again. You do believe us, don't you?"

Joseph looked back toward the village and saw the star hovering high in the sky. "Daniel, I tell you the truth. I don't understand it, but I believe every word."

Chapter 9

The morning broke clear and cool with a slight breeze out of the west. Joseph opened his eyes to a breathtaking sunrise beginning to paint streaks of reds and yellows across the sky. He reached over and ruffled the fur behind Moondog's ears.

Moon lifted his head and stretched his front paws out in front of him while he spread his toes out wide. After he relaxed from his stretch Moon closed his eyes and yawned as wide as he could, curling his tongue at the end and making a squeaking noise at the peak of his yawn. He then looked at Joseph and began patting his tail against the blanket.

Joseph smiled as he gently scratched the top of Moon's head. He had often seen Moon wake with fresh excitement about a new day. Joseph had learned to adopt the same perspective himself, although his good attitude faded from time to time. Moon always seemed to be consistent in his happy anticipation of a new day of life ahead. Joseph again reminded himself to make a conscious effort to embrace that attitude.

Joseph stretched and detected the smell of food being prepared over a fire. Ruben had commenced cooking a short time ago. The food smelled good to Joseph, but he didn't feel very hungry. Joseph looked at Moon, who lay by his side taking in the morning. Even he paid little attention to the smell of food wafting over them. Joseph knew Moon well enough to know that if he felt hungry, he would be over near Ruben, staring holes into him until he got something to eat. *I can't remember when we've last eaten. This is really strange,* thought Joseph.

"I started to wonder if you young fellas would wake up today or not. Breakfast is about ready. There's a stream not far down past the hill over there." Ruben pointed a rough hand toward the east. "You boys go get washed up and we'll have something to eat."

Daniel had awakened at the sound of his father's voice and sat up, rubbing his eyes. "I'm sorry, Father. I meant to get up early and get the fire started. I guess I overslept. I didn't dream about what happened last night, did I? Angels came here and we did go into town to see the Child last night, didn't we?"

"Yes son, angels came here and we did go see the Child last night. And yes, you did sleep late. Simon and I talked most of the night, and there

41

is still much to discuss. You fellas go and get washed up. And get Simon on your way. He's watching the flock. The food will be ready when you get back. We'll talk more about last night."

Daniel, Joseph, and Moon rose to start the new day. Joseph noticed that although Daniel had an unsteady gait due to his limp, he could walk along at just about the same speed as Joseph.

"Brother," hollered Daniel as he flagged Simon down, "come on." After morning greetings the young men and Moondog walked silently toward the stream.

Joseph spent each step taking in their surroundings which the darkness had concealed the night before.

The three young men couldn't help but grin as they watched Moon race in big circles around them, tufts of earth flying into the air from his paws. After several laps, Moon fell back in next to Joseph. Then they all looked skyward now that the color of the sunrise had reached its peak. Their eyes reflected gold and red from the eastern sky as they heard what sounded like a hundred birds welcoming the day.

Joseph noted how several sheep bleated as the sun broke over the hilltop and began flooding the meadow with light. He turned to see a few of them shake off the dew from their fleece, sending rainbows of color into the day's first light. He saw the sun reflecting off a far hill as light fog rolled up into the yellow beam.

The pureness of this new day exhilarated him. Joseph felt he and Moon could jump over the hills if they wanted. Although he could not remember it at the time, they had spent many nights in the woods on the farm, and had wakened to some spectacular mornings. But nothing compared to this. The world, it appeared to Joseph, had somehow started over again, with a clean and bright new beginning.

The three reached the stream and spread out looking for a place to kneel down next to the water. Joseph noticed the track left by Daniel in the soft soil. The inside of his right foot made a clear mark as the foot pointed outward, almost at a right angle from his left foot. As he started to bring his right leg forward, the inside portion of his right foot dug into the ground as he stepped.

"Ugh," Joseph involuntarily grimaced to himself. If it didn't hurt to walk in that way, Joseph would be surprised. And even if it didn't hurt much now, Joseph knew it would over time. He had never seen a track quite like it before, but he pretended to take no notice of it.

Moon followed Joseph as he walked upstream until he located a large flat rock which projected out into the water. The cool water on Moon's warm pads made him stop and swing his tail while he grinned at his master.

Simon and Daniel remained several yards downstream getting cleaned up as Joseph knelt down and splashed the water on his face. As he finished washing he heard a whisper from next to him.

"Hey," said the voice.

Joseph jumped up and spun around. He lost his balance and stepped into the mud as he looked behind him with wide eyes and mouth agape. It was Tysius.

"Doggone you," said Joseph, none too nicely as he quickly scrambled back out of the cold water and onto the rock. "How did you get so close to me without me or Moon seeing you? That's the second time you about scared me to death. Where'd you come from this time?"

Tysius had trouble covering his amusement. "Ah, sorry about that," he said as he looked down at Joseph's dripping shoes. "I'd forgotten how jumpy you humans can be at times. I'll try and keep that in mind. But do try to keep your voice down. The others can't see me."

Joseph looked downstream to Simon and Daniel. They both stood like statues, staring at Joseph. "Hey you two," Joseph called, "do you or don't you see this guy standing here talking to me?"

"You shouldn't have said that," responded Tysius.

Simon and Daniel looked at Joseph in silence for a long time. Then Daniel looked at Simon and shrugged his shoulders. They both began washing again, but Simon changed his position so he could keep an eye on Joseph.

"You see, I'm not kidding," said Tysius. "They saw you jumping off this rock and now they think you're talking to yourself and seeing things. You should be more careful. I thought this might happen, but I need to talk to you right now. Turn your back to them so you can talk without them seeing you. Just pretend I'm not here."

Joseph squinted his eyes at Tysius a moment, his lower jaw jutting out. Finally he turned around and faced upstream. "Pretend you're not here? *I* should be more careful? What about you?" Joseph faced upstream but his eyes cut to the right, peering at Tysius. He spoke out of the right side of his mouth.

"What are you anyway, some kind of special tracker or something? How come they can't see you? You got some kind of special camouflage?"

Tysius smiled. "You might say that. I think your best description of me is what you'd call an angel."

Joseph's mouth dropped open and his eyes grew wide. He cut his eyes straight ahead and then back over to the right, giving Tysius a quick once over. Then he looked straight ahead again, not moving his head a fraction of an inch. His breathing had stopped.

Tysius tried to conceal his amusement.

"You mean like those ones I saw last night – like those ones?" whispered Joseph, his heart pounding in his ears.

"Yes, that's correct. Except I didn't come with them, exactly, though I joined in the singing. I couldn't help but join in the singing. What did you think of the singing?"

"Ah – yeah – I liked it. I liked it a lot – I mean it was great. It was wonderful."

"I would have told you sooner who I am, but you wouldn't have believed me then. I'm not sure you're ready now, but I need to tell you a few things before you do anything else. The others are done washing up. Send them on and tell them you will be following shortly. You need to wash your feet now anyway, so that is a good excuse."

Joseph turned slowly around to Simon and Daniel, who were cleaned up and ready for the walk back. "I'll be along soon. I've got to wash my feet and shoes off." Joseph's voice wavered as he felt his knees almost buckle.

Simon looked at Daniel and back at Joseph. "Okay, but don't take too long. Breakfast should be ready." The two started back with both of them giving quick glances over their shoulders from time to time at Joseph and his dog.

"So you're really an angel, like a real live angel!" Joseph exclaimed when the two brothers had gotten out of hearing distance.

"Yes, that's true. I cannot speak anything but the truth. I would not lie about this or anything, Joseph. Now listen carefully because I don't have time to repeat things and neither do you. And clean out your shoes. You can't go around telling lies either."

"Ah, right, right," said Joseph as he pulled his shoes off without bothering to untie them and began washing them in the stream.

Moondog waded out of the water and shook himself off, spraying Joseph in the process. He then walked up to Tysius. The angel scratched behind Moon's ears and smiled. Moon twitched and joyfully whipped his tail around. Joseph saw the tiny sparks dance from Tysius fingertips.

Tysius looked back at Joseph. "I'm not sure how long you'll be here. You need to learn all that you can without interfering with the Child. In your short life you've already learned to observe better than most people do in a lifetime. Continue to sharpen this skill, and gather all the information you can. I can only think that you will need it in times to come, although I cannot be sure how or when. You may interact with some of the people, but not directly with the Child or his parents. This whole situation is far bigger than you or me, and it is absolutely vital that you abide by these rules. Do you agree to this? I must have your word."

Joseph began to get over the shock of speaking with an angel. Somewhere inside fear tried to rise up. He looked at Tysius.

"Will it – is it – I mean – this is for good, right? There is nothing bad I'm doing here, is there? I don't know much about God but I've always been afraid of Him and what all He can do to me. I don't want to be doing anything against Him."

Tysius smiled broadly. "Yes, Joseph, it is for good. Of all the questions you've asked me in the short time we've known each other, this one is the best. Perhaps you'll have more like it in the days to come. Fear of God, if you understand what that means, is very good. It is the beginning of wisdom, Joseph. He is awesome and should be feared for what He can do. But do not fear Him in such a way that some do, as if He is some giant terrible ruler who wishes to crush you at any moment for any mistake you might make.

"Continue to search out His character, and realize who He is and who you are in relation to Him. Recognize how very much He loves you. That is where the fear, the respect, the awe of Him and who He is will begin to develop your wisdom and understanding. But do not fear Him for the sake of fear itself, for He truly loves you more than you can ever comprehend. For those who believe, who trust on and in His Child the Savior, God will teach more than just the beginning of wisdom. Indeed, they will have the privilege of becoming His very own children. But now I'm getting ahead of myself. Will you agree not to interfere with the Child or those close to Him?"

Joseph finished his washing and put on his soggy shoes. All the time Tysius had been explaining about God, Joseph felt a peace and joy growing in his heart. He stood up and looked at Tysius.

"Are you going to be around to help me when I need it?" asked Joseph.

"I will be nearby, or "around" as you say, sometimes, but not always. But you will have to be obedient on your own; I cannot help you with that. And things could get very difficult for you. Very difficult, and dangerous as well. The danger is real, not something make-believe. This you should know."

"You said before that Moon could go with me, that's still okay, isn't it?"

"Yes, as I said, you'll probably need him to help you if you decide to agree. Just know that the danger, very real danger, is for him as well as for you. So what is your answer?"

Joseph looked around. He always liked new adventures. This seemed like the chance of a lifetime for him and Moon. He couldn't remember much about his earlier life anyway.

"I agree. Let's do it." Joseph smiled at Moon who wagged his tail and began prancing about next to the water.

"Good. You should go back to Ruben and his sons now. Listen and learn."

"No problem. But next time you pop in on us, try to give us a little warning, okay?" asked Joseph.

"No problem," mimicked Tysius playfully.

Joseph looked up at the hillside where Simon and Daniel had gone, and then back to the angel. "One more thing…"

Tysius had already disappeared.

Chapter 10

Joseph felt his shoes squish as he and Moon walked back to the shepherds. Moon ran a big circle of greeting around everyone and then returned to Joseph's side.

"Good thing you showed up when you did," said Ruben. "My two boys about had a mutiny for the food. Sit down and I'll say the blessing."

Joseph sat on the ground next to Daniel. Moon sat next to Joseph and looked out over the meadow at the sheep. He still seemed uninterested in food, and much to Joseph's surprise, he himself didn't feel hungry either.

The three youths bowed their heads.

Ruben stood and looked to the heavens. "Dear God, You, who brought us out of Egypt and have given us so much, thank You. Thank You for this food. Bless this food and bless our day today. Thank You for allowing us, me and my family, to see the sights we saw last night. Give us wisdom as to what we should do now."

Joseph shot a peek at Ruben. Ruben looked to the heavens while he prayed, as if he could see the One he was talking to.

"Give us wisdom this day about the Child we visited last night, about the signs we saw and angels who visited us. I'm just a simple man, God, and I don't know about all these things. Watch over us and our new friend Joseph, our flock and his dog. Our times are in Your hands."

Then Ruben knelt down next to the pot of food over the fire and began ladling out the portions. He gave Joseph his food first.

"Ah, you know, I really shouldn't be eating this...,"started Joseph.

Ruben looked surprised and hurt at the same time. Simon and Daniel looked at each other. "I know it isn't anything special, and we don't have guests often, but it will do," replied Ruben.

"Oh no, I didn't mean that," apologized Joseph. "It's just that, well, I'm sure you folks weren't expecting guests, and you all work hard. I haven't done anything to deserve to share your meal. You three should eat. I'll just stay here and visit some if that's alright with you. I'd like to hear more about what happened last night."

"Yes, last night," mused Ruben. "We will talk more of last night. But I want you to eat something, if you will accept our friendship."

"Of course, yes, I gladly accept your friendship." Joseph fumbled for words. He took the food, and Ruben spooned out portions for his two sons, and then for himself. The food tasted delicious although Joseph couldn't identify it and didn't know if he should ask.

All the while Moon looked off indifferently toward the village.

"This is very good, Ruben," stated Joseph truthfully. "You should be proud to serve this to a king."

"Oh ho!" burst out both Simon and Daniel at the same time. "A king, no less," said Simon. "You made a few points there, you did."

"I knew you would like it." Ruben beamed.

Joseph changed the subject. "Tell me more of what happened last night. What did you and Simon decide about all of this, the Child and the angels and all?"

"We don't know for sure," began Ruben. "We know there is to be a Ruler born to us from God. He will be the King over all His people, over everyone. He will remove this yoke of Roman oppression from us. Under Him, we'll be a free people once again, for we are His chosen ones. The prophet Isaiah wrote about Him, and others have also spoken of Him long ago. Simon knows of other things as well." Ruben looked to his older son.

"Yes, I've heard of strange things, strange and great things for our people," began Simon. "The Savior for us is to be of the house of David. And He is to be born here, right here in Bethlehem. And the star, look at it, it still burns bright, even in the morning sky. It's no ordinary star."

They all looked at the star over the town as Simon continued.

"Last night the angels said that this is the Christ, to be born for us, the Chosen One of God. And yet..."

"And yet, how could it be that this Child, the Christ, would be born in a stable, a small dirty stable?" continued Ruben. "This is no place for the Savior of our people to be born. He should be born in dignity, in the nicest room in the town. And His parents. They are poor people, like me and my family. They have no riches, nothing to make them look like a king's family." Ruben looked as if he wanted to continue but stopped.

"And yet the angels," stated Joseph softly.

"Yes, the angels and the singing, the glorious singing," chimed in Daniel, his voice rising. "I have never heard such singing. I felt like I could jump off the ground and float in the air, and the singing would hold me up."

"And not just the singing," continued Simon, "but such tremendous praising, all directed to glorify God. That made it so much more meaningful than just singing. Can you understand that, Joseph?"

Joseph, with his extraordinary sense of observation, remembered how his heart had soared when he heard the worship. He recalled how it made him want to stay there forever and listen, never growing tired or wanting anything else. "Yes, Simon, I can understand it," replied Joseph softly as he relived the experience in his mind.

"Well, now that we have eaten, let us pray as told to us by our ancestor Moses," stated Ruben respectfully. "Dear Lord, we have eaten and are satisfied. Thank You for this good land which You have given us. May we not forget You, oh Lord, or Your commandments this day. Thank You for this food." Then Ruben looked at his sons.

"You boys clean up and tend to the flock. I'm going into town and check on the Child and his parents. There have to be others who saw and heard things last night too. I'll try to find out what's going on and find someone at the synagogue who can help answer our questions. I'll be back after a while. You fellows stay out of trouble. And you can give what leftover food there is to that dog. He sure is well behaved. We could use one like that if he could learn to herd sheep."

"Don't worry, Father, we'll stay out of trouble," replied Simon as he gave Daniel a stern glance. "I'll keep an eye on things."

"Very well then, I'll be back by evening." Ruben started off toward town as the three gathered up the plates.

Joseph gave Moon the leftovers. Moon looked at them and then back at Joseph.

Joseph stood shocked. Normally Moon would have scarfed down everything almost before it hit the ground. He looked at Moon and then gestured with his head toward the food, as if to say 'Eat the stuff, will you? There's friendship involved here'.

Moon saw Joseph's motion and ate the food without much enthusiasm.

This is so strange, thought Joseph.

With Moon at their side, Joseph and Daniel took the breakfast plates down to the stream for washing as Simon tended to the flock.

"Do you see this?" Joseph asked Daniel as he flipped over a rock and quickly caught a wiggling insect in his hand. "What do you call it?"

"Well, I don't really know. I guess I've never noticed those things before."

"Hmm." Joseph flipped over another rock and caught something else that Daniel had never seen before.

Daniel put down the plates and studied the little bug.

"Are those things under every rock?" he asked.

"Well, there's one way to find out," said Joseph. "See what you can find under that one."

Daniel turned over a big stone. "Whoa, look at that," he said earnestly. As he reached down to pick up the critter Joseph grabbed his arm.

Daniel looked up at him. "Do you see those pinchers on that thing?" responded Joseph. "Better take it slow until we learn what's what."

Daniel grinned. "This is amazing. I never knew there was so much stuff going on under these stones."

Moon watched his master exploring with Daniel. He began searching the bank; it didn't take him long to find a treasure of his own.

Soon Joseph spotted Moon's flying tail, held high like a plume, the tip twitching back and forth as fast as it could go. "Daniel, check this out." Joseph motioned toward Moon. "Let's see what he's found."

Joseph walked up and touched Moon's side. Immediately Moon stepped back, grinned at Joseph, then back at the clump of grass. "Hafoof."

Joseph knelt down and slowly parted the grass. Then he smiled and motioned for Daniel to have a look.

As Joseph opened up the grass and Daniel's eyes adjusted to the shadows, his face lit up. Daniel saw four birds half the size of his little finger huddled together in a nest no larger than the palm of his hand.

Joseph gently closed the grass back over the top of the tiny birds and the two took several steps away. Joseph then knelt down and hugged his Moondog. "Good dog, Moon, good dog, way to go buddy."

Moon backed up a step and looked into his master's eyes. A big grin covered Moon's face as his tail looped big circles behind him. Then Moon pushed the top of his head into Joseph's chest while his master praised him some more.

"If you moved away and sat here long enough, you'd see mama fly back to the nest after a while. In fact that's probably her now, on top of that little bush over there."

Daniel followed Joseph's gaze.

"When you look directly at her," remarked Joseph, "she hops facing the other way, like she's not interested at all in what we're doing. But if you look away, you'll notice she's very interested indeed."

The different things he began to see near him fascinated Daniel. He had difficulty maneuvering around some of the large rocks, but that never stopped him. "This is amazing, Joseph. I never paid attention to these things before. I had no idea there is so much life right here. Some of these bugs are really strange looking."

"Before you walk into an area," instructed Joseph, "take a few moments to just stand and observe. You'll be surprised at what you can see and hear if you do. Once you learn that, you'll begin to recognize some of the signs as to what might be there. You'll get an idea of which areas hold the largest variety of life, and which areas may have something specific to look for. If you practice this, you'll know a lot about what you're going to find even before you find it."

Daniel looked up and noticed the position of the sun. "Uh oh," he said. "I'm in big trouble now. I've got to get back and take my turn at watching the flock. I'm not old enough yet to do that at night, so Father and Simon have to take turns then. But I'm supposed to help during the day. I gotta go."

"Sorry about that. I can lose track of time when I'm exploring new areas too," replied Joseph. "Let's clean these dishes real quick and then Moon and I will go with you. But I don't think you have anything to worry about as far as Simon is concerned. Your brother's been checking up on you from time to time most of the morning."

"What do you mean by that?" asked Daniel, puzzled.

"I've seen him four times now," stated Joseph. "Three times he's tried to hide behind that big bush up above, and once he crept up to that large rock over there and peered around it." Joseph pointed toward the bush and rock at the edge of the ridge.

Daniel hadn't even noticed them before, let alone his big brother hiding behind them.

"He's not all that good at stalking, but I appreciate his concern for you," continued Joseph. "I don't blame him. He's just being a protective big brother to you while your father's gone to town. You know how I've been showing you how to concentrate on one area, and to see, really see what's there?"

Daniel nodded.

"Well after you get good at that, and some other tricks I'll show you, then you can learn to not only concentrate on one small place, but to see the entire surroundings almost at the same time. You'll even be able to know when someone is trying to slip up and watch you from a distance. It will take practice, but I think you can do it if you try."

"Did you really see Simon sneaking around up there looking at us?" asked Daniel.

Joseph smiled. "Sure did. And Moon saw him too. In fact he alerted me to him twice. After he did I signaled him to look away. That way Simon didn't know we saw him. Moon's usually pretty good about things like that. In fact, he's been really obedient for the past several days, except last night when we were near the Child. Moon's a good dog, he is," Joseph said proudly as he scratched Moon's ears.

Moon grinned big and whirled his tail around as he looked up at his master.

"How come I never saw Simon or noticed Moon when he saw Simon?"

"Well," said Joseph, "I don't know why. But you're right, I know you didn't notice. Maybe you just aren't used to watching for things like that. But now we should go back and check in with your brother."

The two boys and Moondog left the stream and found Simon watching over the flock in the afternoon sun. Daniel looked down at the ground as they approached. "Uh – sorry – I – we took so long, brother. We got carried away looking at things. I should have been back sooner."

"Ah, it's okay," replied Simon, much to Daniel's surprise. "I needed time to think without my little brother pestering me all the time anyway," Simon feigned irritation at Daniel.

Joseph caught Simon's glance and gave him a wink. Simon couldn't help but grin back.

The three youths spent the next few hours lazily watching the flock and trying to see angels in the clouds. Then they saw a man and a young girl approaching from the west.

"Who is that?" Daniel asked his brother.

"I don't know who the man is, but the girl looks a little like our cousin Sarah. Something's wrong here."

Soon they arrived. "You are Simon, yes, and Daniel?" the man asked. Simon nodded.

"Where is your father Ruben?"

"He's gone to town and may not be back for a while. How can we help you?"

"It is your Uncle Benjamin and his wife Rachel. They have died in an accident. I am their neighbor, Samuel. And I am sure you know their daughter, your cousin Sarah."

Sarah had her head covered and stared at the ground as she sniffed. Joseph noted her red eyes when she looked up for only a moment.

"I believe Ruben and you two are Sarah's only relatives in this area," continued Samuel. "I am sorry to bring the news of the death of Ruben's brother and his wife. This is tragic. They were such good neighbors to my family. Such good friends."

Simon took a deep breath and nodded. Although he and Daniel didn't know their uncle well, or Sarah for that matter, he knew the news would hurt his father. "What can we do?"

Samuel gazed from Simon to Sarah, and then back to Simon, the distraught look on his face saying all he needed to.

Simon nodded. "Thank you, Samuel. You have done what you could. I believe you were as good a neighbor to my uncle as he was to you."

Samuel tried to smile. He put his hand on Sarah's head for a moment and closed his eyes. Then he turned and walked back toward his village.

Simon cleared his throat. "Ah, Sarah, we're sorry to hear about your parents. Why don't you come and sit down at camp for right now."

Sarah nodded without looking up. The three along with Moon walked back to their campsite. Sarah sat down and drew her knees up to her chest as she closed her eyes.

"Are you hungry?" asked Simon.

Sarah shook her head.

Simon looked at Daniel and Joseph. "I think I'll go back and tend the flock for now," he said softly.

"I'll come with you," added Daniel, not knowing what else to do.

Joseph watched the two brothers walk toward the flock. He sat down and sighed. "I really am sorry to hear about your parents, Sarah." Joseph noted a tear roll down Sarah's face as she nodded slightly, her eyes still closed.

Moon walked over and put his head on Sarah's knees as he looked at her face.

Sarah startled at Moon's touch as her eyes flew open. Moon gazed unblinking at Sarah.

"That's the most mournful look I've ever seen in an animal," Sarah said softly. The two looked at each other for a long time. Sarah then reached out her right hand and gently kneaded the fur in Moon's thick mane.

Moon stood still, his tail slowly swaying as he continued to look into Sarah's eyes.

Sarah couldn't help but smile in spite of the huge tears rolling freely down her face. Then she pulled Moon close and buried her face in his golden mane. Sarah's whole body shook as she wept deeply for the first time since the accident.

Moon stood still as Sarah hugged him tightly, as if he knew of the healing that flowed out of him into the distraught girl.

Finally Sarah regained some of her composure. "Is this your dog?" she sniffed as she looked over at Joseph.

"Yes, he belongs to me. His name is Moon. Except when he wears me out, and then I call him all kinds of things."

Moon looped his tail as he heard his master say his name.

Sarah laughed a bit longer than was fitting at the joke, but didn't seem to care.

Joseph was surprised at how pretty Sarah's smile looked despite her current condition.

"So are you and your family from the village here?" asked Sarah.

"No, we're not. I guess you could say Moon and I are just visiting right now."

"Just you and Moon?"

Joseph nodded.

"Are your parents still alive?"

Joseph looked at the ground as he thought. "I – don't know. I know this sounds strange, but I can't remember right now." Joseph then looked over Sarah's head. "I think your uncle is returning from the village."

As Ruben made his way across the field, Simon intercepted him. Joseph and Sarah watched as Ruben's shoulders slumped and he put his hands on top of his head. They saw him shake his head slowly, then look toward Sarah. Soon Ruben and Simon approached.

"Why don't you boys leave me and Sarah alone for a bit," Ruben said quietly. "I need to hear what happened."

Sarah stood and she and Ruben embraced and wept while Simon, Joseph, and Moon joined Daniel tending the sheep.

When evening came they settled around the small fire and supper. "For now, Sarah will stay with us," stated Ruben to the three young men. "We are her only relatives that I know of. She can help around camp until we figure out what to do. Sarah said she'd do her best to help and I told her we'd all do the same. This will take some adjustment for all of us, so we need to be patient with each other. Is everybody with me on this?"

All three nodded in agreement.

"I also told her of what happened to us yesterday with the angels and the Child and all. I hope she doesn't think she's joined a bunch of crazy people."

Joseph could see Sarah's smile in the firelight as she shook her head.

"Well, I'm more confused now than before I went into town today," continued Ruben. "The young couple is doing fine, far as I could tell. I didn't spend much time there; they are both still pretty tired. And that Child, I could hardly take my eyes off of Him. I got that same feeling inside me today like when we all laid eyes on Him last night. Remember that feeling, boys?"

Both Simon and Daniel nodded in agreement but said nothing.

"Well, like I said, I tried not to get in the way there, but I had to force myself to leave that Child. I have never felt anything like that in my whole life." Ruben stopped for a long moment and gazed at the fire.

"So after seeing the little family, I went over to the synagogue to see what I could find out. I tell you, there's more confusion over there than you can shake a stick at. Anybody with an opinion of that star is giving it, and the ones who can read are looking into the ancient writings to try and make some sense out of what's happening. Folks are going off to find some of the real old-timers and see if they know what's going on.

"When I asked if they'd seen the angels last night it got dead silent. They looked at me like I was crazy or something. A lot of them acted like I'd been out in the fields too long. If any of them did see the angels, they sure didn't say so. It seems to me that there aren't too many other folks who saw the angels at all. I can't see how that could be; they filled the whole sky from one end to the other, and then some." Ruben stopped for another long pause.

"Anyway, after I left there I went and told a lot of our friends about it. Some of them may have believed me, I don't know. All this doesn't make sense to me. We're just simple folks – why would something like this happen to us?"

Ruben shook his head as if to clear all the confusion, but it didn't seem to work. Finally he sighed. "Something big is going on around here, something far bigger than I can imagine. And we're a part of it and I don't know why. But for some strange reason, I sure am glad."

Each of them stared at the fire. Whenever someone would start to give some sort of definite statement about the situation, they would stop after only a few words.

As it grew late Ruben took the first night watch as everyone made up their sleeping areas in the tall grass. They all gave Sarah the choice place next to the fire. Daniel squatted next to his older brother as he readied his grass bed and whispered a question.

"Simon, did you check up on us today while we were by the creek?"

"No – well – ah –well yeah – sort of. Why?"

"Four times?" asked Daniel.

Simon narrowed his eyes as he stared at Daniel. "Yeah, four times. But how did you know that? You never saw me. I'm sure of it."

"Once behind a rock and three times behind a bush?" whispered Daniel.

"Yeah, yeah, okay, so you saw me, big deal," said Simon.

"Just checking," replied Daniel. He lay down but his eyes remained wide open.

Joseph, who had silently observed the exchange from under his blanket next to where Moondog lay awake, shifted his gaze over to the star. "I agree with you, Mr. Ruben." Joseph said softly so that only Moon could hear. "I don't know what to expect, but I sure am glad me and Moon are a part of it."

At the sound of his name, Moon looked at Joseph and flapped his tail once underneath the blanket, the light from the star reflecting in his eyes.

Chapter 11

"HO, YO! Get on now. HO!" hollered Ruben into the cold night air.

The sound of the shouting tore Joseph from his sleep. He reached for Moondog but felt only warm ground. As his head cleared, he saw both Simon and Daniel shoot out of their sleeping places and run toward the sound of their father's voice. Sarah sat huddled near the fire trembling, her eyes wide.

Joseph jumped up and quickly followed the others. The star gave enough light for Joseph to see Simon outrun Daniel and speed off toward their father. Joseph could barely make out the surrounding hills and dark figures moving about. He caught up with Daniel and had to slow himself down so that they could run together, the young boy struggling to sprint on his twisted foot.

"What is it?" Joseph pressed as he and Daniel reached the sheep. Ruben and Simon yelled and waved their arms and shepherd's staffs as they moved swiftly around the flock. The sound of lambs bleating filled Joseph's ears as he scanned the area, straining his eyes in the dim light to see Moon.

"Don't know," came Daniel's pained response. "Go to the left, after Simon. I'll find Father."

"What is it?" panted Joseph as he caught up with Simon. "What's going on? Is Moon with you or Ruben?"

"Wolves," said Simon with fierceness in his voice that shook Joseph to his core. "They've come to raid our flock. It's been a while since they've found us, but now they're back and they want something to eat. We must act fast if we're not to lose any sheep – if we haven't already. Be careful. Some wolves are mad; they will attack you if they think they can get away with it. There may be several. Sometimes they hunt in big packs. We should go in two's. Where's Daniel?"

"He's circling around toward Ruben. Where *is* Moon?"

Simon had his staff in hand, but Joseph had nothing to use for a weapon. Joseph sucked in a deep breath to holler for Moon when suddenly they all heard a blood curdling howl from the blackness below. Joseph knew instantly that it was Moon.

Joseph's heart pounded as he ran down the slope, tripping and falling as he went, scrambling to his feet and running again into the darkened valley. "MOON!" he screamed into the dark night, "Moon, come here!" Joseph heard teeth snapping and wild snarls and yelps. The sounds of a massive canine war erupted in the inky black below him.

"Joseph!" Simon yelled. "Come back! Wait for me! Don't go down there alone."

Joseph didn't hear Simon's warning, but even if he had he would never have stopped.

Simon tore after him into the darkness.

"Moon!" screamed Joseph as he stumbled through the blackness and fell again over some rocks. "Moon, come here boy. Moon!" Joseph tripped yet again and smashed his left side into a large rock, but his adrenalin carried him through the pain. As he hurried to regain his feet, he felt a rock the size of his fist and picked it up in his right hand. He ran on into the darkness, oblivious to the danger that surrounded him.

When Joseph reached the bottom of the valley he stopped to listen, focusing hard on the dark landscape. He forced himself to hold his breath for a moment so he could hear over his pounding heart. He felt the hair on the back of his neck stand up as his eyes adjusted to his surroundings. In the dim light Joseph could barely make out his golden dog about twenty yards ahead.

Moon stood with his backside toward some large boulders, three sheep right behind him and jammed up against the rocks as tightly as they could get. In front of Moon circled at least six wolves or wild dogs.

Joseph squinted his eyes to see. He couldn't be sure how many wolves surrounded Moon since their dark fur blended in with the shadows. Moon was standing on only three legs, his right front leg torn, along with his right ear and side.

Moon's eyes locked on the alpha wolf as it slowly circled closer. Joseph's dog stood as the only defense between the wolves and the three sheep. Even though more than one wolf closed in on him, Moon did not let his eyes break from his intense glare at the alpha dog.

Joseph stood panting as his mind scrambled for a plan. Silently a half-starved wolf darted out of the blackness and struck Joseph from behind, driving him to the ground.

"Waaahk!" Joseph screamed as his head whipped backward from the shock and surprise.

When Moon heard his master's shriek he looked up toward Joseph. The alpha wolf saw his opening. Instantly the lead wolf and his pack, wild from hunger, the hunt, and the taste of blood, pounced on Moon.

Joseph rolled on his back to fend off the wolf with his left arm and swung wildly with his right. The rock made contact just below the wolf's left ear. For a moment the blow staggered the animal, but it regained its balanced and attacked again.

Suddenly Simon's staff whistled through the air and landed solidly on the lone wolf's back. The wolf let out a startled yelp and jumped several feet to the side.

Meanwhile Ruben's staff whipped in a frenzy at the wolves piled on top of Moondog. After a few seconds Daniel joined the fray. The lone wolf who had knocked Joseph down saw that the odds no longer played in his favor and tore off into the night. Simon quickly joined his father and Daniel in a battle to save Moon's life.

Joseph's anger and adrenaline reached their peak as he scrambled to his feet. He began tearing the wild dogs from the cluster and throwing them violently away from Moon. The alpha wolf looked frantically about and realized he was about to be pounded into oblivion. He took off with a yelp as Ruben's staff came down on his spine. With the alpha wolf fleeing, the rest of the pack soon followed into the darkness.

Joseph knelt down next to his broken dog and put his head gently on Moon's torn body. "Oh Moon, oh Moon," Joseph gasped.

At hearing his master's voice, Moon managed one weak thump of his tail. Moon tried to lift his head but he couldn't. Only a weak whimper came from his throat.

Joseph tried to gather Moon up but he couldn't use his left arm.

Ruben knelt down next to Joseph. "I'll carry him," he whispered to Joseph. Then he looked up at his boys. "Simon, you help Joseph walk. Daniel you bring these sheep. Let's get back to camp."

Ruben tenderly lifted Moon's limp body and cradled him in his strong arms. Then the four friends began the painful trek back up the hill.

Joseph walked next to Moon. With his one good arm, Joseph reached out to stroke his precious dog's head. He spoke softly to Moon – so softly that not even Ruben could hear what passed between the two friends. When they reached camp, they wrapped Moon in Joseph's blanket. Sarah threw her own blanket over Joseph, and she and Daniel sat at either side. They offered the compassion of a quiet presence while Joseph caressed Moon's head in his lap. Ruben started a large fire to keep the dog warm during the night as Simon headed out to guard the flock.

"I'm really sorry about your dog," Simon said quietly as he touched Joseph's bent shoulder.

"We're all sorry, Joseph," said Ruben. "We're all sorry."

Daniel and Sarah put their arms around Joseph's shoulders.

Joseph stared at Moon's battered head in the flickering firelight. "I know," whispered Joseph, fighting back the tears. "I know."

Chapter 12

The weather the next morning looked like a carbon copy of the day before. Ruben had spent the night stoking the fire in hopes of keeping Moondog warm and the wolves away. Daniel and Sarah had slept little, dozing off while leaning on Joseph.

The ache in Joseph's left arm had little to do with his not falling asleep during the longest night of his young life. He had caressed his dog's soft mane the entire night, and he never stopped praying.

Simon returned from the flock as Sarah began cooking breakfast.

"As far as I can tell, we didn't lose any of the flock, thanks to Moon. How's he doing?" he asked Joseph.

Joseph started to speak "I..." He just shook his head.

"There's been no change," said Ruben quietly. "He made it through the night though. He's a strong dog with a strong heart."

Ruben looked at Joseph as he searched for words. "We all saw how he positioned himself between the wolves and our sheep. I'm sure Moon could have gotten out of there to save himself when he had the chance. But he chose to defend the ones who had no defense of their own." Ruben closed his eyes and shook his head for a moment. Then he looked back at Joseph. "He's got a strong heart, that one."

Daniel and Simon caught each other's eyes at their father's words about an animal.

"Joseph, after we eat I'll go get some water so we can heat it and wash him off some, if that's okay," said Daniel.

Joseph tried to smile and nodded to Daniel. He couldn't bring himself to talk. He knew his companion lay close to death, and he couldn't imagine his life without Moon by his side.

After breakfast Daniel brought the water, and together he and Joseph carefully cleaned Moon's wounds as best they could.

Simon, even though exhausted, took another turn at watching the flock as Ruben and Sarah dug up some roots down by the stream. Then Sarah cleaned and boiled them and Ruben crushed them into a paste. He put them on Joseph's and Moon's wounds, and then wrapped them with what little cloth he had so the dressings would stay in place.

All the while Joseph sat with his dog, kneading his thick mane as he continued to pray. Moon lay with his eyes closed, his breathing so shallow that Joseph sometimes had to look hard to make sure he was still alive.

After they had done all they could, Ruben spoke to Joseph. "You should go to the stream and try to wash that biggest wound on your arm. I could not get it clean without more water. Then I can put some of this medicine from the plant on it, and it should get better. But first you must wash. If I try to cover it now, infection will set in. It still may, so you must wash well first. We will look after your Moondog, we promise. Now please, go wash. If you need help walking, Daniel can help you."

Ruben's eyes pleaded with Joseph. Although Joseph didn't want to leave Moon, he knew Ruben was right.

Sarah looked at Joseph. "We will take good care of him," she said softly, her eyes filled with compassion.

"Alright, I'll go. And I don't think I need any help. Daniel should go and spell Simon for a while. Simon could use a little rest."

Daniel helped Joseph to his feet and then started off toward Simon. Joseph walked slowly to the stream, feeling the full results of his numerous falls on the rocks and the struggle with the wolves. It took him a long time to reach the water. When he did, he knelt and threw some of the cool water on his face. For a moment he began to feel better, but as his mind quickly returned to his broken dog, the sense of refreshment left him.

"Joseph."

Joseph grimaced as he turned to see Tysius standing behind him.

"Don't be frightened. I didn't mean to surprise you," said Tysius softly.

"Tysius, where the heck were you last night? Do you know that Moon is almost dead from a fight with the wolves? Where were you?" Joseph clenched his fists.

"I know his condition now, but at the time it happened I did not know, Joseph."

"What do you mean you didn't know at the time? I thought you knew everything – you're an *angel* aren't you? You're supposed to know everything." Joseph could hardly control himself. "My best friend might die and you say you didn't know? Well I don't believe you. I think you knew all along and just wouldn't come to help." Joseph stood up and hurled a rock into the bank next to Tysius. "Moon might die, you know – he might die." Joseph's vision became blurred.

"Yes, I know"

Joseph stared at Tysius. "*I* know. You can heal him, can't you? You're an angel and all. You can just touch him and heal him can't you?" Joseph said excitedly.

"Now Joseph," replied Tysius, "no, I cannot. I've not been given the ability to do that."

"Well then, what kind of weak angel are you, anyway, some kind of reject or something? What good are you?"

"Joseph, now listen to me," stated Tysius firmly. "Of myself I have no power to heal. The power for true healing comes from only One, God Himself. God and God alone can heal. And I'll tell you why I didn't know what was going on last night. First of all I was not here. I was off doing other work. Secondly, you and Ruben and the rest may have been concealed by evil ones overhead. If they were here, then from where I was I could not see through them. If I had known, I would have seen what was happening and might have been able to help.

"Since the Child has been born, the evil one has been keenly interested. He has not bothered to come himself, which is good, but has sent some of his chief henchmen to survey the situation, and they are nearby now. They always cause trouble wherever they go. Last night was no exception. In fact, had they realized who you were, they probably would have tried harder to see that you would not have lived through the night. That could have cost the lives of Ruben and his family and Moon too. Fortunately, they were satisfied with the pain they did cause, and left it at that."

"I doubt it, Tysius," replied Joseph. "I can see *you*, so why didn't I see any evil ones last night? Are they invisible to me or something?"

"At night, to you, yes," answered Tysius. "You can see me in the day or night. And you can see them in the day, though you may never get the chance. Some are very bold, however, and don't seem to be as guarded anymore. But if in fact you do see them during the day, beware. For they usually like to do most of their work at night. And at night, they are the color of the night, so you cannot see them, or at least not now. Once you use your keen sense of observation to train yourself, then, up close anyway, you may, just may be able to see them. But right now, you cannot."

"Are you telling me the truth?"

"Joseph, I am a servant of the Most High God. I cannot and will not lie."

"So you mean what happened last night may have been a set-up? Just meant to hurt us as some sort of game these evil ones play?" asked Joseph.

"I am not absolutely sure, for I was some distance away, and this world is a broken place by its own nature right now. Because of that I am not sure. But it is possible, yes," replied Tysius. "And if I had been closer and had seen them, I don't know how much I could have helped. You see, what is happening here with the Child is far bigger than you or I or the world, for that matter. If I interfere and cause these evil beings to become more suspicious about what is going on, it would be too costly. There is nothing that I, or you, should ever do to alter the will of God, if that were possible. We must not and we cannot. Do you understand, Joseph?"

"No, I don't. You mean that if I, Ruben or his sons were going to die, you wouldn't help if it would mess up the will of God?" asked Joseph.

"Your time on this earth and your time to leave this earth are in God's hands, Joseph, not mine. You never asked to be *born*, did you?"

"Well, I don't understand that. And I thought God wanted only good things for people. How could all this bad be part of His plan?"

"I didn't say that people suffering is a part of His plan, did I?" answered Tysius. "There is such a thing as the evil one and sin. People truly don't understand how much pain and suffering is caused when they give in to temptation and sin. God desires fellowship with people and He loves you far more than you can comprehend. That I can see clearly. Hopefully you will learn and gain understanding as you observe things here. However, when I give you an answer, it is the truth," replied Tysius.

"So being obedient to the will of God, having faith, trusting in God, is important, no matter what the cost," replied Joseph.

"Yes, that is true."

"So you have to tell me the truth, always, right?"

"I do, yes," responded Tysius, "but I can only speak the truth in love. There are those of your kind who like to justify telling others what the truth is as they see it only to justify themselves or put others down. That is not God's way, thus it cannot be mine."

Joseph took a deep breath and swallowed hard. "So, will Moondog live or not? Remember, you have to tell me the truth."

"That is something that I cannot tell you because I do not know," answered Tysius. "I know you care deeply about him. I am troubled that he got hurt. I am telling you the truth about that."

"I think I'm beginning to understand that now. How often do you see God?" Joseph's question surprised Tysius.

"You live on a different plane of time than I, and *seeing* is an entirely different concept than what you imagine, so I'm not sure you can understand my answer. I suppose the best you can understand it, is that it depends on what I'm working on, although that is far too simplistic an answer to describe it. Because God is so near as is His very nature, I don't believe I can answer that in a way you can comprehend. Why do you ask?"

"Because the next time you see Him, would you ask Him to heal my dog for me?" Joseph wasn't kidding.

"Joseph, you don't have to ask *me* to do that. You can ask Him yourself. 'The prayer of a righteous man avails much.' That goes for righteous women and children too, you know."

"Children!"

"All right, young men too." Tysius smiled.

"Tysius?"

"Yes Joseph."

"I'm sorry. I shouldn't have said you're stupid or a reject or something. I'm upset that Moon got hurt and I thought you let me down big time. I am really, really worried about him, but I'm sorry I said those things to you."

"It's alright Joseph. Now let me ask you something. You've seen and heard angels singing of God's glory and you've caught a glimpse of the Child. Do you have the courage to go on? Are you able? As you've already seen, there is much danger involved. And things could get worse. You still must not interfere with the Child in any way."

Joseph remembered the glory of the angels singing and his brief glimpse of the Child. Just a thought of the Child sent a thrill of excitement through him even now. Then Joseph remembered his crushed Moon. After a long pause he finally answered. "If I do go on, it will not be from my courage or ability, for I don't have any on my own. The strength and courage will have to come from God. Is it in the will of God that I do?"

"Excellent question, Joseph," responded Tysius. "You should pray about that yourself and see what answer you get."

Joseph sighed. "I'll try, but right now I'll continue to pray for Moon. But if Moon doesn't make it," Joseph had to force himself to think this for the first time, "if he doesn't, you'd better ask me again, okay?"

"Agreed," said Tysius gently. "Now once you get washed up, you'd better be getting back. You're needed there right now more than you realize."

Joseph turned to wash and then thought of another question. When he turned back, Tysius was gone.

As Joseph drew near to camp, he saw Sarah cradling Moon's head in her lap while she rocked gently back and forth. There was no change in his dog. Joseph took his place holding Moon's head in his lap as Sarah sat quietly next to him.

By evening, Ruben and Simon finished another turn standing guard and returned for supper as Sarah and Daniel tended to the food. Everyone looked compassionately on Joseph and Moon, but there was little they could say to comfort their new friend.

Meanwhile Joseph stared blankly at the fire as Moon's head rested on his thigh. Joseph had prayed over and over to know what to do for his dog, and now he felt exhausted. Yet he didn't have a clue. Sarah and the family of shepherds ate in silence, each lost in his own thoughts while Joseph sat with his meal untouched before him. Only the occasional sounds of a few bleating sheep and the crackling of the fire could be heard.

Simon broke the silence. "Father, do you remember when Daniel fell into the ravine?"

Everyone jumped at Simon's words. Even by firelight Joseph and Sarah saw Ruben's entire countenance change.

"Of course I remember," Ruben hissed. "What do you think? That I've forgotten that I should have kept a closer eye on him? That his leg would be fine right now if I had?"

Joseph felt a knot growing in his stomach as he saw Daniel hang his head.

"Father, please do not be angry," begged Simon. "I ask for a good reason. When you held Daniel that day and night and the next day, we didn't know if he would live or not. But you knew that he had to eat something, drink something soon, or he would lose all his strength. Do you remember?"

"Of course I remember, Simon." Ruben's answer sounded like it was forced out of clenched teeth. "How could I forget?"

"And do you remember what you thought of to revive Daniel, how to get him to open his eyes again after the fall?" Simon's voice wavered between urgency and fear.

"*I* do," exclaimed Daniel, his head now up and eyes dancing with excitement. "I remember, or at least I've been told by Simon so many times that I *think* I do. You remember what you did, don't you, Father?"

Ruben's eyes cut to Daniel and back to Simon.

"Yes," said Ruben softly, the anger cooling from his voice. "That might work. That just might work. We don't have anything to lose, and Moon can't go on much longer the way he is. He has lost too much of his strength already."

Joseph listened to the conversation but didn't grasp a word of it. Then Ruben turned so quickly toward him that he jumped.

"I want to try something, if it's okay with you. When Daniel remained unconscious for so long I – we," Ruben looked at Simon, the fire in his eyes now replaced with understanding, "we didn't know if Daniel was going to live. We both had been calling out to God for help, to know what to do. So I took some soup..." Ruben looked down at his bowl of food. "In fact, it was this same kind of soup we're eating now. Anyway, I took some and put it on Daniel's lips and tongue. After only a few moments his eyes opened and he said he was hungry. Then he started to eat again and got his strength back. We know that our God brought my boy back, but He still used us to help Him do it. He gave us the idea of what to do. Can I try it with your dog?"

Joseph looked at Ruben and his two sons, then at Sarah. Joseph then looked down at his companion. Moon had been unconscious for almost 24 hours. With the extent of his wounds, Joseph knew he couldn't last much longer unless he began to regain his strength.

Joseph smiled weakly at Ruben. "Go ahead. It can't hurt anything so far as I can tell."

Ruben dipped his finger into his soup and gently, very gently, opened Moon's mouth and touched the soup to Moon's tongue. Then he closed the dog's mouth. The five stared at Moon. They waited.

No change.

Joseph felt his heart sink.

"Father, let me try," said Daniel, not willing to give up. He knelt down clumsily in front of Joseph and his dog as his right foot dragged behind him. He put some soup on his finger and touched it to Moon's cold nose.

"Down by the stream I've seen him find things with that nose of his that I could never have found myself in a million years. If this doesn't do it, nothing will. Ah... I mean, this might help too," Daniel said quietly as he looked away from Joseph.

Once again all five of them stared at the big dog. Moon looked more golden than ever lying motionless in the orange firelight. He quivered violently and gave a quick sigh, then appeared to quit breathing.

"Oh dear God, NO," said Joseph as he thought he heard Moon's last breath. His vision clouded.

Suddenly Moon's liver-colored nose started to twitch around like a rabbit smelling the wind for signs of danger. Then they all saw his dark eyes open and his tongue flick out to lick his nose and lips. Moon looked up at Joseph and ever so slightly lifted his tail twice off the ground.

The five stared dumbfounded for a moment. But only for a moment.

Then all of the flock lifted their heads from eating and stared at the small group of cheering people surrounding the campfire.

Ruben pumped his fist in the air as Simon danced a little jig around the fire. Daniel knelt staring at Moon, first with his mouth open, then with a huge grin. That grin spread across his face as he sucked in his breath.

Joseph simply buried his face in Moon's mane. "Thank You God, thank You God, thank You God."

"Well," said Simon to his younger brother, "don't just kneel there staring at him. Give that dog some more of that soup."

Joseph gently tilted Moon's head up as his friend began spooning in soup. "I've been praying all day to know what to do, but I just couldn't think of anything. Thank you, thank you," Joseph said through his tears as he watched Moon taking the food.

Ruben rose to ladle out some more soup for Daniel's bowl. As he walked by Simon, he grasped his shoulder for a long moment; the eyes of the two men met.

Then they all heard something they'd never heard before.

Sarah began to giggle.

Chapter 13

Exhaustion caused Joseph to sleep well that night. When he awoke, he pulled in a deep breath of the cold morning air. Even as it tingled his teeth and lungs, he felt life and health returning. Joseph still had no appetite, but he ate meals with the others. Ruben's herbal dressing seemed to do wonders for his wounds.

"Your recovery is rather remarkable," stated Ruben after a short time. "But it seems to me that your Moondog's recovery is even more so."

Joseph smiled as he nodded his agreement. "Once he got to moving around a little, his strength is really coming back fast. Are you sure you won't let us tend the flock today?"

Ruben shook his head. "No, not yet my friend. Both of you should mend for at least a few more days. We can take care of everything that is needed. You and Sarah just tend to things here at camp. That has already lifted a burden from us."

Once, when Ruben, Daniel, and Sarah were looking after the animals, Simon took rest at camp with Joseph and Moon.

"Simon," Joseph started, "have I thanked you for coming up with the solution to heal my dog? I really didn't know what to do, and if you hadn't thought of it there's no telling what might have happened to Moon."

"Joseph, yes, you've thanked me about ten times now. But you know you prayed about what to do, right? And just because *you* didn't think of the solution doesn't mean your prayer wasn't answered. I don't know why I thought of it when I did. I think God gives us wisdom if we ask for it, don't you?"

"Yes, I think He does."

"Well, I prayed to know what to do for Moondog too, so I figured He gave me the answer. Only I didn't know if I wanted to say it or not."

"You mean about bringing up Daniel's accident to your father?"

"Exactly. I take it you noticed the tension in the air when I mentioned it. Father has always blamed himself for Daniel's injury, and it just tears him up to see Daniel not able to run like the other kids his age. He's never once talked about it. Not once. That isn't right, I don't think."

"But you could have tried the soup on Moon's tongue when your father wasn't at camp, then you wouldn't have had to confront him with Daniel's injury," stated Joseph.

"You're right, but if Moon recovered, Father would have wanted to know what happened. And when I told him, he might have just crawled tighter into himself and hurt even more and never said anything. He might even have wanted you two to leave because you and your dog might have reminded him of when Daniel got hurt. Who knows what would have happened if I'd done it that way? No, I had to bring it up in front of him and in front of Daniel too, if our family was ever going to be healed. I didn't know what would happen.

"I just had to depend on God. He worked it all out. I think God may choose to give us wisdom to know what to do. Like what kind of herbs and medicine to use and all, but we're still the ones who have to step out and act with faith in Him. I believe real healing comes from God. And sometimes it isn't even the physical healing that we need the most; it's healing in the heart. I think He's the one who heals. Do you believe that, Joseph?"

Joseph smiled as he scratched Moon's ears. "Yes, I'm beginning to believe it more each day."

"Another thing you might not realize," continued Simon. "If I would have put some soup on Moon's tongue like we'd done to Daniel when he lay unconscious from his fall, nothing would have happened. Daniel thought to put some on the end of your dog's snoot, not me or my father. Daniel wouldn't give up. I thought it was all over when Moon didn't respond the first time."

"I need to thank Daniel for that," stated Joseph.

"You already have." Simon laughed again. "At least ten times. But you could tell him again if you want." Simon grew solemn. "He doesn't get much of a chance to feel important, you know. Don't get the wrong idea. Father loves him dearly and would do anything for him, and so would I. It's just that some of the kids in town are mean to him because he can't run and do all the things they can. Even some of the grown-ups too. You'd think they'd know better. People can be pretty cruel sometimes."

Joseph thought for a while. "He's good at seeing things out here. When we're down by the stream he's just fascinated by all the things I show him."

"I know. He's told me about it."

"I can't wait to get back out there with him," stated Joseph. "We had a great time and I like teaching that kind of thing."

"I've been hoping you'd say that. He could use a friend."

Some days later Ruben came back from town with some more news of the Child. "They've all gone off to the north, to Jerusalem, to dedicate the Child to God in the temple. It's our custom," continued Ruben as he glanced toward Joseph, "to take the firstborn to the temple. This is where the Child will also be given His name before God and man."

"Do you think I could get there to see that?" asked Joseph. "You don't know how I'd like to be there. And then where will they go afterwards? Do you think they'll come back here?"

"I think we'd all like to be there, but it wouldn't work for any of us to go. They're kind of exclusive about who they let in for things like that. And I don't know for sure, but I think their plan is to return right back here to Bethlehem and be nearby. At least this is the plan as far as I know it. And that will be good news for all of us. I have so many unanswered questions, and being close to the Child will be the best way to learn what's happening."

Ruben went back to town a few days later and returned that evening grinning. "They have returned from Jerusalem, just as we'd hoped. The town is buzzing with what happened. There are at least a couple of stories of how two old people saw the Child in the temple and proclaimed great things, incredible things, about Him. They both said that He is to be the Savior and Redeemer of His people in Israel. This sort of thing has never happened before as far as I can remember. And they have named the Child. His name is Jesus – that is Joshua or Jehoshua – which means 'Jehovah is salvation'."

"What we saw the other night, what happened with the angels and all is no mistake, no accident. Something huge is happening here. All my life I've heard of the Promised One from the writings of old, but I admit sometimes I doubted if anything would ever come of it. Others have lived and died in hope of seeing these things fulfilled but never saw them. I still don't know what all this means; but as I said before, I sure am glad to be a part, whatever part that may be."

He looked back toward the town and pointed a weathered hand. "Look, even this early in the evening you can already see that the star is burning bright with its long tail pointing right at the village."

Chapter 14

Joseph noticed that all but one of Moon's injuries healed without a scar. This surprised him since Moon had received such a mauling from the wolves. However, on one place on the top of his snout the fur didn't completely grow back. Joseph saw it as a permanent reminder of when Moon put his life on the line for those without any hope, without any defense. The scar looked like the outlined figure of a fish, about a half-inch long. It looked perfectly proportioned with the lines crossing each other where the tail met the body. Joseph mentioned it to Ruben and Sarah as they cleaned up camp.

Sarah studied the mark. "I think it looks kind of cute."

Ruben glanced casually at the mark, and then he stopped and caught his breath. He bent down with his eyes a few inches from Moon's snoot and studied the mark carefully.

Moon wagged his tail gently at all the interest in his snoot.

Ruben stared blankly at the ground as he slowly sat down. Then he closed his eyes and scratched his head. Joseph cast a puzzled look at his dog, who returned his gaze with more tail-wagging.

"*Ichthys*. Most remarkable," Ruben said softly to himself, then looked at Joseph and Sarah and repeated his words.

"Have you seen this symbol before?" asked Joseph. "What does ichthys mean?"

"Ichthys is the symbol for a fish. And, I guess you could say I've seen it before," started Ruben slowly. "I've seen this precise symbol the past three nights in a row now, to be exact. In my dreams, that is, not anywhere else." He looked over at Moon. "Not anywhere else until now."

Joseph and Sarah sat down next to Ruben while Moon curled up at their feet. "So what are your dreams? Are they something good?" asked Joseph.

Ruben closed his eyes. "Well – yes – and no. I mean – they are – but they aren't." He let out a deep sigh as he looked at Joseph and Sarah. "I don't understand what they mean."

"Are all three the same dream, or are they different ones with this same symbol in them?" asked Sarah.

"Well, they are all pretty much the same. I mean, there are some little differences in them, but not much as far as I can remember. They all had something to do with the Child, but not at this time. It is as if it is going to be a time in the future, when the Child grows up and dies. But then He's alive after He dies. But that doesn't make sense, because when the Messiah comes, He will reign forever. So that's one of the things that has me confused. But it gets even harder to figure out.

"In the time in my dreams, when the Child has grown up and died, this symbol is one that people who believe in Him will use to help them identify with each other. I didn't recognize anyone in the dreams, but they drew this very symbol in the dirt near their doors. That way others who believe will know that the family living there believes as well. And they put the sign on their clothes, and on other things too I guess."

The three friends sat for some time, Moondog snoozing comfortably at their feet. "Well, why doesn't everyone just say Who they believe in? Why use some kind of symbol?" Joseph asked. "Did you get a feeling for why that is in any of your dreams?"

Ruben looked at the ground for a long moment before he answered. "It is because those who believed in the Child were being hunted down and killed. They believed in secret, sort of. Those who spoke openly about Him were just removed, they were gone. I don't know how it was done, but I just knew in my dreams that this pursuit was bad, very, very evil. But those who believed were many in number, and they gave shelter to each other. This, I somehow knew in my dreams, was good, very good. And they used this symbol so they would know each other, even if they had never met before. It was as if those who were doing evil didn't know about the symbol. But to those who believed, it was the symbol of refuge where they could gather together and strengthen each other.

"None of this makes any sense. Why should anyone persecute believers in the Messiah? In the dreams there was much pressure on people not to follow the Messiah, very much force from many people. But there were those who would not give in to the forces against them, no matter what happened to them.

"How could any of this be?" Ruben looked right through Joseph and Sarah as he asked his question. "None of this makes any sense; perhaps it is just some dreams. But they seem very real. I have told no one about them, and probably would not have told you, except for this mark on your Moondog. I will tell you if I have any more such dreams and maybe then I can understand better what they mean. You know how dreams are. You wake sometimes with many questions, and try as you may, you can't go back and ask them."

Joseph and Moon continued to recover from their injuries and soon resumed helping where they could with tending the flock and other chores. Each day from afar they checked on the status of the young couple and the Child. Whenever Moon saw the place where they lived, he always acted like he wanted to go down into the village.

"You know what I think I appreciate the most about Joseph and Moon," Ruben said to Simon one day, "is not really their help with the flock. I mean, it's nice to be able to work less and get a little extra sleep, and to have time to go into the village more than usual. But what I like most is the time he and Moon spend with Daniel. They keep teaching him about all the different creatures and things that Daniel hadn't ever noticed before. In fact I haven't seen half the things Daniel has been telling me he's learned from Joseph. And I don't think I'll ever forget how Moon put his own life in jeopardy to protect our sheep that night. I've never seen anything like that before in my life."

"I know what you mean," replied Simon. "But it's not all one way. Daniel told me how he's shown Joseph some of the ways the flock acts if they think there's danger nearby, or how he's learning to predict the weather by watching the actions of some of the sheep. Of course I imagine Joseph has observed most of that himself already, nothing seems to get by him. But Daniel said Joseph always acts surprised when little brother shows him something like that, so that's a good thing too.

"As incredible as Joseph's ability is, he doesn't come off as a know-it-all. He seems a lot older than he is, if you know what I mean. And his dog, you're right about that, I've never seen anything like him before either. And not just the night the wolves attacked. Sometimes I think Moon seems almost more in-touch with things going on around us than Joseph does, if that's possible."

"They've been a big help with Sarah, too, don't you think?" asked Ruben. "Both Joseph and Moondog. I don't see how you, I, and Daniel could have taken care of Sarah on our own. But she seems to get along okay with Joseph; and, like you said, Moondog seems to know just when she needs some help getting through the day. I've seen her hugging that big dog and crying her eyes out and he just stands there. I couldn't take that."

Simon grinned. "So, you think Sarah gets along okay with Joseph, huh?"

Ruben looked surprised. "Well, I think so. Don't you?"

"Oh, I think so alright. I think she may like him a lot."

"Really?" asked Ruben. "I haven't noticed that. How come I'm the last one around here to find out about these things?"

"Well, you may not be the last one. Daniel knows, but as observant as Joseph is about everything else, he may be clueless about this one."

"I find that hard to believe."

"Yeah, me too. He probably knows. He's just not letting on," agreed Simon. "But do you think Joseph has caught on yet to what Daniel and Sarah have been up to lately?"

"Well, if it were anyone else but Joseph, I'd say no, no way. Especially when I think how careful all of us have been. But Joseph seems to be aware of everything that's going on around him, you know what I mean? And I mean *everything*, maybe with the exception of Sarah. Maybe. It's almost unreal."

"I know, I know," said Simon. "At least we're almost done with the thing. I'm getting tired of sneaking around. Daniel and Sarah are supposed to do some more work with me this morning if they can get away again without raising too much suspicion."

"Well," said Daniel to Joseph as they washed up by the stream, "I think I'll see if Father needs some help with the flock."

"I thought we'd do some more exploring in that canyon over there this morning. Your father said it'd be okay with him. I asked him about it yesterday," replied Joseph.

"I really don't want to today," Daniel lied. "I think I'll see what big brother is up to."

Joseph watched Daniel limp back up the slope toward camp and sighed out loud to Moon. Then he knelt down next to his dog. "I just don't understand it," whispered Joseph softly as he ruffled Moon's thick mane. "He seems to want to learn what's all around us here, and he really seems excited when you or I find something he's never seen before. But here lately he's acting kinda weird. He acts as if he doesn't like being around us anymore or something."

Moon looped his tail at Joseph's touch.

"Well, I guess if he doesn't want to go exploring, we can climb up to the ridge again and try to get a glimpse of the couple and Jesus. It sure seems to me that Daniel is wasting time though. And there's something else strange going on here too, Moon buddy, and I know you've seen it yourself. Like once in a while when we're alone down here, and we've noticed Ruben peeping at us from just over the hilltop or from behind some large rocks. You know, he's not any better at stalking than Simon. Then they send Sarah once in a while too, and she's worse about sneaking up on us than they are. Maybe they still think I'm nuts because of that time Tysius stood next to us and I asked Simon and Daniel if they could see him. Oh well."

Joseph cut his eyes up the slope that overlooked the village, then back to Moon. "Gotcha, buddy," he said as he shoved Moon off to the side and raced up the slope. As soon as Moon realized the game was on, he reared up on his back legs and bolted toward Joseph, little chunks of sod flying into the air from under his pads. He easily caught Joseph, ran past and spun around, stopping right in his path. Moon put his head low to the ground and his rear end up in the air, tail up and waving like a plume as his master ran toward him. Joseph took a jab at Moon and almost caught him, then the big dog tore off again in his joy, running full speed in big circles around Joseph.

They raced up the hill. Moon once got close enough for Joseph to grab him. They both tumbled to the ground and wrestled around until Moon got free and raced off in another big circle, his tongue hanging down from a huge grin. They reached the top of the hill and plopped down next to each other, panting for breath.

Joseph hugged Moon and plunked the big dog's head down on his chest as he tipped over on his back. This time Moon didn't struggle to get away. Joseph lay on his back watching the clouds and trying to catch his breath while Moon's head rested on his chest. Joseph knew the sound of his own heart beating was likely a comfort to his dog. "Oh my Moondog, my Moondog," said Joseph softly as he kneaded Moon's mane. "What would I ever do without you?" Moon's tail thumped his response.

That evening Joseph's new friends revealed their top secret project. They were all gathered around the fire when Ruben stood up and cleared his throat in a rather dignified manner.

"Today is a very special day in my family. We have a gift to present to Mr. Joseph and Mr. Moon for helping save our flock from the wolves. My family doesn't have a lot of nice things to give away, but this took Simon, Daniel, and Sarah some time to make." Ruben smiled and nodded, first to Joseph, then to Moon. "We hope you will find it to your satisfaction."

Daniel rose and limped over to his blanket. From inside he pulled out a beautiful shepherd's staff, straight as an arrow along the shaft and formed into a perfect hook on the end. Daniel hobbled over and presented it first to Moon, who gave it a long sniff and several tail thumps of approval. Then Daniel handed it to Joseph.

Joseph stared at the staff wide-eyed with his mouth open. Even by firelight Joseph could see the luster on the staff and multiple swirls of wood-grains spiraling throughout.

"It's beautiful!" Joseph smiled broadly. He stood up and used it as a walking staff around the camp. "It's perfect, just perfect. I can use this wherever I go exploring, as well as tending the flock." Joseph looked at

Daniel and smiled again. "Thank you very much, Daniel. This is something I can use pretty much anywhere I go."

"Simon did a lot of the forming of the wood. Sarah and I finished it and carved the lamb."

"Did you see the lamb, Joseph?" beamed Sarah.

Joseph had noticed the carving but hadn't had time to study it closely. He tipped the staff up and held the image toward the firelight. Right at the beginning of the bend in the hook he saw a beautifully carved lamb. Perhaps it was the play of the firelight, but Joseph noticed that the face of the lamb, especially the eyes, seemed to look right into his. Joseph held the staff in both hands. "Wow."

"I told you he'd like it," said Simon. He grinned at Sarah and his little brother.

"How did you make this without me knowing it?"

"Oh ho, it took a bit of doing, I can tell you." Then Ruben's laughter boomed across the hillside before he continued. "Daniel and Simon told me how observant you are, and now I believe them. Between running around seeing where you were and running over to see where everyone was working on the staff, and tending to the flock, I've about worn myself out. You almost saw it a couple of times, even with all our precautions. I'm glad this thing has finally been given to you. I don't think I could have taken another week of this." Ruben laughed again as he started out toward the flock.

Simon looked at Daniel and mouthed the words – 'He's laughing!' Daniel couldn't hide his grin.

"Well," said Joseph as he caught the exchange between the brothers, "I will think of each one of you whenever I use it. I promise you that."

At those words, Sarah spun around to look toward Ruben. She continued to watch him as he ambled away, her growing smile nearly hidden from Joseph.

"Perhaps tomorrow Daniel and I can go exploring and I can try it out?" Joseph called out to Ruben.

Ruben turned back to the group and looked at Simon and Sarah. "Do you think we can handle things all by ourselves for one day?"

"I guess we can get by," stated Simon. "Besides, Daniel has been putting a lot of extra time in for me while I worked on the staff. I guess we can struggle through."

The next morning Joseph peeked out from under his blanket to see a sky streaked with brilliant yellow and orange ribbons of clouds across the eastern horizon. He pulled in an enormous breath of cool air. How he loved the freshness of a new morning.

Moon tightened all his muscles for a second as he stretched his warm back against his master's side. Joseph felt his Moondog relax for a moment, then roll on his stomach. From there Moon squinched up his eyes and let out a giant yawn that ended in a high squeak. Moon jumped to his feet and shook himself, sending yellow fur flying into shafts of morning sunbeams.

Joseph looked over at Daniel. His friend sat up and rubbed the sleep from his eyes. Joseph gave him a thumbs-up sign, and Daniel returned the gesture with a grin that couldn't hide his excitement. The explorer's big day had begun.

As Simon and Ruben tended the flock, Daniel finished the last of the dishes.

"Joseph?" Sarah had a moment with him alone.

"Yes Sarah."

"Do me a favor today please?"

"What is it?"

"Be careful."

Joseph smiled. "Thanks, I will be. I've got Moondog with me; there's nothing to worry about." Joseph realized Sarah wanted to say something else, but just then Daniel appeared.

"Are we ready?" he asked Joseph.

"We are. Let's do it."

Joseph, Moon, and Daniel set off. The three took full advantage of their opportunity as the weather remained perfect for exploring.

Joseph and Moon showed Daniel different creatures, from small colorful insects to large eagles soaring along the morning thermals that lifted them high above the sun-warmed hillsides. Joseph taught Daniel how to use the drafts in the canyons to their advantage to mask their scent as they hiked.

Moon's keen sense of smell soon showed Daniel exactly what Joseph meant. "Hafoof."

Joseph noticed Moon's reaction to the slight breeze coming up from the warm valley below. "Let's go slow here," Joseph cautioned Daniel. "There is something unusual down below us. I'm sure of it. Let's take our time and stay in this line of brush along the left side as we go down. Then we'll see if we can spot anything out of the ordinary."

It didn't take Joseph long to find the objects of Moon's interest. After pointing them out to Daniel, the three explorers made a soft nest for themselves under the brush on the sunny hillside. There they spent nearly an hour watching a deer frolic with its two young along the canyon's opposite edge.

After a while Moon stretched himself out in the warm sunshine and fell fast asleep, the top of his head resting against Daniel's bad leg. Daniel playfully kneaded Moon's mane and smiled at Joseph. "I think I could stay here forever."

The unsuspecting deer disappeared into the brush as the sun climbed into the sky. A few ridges over, the three explorers discovered hyrax scurrying among the rocks, gathering food and protecting their territory from each other. Moon's ears went up as several hyrax simultaneously whistled a shrill warning to their clan. Joseph pointed out an eagle soaring overhead. The bird's large shadow raced across the ground and sent all the hyrax scurrying deep inside their burrows.

Joseph's new staff helped him climb the steep rocks on the canyon walls with amazing ease. "Now I know why you have these things for walking about," he said to Daniel, who expertly used his own staff as they trekked along. "I never knew how much they help in this steep country."

Daniel smiled broadly seeing that Joseph found his gift useful. "They are helpful, although we're still not as good as Moon," replied Daniel as he pointed toward the big dog.

Moon leapt easily about the rocks and boulders like a goat, his golden coat shining in the bright midday sun. Halting at the sound of his name, the dog perched precariously atop a large rock. He gave Daniel a quick wag of his tail before bounding to the next rock where he stopped once again to scent the air, alert for anything else that might interest his master.

Joseph watched as Daniel struggled to walk on the rocks or to cross the water when they came upon a small stream in the canyons. On numerous occasions Joseph saw Daniel stumble, and his heart ached to see his friend struggle so. "What say we just rest up here a bit and then start back? We don't want to overdo it. If we come back to camp and can't work the flock for a while, your father might not let us go again," suggested Joseph, but Daniel would hear none of it.

"I haven't ever been able to do this on my own, I mean, without Simon or Father with me. Even then we don't explore things like we're doing today. Don't worry about my leg, Joseph. I'm used to it. Besides, there are a lot of things going on out here that I've never seen before.

"I wonder if we couldn't spend the night out here in the wilds so we could hear what goes on in the dark. Then we could see how this whole valley comes to life at daybreak. Wouldn't that be great?" Daniel prompted Joseph.

"Well, maybe soon. I think today we'd better be getting back before it gets dark." They both looked at the sun in the sky, then back at each other.

"I can't believe how late it is already," said Daniel as he looked at the hills beyond them. "There's so much more to see. Today we've come a good ways, but next time we need to go further out and get away from town."

"That would be fine with me and Moon," agreed Joseph. "The less we're near people, the more we'll end up seeing out here."

The three explorers reluctantly began their journey back to camp. Along the way, Joseph dared to ask Daniel his opinion on something. "Daniel, your brother told me that all true healing comes from God. I think I believe that, don't you?"

"Yeah, I do. Just like I think that's why you and your dog got well so soon."

"After your fall into the canyon, you hit your head and were unconscious for a while, right? Then your head got better and you got well again, right?"

"Right. But what are you getting at?"

"Well, listen, if it's none of my business, you tell me and I'll shut up, okay? But why do you think that when God healed your head from the fall that He didn't heal your right leg too? You know what I mean, since He can do anything and all, it wasn't too big for Him."

Daniel fell silent for a while as they walked back along a stream. Joseph, sensing the awkwardness, wished he had not asked the question. Finally, Daniel answered.

"My mother died when I was born. I always figured it was my fault. But Father and Simon said that wasn't true. Then when my accident happened, I just figured that it was to punish me for what I did. I've never told anyone that, so don't you go telling anyone either, okay?"

Joseph felt his stomach tighten at this confidence. "I'm sorry about your mother. I had no idea," he said softly. "But it wasn't your fault that your mother died. How could it be your fault? You were just born. You didn't know what was going on; you didn't do anything wrong."

Daniel looked at Joseph but said nothing.

Joseph silently prayed about whether or not he should pose his next question. "So, like, you've never prayed for God to heal your bad leg?"

"No. I just figured that was God's way of punishing me for what I did to my mother. And my father too, and Simon, they hurt a lot when my mother died, though they never told me as much. All I know is that I was born and my mother died. If it wasn't my fault, then whose fault was it?"

Joseph sought to find the right words. "It surely wasn't your fault. I don't know why bad things happen sometimes, but you didn't do anything to cause it. Look, you believe what you want. I know it wasn't your fault. And I'm going to pray that God heals your leg, too. You can't stop me from doing that."

Joseph could sense Daniel studying him as they walked along the stream toward the village, the darkness of night beginning to settle in around them. They walked along in silence as Moon trotted happily in front, searching for any would-be treasures to discover before they got back to camp. As they neared the village and began to turn toward their nearby camp, Moon began walking up the hillside that overlooked the town.

"Moon, come here buddy, we've got to get back," urged Joseph.

Moon started prancing about as he tried to lead Joseph up the hillside.

Joseph studied Moon's actions and turned to his friend. Daniel began to speak, but Joseph put up his hand and listened. He had often heard the sounds of the village at this time of the day. Although they couldn't see the town from where they stood, Joseph thought he heard something different. He knew the trust Ruben had put in him to get Daniel back on time. Still…

"I can't quite put it into words, but something out of the ordinary is going on here. Are you alright with one last climb before the end of the day?" he asked Daniel.

"Well, yeah, okay," Daniel answered hesitantly as he gazed at the darkening sky.

As they turned uphill, Moon raced ahead with seemingly boundless energy. When they reached the top they studied the village below. "Do you see anything unusual going on down there?" Joseph prodded his friend.

"No, I don't see anything out of the ordinary. What do you see?"

"Something's going on, or more correctly, I think something will soon. I don't think we want to miss this. I'm not sure what it is, but there are some people down there who are all excited. Don't you sense it?"

"To tell you the truth, no, but maybe you're right. Let's go back and get Father and Simon and Sarah, then come back," suggested Daniel.

"One of them will have to stay with the flock, and besides I don't think there is time." Joseph pointed to the road coming into town. "Man, will you look at that, off toward the south." Right before their eyes came a caravan of camels and runners and – royalty. Each one wore fancy clothes with his envoys in front of him. The booming voice of the man in front of the procession could be heard from where they stood.

"Ho now, clear the way, clear the way. One time now, clear the way, ho now!" he hollered into the crowds. Each envoy dressed in similar although somewhat subdued colors compared to the person of honor behind him. And even as the light faded in the western sky, Joseph and Daniel could easily see the brilliance of the strangers and their courts as they proceeded below them. With so many oil lamps lit in the village, the three on the hilltop could see the commotion down below. They had never seen a more brilliant man-made sight.

Joseph cupped his hands around his eyes to shield out any other light as he concentrated on the spectacle below. Likewise Daniel squinted to see more clearly in the fading light. Meanwhile Moon just looked on and swung his tail slowly from side to side, his evening vision more refined than either of his cohorts.

Joseph saw the first man clothed in a deep purple robe with gold trim on the sleeves. He rode directly below them now, his runners surrounding him and making room for his camel by forming a wedge through the crowd with their bodies. The town's people crowded in along the streets. Shouts from the other runners to make room for their dignitaries caused the people to step back.

Behind the first celebrity, the three explorers saw more runners clothed in red and holding flaming torches. Among them came a man wearing a large pillow-like red hat adorned with gold tassels that danced in the rhythm of his swaying camel. He had a long red robe that draped off the left side of the camel. As he passed below them, Joseph noticed two young men walking alongside the man, carefully holding his robe off the ground.

Following this red-robed royalty walked about a dozen muscular men dressed in blue. Eight of the men supported two long poles on their shoulders, holding up a small coach. Inside it sat an official attired in blue and gold. Joseph and Daniel could barely see him through a side window as he passed below. With all the shouting and confusion, it was possible that even more royalty was present.

"Whoa, would you look at that! I've never seen anything like this. I didn't know people like this existed in the whole world." Daniel's eyes shone. "Listen, Joseph, I've got to go back and get Father and Simon and Sarah. They've got to see this."

Joseph didn't want to miss it himself, but he considered Daniel's bad leg and knew it would take a while for them to get to camp together.

"You're right; I want them to see this too. But you and Moon stay here. I'll run and get them and you keep track of what's going on down there. Pay attention to every detail you see and hear. I'll be back just as soon as I can. Will you be okay here by yourself for a bit? Moon will stay with you."

Daniel had never been allowed to stay away from his family alone and at night before, especially near the village. He stood a bit taller. "I'll be okay. And I'll tell you every detail of what happens. I promise, I won't miss a thing."

Joseph knelt down and put his face right in front of Moon's. "Now listen buddy, you know I don't like leaving you. But now you've gotta stay with Daniel. I'll be right back. Stay, Moon."

Joseph took off down the hill. Moon dropped his tail as a low moan came out of his chest. Joseph turned and looked at Moon. He gave him a hand signal and again told him to stay, then turned and ran into the fading light.

Daniel knelt down next to Moon. "It's okay Mr. Moon. We'll be alright until he gets back. I'll take good care of you." Daniel turned back toward town.

Moon gave another soft groan and sat down, leaning on the back of Daniel's legs. Although Daniel studied the progress of the dignitaries in the village below, Moon's eyes remained riveted on the spot where his master had disappeared into the darkness.

Joseph's feet barely seemed to touch the ground as he flew back to camp. He had taught himself to first walk, then run, almost silently on top of most any natural surface. Now he deftly slipped through the darkness and into the campsite. Joseph ran so quietly that he scared everyone as he suddenly appeared next to them. Ruben tipped the remainder of his meal onto the ground as he jumped up and Simon grabbed for his staff out of instinct. Sarah let out a quick shriek.

"Sorry to scare you," panted Joseph, "but you've got to come and see what's going on in the village. The entire place is buzzing. You've got to see it. I left Daniel there to watch until we can get there. If you think the flock will be alright for a while, you all need to come right now."

Looking startled, Ruben spoke first. "You left Daniel in the village, at night? What were you thinking, Joseph? I trusted you to take him to explore the hills today, not to leave him in the village. What have you done? Is he alright?"

"Yes, yes, he's fine. And he's not in the village. He's up above, on top of the ridge, watching. And Moon is with him. He'll be okay. But please come quickly. You don't want to miss this," Joseph urged.

"Alright, we'll come. But I want a full explanation of this when we get to Daniel. Do you understand, Joseph?" Ruben's voice boomed.

"Yes, I'll explain everything, but come on. We need to go *now*."

Simon quickly doused the fire and the four were off into the valley below. Ruben and Simon moved quickly but Sarah struggled to keep up. Joseph took her by the arm to help keep everyone together. When he touched Sarah he had a strange sensation and wondered if Sarah felt it as well. He kept his gaze straight ahead.

As soon as Moon saw Joseph striding up the hillside he stood up and began to thump his tail against the back of Daniel's legs. Daniel had become so engrossed in trying to catch every detail of things happening down below that he almost didn't notice.

Joseph signaled to Moon with his hand, and the dog took off toward him like a shot. He ran around Joseph in tight circles as if it had been years since they'd seen each other. In Moon's joyous excitement he almost ran Simon over as they all emerged from the shadows. Soon all five, along with Moondog, stood atop the hill, looking down into the village.

Ruben looked at Joseph as he drew labored breaths. "Alright. Now tell us what's going on here. And this had better be good."

Joseph looked at Daniel. "Ah, perhaps your son should tell us what he's seen. Daniel?"

"Well, after Joseph left, they all went right down the main street. Then they did something strange. They didn't stop at the inn for the night. I thought sure they would. It's the best place to stay, although not nearly good enough for those men. They went right by there and into that area of small houses. Once in a while the one in front would glance up at the star and point for his men to go this way or that. When they got right under that big ole star, they all got down, at least two off of their camels, and the one or two got out of the coach. It's hard to see in the dim light."

"Daniel," Ruben said impatiently, "who are you talking about, lad? I don't understand a word you've said."

"The magos," exclaimed Daniel. "The magos! I've heard several in the village calling the fancy men that name since Joseph ran off to find you."

"The magos?" replied Ruben and Simon at the same time.

"Yes, Father. The royalty, or at least that's what they look like. Joseph and I saw them come into town. Didn't he tell you? We thought they looked like dignitaries anyway, and then I've heard little bits of conversation from the people below saying they are kings too. See all their men, all dressed up standing together under the star? See them in the light?" Daniel pointed at them while everyone tried to focus through the night air on the gathering of men carrying torches and lamps. Directly above them shone the brilliant star.

"What does that word mean, 'magos'?" asked Joseph.

"It is a name for astrologers, seers, men of great wisdom who study various things, including the heavenly bodies like the stars," replied Ruben.

"They went into the house," continued Daniel. "But before that, each one had his men bring him something, though I couldn't see exactly what. The first magi had what looked like a small treasure chest or something. The others each had some kind of urn or vase. The men who carried them to the magi walked like the urns were real valuable, like if they dropped them they might die or something. Then one of their men, one dressed in red, knocked on the door of the building. A man opened the door and let them in. That's where they are right now, inside there."

"Well done, Daniel." Joseph complimented his friend on his observation of detail.

"Father," said Simon. "That is where the Child is, isn't it? That's where Jesus is."

Ruben stood squinting into the crowd down below and across town, his right hand stroking his chin, his left hand cupped under his right elbow. "Yes, Simon. I believe it is. I believe it is." Ruben said softly. "And kings will bow down before Him...I wonder..."

"Father," stated Daniel, "I know you don't want me out here by myself. But Joseph – I mean – we – thought it best for one of us to stay and watch and the other to come and get you. Plus I had Moon here with me the whole time. Are you angry with me, Father?"

"What? Oh – um – I'm trying to think here, son. I'll have to think about that a little."

"What does all of this mean, Father?" asked Daniel. "Is this in the writings of old? The angels and the words of the people from the temple in Jerusalem. And the star. And now magos come here to see the Child?"

Just then they saw a shaft of light coming through the door and the strangers and another man emerged from the house. After a few moments, the man went back inside and the magos returned to their camels and coach.

The shepherds stood a long while in silence, observing the magos leave town and set up camp in a high meadow on the other side of the village.

Finally Ruben spoke. "I don't know what it all means," he said softly, breaking the silence. "I must go to town tomorrow and find someone who can read and explain this to me. For now, let's get back to the flock."

"Ruben," asked Joseph as they turned to leave. "Do you think that you can watch the flock by yourselves tonight?" As soon as Joseph spoke, he realized the foolishness of his question. Of course they could, they'd watched the flock without him for years. And now Sarah was with them as well. Before Ruben could answer, Joseph restated his question.

"I mean – well – I don't know how long those magos, as you call them, are going to be here. And I'd like to sort of find out more about them if I can. Even with as many men as they've got around them, I think me and Moon can get close enough to hear without anyone ever knowing it. And I might be able to find out some answers for you."

"Can we, Father? Can I go too?" asked Daniel excitedly.

"No, Daniel, you cannot go. And Joseph, I don't recommend it for you, either. You are not one of my family, so I have no authority to tell you what you can and cannot do on your own. But those men are there to protect their leaders. They may not stop to ask any questions if they catch you sneaking around their camp. It could be a very serious thing."

"I know, but Moon and I have gotten close to things that can hear and see a lot better than those men. Besides, we may never get this chance again. I will go, and perhaps you can learn something in the village tomorrow as well. I'll see you then." Joseph turned to go, handing his staff to Daniel for safekeeping.

Moon sensed the excitement of a new adventure and remained close to Joseph's side. He looked up at his master for instruction.

Almost simultaneously, Ruben, Simon, Daniel, and Sarah cautioned – "Be careful."

Chapter 15

Joseph and Moon circled the village until only a steep-sided canyon separated them from the magos' camp. Joseph surveyed the area in the bright starlight and noted several small shrubs in the meadow surrounding the camp. "Well, buddy," Joseph said softly to his companion, "it looks like these folks aren't too worried about security. If they were, they'd have picked either an open area so that their men could better see anyone approaching, or they would've posted more than just the few guards that we can see from here."

Joseph smiled as he looked at Moon, whose tail swung gently behind him. Even after hiking all day, Joseph knew his companion was ready to go anywhere with him. They descended into the shadows of the valley and started up the other side.

Moon stayed close to Joseph and moved just as silently. Although they'd stalked many animals together, they hadn't tried to sneak up on humans before. Joseph realized this could be their most dangerous stalk ever.

When Joseph and Moon reached the crest of the canyon wall, Joseph lay down on his stomach and peered over the top. Moon followed his example and the two remained all but invisible to the few watching guards. From here they could see a scattered row of low trees and shrubs leading to one of the tents. Joseph observed the area for a while to make sure no one was hiding in the shadows of the trees. He reached over and ruffled Moon's soft mane.

The two spies began a low, slow approach toward the tent, using each piece of cover to its utmost. Only once did they have trouble in their advance. As they crouched in the shadow of a low bush, both heard the approach of one of the guards as he walked within a few feet of them. Joseph turned his head toward the ground and held his breath as he knew that one sound from him or his Moondog would spell disaster. They heard the guard stop as he looked about. Although a very cool evening, Joseph felt sweat beading up on his forehead.

For his part, Moon sensed the guard coming before Joseph did. He now lay as flat against the ground as he could, his head set directly on his front paws. If any danger came upon them, Moon could spring up in an instant to defend Joseph. Moon's golden fur reflected the starlight quite well, but fortunately, the dried grass around them almost matched his color. At last they heard the guard's footsteps fade off into the night and Joseph let out a nervous breath.

The two night stalkers moved to the shadows of the last large tree. From here one small bush remained for cover next to a tent. Joseph and Moon once again surveyed the situation. As they did so, two of the magos emerged from their tents and entered the tent nearest the two spies.

Joseph signaled Moon to stay while he made his way to the bush beside the tent. The small bush didn't provide much cover. From his new vantage point, Joseph could barely hear the magos conversing.

"But how can this be?" stated one. "First, He is born in a stable, a dwelling that even these plain people would find a lowly birthplace. Now living in a small house, almost a shack. And for a King, no less. And the parents look no more like royalty than any of the peasant people in this tiny village. This is strange. We have traveled so far. Could we have been mistaken?"

"I think not," responded another. "Remember the writings of old. They proclaimed the star from long ago. And also the writings of these people... 'But you, Bethlehem Ephrathah, though you are little among the thousands of Judah, yet out of you shall come forth to Me the One to be ruler in Israel, whose goings forth have been from of old, from everlasting.'"[1]

A third voice entered in excitedly, "Yes, and how can we forget the Child? Those eyes? When He looked at us, He looked right through us. Right through. Didn't you feel it?"

"More like right into us, into our very souls," responded the first voice softly.

"Yes, we all agree on that. Like being in the presence of peace itself, of life itself, so pure and absolutely wonderful, beyond words," said the second magos. "Not only the freshness and simple innocence of a newborn. But something far greater than that. I felt as if I could have stayed near Him for the rest of my life. What a strange thing that is. Think of it! Abandon everything, my kingdom, everything, and follow this Child. Extraordinary."

Joseph listened so intently to the barely audible conversation as he faced the tent that he didn't notice a guard approaching from behind. Even if he had, he could have done nothing. The guard stalked almost as well as Joseph. When he got close enough, he reached down to the crouching lad and grasped his shoulder in an iron-like grip.

The guard may have approached undetected by Joseph, but he was studied intently by another set of eyes – canine eyes. The guard's hand had no sooner touched Joseph's shoulder than the seventy-five pound rocket of gold fur and fury launched out of the shadows. Moon bounded twice as he accelerated, and then slammed into the guard's right side. The power of the collision knocked the man to the ground while freeing Joseph from his grip.

Joseph sprang to his feet and let out a shout of fright. However, the guard's scream of terror as he came crashing to the ground more than drowned out Joseph's shriek.

Moondog landed heavily on the guard's back. It took Joseph only a second to gather his wits and realize what had happened. In the low light he looked quickly at Moon. His dog stood squarely on the unfortunate guard's back, head near the man's right ear, teeth bared and a low growl rumbling from deep within.

There wasn't a moment to lose. "Come on, Moon!" Joseph urged. The two turned and flew through the shadows across the field. Disregarding any thoughts of cover, they headed straight for the protection of the shadowed valley. Now other guards came running, and the magos themselves emerged from the tent. Two of the faster guards began pursuit as the others surrounded the magos with a wall of protection. Two others ran to help their downed comrade who was really only shaken but not hurt. The unfortunate man had never seen what hit him and was lying motionless, frozen in fear lest the wild beast return.

Joseph and Moon reached the edge of the meadow and ran headlong into the steep valley below. Once at the bottom they stopped. Joseph took a moment to scan the ridgeline for pursuers, and to his dread, he saw the silhouettes of two men emerge and then briefly pause to speak before continuing. Joseph's heart quickened when he saw the shortening silhouettes of the descending men. The concealing shadows shrouding him and Moon would be little protection when the men reached them, so Joseph had to think quickly.

If they went up the other side directly away from the men, he and Moon would soon be visible in the star's light. If they went away from the village Joseph knew they would again climb out of the valley. Although Joseph preferred wilderness, they would soon be visible again by the light from the star. Joseph hesitated only a moment. Then he and Moon began to make their way swiftly down the valley and toward the village.

For once, Joseph thought, *the multitude of people and the inevitable confusion in the streets brought by these special visitors will be a good thing.* Joseph and Moon never stopped until they stood on one of the main streets in the village. There they ducked into the shadows of a side alley and waited. After a while Joseph poked his head out and looked around. He saw no sign of their two pursuers. Joseph breathed a sigh of relief, and the two made their way out of the far side of the village and to one of the surrounding hills. From here Joseph could see the magos' camp about a half mile away.

Joseph sat down and took in the scene: the star shining brightly overhead, the village below, and a few dim lights from the magos' camp off in the distance. Moon sat down next to his master and leaned his body against Joseph's right shoulder.

"Thanks, buddy," Joseph said as he gently scratched his dog's ears. "I owe you one. It's a good thing you were watching. I never saw that guy coming."

Moon thumped his tail easily at Joseph's quiet praise. Between exploring new territory and the evening's adventure, Moon had had a big day.

Joseph continued to study the scene below. As he stood to go back to Ruben's camp, he sensed something strange in the air. Moon felt it too and jumped up, looking out toward the magos' camp. They saw a light descend from the heavens to their camp. The light stayed a few moments and then ascended again. The night became still once more, the star shining brightly overhead. "Wow," Joseph whispered to Moon, "I believe we'll try to stay up the rest of the night and watch." Moon thumped his tail in agreement.

As morning began to color the sky, Joseph noticed the men in the magos' camp making ready for travel.

"Hafoof."

Joseph followed Moon's gaze and picked out Ruben and his son on the main street below. "You're on the top of your game, buddy. Let's go." Joseph and Moon made their way down to greet their friends.

"So, you have made it through the night alright I see," said Ruben, flashing a big grin. "We were worried about you. We all prayed for you last night that you would be safe."

Moon wagged his greeting as he rubbed his shoulder against Daniel, then Ruben, and then back to Daniel again. The boy smiled and stroked Moon's head and back.

"Thanks, we needed it, but we're fine. Moon helped with that. I heard the magos talking. They spoke of writings from long ago about the star and the King to be born under it. They've come a long way I guess. But they too are confused about the circumstances surrounding the birth of the Child. I think they're used to palaces or something."

"You heard them speak!" exclaimed Daniel. "Did you meet them? What are their names? I wish I could have gone with you."

"No, I didn't get to meet them," said Joseph, putting up his hands to stop Daniel's onslaught of questions. "It's kind of a long story."

Joseph turned to Ruben. "If I could take Daniel along, I'd like to show him something. We won't be gone long, and I promise I'll bring him right back."

Ruben thought about it for a moment. "Alright, if it's not far, he can go with you. I've just come to gather a few supplies and see if I can learn anything else about the Child and his visitors. Daniel came along in hopes of finding you anyway. I'll see you two back at camp, but don't wander off now, you hear?"

Joseph sensed a bit of tension in Ruben's response. He nodded to Ruben and then he, Daniel, and Moon made their way back up the hill where Joseph and his dog had spent the night. Joseph studied the surroundings and smiled. "Just as I thought, just exactly as I thought."

"What? What do you see?" asked Daniel as he watched Joseph and tried to follow his gaze.

"You know who's over there, right?" Joseph asked.

Daniel looked across the valley. "Yup, it's the magos' camp, moving out it looks like."

"What else do you see?" prodded Joseph.

Daniel studied hard for a long moment. "What should I be seeing?"

"You already see it, Daniel. You just don't know what you're seeing," answered Joseph.

"Well now, that helps a lot. What am I supposed to do with that?"

Joseph smiled. "When we saw the royalty last night, which way did they come from?"

"From the south, probably from Herodium and beyond there," replied Daniel. "So what?"

"Think about it, Daniel. The men came a long ways to find the Child under the star. They found him. Apparently, they've seen what they wanted to, and they're not staying around. So now, most likely, what are they doing?"

"Going home, I guess. Unless they have somewhere else to visit, but since they probably live a long ways from here, they may not know anything or anyone else around these parts. So I'd guess they are going back where they came from, going home. So?"

"I would guess you're right in what you're saying. So now look and see. Really see."

Daniel blew out a breath. "I can't hardly make out what they're doing now, the sun's in my eyes."

"Right." Joseph smiled.

Daniel knew better than to ask again. Instead he just studied and studied.

"The sun's in my eyes," said Daniel again. "Wait a minute. The sun's in my eyes. They're not going back the way they came into town. They're leaving a different way than they came here, and it looks like it might be a tougher way without the big road to travel on and all. Why would they be doing that?"

"What do you think it means?" asked Joseph.

Daniel laughed. "Is 'how should I know' a legitimate answer at this time? Perhaps they've got someone else to see, someone they all know?"

"Possible, but not likely. Like you said, they are not from around here, not anywhere around here," replied Joseph. "From what I heard yesterday, their speech doesn't sound anything like yours or the people of the village."

"I'd say 'I give up,' but I know you get upset when I say that, but I'm at my wit's end. I can't think of anything else right now. Why do you think they're going home a different way?"

Joseph could sense Daniel had given it his best, and he knew when to stop pushing his friend. "You did well, Daniel," replied Joseph. "You're getting better all the time. Pretty soon you'll be showing me things that I missed."

"I doubt that." Daniel smiled at the thought.

Joseph continued. "I'm not sure myself, but I believe it's significant." Joseph remembered Tysius saying that he would not show himself again lest the evil ones be forewarned of his presence here. Joseph wasn't certain if he and Moon saw Tysius last night descending from the heavens. "What they're doing over there is important, though I don't know why. Keep alert for signs of anything unusual which may tie in to this. I wish I could tell you more, but that's the best I can do myself right now."

Daniel smiled again. "I'm glad there are times when you can't figure things out too."

"You mean like most of the time."

"Yeah, right."

Joseph, Daniel and Moon made their way back to the edge of the village and found Ruben. As they started towards camp, Ruben sent Daniel ahead to get Simon. He turned to Joseph after Daniel was out of earshot.

"I spoke to one of my friends in town," started Ruben. "He's a strange old man who likes to stay out half the night. He told me he saw a young man and a golden dog sneaking about town last night and slipping into a dark side-alley. After that, a couple of the magos' men came snooping about. He said the young man sort of looked like that fellow who stayed around my camp. And there aren't any other dogs that look like your Moon in these parts. You want to tell me what happened or shouldn't I ask?" Ruben had an expression of amusement on his face, as if to say "I told you so."

Joseph thought for a moment. "Well, let's just say things didn't turn out exactly as I had planned."

"So you did get caught snooping around then, didn't you?"

"Well, I wouldn't exactly say I got caught, in the truest sense of the word. Moondog made sure of that. But I did get to hear a bit of their conversation before things got exciting. It seems they have come a long way following the star. And the Child had a tremendous effect on them. One even said that he felt like abandoning his entire kingdom just to be around Him. Pretty impressive stuff, I'd say."

Joseph decided to change the subject. "Did you hear anything else today about the Child?"

Ruben looked at Joseph for long moment. "Yes, actually I did. It seems that some of the elders at the temple have been studying up on these happenings and have found that the Child's father is from the line of King David from of old. And so is his mother. It has been prophesied that Israel's King would come from this line. By the way, I don't think I told you this before, but the father's name is Joseph."

"Well then, he must be a good fellow if I have to say so myself."

Ruben threw back his head as his laughter bounced off the hillsides. "I should have expected nothing less from you, Joseph."

Simon and Daniel approached, and Ruben did not return to his questioning about last night, at least for the moment.

The evening passed with more discussion about the star, the magos, the prophecies, and especially the Child. Ruben and Simon spoke of their dreams for themselves and their nation, with a leader strong enough to stand up to the Romans. What a great new world this would be for them and all their people. Joseph, Daniel, and Sarah listened intently, while Moon passively watched over the flock from a comforting spot near Joseph's side. The next few weeks passed by with talk of little else.

Sarah remained close to camp as she adjusted to her new life. Joseph and Daniel spent countless hours exploring the nearby country. Joseph always checked the village from an overlooking hillside before and after their treks. He wanted to keep alert for any changes in the village, or of the Child and His family. All seemed peaceful, and Joseph lost track of the days. Although he preferred to explore new territory, he decided to stay close for the time being as Ruben seemed cautious about trusting Daniel to his care again.

Joseph allowed Daniel to take Moon for short hikes to explore. Moon seemed to sense Daniel's need for self-confidence, and the wise golden dog generally seemed happy to go along. Still, when Moon saw Joseph after being away from him for just a short while, he would rear up and bound toward him. His tail would fly in the wind, his eyes bright, and mouth open in a big grin. The two would wrestle on the ground and greet each other like they had been apart for years.

"You know," Simon said to his father one day, "I believe you ought to think about allowing Joseph and little brother to go off for another day exploring. It seems to me that Joseph needs to get out and see some new territory, and it might do him good to know you still have confidence in him. Ever since that magos incident when Joseph left Daniel unattended, you've been a bit cool toward him. I think he feels it too."

"So you think I've been cold toward him, do you?" asked Ruben. "Well, if you've thought that, no doubt Joseph has noticed it. That young man seems to notice everything. Except Sarah. Maybe. But it *was* a bit irresponsible for him to leave Daniel by the village alone at night, don't you think? And all this exploring business. Why can't he be satisfied to stay here around camp?"

Simon studied his father. "Have you ever seen Daniel so joyful, so excited about life and all the things around him? As a matter of fact, I've even seen *you* looking more closely at the plants and insects and critters since Joseph and that dog of his showed up."

"When have you seen me do that?"

"Oh, usually after you glance around to see if anyone is looking."

"You've seen that, huh?"

Simon tilted his head to the side and downward and looked at his father from just under his eyebrows, a slight smile spreading across his face.

Ruben laughed long and hard. "Alright, alright, I'll talk to them this evening when they come back. I think you boys have got it in for me. I remember when life was a lot more routine around here."

That evening Ruben took Joseph aside and told him that he thought exploring some new territory would probably be good for Daniel. The two looked at each other for a long moment.

"Thank you," said Joseph.

Ruben nodded his head ever so slightly. "Thank *you*."

Joseph slept well that night. Too well.

A flash of light from the heavens descended quickly to the village below and remained only a few moments.

"Hafoof."

By the time Joseph cleared his head to look in the same direction as his antsy dog, he saw nothing unusual. "Moon," whispered Joseph, "we've got a big day tomorrow. Go to sleep." Little did Joseph know just how big, and that it would change all of their lives forever. Moon laid his head down on his front paws with a harrumph, but his eyes remained opened to the dark night around them.

Chapter 16

The sun rose bright and clear, but Joseph, Moon, and Daniel awoke long before dawn. Sarah, having heard of their plans, rose even earlier and prepared a hearty breakfast for the explorers as they made ready for the day.

"Would you young people be quiet and let a man get some sleep?" Ruben groused at the sounds of their early preparation. His pretense of annoyance fooled no one.

As the sun broke over the eastern hilltop Moon began bounding about. His tail flew like a flag as he rocked back and forth in his spirited romp around camp.

Joseph smiled as he watched his dog react to the change in morning routine. Then he began his last conversation with Ruben. "Now don't worry about us. The Good Lord will take care of our coming and going. He always has."

"The more I've studied on things these past few months, the more I'm beginning to truly believe that, Joseph. I'm not worried. When you first came here and started teaching my Daniel about all these things around us, and tying them all back to the Creator, I wasn't sure I liked this idea." Ruben smiled broadly at Joseph. "But I feel different about that now. You two have a good day and just keep teaching him about things out here, things that God has made. And be back before dark today, got it?"

"I couldn't help but keep teaching him. He never gets tired of learning. Besides, he's so curious about things that I have to learn a lot myself to keep ahead of him. And don't worry. I'll have Daniel back before dark."

Simon gave the explorers a wave from across the field as he stood guard by the flock. Joseph and Daniel returned the gesture.

"I'll have supper ready when you get back," said Sarah.

"Thank you." Joseph nodded his appreciation. "I – ah – I mean – we would like that." Joseph gave a final quick wave to Sarah as he turned to go.

Joseph, Moon, and Daniel had gone only a short distance when they heard someone following. They turned to see Sarah walking quickly toward them.

"You almost forgot," she said as she handed Joseph his staff. "Remember what you said you'd do every time you use this." Sarah's brown eyes sparkled as she spoke.

"I remember." Joseph smiled. "And don't worry about us. God's always taken care of us wherever we've been, and we've got Moondog with us too."

"Let's have a look over the village for a minute before starting out," Joseph suggested as they headed out away from camp.

Daniel looked like he wanted to say something but kept quiet as the two, plus a tail-wagging Moondog, walked briskly up the slope. They saw what they saw every morning: a sleepy village beginning to show signs of movement under the brightening eastern sky. Daniel sighed just loud enough for Joseph to hear.

"There is something odd here, something different," stated Joseph slowly, knowing full well Daniel's desire to get off to new places and start exploring. "This is strange. It's not that I see anything unusual, just that I sense something's not right. Do you feel it?"

Daniel paused for a long moment. Joseph watched Daniel go down his checklist as he'd taught him. First, after not seeing anything Daniel closed his eyes and concentrated on his hearing, then he bent his mind on his sense of smell. He tried combining all his senses together, even taking note of the cool morning air on his skin and direction of the breeze. Daniel shook his head.

Joseph spoke again in very measured words. "Last night, Moon woke me up. He sensed something, but I don't know what. I wish I hadn't been so sleepy. Maybe I would have seen something..." Joseph looked at Moon. The dog stared intently at the village below, the way he often looked when he couldn't quite make out something that seemed awry. They could all see the small house the Child lived in not far from the stable where He was born. All looked peaceful, and yet...

Joseph wished they could sit and observe the village for a time, but he knew how much this day meant to Daniel and what a disappointment that would be to him. They might not get another chance to explore away from camp for a while.

"So, where are we headed today?" Daniel asked as cheerfully as he could.

Joseph turned to his friend and smiled. He then looked toward an area which he had wanted to investigate for quite a while. However, that would mean a long walk from the camp and even further from the village. He then turned back and saw some interesting territory, not quite so far away, and still unexplored by the three friends. "This way," he pointed.

Joseph heard Daniel breathe a sigh of relief as they began their journey around the village and toward the southeast.

As they walked, Joseph and Moon studied Bethlehem from up above but never saw anything out of the ordinary. After this the three hiked around a small settlement where some houses sat under the hills not too far from Bethlehem.

"Do you know the name of this little village?" Joseph asked.

Daniel shook his head. "Nope, not this one. It's so small it may not have a name. That's the road to Herodium down there though, the one the magos came in on. But I'm sure you knew that already."

After hiking above the main road for a bit they decided to leave it in hopes of seeing more wilderness. They traveled east and dropped into a valley where it looked like no one else had been for some time. They soon discovered plants, birds, and insects which they hadn't seen before.

"Most likely this is due to the different aspect that this valley has relative to the sun as it passes overhead during the day," explained Joseph. "You may not have noticed it yet, but the climate is actually a little different here than just a short distance away. A lot of this is due to the lay of the land and its relationship with the angle of the sun's rays."

"So if we find another place like this, with the same angle toward the sun and all, then will we find the same type of plants and animals?" questioned Daniel.

"Plants, most likely. And some animals too, especially the smaller ones. The bigger ones, along with the birds, probably have larger home territories and move about more, sometimes due to the various seasons as well. But if we find nesting birds, they may return to the same areas each year during that season," responded Joseph. "And of course a lot depends on some other things too. Do you remember what they are?"

Daniel took a moment to answer. "Um, one would be elevation and even more important, how available water is, and if it's here all year or not."

"That's two. Good for you. You keep thinking about it as we look around and I'll bet you can come up with a few more." The young men made new discoveries most of the early morning.

Joseph noticed Moon behaving oddly. His big dog continued either looking back toward the village or ahead toward the south. Moon's ears were up but his tail remained low. Joseph knew something troubled his dog, but couldn't figure out what. He sensed Moon growing more and more restless as the day wore on.

Joseph saw that two families of birds had his friend's full attention. "Hey, Daniel, you stay down here in the valley. Me and Moon are going to climb out toward the south side and have a look around." Daniel motioned for Joseph to go ahead, that he'd stay put for a while.

Moon let out a barely audible moan and pranced about, not able to keep his feet still. He looked anxiously at Joseph, back toward the village, then away again toward the south. "Easy, buddy, take it easy Moon," Joseph said as he tried to reassure himself and his dog. Moon could barely stand still long enough to let Joseph touch him before he started prancing around again. They began climbing up the slope.

Moon raced ahead since Joseph could not keep up with his dog's rapid pace. When Moon reached the top of the ridge, his hackles went up from head to tail. He began pacing and a low rumble came from deep within. He looked back at Joseph and then off toward the south again. Running back and grabbing Joseph's shirt sleeve, Moon tried to pull his master up the slope. He then tore back to the top and resumed pacing and growling again.

Joseph sped up the hill as quickly as he could, his shepherd's staff digging in to give him traction as he went. When he reached the top, what he saw took away what little breath he had left. "Oh no!" he panted.

There before Joseph and Moon, not far in the distance, circled dark creatures, horrible creatures, too numerous to count. Most looked two or three times the size of a man, some even larger, with shiny, purple-black wings. The heads of these creatures shone blood-red and seemed almost too hideous to look at. Joseph and Moon saw their powerful feet with huge claws hanging beneath as they flew. The creatures fought as they flew near each other, and they appeared to be battling to be directly over their prey.

These creatures went by many different names, as they would often change their own names to fit their liking. Joseph and Moon could easily see one huge creature circling that currently went by the name of Krog. He appeared more powerful and evil than the rest, and the others kept him at a respectful distance. He flew in an ever-tightening circle, a menacing smile appearing now and then on his wicked face. Suddenly he dove below Joseph and Moon's field of view, and the rest of the creatures followed. As Joseph struggled to grasp what he had just seen, he noticed a cloud of dust coming from the area where the creatures had disappeared. The dust drew closer, following the road a short distance away.

Joseph and Moon ran along the ridge to where they could catch a glimpse of the road. There they saw soldiers on horseback racing to the north, clad in full armor. On the soldiers rode the creatures, their wicked claws dug into the soldiers' heads and backs. They half flew and half rode on the men's backs, screaming obscenities and the word "kill, kill, kill" over and over. The power and force of the creatures' screams sent a shiver down Joseph's spine. Moon stood next to his master, his hackles up and teeth bared, snarling at the sight below. Then it hit Joseph. The soldiers with the creatures rode directly toward the Child!

Joseph and Moon flew back along the ridge top, puffs of dust flying from beneath their feet. "Go back, go back!" Joseph's frantic shouts shattered Daniel's concentration.

Daniel turned and looked at Joseph and Moon racing toward him, his friend's shrieks causing the hair to rise on his arms and neck. He jumped up and began to climb the opposite slope, back toward the north, the direction from which they had come. Joseph's frenzied screams grew closer and Daniel climbed the slope faster than he'd ever moved before, in spite of the pain in his bad leg. Even with his best speed, Joseph and Moon caught him soon after he reached the top of the hill.

"Come on, come on," demanded Joseph as he caught Daniel.

Daniel fell and got up again. Joseph helped him up and pressed on. They finally reached the ridge overlooking the small group of houses in the town with no name.

The three stood panting. Joseph felt a huge knot in his stomach that almost made him nauseous. From their vantage point, both he and Moon could see the creatures, circling as if drunk with glee, over Bethlehem. Even from this distance, the two could hear the creatures' laughter at the coming violence, their ridicule and contempt for the people. They could hear them mocking the mothers as they watched their young sons die at the hands of the soldiers, the creatures' instruments of destruction. Joseph clenched his fists and screamed, "No, NO!"

Daniel stepped back from his friend as he fought for breath.

"I was supposed to watch," continued Joseph, now in a barely audible voice as he knelt down and stared at the ground, his hands on his head. "I was supposed to be there, to watch the Child, but I wasn't. Now it's all over. I was supposed to be there. No, oh no." Moon stood trembling and staring off toward the north. He seemed just as upset as Joseph.

"Joseph, have you lost your..." Daniel closed his eyes and shook his head. "I don't understand. Please tell me what is going on." Then Daniel looked up. "Joseph, there are many coming from the village now. I am sure of it. I can tell by the dust coming up from the road."

Joseph slowly stood up and looked toward Bethlehem. Dust from the horses' hooves rose as the soldiers returned from their deadly ride. As they rode south, the creatures remained soaring over the village behind them, intoxicated at the destruction below. The soldiers, no longer accompanied by the vile beasts, passed on the main road going south. All the soldiers passed, except the last one, a young soldier named Marcus.

The largest of the creatures, Krog, still clung to Marcus, spewing vile words of hatred into his ears, cursing the God of the universe. As the other riders rode past, Marcus stopped at the small road leading to the few houses directly below the three explorers. The creature tightened its hateful grip on the rider's head and cursed the people this man ruled over.

"They should all be destroyed, all of them," hissed Krog. "No one would know if you got the children here too. You'd probably be promoted. You must kill them, *kill* them."

The rider turned his horse up the road, toward the houses below the three friends.

Joseph didn't hesitate. He whirled around and grabbed his friend by the shoulders. He spoke quickly and passionately as he looked Daniel in the eyes.

"Listen to me, Daniel, there's not much time. Something terrible has happened in the village. You must go there at once. Your father, Simon, and Sarah, will need you there more than ever."

"But – but Father said we must stay together this time no matter what ..." began Daniel.

"I know, I know, but this is critical. Tell them all that they must believe God is still in charge, no matter what happens." Joseph knew that both he and Moon would not survive a battle with this soldier on his horse, or with this creature. But he would not allow his young friend to see the outcome. He could see the confusion and pain in Daniel's ashen face.

Joseph shot a glance down the hill as the horse and rider galloped toward the houses below. The sound of the horse's hooves grew ominously louder. Joseph turned back to Daniel. "You know I've never let you down before, my friend. Trust me, please, trust me. Now go as fast as you can, and remember what I've taught you. And tell Sarah – tell her I will not forget."

Daniel shook his head as his wide eyes filled with tears. "You're the best friend I've..."

"Please, Daniel," interrupted Joseph. "Tell them. Now go, go quickly."

Their eyes met. "I will tell them," Daniel managed to say.

Joseph nodded slightly. Then he and Moon spun and raced down the hillside, in a direct line to intercept the horse and rider galloping toward the houses.

Daniel swallowed hard as he watched for only a moment. Then he turned and stumbled off the ridge down the hillside toward the north, toward Bethlehem and his family, his vision blinded by tears.

Chapter 17

It took Daniel a while to make it back to Bethlehem, but long before he reached the village he already knew that Joseph had spoken the truth. Something terrible had happened there, something more horrifying than he'd ever known.

Daniel could hear the loud shouts and cursing of men long before he knew what had occurred. People ran along the road, back and forth, in utter chaos. But above all this noise he could hear the wailing and mourning of the mothers and fathers and children. Daniel saw his family as he wearily climbed the last hill overlooking the village. He came up behind them and when they saw him, they all hugged Daniel tighter than they ever had.

"Thank God you're alright." Ruben wept as he held his youngest son close to him. "Thank God. We don't understand what's happened. The soldiers came out of nowhere. We don't know why. They've slaughtered all the little children. All the young boys. We all heard the commotion while in the fields, the screaming, the shouting. We don't understand."

Simon and Sarah looked around them, and then Simon put his face in front of his younger brother's. "Where's Joseph?" he nearly screamed.

Daniel shook uncontrollably. "He knew," he sobbed into his father's chest and grabbed hold of Simon and Sarah to pull them close. "He knew all along. He knew something was wrong this morning but he couldn't figure out what. He could sense it. You know how he could sense things we never could? He said he should have stayed here so he could have done something. But what could he have done here? What could he have done? And how did he think he could stop that soldier, the one riding on his horse? That's the last I saw of them, Joseph and Moon, running down that hillside, right in line to meet that soldier. I know what he tried to do. He tried to keep that soldier from hurting anyone else. I know it."

Simon looked up at Ruben with shock in his eyes.

Sarah wept as she clung to Simon and Daniel.

"He didn't want me to watch. He knew I'm too valuable to you to let me get involved too, so he sent me away," continued Daniel. "He didn't want me to get hurt so he sent me back here. And he didn't want anyone else to get hurt, so he and Moon went to try to stop the killing."

The four continued to hold each other close. Painful cries of those who had lost loved ones pierced their ears, cries of those who had watched their own children butchered before their very eyes.

"If what you're saying is true, Daniel," said Ruben softly, "then I may have lost one as close as a son today too."

They held each other for a long time until Simon broke the silence.

"I've been checking on the Child, Jesus," he said quietly, fighting back tears. "No one has seen Him or his parents. It may be possible that they escaped."

Daniel looked up at his brother, and then his father as he wiped tears from his face with the back of his sleeve. "Joseph's biggest concern was about Him, the Child. He said he was supposed to be watching. That's why he was so upset that he wasn't here. Maybe the Child did get away after all. Maybe Joseph got away too.

"I remember my last glimpse of Joseph and that big golden dog of his tearing down the hillside to intercept the soldier on horseback. The soldier in full armor. The soldier trained for combat, trained to…" Daniel, covered with sweat and dirt, continued to shake.

Ruben looked over the heads of his family huddled around him, toward the south as shrieks of pain continued to fill the air. "I have prayed for wisdom as to what we should do," he began slowly. "It would be almost dark by the time we got to the place Daniel last saw Joseph. Simon, even if you ran the entire distance you would get there far too late to help Joseph and his Moondog. And I will not risk losing my oldest son in the process," Ruben groaned. Then he lifted his eyes to the star.

"Look, even now the star appears to be fading. I feel strongly that we must stay together at this time. We must not leave each other alone anymore this day. We will help here with what we can, help these people as best we are able to. Then let us go back to camp. We will go back, together. Perhaps we will find Joseph and Moon there already. If not, tomorrow at first light I will check at the place you are speaking of, Daniel. I will go there and check on Joseph and Moon if they don't come back to us tonight. And we will check on the Child Jesus too. But now, let us stay close to each other and do what we can to lend a hand here."

After helping the townspeople as much as they could, the four walked back to camp in silence. Simon started the fire as Daniel and Sarah sat with silent tears rolling down their faces. Ruben sat on their right and then Simon on their left, all touching shoulders with each other. Every few moments one would look into the darkness and could almost see their friend and his big yellow dog walking into the firelight. When Simon or Ruben thought they heard a sound they would jump up and stare into the blackness, sometimes calling out Joseph's or Moon's name.

Daniel stared at the fire as Sarah held Joseph's blanket close. Finally Daniel broke the silence. "Just before we left each other, Joseph told me to tell each of you to believe that God is still in control, no matter what happens. And Sarah, he told me to tell you that he would not forget. And he told me to remember everything he taught me. I don't see how any of that's possible now."

Sarah buried her face in Joseph's blanket, her shoulders shaking.

There was another long silence before Simon spoke. "The things Joseph told us to do sound pretty difficult to me right now. But maybe we all ought to try. At least for his sake, we could all try. For his sake, and the sake of that golden dog of his, we could try."

After a pause Ruben added, "It is the best idea I can think of as well. Let us agree together. Are you with us, Sarah? Daniel?"

Sarah nodded her head as she kept her face buried in Joseph's blanket.

Daniel shuddered as he gave a deep sigh. "Alright – alright I'll try. For my dear friends Joseph and Moon. And for you three, I'll try." Then Daniel did something none of them had ever heard him do before. Daniel prayed out loud.

"Dear God, if it's not too late, please help our friends Joseph and Moon. And the Child. May they not be..." Daniel paused a long time before he could continue. "And please help us to try."

Chapter 18

As the soldier Marcus rode up to the little village, he saw a woman and small child behind one of the houses. The beast on his back squeezed his wicked claws deeper into the man's head and hissed, "Kill it. Kill that one. It is an inferior race. You must kill it now before it can grow and be a soldier against you and your army. It is inferior to you, it doesn't deserve to live, you must take it."

Marcus began to tremble.

Joseph and Moon heard Krog laugh his horrible, arrogant jeer.

Marcus turned his horse and galloped around the house toward the unsuspecting woman and child. He jumped off his horse and picked up the child, drawing his sword in the same motion. The woman ran screaming at the man, but he knocked her nearly unconscious with his forearm. She buckled and sank into a heap upon the ground.

Joseph couldn't see the soldier's face as he and Moon ran toward him from behind. Joseph hoped they could take both him and the hideous creature by surprise. It seemed their only chance and they had no time to spare.

Marcus remained focused; if he did see Joseph and Moon, he showed no sign of it. But the creature Krog did turn his ugly head toward the two. With a slight motion of one of his wings he reached out and caught Joseph under the jaw. He lifted the young man off the ground and flipped him over and back onto the side of the hill Joseph had just descended.

A numbing pain shot down Joseph's right leg as he hit the ground and began sliding back down the hill.

Moon darted in with lightning speed and made a lunge at the beast's slimy left leg, biting deeply and tearing into its flesh.

Astonishment and rage flashed across Krog's face. How dare this dog come so boldly at him after seeing its master so easily beaten. For an instant the beast let go of Marcus and reached down to seize Moon with his other claw. He began to lift Moon up to eye level, slowly crushing the life out of him, grinning maliciously all the while.

As the beast released him, Marcus wavered and hesitated as he looked at the boy in his grip. "A child…innocent child…"

Krog saw him and screamed, "No, no, kill, kill, you must kill." The beast tossed the heavy dog aside as if flicking water off his fingertips. Moon was hurled violently onto some rocks; the impact knocked the wind out of him and inflicted a tremendous blow to his spine. Moon tried to stand but couldn't move his back legs.

Quickly the hate-filled creature grabbed Marcus with his right claw while he balanced on his left, hissing and cursing at him to kill the child. As the creature from hell screamed his commands into the soldier's ears, Marcus began trembling again. The man drew back his sword.

Meanwhile Joseph struggled back down to the battle using his left leg and staff to hobble across the ground. "God help me," cried Joseph as he stood on his one good leg and swung his staff around with all his might at the towering creature. The staff whipped through the air, the carved image of the lamb making contact with the creature's left wing tip and knee. It cut through the wing and shattered the knee, severing the lower leg completely. Immediately there spewed forth foul-smelling fluid and smoke from the wounds, wicked and vile substances as corrupt as sin itself.

Krog let out a scream of pain so intense that the other hideous beasts still circling and gloating over the destruction in Bethlehem heard it. They stopped their laughter and listened. Had there been another scream, a cry for help from Krog, all would have converged on Joseph and Moon. But Krog did not let out another cry. Fury exploded along with his pain as his grip on the soldier relaxed. Rage nearly blurred Krog's vision. He released Marcus and turned his full wrath toward Joseph and Moon.

Truth halted Marcus where he stood. His breath became short, but this time not from hatred. As if watching someone else, Marcus put his sword away, helped the woman up and handed her back her child. With wild eyes she snatched her child from him, continuing to weep. Marcus staggered to his horse.

"I – I'm sorry. I'm very, very sorry." He mounted his horse and slumped over in the saddle, staring at the ground beneath him. He turned his horse and rode back to the main road in a daze. Marcus closed his eyes and the horse had to find its way back to Herodium on its own.

Krog ground his filthy teeth. He towered over Joseph by several feet as he hurled down curses.

Joseph stood still and lifted his shepherd's staff between them with both hands, eyes locked on his enemy as the vile purple and black smoke from Krog's wounds swirled about. Joseph's eyes stung and his lungs burned from the acrid smoke pouring from Krog's wounds, but he stood his ground.

"No fear, little one?" hissed Krog, anger and loathing dripping from each word. "Sooner or later I destroy all who fail to fear me. For you it will be sooner." So much fury burned inside Krog that as he began to bring his killing claw down on top of Joseph, he leapt into the air for even more power. But because Krog had just lost part of his wingtip and one of his legs, his balance became unsteady. His crushing blow landed off its mark, barely missing Joseph and slamming to the earth instead. The powerful impact threw Joseph back several feet, knocking him down and tearing the staff from his hands. Joseph couldn't feel either of his legs and couldn't stand.

The botched strike made Krog all the more enraged. He stood over Joseph in an instant with yet another crushing blow on its way.

Before it reached Joseph, Moon gave one last leap and struck Krog from the side, knocking the wicked creature down onto his severed leg, causing even more pain for Krog. The lunge broke the brave dog's back. Moondog lay in the dust a few yards from Joseph, gasping for breath, his strength spent. Moon clawed at the ground with his front feet as he tried to pull himself closer to Joseph, his hind legs dragging uselessly behind. Moondog had given his last, his all, for his master.

Joseph crawled over to Moon. He grabbed the fur around his neck, his face only inches from his dog's. Their eyes met as Joseph sobbed, "We're together till the end, buddy – it's okay."

At the sound of Joseph's voice Moon tried to thump his tail but couldn't.

Meanwhile, Krog slowly righted himself, spewing hatred and curses, while flinging Joseph's staff to the side with his one remaining claw. He threw his head back and laughed as he stood over the broken dog and his master.

Joseph lay on his side as he clung to Moon's neck with one hand. "Dear God help us." He looked up through the sickening purple smoke at Krog towering over them. The creature, though still in tremendous pain from his injury, threw back his ugly head and laughed maliciously again. Then he drew back his terrible claw to crush both Joseph and his dog together.

Joseph instinctively put up one hand to protect himself and Moon, but it was like putting up his hand to stop a speeding locomotive. Joseph couldn't tell if he closed his eyes or passed out or if he actually saw the blinding white light streaking across his vision. A thought flashed through his head as Krog's horrible claw came down. *Maybe this is what it feels like to die.*

At the same time Moon managed to lift his head slightly. He looked over the top of Joseph.

"Hafoof."

Chapter 19

"What did you find out?" Daniel asked his father when Ruben returned home the next day. Daniel stood with Simon's arm around his shoulder on one side and Sarah's on the other.

"Well, I'm not sure of anything, so let's get that straight right away," began Ruben. "First, I checked in the village. As far as anyone can tell, the Child and his parents got away before the massacre happened. That's not for sure, but no one saw them or heard of them the day it happened. And I would think that someone would have known about it by now. I just think, and hope, that maybe they did get away. But we need not tell anyone about that, the soldiers have spies everywhere. As to where they may have gone, I have no idea. If Jesus is the One the soldiers tried to kill, let them think they succeeded, lest they come back again."

"Well that's a relief," responded Simon. "If this Child is the Savior of our people, the One the angels told us about, it would be beyond imagination if the soldiers had killed Him."

Daniel nodded his head in agreement as he unconsciously gripped his brother's arm. "And – what about Joseph?"

Ruben shook his head slowly. "I went over to where you said, Daniel. I spoke with some of the people there. At first they didn't want to say anything. Maybe they thought *I* was some sort of spy for the government, I don't know. Everyone is so confused and suspicious that they don't trust anyone, and I can't say that I blame them. Finally I convinced them of who I am and what information I wanted.

"You are right, Daniel. A soldier on horseback did ride into their town and tried to do the same wicked thing they did here. They took me to a woman, poor lady, who said she saw a soldier ride up, jump off his horse, and take her child. She tried to fight him, but he just knocked her down. She kept struggling to get up but couldn't. She felt sure he would murder her son right before her eyes. But then she said a strange thing happened. A strange and miraculous thing. The soldier got a look in his eyes like he no longer wanted to kill her child. Then he got mad again, and it looked like for sure that he would kill her son. But then, he put away his sword, helped her to her feet and gave the boy back to her. Handed him right back into her arms. And then he said he was sorry. Sorry! Then he left. She has a

nasty bruise on her forehead where the soldier hit her, and she is still in
shock, as are the other people around here."

"Did she see Joseph?" pressed Daniel. "Did she see him and Moon?"

Ruben held up his hands to slow Daniel down. "My son, she thinks
maybe she did, she doesn't know. Once the soldier handed her son back to
her, she said she ran and hid, lest he change his mind and come after them
again. She was almost hysterical today and I'm sure she was even more
panic-stricken yesterday. No one else saw what happened. She said the
soldier acted crazy, just crazy. If he was crazy with killing, and then crazy
with not killing, who knows what happened? Maybe he took Joseph and
Moon with him, who knows? She said the man was crazy."

"But no one saw any – uh – no one saw anyone killed there, or any
yellow dogs that were killed, right?" asked Daniel.

"Yes, that's right son. But I don't need to tell you how the soldiers
treat people, do I? Just look at what happened to our village yesterday."

"Well, maybe the soldiers let them go then. That soldier let the child
go, didn't he? Or maybe they got away. Joseph and Moon are real good at
slipping around you know."

Ruben shot a pleading look at his older son.

"Daniel," responded Simon as gently as he could, "if Joseph and
Moon escaped yesterday, they would be here by now. It's not that far,
especially for those two."

Daniel looked at the ground, fighting back tears for his best friend and
his dog. "I know you're right. But I can hope. And I can pray too, you
know."

"We can all do that," said Sarah.

"Yes, we can all do that," agreed Ruben.

Daniel wanted to know more about what had happened, and he knew
no one there could help him. Still, he wanted some hope.

"Father, do you think we'll ever see Joseph and his Moondog again?"

Ruben breathed a deep sigh. "I'll check with friends in Herodium, and
in Jerusalem. I'll see if they know anything about a young man and a
yellow dog taken by the soldiers. As for your question, I don't know, son. I
just don't know."

Chapter 20

"How do you feel?" asked Tysius

Joseph shook the cobwebs from his mind. He sat up slowly and looked around. Next to him lay Moon with his head in Joseph's lap, his tail thumping on the ground. Joseph's wakening obviously delighted his companion.

"How... what?" asked Joseph.

"I asked how you feel. You've been sleeping for some time now. Do you feel alright?"

"Yes, yes I feel okay. My right leg is a little sore, but not much. Where are we? Did we die? Is this heaven or something?"

"Slow down," said Tysius. 'No, you didn't die, though you were about to. And no, this isn't heaven. You are a little more than thirty of your years beyond where you were, although you have aged only a few moments. And we are some distance north as well, around the Sea of Galilee to be exact."

"Really?"

"Really."

"How did we get here? The last thing I remember is fighting with some monster that had his hooks in a soldier who wanted to murder some little kid. What happened?"

"Well, my dear friend who said he wouldn't interfere with anything." Tysius shot Joseph a stern glance.

Joseph looked up at the sky as if seeing a bird for the first time and Moon quickly followed his gaze.

"As I was saying, you two met up with one of the dark ones. A demon from the wicked side of this world, from the evil one. There are ones who are lesser than that one, and there are ones who are greater. As it turned out, it seems the both of you were no match for him at the time."

"So what happened? Did you take him out for us right there at the very end or something? I should have been watching."

Tysius stared at Joseph. "No, I did not take him out. It is not yet his appointed time. In fact he's still very much alive. And he loves to hold a grudge. For years after your clash with him, he searched for you. He only has one leg now, and a bit of a clipped wing. If anything, that has made him meaner, if that is possible. He would still very much like to destroy you, destroy the both of you. And he will do it if given the chance."

"So, what happened? How did we get here and not be taken out by that thing back there, or that soldier?"

"The soldier's name is Marcus and that thing is called Krog, or I think that's what he called himself when you met him. Don't know what he calls himself now, but his cohorts have some unkind names for him since he lost his leg. Another reason Krog hates you is that since that day, Marcus has turned from evil and has become a servant of the Most High God, and in the Roman army, no less."

A slight smile lingered on Tysius' face for a long moment, and then he continued. "As you know, Krog once had him completely, had him so securely that Marcus couldn't see any light in anything. Darkness smothered him. Now Krog can't get near Marcus and it infuriates him just about every moment of his existence."

"How did Marcus shake a thing like Krog? That monster had his claws – powerful claws – crushing Marcus' brain. I saw them. How does he defend against something that powerful?" asked Joseph.

"How does any human, Joseph?" replied Tysius. "Submission to God and resisting the evil one. That's the best way I can tell you. He has confessed his sins, prays, and fasts. He resists temptations that would lead him back to his old ways. Through his commitment, belief and trust in God and God alone, relying solely on His power. A complete surrender to God and believing on the Truth of His Word. And the Truth of His Word is His one and only Son, Jesus. Marcus almost never stops praying, almost never. And Krog can't come near him. In fact, it began to drive Krog mad, so he gave up for the time being. Hasn't been around Marcus for quite a long time now. It just tears Krog up; he can't stand it."

Tysius paused again as the smile reappeared. Then the angel continued. "As to how you got here, it's all quite complicated. Several things had to happen for this to take place. As far as you need to know, let's just say that I got the go-ahead to use my speed and power to come in and pick you two up before Krog destroyed you. It involved a lot, actually, a lot more than I can tell you at this time. And now Krog has seen me and knows who I am and some of the things I can do."

Tysius looked at Joseph and Moon again. "I'm glad I could rescue you this time. But keep in mind that may not happen next time. I have no idea if it will or not. It is not up to me. Also remember that Krog learned a few things about me that are no longer a secret to him. He will be more prepared the next time, if and when that time comes."

Joseph thought about that for a moment. "Well, if he's looking for me and he's around here, why can't he find me? And why did you bring me here? Couldn't you have taken us someplace where this Krog is gone forever?"

"Forever is a long time, Joseph. He has looked for you and didn't find you, so he's quit looking, more or less. He doesn't know you're here, as in here now. So he won't be looking for you, and he probably won't find you as long as you just observe and don't interfere with the Man, Jesus. Got it?"

"What do you mean 'Man', Jesus? He is only a Child."

"I told you thirty years have passed. Jesus is well into His ministry now. A lot has happened. A lot more is going to happen. You will see things you've never seen and will never see again. Are you ready?"

"You mean He's here, around here? Where is He?" Joseph couldn't contain his excitement.

At Joseph's enthusiasm, Moon looked up at his master and thumped his tail against the ground.

"Relax, Joseph. Yes, He is nearby. Are you ready to just observe this time? I am serious."

Joseph sat a moment and tried to understand all he'd just been told. "Okay, yes, okay. But what of our friends Daniel and Ruben and Simon? Did they, I mean, are they okay? What did they do when I sort of disappeared?"

"Yes, they're all 'okay', as you say. Over thirty years older, but all well. They still live near Bethlehem, a distance from here. They missed you. In fact they still do, especially Daniel. He tried to go back and track you, just as you taught him to do, after you disappeared. But by the time he got there with his older brother, many people had walked in the area, so they never could pick up a trail."

"I'm going to miss them too." Joseph felt his stomach tighten up. He wanted to know about Sarah but didn't feel quite prepared for the answers he felt sure he'd get. Answers about whom she married and how big a family she raised, etc. He decided to put the questions about her on hold for now.

"Tysius, do you think I did wrong to get involved the way we did back there? I didn't know what that soldier, Marcus, was going to do, but it had to have been bad. I saw the creatures over the village and all, and that Krog thing hanging on him."

Tysius remained silent for so long that Joseph didn't think he would answer. Finally he did. "It is not for me to judge, Joseph. You gave your word that you would not interfere with things, and you did."

"I had no idea that saying I wouldn't interfere meant that I would turn my back on the defenseless," replied Joseph quietly. "I know what it feels like to have something come at me that I have no defense against. I couldn't stand there and witness that and not do what I could to help."

Tysius studied Joseph. "You risked your life for the life of another, that I know. Perhaps this may be one of the reasons the command came down to allow me to rescue you. I don't know for sure. You did what you thought to be the higher good before God, didn't you?"

"Yes, and I'd probably do it again if it came to it, at least I hope I would."

"I'll try and keep that in mind."

"But why did you show yourself for our sake? That's what I can't figure out," asked Joseph. "You said you wouldn't because it would draw too much attention to the Child. Why did you do it then?" asked Joseph.

"You don't know what happened in Bethlehem that day, do you?" responded Tysius.

Joseph shook his head.

"Well, Herod the so called king of Judea waited for the magos who had paid homage to Jesus to return to him. Herod felt threatened by Jesus and wanted to kill Him. When the magos went back a different way, Herod went crazy with rage. He sent the soldiers to kill every child two years of age and younger in the village of Bethlehem so as to remove any chance that Jesus could survive. So you see, the evil one had already tried to kill the Child, therefore I didn't need to be quite so secretive at the moment."

Joseph reflected on what had happened to all those children and their families. "You know, this whole thing about Jesus is not just some nice story to feel good about and then go your way, is it? I mean, there are some serious consequences to all of this. Those little children may be forgotten by some, but it couldn't have been any more serious for the people involved. What could be more serious than life or death?"

"And not just life and death here on this earth," responded Tysius. "We're not just talking about that, but for eternity also. Yes, it is far more serious than most think."

"I'm not sure I follow you about more than just life and death here on this earth," replied Joseph.

"If you'll watch closely what is to be played out before you, you will know exactly what I mean. Let us go from here. There are things I want to show you. And by the way, you may find this useful."

Tysius reached behind him and tossed Joseph his shepherd's staff, complete with the engraved lamb.

Moon sniffed the staff and wagged his tail as he and Joseph stood up.

A huge grin enveloped Joseph's face. "You got it too!"

"Well of course, Joseph. What type of rescue operation do you think we servants of the Most High carry out, anyway?"

Chapter 21

Tysius took Joseph and Moon to the northwest side of the Sea of Galilee. From here they could see some workers toiling in the fields. Tysius stopped.

"See those men?" he asked Joseph as he pointed to some of the workers beyond the next valley. "You will find it beneficial to get to know some of them, one in particular. Be careful."

"Wait, whoa. What do you mean, 'get to know some of them?'" sputtered Joseph. "Who are they, and how do I do that?"

"Just do what comes natural for you, Joseph. And besides," Tysius looked down at the wagging Moon, "I think you'll have some help in getting to know them. Farewell."

Joseph looked out over the fields. "But I don't even know where we...." he looked back toward Tysius. Then he spun quickly around in a circle.

"Aw, doggone you, Tysius. I could use a little more info here, you know?" Joseph looked down at Moon and shook his head. "Well, he's done it again Moondog. I should have known."

Moon looked up at his master with eyes bright and tail wagging.

The two set off near the shore on their quest to 'get to know some of those men, one in particular.' Along the water's edge Joseph and Moon saw creatures moving about in the mud, and birds that they'd never seen before darting about the shore. The pungent smell of the sea filled their lungs as the wind carried it off the water toward the meadow behind them. After a while they came to the field Tysius had pointed out. Joseph approached the nearest worker as Moon walked obediently at his side.

"Hello," called Joseph as he drew near. The man slowly straightened his back, a grimace of pain on his face.

"What do you want?" Liam asked.

"Uh – I don't know – uh – I guess I just wanted to see how you're doing," stuttered Joseph.

"How I'm doing? What are you, crazy or something? I'm out here in the hot sun and you want to know how I'm doing. Do I know you from someplace or something?"

"Uh – well – no – I don't think so. I just thought I'd look around some – you know – and say hello. That's all."

"Look, kid," Liam said as he bent back to his task, "if you want work, you'll have to talk to the foreman, the one over there." He waved a callused hand off to the side. "Lord knows we could use some good help around here. Seems no one else wants to work but me. You got a good back, don't you?"

"Uh – yes – yes sir I do. My back's fine. Thanks." responded Joseph. The conversation was going nowhere fast.

The man straightened up again. "And what does *he* do?" he asked, pointing his rough hoe at Moon.

"Well, he can help. He helps me a lot. He's a fine dog."

Liam gazed at Moon for a moment. "Looks like another mouth to feed to me. But listen, kid, I've got work to do here. If you want a job, go over there and talk to that fellow. His name is Isaac. He does all the hiring and firing. I just work here."

"Thanks," responded Joseph as he and Moon made their way over to Isaac. *This has got to get better.*

"Uh, hello," called Joseph as he and Moon approached Isaac.

Isaac turned and studied the young man and his yellow dog. An eyebrow went up as he looked at Moon.

"Yes, what do you want?"

"Uhh – I – uh – I'm just wondering how you are doing?"

"How am I doing?" Isaac repeated the question. "How am I doing what? What do you mean by that?"

"Uh – well – I just thought I'd stop by and say hello," replied Joseph, thinking he could hear Tysius getting a good laugh out of this.

Isaac studied Joseph. "Do I know you from somewhere?"

"Well – no – no you don't."

"Look young fella, we're short on help and there's a lot of work to be done around here. I'm the one responsible for seeing it gets done, so I'm quite busy." Isaac turned away and looked out across the fields.

Joseph thought for a moment. "Maybe we could help you out. I've got a good back and my dog here is always ready to help if I show him what to do. Perhaps we could work for you."

Isaac looked back over his shoulder and glanced at the youngster who stood with a staff in his hand and a dog by his side. Then he shifted his gaze into the distance. "Hmmm – that might work. We don't have any sheep around here, but we've got lots of work. Get a hoe out of that wagon and follow me. I'll show you what to do."

Joseph took up a heavy bladed hoe with a short handle and he and Moon followed Isaac into the field. After Isaac explained what to do,

Joseph worked the soil, all the while taking in as much of the surrounding activity as he could. Ten other men worked the fields, two working with a lone mule, the rest with hand tools.

Moon apparently grew bored and stretched himself out next to Joseph's cultivated row, keeping his head up and alert. Joseph laid his staff down next to Moon as he continued working until sunset when he saw the other workers coming in from the fields.

Joseph put up his primitive hoe and he and Moon walked over where the other workers gathered around Isaac. The foreman handed out the day's pay as Liam grumbled none too quietly about his salary. Joseph studied all the men as he waited his turn. He had little desire for pay; he just wanted to know why Tysius had sent them there. As they drew near, Isaac looked up from his money box and smiled. He had noticed how hard the young man worked and started to speak when Liam interrupted.

"You're not going to give this *boy* what you gave me, are you? The *boy* ain't worked but a few hours at the most. And he ain't done much at that. You ought to give some of his pay to me. I done twice as much."

Isaac's smile faded as he turned toward the older man. Slowly he spoke in a low voice. "Liam, you've received a fair wage for today, as have all the rest of you. It is the wage you agreed upon. Now leave this one alone. He worked half a day and will be paid for it. There's more than enough work around here for all of us. I don't want you running anyone else off. You understand?"

"Yeah, sure," replied Liam. "Why not pay the boy for his dog too? The two ain't done much but lay around all day anyway." Liam threw up his hands as he started down the dusty road toward his home.

Joseph saw Moon stop wagging his tail as his dog studied the man. Joseph knew his dog's sensitive nose; Joseph himself could catch the scent of the unwashed laborers and so could Moon. But his dog could go a step further and pick up the stench of a rotten heart.

Isaac sighed and turned back toward Joseph, handing him his half-day's pay. "I hope you'll be back. We've got plenty to do and I could use a good worker."

Joseph took the money, though he had no idea what he'd do with it. "We'll be back. Sunrise okay?"

"Sure." Isaac laughed. "Sunrise will be just fine. See you then."

Joseph and Moon ambled along near the sea and listened to the fishermen talk of the day's catch. After a while they walked halfway up the hillside and stopped near a small grove of trees. From here Joseph and his dog could see a good portion of the sea and a fine house nearby. They sat down and studied the scene. Once in a while Joseph could make out Isaac, busying himself about the property. *Hmmm, Isaac must own that fine house.*

They rested and looked over the valley below as the sun set behind them. A cool breeze came off the sea and the tangy air filled their lungs. Joseph felt a chill as Moon curled up in a tight ball against the breeze. For the first time Joseph realized that the blanket the innkeeper had given him had been left behind. Joseph sat with his back against his dog and drifted in and out of an uneasy sleep.

Tomorrow, Joseph determined, *I'll use the money to get us another blanket.*

Chapter 22

Joseph watched the morning sky change from grey to pale blue as he shivered and stirred in the dampness of the early hours. He and Moon walked to the water's edge and listened to the fishermen as they readied themselves for the day. They arrived several minutes before sunrise as Isaac toiled about the house. Joseph noticed how much care he took while doing his work. He saw that Isaac treated everything with great respect and knew he must have worked hard to own such a fine place.

Isaac worked so intently that when he saw Joseph and Moon standing in the dim light he gave a short grunt as the two startled him. "Whoa... well, hello there. You two are early. I didn't know if I should believe you about being here at sunrise."

Moon ambled over to Isaac, who gently stroked his big golden head. Isaac looked down at his moist hand in surprise while Moon wagged his approval and returned to Joseph's side.

Isaac came closer and looked at Joseph. "Where do you live?" he asked as he studied his newest worker.

The question caught Joseph off guard. "Oh, just around I guess. We like to sleep outside when the weather's nice."

"When the weather's nice..." Isaac looked at Joseph's damp clothes. "You got anything to get under if it rains?"

"Uh – well – not yet – but I will soon – after today's pay and all," Joseph stammered. "We're fine. We love it outside, we really do." Joseph changed the subject. "Can we do anything for you before we go out to the fields? You seem to be plenty busy around here."

Isaac smiled. "You sure can. The others won't be here for another half hour or so. By the way, I'm Isaac," he said as he dried his hand and extended it in a warm greeting to Joseph. "And I suppose you and your dog have names?"

"I'm Joseph. And his name is Moon, except when he wears me out. Then I call him all kinds of names," Joseph looked down with love at his companion, rubbing the top of his golden dog's head.

Moon's tail swayed from side to side as he grinned back at his master.

Isaac smiled. He studied the young man and dog who had obviously spent the night out in the fields. "First, you can go down to the sea and fill these urns with water. The inside help will need it by the time you get back. Then you can start over in this shed," said Isaac as he pointed to a nearby building. "Clean it out and straighten things up inside. I could use someone around here at night to help me look after things. There's a cot and blanket in there. You two can stay in there tonight if you'd like."

"Well – yeah, that would be great, if it wouldn't be any trouble to you. You sure do have a nice place."

"Oh, I'm not the owner, but he trusts me to make most of the decisions around here. He should be back next week. If things work out for you here, perhaps you can meet him. He's a good man. But you'll have to earn your keep, mind you."

Isaac handed Joseph an oil lamp. "By the way, Joseph, be careful when you're down by the sea getting the water, especially before daylight. Some of these fishermen around here are a pretty rough group. So just be aware of that, alright?"

"No problem," replied Joseph as he toted the two urns with Moon stepping in beside him. "We'll be careful." Once down by the water, they stepped out on an old wooden dock that the fishermen used to help launch their boats. Joseph knelt down on it to fill the urns. The scent of wet lumber and lake water swirled around them with fresh new aromas as the day began to break. Soon they returned and gave the water to a young man at the door of the house.

Joseph opened the creaking door of the shed and peered in. By the light from the smoky lamp he could see that the inside of the shed already appeared clean and in order. After walking in, he hung the lamp on a ceiling hook and looked down at Moon and shrugged.

"Well buddy, things look pretty good in here. I guess I can shuffle around some and at least sweep the place out." Joseph began sweeping the floor as Moon wandered from corner to corner, sniffing scents of workers from long ago. "Hope it's not too musty for you, Moon," kidded Joseph. "At least we've got a dry place for tonight, and for that I'm grateful."

The workers soon gathered outside and the workday began as Isaac directed each to his specific job assignment. No one but Liam commented, stating his weariness of always having to do the most work. Isaac ignored him as the workers left for the fields, Joseph and Moon returning to the area where they had worked the day before. From there, Joseph and his dog could see a large portion of the sea below and the daily activity of fishermen coming and going.

Joseph continued working with the heavy hoe as Moon stretched out on the ground, head up and alert. Except for one man's expertise working the lone mule in another field, there seemed little unusual for Joseph to see.

The day passed uneventfully, and at sundown Joseph and Moon returned to Isaac to collect their daily wage.

After the other workers had left for home, Isaac sent Joseph down to the sea to get more water for chores around the house. While there Joseph heard some of the local fishermen speaking of Jesus.

"I'm telling you guys, I've seen Him heal a man, a crippled man. The fellow got right up and started walking and jumping around and yelling and all. I'm telling you, I seen it myself."

"You're as crazy as this Jesus is, you know that?" said another. "You're nuts."

"I don't know, others have told me some strange things," offered another man. "One of these days I'm going to get close enough to hear what He says for myself."

"You'd better watch it, buddy," added someone else. "I've heard He teaches things that even those religious folks don't like to hear. And if they don't like to hear it, what good will it do you or anyone else? Only trouble, that's what He is."

Joseph wanted to ask them about Jesus, but he remembered the words of Isaac and decided to wait for now. Returning to the house with the two urns of water, he spotted Isaac gathering figs from a nearby tree.

"Have you heard anything about the Man, Jesus?" asked Joseph as he put down the water.

Isaac looked over at Joseph as he continued his gathering. "Yes, I've heard of Him. Most everyone around here has. And most everyone has an opinion of Him too."

"What do you think about Him?"

Isaac stopped picking and looked at Joseph. "Well, I know some folks who have talked with Him. Reliable folks, I mean, not some rumor-mongers. And they seem to think this Jesus might be some kind of prophet or something."

"You haven't answered my question."

Isaac smiled. "No, you're right. I guess I haven't. Well, I've not met the Man myself, so my opinion is only from what I've heard others say. That along with the fact that I can read. The owner of this place, Lucius, actually paid someone to teach me. Can you believe that?

"Anyway, I try to read a lot. And a little over thirty years ago I heard rumors of some great and terrible happenings down around Bethlehem. I guess the terrible happenings aren't rumors as far as that goes. Too many people witnessed some kind of slaughter of the small children down there for it to be a rumor.

"But the other report was about a Child born there, a Child who would set our people free. And supposedly angels appeared to a few poor folk to tell about it. I've read some of the old prophecies. This Jesus may have been that Child, although if that's the case, it doesn't make a lot of sense to me, at least not yet."

Isaac stopped speaking and looked off beyond Joseph and Moon. He squinted his eyes and stared with such intensity that Joseph and Moon turned to look for themselves. There, off in the distance on a dusty path came two men, still a long way off. Joseph looked back at Isaac for an explanation.

Isaac stared for a moment longer. Then a smile began to spread across his face and his eyes shone. "It's him. It's Lucius. He's back early. He's back! Go tell the other workers inside that Lucius is back. Then wet a clean towel with some of the water you just got and come and meet us. Go lad, go quickly."

Joseph hurried to tell the workers inside the house while Isaac ran to greet his master. Moon waited outside for Joseph to emerge, sounds of joyous excitement from the inside workers reaching his ears. Joseph hurried out with the towel and dipped it into the cool water. Some of the inside workers came out for a few moments to get a look at their master as he made his way toward them.

"He's made it back! He's made it back safely. Praise God!" they exclaimed.

Joseph and Moon hurried along the path to meet the three men, already deep in conversation and slowly making their way toward the house. Joseph stood a short distance away so as not to interrupt. Finally, the tallest man nodded toward Joseph. Isaac turned around quickly and introduced Joseph to Lucius.

"This is our newest laborer, Lucius. He is staying in the extra tenant's house tonight. If he works out, he may stay on for a while." Isaac gave Joseph a warm smile.

Joseph handed the towel to Lucius. The older man studied the youth for a long moment.

"Pleased to meet you, Joseph. Welcome to our humble farm. I'm glad that you're here."

Immediately Joseph felt the warmth and sincerity of Lucius' greeting. Joseph felt very important and genuinely welcomed by the man. Yet they had just met.

Lucius smiled at the cool damp towel and handed it to his companion. "Wipe your face, my friend." He laughed. "You look like you could use it more than me."

The man nodded at his boss's concern as he took the towel. Lucius turned back to Joseph.

"And what is your dog's name?" asked Lucius as he squatted down to Moon's level. Moon walked over with a big grin as Lucius gave him a pat on the head. Moon's tail whirled about and then he returned to Joseph's side.

"Well," said Joseph lightly, "his name is Moon, but I call him all kinds of names when he wears me out."

Lucius laughed heartily at the joke. Then he introduced Joseph to the man he had given the towel to.

"This is my best soldier, John. He shadows me wherever I go."

Joseph's eyebrows went up as he couldn't hide his surprise. "Soldier?" he asked as he looked at Lucius.

"Forgive me, Lucius," said Isaac rather sheepishly. "Joseph is so new here I haven't had the chance to tell him that you're a centurion in the Roman army."

Chapter 23

Sounds of celebration filled the night air as the entire household gathered in the yard to hear Lucius' stories of faraway places. Joseph and Moon sat in the shadows listening. Once Joseph had heard that Lucius was a centurion in the Roman army, he and Moon became very withdrawn. No one seemed to notice them sitting apart from the group.

Why in the world has Tysius sent us here? Joseph wondered. He made plans to leave the next day, although he didn't know where they would go. *Any place would be better than this,* he thought. *We'll go and find Jesus, that's what we'll do.* Joseph thought he had it all figured out, but then something Lucius said caught his attention.

"There is still much to be done. But I am proud of all that has already been accomplished, and especially through the efforts of so many people. They are hard workers, tireless since we began. Without their help, none of this could have happened."

Joseph saw Isaac smile and shake his head. "How much is still needed?" Isaac asked.

"Well, there's some timber we need to get from the north," stated Lucius. "It should be in Capernaum in a few days. After that, the rough work on the outside may take a couple of weeks. Then the inside work can begin."

"When do you think the synagogue will be ready for use?" asked one of the workers excitedly. "From what you've told us, it will be like nothing we have ever seen."

Joseph looked at Moon, who looked back at him and thumped his tail. *Synagogue?*

"I'm hoping within a few months, if we can get the materials and the laborers," answered Lucius.

"Oh, you'll get the laborers alright." John laughed. "You know that the people around these parts care a lot about you, Lucius. And you know they'll find the materials too, one way or another. You just say the word, and people will come out of the hills to help."

Even in the firelight Joseph thought he saw Lucius blush as he heard John's compliment.

"Well," Lucius said after a moment, "this is for everyone. Everyone and God, that is. People need a good place to worship. Besides, we're way behind the times around here. I'm just trying to keep us in this part of the world up-to-date."

The conversation turned to the crops and to current events. The topic of Jesus came up and Joseph saw that Lucius seemed to sit up straighter as he took a keen interest in all that his workers had to relate. Most of the information came second and third-hand. Finally Joseph and Moon slipped into their new dwelling as the others made for the big house. Joseph slid the latch on the door and sat on his bed, scratching the back of his head.

"What in the world is going on around here?" he asked Moon.

Moondog planted his tail and rear end on the floor. With his front feet tucked up on his chest, he looked a good bit like a kangaroo in profile. This was one of Moon's customary postures when his master was pondering the unknown.

"This guy Lucius is a centurion, supervising a hundred other Roman soldiers. And he's building a synagogue, a place to worship God!" Joseph looked at Moon in amazement. "I don't know. Maybe we should stick around another day and see what happens."

Moon's tail twitched back and forth on the floor, stirring up a little dust. He leaned forward and stood on all four feet, then gave a huge sneeze that lifted the front of his body off the floor as his head whipped from side to side. Then he gazed up at Joseph with his head cocked to the right and a bewildered look on his face.

Joseph couldn't help but forget his concerns and laugh out loud at his dog. Moon laid his head on Joseph's lap and Joseph's responding smile was instantaneous; he stroked Moon's golden head. The big yellow dog swung his tail back and forth as he looked up at his master.

Joseph felt at peace again as he turned out the oil lamp and lay on the bed, staring at the black ceiling. Moon curled up on the floor next to Joseph, his head toward the door so that he could hear if anyone attempted to open it. They drifted off to a short sleep before a blood-curdling scream brought them both to their feet.

"No – Noooo!" the voice cried out.

Joseph bolted through the door and sprinted toward the house. Moondog, hackles up and eyes wide to the inky darkness, was right by his side. They reached the door of the house as a final, more muffled cry emerged. Then they heard the sound of sobbing from within.

Joseph found the door open and didn't bother to knock. Both he and Moon rushed toward the sound to find all the servants gathered around the master bedroom. Isaac sat on the edge of the bed holding Lucius in his arms, rocking him slowly back and forth in the dim light and trying to comfort his friend.

"It is alright, my lord. It is alright. You are home now and it is alright, I am here for you." Over and over Isaac tried to comfort Lucius as the centurion shook uncontrollably and sobbed in his arms.

Joseph and Moon looked on, along with the rest of the stunned servants. Silently, without Joseph noticing, Moon weaved his way past the people and up to the bed. He put his muzzle gently down on Lucius' hand. Instinctively the man put his hand on Moon's head and began to knead his fingers through Moon's thick mane.

It took Isaac a moment to see Moon. He looked sharply at Joseph and began to reprimand him for allowing a dog in his master's house, let alone his room. But Lucius quickly stopped his favorite servant from saying anything more.

"It's alright, Isaac," whispered Lucius. The soldier took a deep breath and shuddered, all the while stroking Moon's big head.

Moon did not wag his tail, or make any other gesture that might reveal his state of mind. Joseph watched as Moon looked into the man's distraught face. Moon remained still, and the silence seemed to go on for a long time. Finally, Lucius spoke.

"I – I am sorry to have woken you all, and to have scared you so. It has been a long while since I've had a dream like this. I am sorry to have worried you. Now please, please try and go back to sleep. Isaac and I have much to speak of. I am alright. Thank all of you for your concern. I am alright now."

Smiling first at Moon and then looking up, Lucius added, "Thank you for allowing me to borrow your friend for a short while, Joseph. He seems to have a most calming effect on me."

Joseph smiled then called to Moon. The two returned to their shed for a restless night's sleep.

The next morning Joseph met Isaac early and began his chores outside the house. Isaac made no reference to Lucius and his nightmares. Finally Joseph asked him about it.

Isaac spoke hesitantly. "No, Lucius never tells me what these dreams are about, but yes, they have come before. None worse than last night I think. It just tears me up to see him like that. He is so good to me, to all of us. The dreams shake him up for hours, sometimes for days. He's afraid to go to sleep sometimes, because he thinks the dreams will return. I wish I could take them from him and put them on myself, but I don't know how."

Then Isaac looked sternly at Joseph. "Not a word of this to anyone else, do you understand? There will be enough talk from all the other inside help once they get to town. But nothing from you, especially to the field workers, understand?"

"Isaac," began Joseph, "I know you don't know me well, but, you don't need to worry. It will go no further than me. I give you my word. And sorry about us running into the house like we did last night. We heard someone in trouble and without thinking we came to see if we could help."

Isaac's face softened. "You are pardoned from coming in without permission. A new worker, and a dog in the house, in the master's bedroom no less! But Lucius has already taken a liking to you. You and your Moondog. He told me so again last night after everyone left the room. In fact he wanted to know more about you two, though I had little to tell. Perhaps..."

Isaac stopped talking as the first of the day's workers began to arrive. After being instructed to be on their best behavior due to Lucius' return, all went to the fields with their assignments. The man who had been working with the mule had gotten injured somehow and would not be back for at least a week. Liam took up the job of working the animal. It appeared that Isaac did not feel at ease with this arrangement, but he didn't quite seem himself this morning.

Joseph and Moon began working their plot of land, all the while keeping watch over their surroundings. They weren't far into their task when they began to hear a lot of yelling and cursing coming from where Liam and the mule worked.

Liam did not give clear commands for the animal to follow as Joseph and Moon had heard the past few days. He could not get the animal to obey his orders and grew impatient with the mule. The more Liam tried to force his way with the animal, the more the mule fought back. Finally the mule refused to go any farther, despite the rough words from Liam.

Joseph and Moon watched as Liam began to whip the animal to get it to move. Joseph looked towards the house but could not see Isaac. Moon stood as a low rumble came from his chest. He looked up at Joseph.

Joseph put down his hoe, took up his staff, and the two made a bee-line for the mule and the angry Liam. As the other workers saw that someone was about to confront Liam, they stopped to watch in amazement.

When Joseph and Moon reached Liam they saw his red face and the veins standing out in his neck like small strands of rope. He continued to whip the mule as large welts began to show on its back. Liam paid little attention to them as he continued to vent his anger at the animal.

"That's enough!" yelled Joseph, surprised at the force and tone of his own voice.

Liam turned on Joseph and began to curse him. "You keep out of this, *boy*," the hot-head screamed between expletives. "This ain't no place for a shepherd boy and his mutt." Liam's eyes burned with rage in his crimson face. Turning back to the mule, he reared back to deliver another fierce blow.

Just as the whip began its forward drive, Joseph's staff snaked out and caught the end of it, jarring the whip violently from Liam's hand. Liam grabbed his wrist, his face contorted in pain. He stood stunned for a moment as his eyes darted around to see what had happened.

Some of the workers now began running toward the scene. They hoped to get there before Liam killed the young man.

Liam turned toward Joseph, his eyes wild with fury. Joseph gathered up the whip, his own anger as great as he had ever known. The two burned holes in each other with their glares.

"How dare you!" fumed Liam in a low voice. "How dare you!" he screamed. In his rage, Liam seemed to forget about Moon. He took one step toward Joseph and then looked down at the dog. Liam wavered for a moment.

Moon crouched low to the ground a few feet from Joseph's left side. He looked like a golden fireball about to be launched into Liam's face. Moon bared his teeth and a low, barely audible rumble came from deep inside. Moon's eyes remained riveted on Liam's. The big dog's legs trembled slightly, his muscles hard as a rock and as tight as a cable stretched to its breaking point. Another step by Liam and Moon appeared ready do his best to remove the angry man's head.

Liam looked at Moon and swallowed nervously. His lips moved slightly but he said nothing. The three glared at each other. Finally, a voice boomed through the tension.

"What's going on here?" said Lucius, his voice resounding with authority. No one moved or spoke. Moon's eyes remained locked on his target.

"I said, what's going on?" Lucius asked once again, this time more firmly than before, demanding an answer from someone.

Liam took a step back but didn't take his eyes off of Moon as he spoke. "This here boy and his mutt are trying to tell me what to do. They're slowing down my work with this mule so that everything is wrong here, that's what's going on. They ain't been nothing but trouble since they got here, and they ain't never done any work themselves. They just keep causing me and the others problems, ain't that right, fellas?"

Liam shot a quick glance at the other workers who had gathered around. Some looked at the ground, not wanting to meet Liam's eyes. No one said anything. Moon had not changed his stance and Liam quickly looked back at him and took another half step back.

Lucius looked at the mule, welts rising along with steam from its back. Then he looked at Joseph with the whip in his hand. "Joseph, have you used that whip today?" asked Lucius.

"No sir, never have. I don't believe in them." Joseph dropped the whip in disgust, his eyes still aflame as he glared at Liam.

Lucius sighed deeply, and then spoke to his friend who had come out to the field with him. "John, pay Liam his day's wage."

He looked back at the angry man. "Liam, you have been with me a while and received more than your fair share of warnings. Do not come back here to work. Do not set foot on this farm again. And if I ever hear of you hurting this young man or his dog, I will come after you with the Roman army. Do you understand?"

Liam, Joseph, and the other workers stared at Lucius in amazement.

"The Roman arm…" Liam started to protest. He took a few deep breaths as he cut his eyes over to Joseph and his dog. He then made a wide circle around the two and stuck out his hand to John for his pay. John gave him the money and Liam turned and stomped away, his face still as red as blood.

Joseph let out a breath which he realized he had held for a long time. Moon stood up slowly, hackles still up on his neck as Liam walked out of sight.

"Well, Joseph," said Lucius. "I just lost a hard worker. Do you think *you* can do anything with this mule?"

Joseph looked at the mule and a grin broke over his face. "Why, yes sir, I do. I mean, I'd sure like to give it a try."

Lucius nodded once as John looked away to hide his smile.

That night, Joseph and Moon sat around the fire, quite a bit closer than they had the night before. Not that they would have done so on their own, but Lucius himself asked them to.

"You did pretty well with that mule today, from what I could see," stated Lucius.

Joseph couldn't hide his embarrassment even by the firelight.

"Of course, it took you a little while to get started, didn't it?" Lucius added.

"Well, sure it did," Joseph exclaimed, not noticing the gentle teasing in Lucius' comment. "The poor beast was all shook up. He'd about lost all confidence in himself and in humans too. I can't say that I blame him for that, especially in humans. I don't know if you saw or not, but I let Moon nuzzle up to him for a while and that really helped him out. In fact that seemed to calm him down more than anything I could do. That mule's got a lot of heart; I think he'll be alright if we handle him right."

"You mean if *you* handle him right." Lucius smiled. "As of today, you are in charge of him. His care, feed, work, everything. If that's alright with you, that is."

Moon's tail patted the ground as he sat next to Joseph. Joseph gently stroked his big golden head. "Yes sir, it would be great. I mean for now. I don't know how long we're staying, but for now, I would like that very much."

"It's your job as long as you want it."

"Thank you, sir."

Lucius watched with curiosity as Joseph suddenly got up and disappeared to his living quarters. Moondog trailed after him and the two returned momentarily.

Joseph held the whip out toward Lucius. "Do you mind if I burn this?"

"No, Joseph. I don't mind at all."

Joseph tossed it into the fire and glowing sparks spun into the black sky.

Just then John came out of the house and Lucius looked up at him with concern.

"How is he?"

John shrugged his shoulders and shook his head. "I don't know, Lucius, I don't know."

Joseph looked at Lucius. "What's the matter?"

"Isaac. He was taken ill this morning. I sent for a physician but he won't be here until tomorrow."

Joseph closed his eyes. He had not seen Isaac since early this morning. So many things had happened today that for once, Joseph hadn't noticed. He made a mental note not to allow that to happen again.

Chapter 24

The next morning John came out of the house before sun-up to discover that Joseph had already gathered water from the sea and prepared the mule for the day's work.

"How's Isaac?" asked Joseph.

"No better,' John said solemnly. "Worse if anything. I hope the doctor can do something. Lucius thinks the world of Isaac. He's known him for many years now. He knows it's difficult to find someone you can trust these days, and Isaac is a good man."

"Seems to me that Lucius thinks of Isaac almost like a son or something," replied Joseph. "I know Isaac thinks a lot of Lucius. You should have heard him talking about his master before you two got here. I think he'd do just about anything for Lucius."

"I know," said John. "And Lucius knows too."

When the men arrived for work, John attempted to give instruction for the day, but he obviously knew little about farming. Fortunately, the other men seemed in a most helpful mood, offering suggestions as to what to do and how. Joseph had never heard them speak up before – at least not when Liam was around. Most seemed quite willing to do their share. A couple of them even came over to encourage Joseph in his work with the mule and offer helpful advice.

During the entire day Joseph kept a watch over the sea for any unusual activity, but saw none. He also hoped to see Isaac or Lucius. He saw the latter only once, when Lucius came outside to greet the doctor and hurry him into the house.

At the end of the day, while some of the inside workers gathered around the fire, Joseph asked about Isaac. Lucius stared at the fire as he began to speak.

"He is not well. Not well at all. The doctor said he doesn't think Isaac is going to live." Lucius abruptly stopped talking. He looked up and off to the side, his face turned away from the firelight as he gazed at the stars over the big sea. Joseph saw the chest of the big man rise as he took a deep breath and held it for a long time. Finally he let out a long sigh and looked back at the ground. No one else said anything for a long time. Some of the workers began to get up and go inside.

137

Joseph and Moon got up quietly and went to their small shelter. Joseph stared at the dark ceiling, and Moon gazed at his master. Finally Joseph got up and dressed. He knew he wouldn't be able to sleep, so he decided to go down to the sea to gather water for the morning. Moondog jumped up in an instant, ready to go anywhere with Joseph.

Joseph put his head out the door, and it seemed to him that he could see a million stars shining. The sky was as clear as that night when he saw the angels in the field. Like someone took a cloth and wiped the smoke and fog away from a window, so that the stars almost blazed with their own dancing excitement.

"Wow," whispered Joseph without thinking. "Come on, Moon. We can see easy enough with all this starlight since our eyes are already adjusted to the dark. We'll leave the lantern here and take two of these urns for some water."

The two walked side by side in the dark, Moon's golden fur barely giving away their position under the stars. The sounds of frogs and crickets resonated in their ears, and the burning stars shimmered in brilliant contrast to the inky blackness that surrounded them. Joseph did a complete 360 degree spin and gazed in awe at the view of the deep black sky stretched from horizon to horizon above them. He took in a deep breath of the chilly air. He felt closer to the sky and to creation than he ever remembered. The wonder of it, and of the One Who created it, nearly took his breath away.

Moon watched Joseph spin around and followed his gaze up into the heavens.

Joseph felt that with each new breath came new strength for his body. He half believed he and Moon could run across the mountains forever on this night and never grow tired, never grow weary. Or perhaps they would decide to jump up and touch the sky. Or maybe they'd do both and a million other things as well. The air itself seemed charged with overflowing life.

After a long pause, Joseph and Moon continued walking toward the sea. They could see a few fishing boats a short distance from shore, their smoky lanterns giving off a dim sparkle across the water. Occasionally Joseph and Moon could hear a fisherman's voice carried across the silky water by a slight breeze. Fishing appeared slow this night.

As they came to the shore, Joseph carefully stayed out of the mud while Moon tramped happily through it. Sniffing the scents of the water and the coast, tail up like a plume, Moon trotted happily along. In a moment they came to the make-shift dock where Joseph drew water each morning.

Moon stood beside Joseph on the dock, holding his head up with his nose as high as he could reach while he took in the smells of the evening.

His nose twitched back and forth like a big rabbit's as he caught and identified scent after scent wafting toward them.

After filling the urns with the cool water, Joseph stood up to go. Moon then caught a scent that he had not smelled for a long time. Not for over thirty years to be exact. The very aroma filled him with such excitement that he began to prance around and quiver from the tip of his nose to the end of his tail.

Joseph looked down at his dog in amusement as Moon skipped in circles around Joseph's feet. Joseph knew that his voice, along with the sound of Moon's snorting like he'd just inhaled a bunch of feathers, would carry over the water. "Moon, settle down will you?" he whispered.

Joseph took a step back toward the house, and Moon let out a low, joyful sound that he sometimes made when the two wrestled together. Joseph tried to be firm, but Moon's earnest attempt to communicate made Joseph smile nonetheless. Moon continued jumping around and prancing about, trying to get Joseph to follow him further out on the dock.

Joseph looked out toward the end of the pier and noticed a small boat approaching, still a good distance from shore, with a lone lantern hung on its bow. Remembering Isaac's words about dealing with some of the fishermen, especially at night, Joseph decided to get back to the house. Moon, however, continued prancing about, obviously wanting to go toward the boat.

Joseph couldn't remember a time when Moon's instincts had led them astray. Still, they carried no light with them, and for Moon to jump out of the black shadows at these people coming in on the boat would no doubt lead to problems. Moon persisted in his high stepping and snorting.

"Moon, settle down," whispered Joseph urgently. "Come on, they're getting close. Come on!"

Moon looked at Joseph heading to the house and then back toward the approaching boat. He looked back and saw Joseph disappear into the shadows. Moon turned and grudgingly obeyed his master.

Joseph kept walking away from the dock until he knew the light from the boat's lantern could not touch them. He put down the urns and crouched down, holding onto Moon. Moon sat down, and though the evening did not feel cold, he shivered under Joseph's right arm.

They watched the sail from the craft come down quickly just before the boat gently nudged the landing. A couple of men jumped out and swiftly tied the vessel to the dock. The men obviously knew how to run the boat. A large man reached up and lifted the lantern from the nail holding it to the bow. He stepped lightly to the dock and held the light for the others to see.

Through long shadows and much movement, Joseph thought he counted thirteen men. They reached the shore and stopped for a short discussion. Moon now squirmed so much that Joseph reached over with his left hand and grabbed on to his thick mane while keeping a close grip on him with his right arm. Joseph whispered a soft "shhhhh" to try to calm him down.

The light held by the big man suddenly caught the face of a tall, slender Man, taller than the rest. This Man stood on the far side of the group, and the light caught Him just as He glanced up and looked straight at Joseph. His eyes reached through the darkness and met Joseph's with such power that it seemed to Joseph they stood only a few feet apart and in brilliant daylight. The look lasted only a moment, or perhaps a thousand years, Joseph couldn't tell. In an instant Joseph got to see what those who had accepted Jesus for who He is, those few who lived with Him, His followers, got to see. Or maybe he saw more than they did. The Alpha and Omega, the Creator of the universe, the Wonderful Counselor, the Healer and the Most High. The only begotten Son, the Lamb of God.

It seemed as if a million different thoughts and emotions hit Joseph at once, and yet he did not feel frightened. It felt to Joseph as if electricity ran through his entire body, touching every cell. Such peace, all consuming and beautiful, more than what any words could ever describe, flooded Joseph's being. How could he feel afraid? Indeed, Joseph felt he might never be afraid of anything ever again. Courage and strength and forgiveness and mercy and compassion swirled inside him. Hope far above his wildest dreams, and freedom. Freedom and peace as great as anything Joseph had ever felt, beyond understanding. Above all these things, Joseph felt the overwhelming sense of love. Love for him, love for others, love greater than any other thing that he'd ever heard of or thought of or experienced before this moment. He felt immersed in pure love, and Joseph didn't care if his heart beat again or he ever took another breath. He wished to remain here forever.

Joseph had known what all these things meant before, or at least he had thought he did. But those things he knew before this moment faded like a shadow disappearing as the brilliant sun breaks through a dark cloud. Joseph realized he had never actually known any more than just the shell of all these things before now. Just as before he might look at the surface of the ocean, but now he could see a mile into it. Perhaps a thousand miles. Now these things seemed as real to him as the ground under his feet.

Joseph lost track of time. He had no idea how long he remained crouching next to his Moondog. Moon sat still as a stone beneath his arm. Joseph saw no one, except for the few boats out on the sea a short distance away. For a moment, Joseph thought he might be hallucinating. But the peace consuming his heart told him otherwise. Just to be sure, he slowly got up, and with Moon by his side, walked back to the dock. Joseph could not feel his feet touching the ground. They walked almost to the end of the pier and looked at the boat. Moon sniffed around it and slowly wagged his tail as he looked up at Joseph. Joseph crouched down again, deep in thought, his right hand touching the worn wood of the boat.

"Oh my," he repeated softly over and over to himself, silent tears rolling down his face. "Oh my." Moon gently put his snoot under Joseph's arm and laid his head on Joseph's lap. Joseph's breathing became so shallow that his chest barely moved. The two remained there a long time, Joseph's hand resting lightly on the boat, as if it were fragile and might shatter at any moment. "I wonder," Joseph whispered softly to Moon, "if He touched this very place."

Finally Joseph rose and returned to the urns, picked them up, then wandered back to the house, Moon by his side. It felt to Joseph that his very being floated as he walked. He reached the house, put the water down and looked back at the sky. He had not imagined it. The stars shone like they had on that still and holy night some thirty years before.

An agonizing scream from inside the house made both Joseph and Moon jump. In an instant they flew through the front door and stood at the entrance to Lucius' room. There they found Lucius, terrorized by yet another nightmare. John arrived just before Joseph and Moon. A loud thump from a room across the hall resounded through the house.

Isaac had tried to come to his master's aid and had fallen in his attempt to walk.

Lucius pulled himself together and told John to see about Isaac. John began to protest leaving the side of his centurion, but a pained look from Lucius made John stop in mid-sentence. He got up from Lucius' bedside and walked toward Joseph. He stopped for a moment.

"Look after him." John whispered, "I will be right back."

Joseph and Moon walked hesitantly into the room; a lone oil lamp in the far corner casting long shadows across the wall. Lucius drew his knees up under his chin and wrapped a blanket around his shaking body.

"Close the door," he managed to say, not wanting everyone looking at him.

Joseph obeyed, then walked over and sat in a chair next to the bed. Moon approached and put his head on the bed next to Lucius. The tormented man looked down at the big golden head and gently stroked the dog's ears. Joseph was relieved to see some tension drain away from the anguished man.

Joseph did not want to stare, so his eyes wandered around the room. In the corner stood the centurion's armor, propped up on something like a coat rack. It seemed too large for Lucius, who looked frail and weak in his current state. Joseph knew Lucius acted with only kindness toward others, even those who were the least important around the farm. This armor seemed far too hard, far too cold for this man who led a hundred soldiers. Finally Lucius gave a deep sigh and stopped shaking.

"Can you tell me about it? Perhaps I can help," Joseph found himself saying. "The dreams I mean. Perhaps if you told someone, it would help."

Lucius looked across the room at the lamp and stared a long time at the flame. "Joseph, you would not understand. You could not. You have never fought in a battle, have you? You have not seen the faces of those before they die right before you, right before your very eyes, life taken from them." Lucius paused. "No, Joseph, you could not understand this, I already know you too well. What I have done I must live with forever. I must endure the fear of sleep and the dreams that can come without end. I alone am responsible for what I have done."

Joseph surprised himself for interrupting. "And you can also be forgiven of what you have done, Lucius. Only you must admit what you've done to God and ask for His forgiveness. It is up to you."

Lucius shook his head. "As I said, you do not understand, Joseph. What I've done cannot be forgiven. Not even God could forgive me for such things."

Joseph stood up from the chair and began pacing the floor. His jaw was clenched, and his bold spirit surprised him. Before this night, before seeing the One he had just seen by the lake, Joseph never would have been so bold.

"So what you're saying is that God is not enough, right? He's not big enough, or strong enough, or merciful enough. Or He doesn't love you enough to forgive you if you humble yourself before Him, right?"

Lucius looked at Joseph in astonishment. "Do not forget who you are speaking to, Joseph."

Moon raised his head up from the bed and studied Joseph pacing the room.

Joseph walked over toward the armor and stared at it. With just the lantern light from the corner he could barely make out a couple of Roman letters on the breastplate. Joseph casually reached up and ran his fingers over the letters as he sought for the right words.

"Look, Lucius, you're no ignorant man. I'm sure you don't become a centurion in the Roman army by being foolish. I suppose these letters mean something about your special achievements or bravery or something. But ranking high and trying to do good now, like building a synagogue or something, isn't going to protect you when you meet your Maker. And apparently it won't stop these dreams from tormenting you now either. If you're ever going to be free of this, you have got to come to God with a repentant heart and ask Him for forgiveness.

Lucius shook his head slowly. "But Joseph, how could God forgive me for what I've done?" He put his hand to his head and stared at the bed. Then Lucius added softly, "And that's just me, it's not anything special."

Joseph turned and looked at Lucius. "What?"

"The letters on my armor. That's just my name, my initials; it isn't some kind of special bravery thing. Matthias Lucius. It's my name."

Joseph looked back at the letters in the dim light and ran his fingers over them again. M.L. Suddenly a cold chill ran down Joseph's spine and he trembled involuntarily. He felt his breathing become rapid as his eyes grew large looking at the letters. It took Joseph a few moments to regain his composure. He turned back to Lucius, staring at him in the dim lantern light.

"Is your first name Marcus?" Joseph asked in nearly a whisper. At the sound of the name, Moon tensed up and walked to Joseph's side.

Lucius squinted his eyes and stared up at Joseph. "How did you know that?" he whispered. "I haven't gone by that name in many years. None of the help around here knows that. Not Isaac. Not even John. How did you know?"

John knocked at the door. "Lucius, are you alright? I need to speak with you."

Lucius continued staring at Joseph. Finally he spoke in a voice loud enough for only Joseph and Moon to hear. "You will tell no one of this, do you understand? We will speak about it later."

Then Lucius raised his voice. "Come in, John. I am alright."

John opened the door and walked briskly to Lucius' bed. Even in the dim light Joseph could sense the man's distress.

"It is Isaac. He has taken a turn for the worse. I'm afraid..."

"Send one of the workers for the doctor at once," replied Lucius. "I don't care what time it is, send him now."

"Lucius...," began John, then decided to stop. "As you wish." John turned and left the room, closing the door behind him.

"The doctor will not be able to help Isaac. You know that, don't you?" asked Joseph.

"Isaac is my best friend. How dare you be so certain about my friend's death," came Lucius' terse response. "There was a time if you had said something like this to me, both you and your dog would be dead."

Moon's hackles went up as he stepped closer to Joseph.

Somewhere, far away, Krog sensed the opportunity he'd been waiting for a long, long time. The vile creature rose up and began flying a zigzag pattern through the night air toward Lucius, trying to get an inkling as to which way to go. He turned his ugly head from side to side, bending all of his attention toward his goal. Little did Krog know that when he found Lucius, he would be rewarded with two more highly prized victims for his wrath.

"You will have to come to terms with your guilt and anger if Isaac is to be helped," stated Joseph.

"How does...," Lucius began to shout and then realized everyone in the house could hear him. He started again in a quieter voice through clenched teeth as he struggled with his anger. "How does my guilt and anger have anything to do with whether my friend Isaac is healed from this dreadful disease? Who are you, and how do you know so much, or think you do anyway?"

Krog flew closer, chewing up huge distances with each flap of his wings and with each passing moment as he sought out his prey. Although Joseph had no clue of this, Moon began pacing about. The big dog groaned softly and looked toward the roof with each watchful step.

Joseph looked down at Moon and immediately picked up on his dog's anxiety. He looked back at the angry man glaring at him, the man whom both he and Moon had nearly confronted once before. That now seemed like a lifetime ago.

"Look, Lucius, it's a long story and I can't say I understand all of it anyway." Joseph glanced at Moon, who now circled the floor as he stared at the ceiling, his hackles up. "Besides that, there's no time to waste here. But I believe Isaac can be healed. I believe that."

At those words Lucius' anger subsided somewhat. Krog lost his bearings a little. He flew close enough to still pursue his prey, yet the strong hope of finding it immediately had vanished. He slowed and continued relentlessly on, determined to destroy Lucius and everyone around him.

"And how do you expect to heal Isaac?" Lucius asked with a hint of sarcasm in his voice. "Are you a doctor too? The man is almost dead. How are *you* going to heal him?"

Moon began a low growl as he stared up at the ceiling. His hackles were up from head to tail, and it was apparent that he expected disaster to descend at any second.

Joseph now prayed fervently for wisdom. *Would this be considered interfering with things or was it too late to even consider that?* "I cannot heal him, and I doubt any doctor can. But I know of Someone who can. His name is Jesus. I know you've heard of Him."

"Jesus," said Lucius softly as he sat up straight against the wall behind him. "Yes, of course I've heard of Him. Everyone has. He is a prophet of the one true God I'm told. I have heard He is a truly extraordinary Man.

Some have told me they have seen Him do things far beyond what any man could ever do. Is He a friend of yours, this Jesus?" As he reverently mentioned the name of Jesus, the anger in Lucius ceased to exist.

Instantly Krog lost all direction in his search and destroy mission. He screamed madly into the night, his prey so close to being crushed, yet now lost to him.

Although silent to Lucius, Joseph and Moon heard the horrific cry of the frustrated and filthy creature as it flew overhead not knowing where to go. Moon bristled at the sound and readied himself for battle; Joseph prayed fervently. They were both instinctively backed up to the wall.

Krog knew he had been on track to find his prey. But in only a moment and with only one Word, he lost all clues as to where to go to carry out his destruction. Having no one to vent his deadly anger on, his hatred tore at his insides. He circled aimlessly and then slowly drifted off toward the north as the night wore on, not knowing if he was drawing nearer to his prey or farther away. He vowed he would be more attentive to pick up on this man's anger in the future.

Lucius stared at the strange young man and his dog. Joseph had knelt and was praying. Staring at the ceiling and emitting a barely audible rumble of a growl, Moon acted the sentry at Joseph's side.

"Joseph, are you alright?"

A long silence followed. Joseph felt his heart pounding inside his chest as he prayed. "Well Lucius...," began Joseph slowly, feeling a little safer as time went on, "I know Who Jesus is, or at least I know some things about Him. In fact, that is the Name I have just been calling upon. And apparently from what I experienced tonight, He knows me although I have never formally met Him. It's a long story which I cannot go into right now. And my story is not as important to you now as Isaac is anyway."

"Will you go and get this Jesus then? Can you bring Him here? Tell Him I will pay Him what He wants. Anything – I can get anything for Him. Tell Him of my position and authority in the Roman government." Lucius became so excited at the hope of Isaac's healing that he spoke nonsense.

Joseph put up his hands to stop the flurry of words being thrown at him. "Whoa, whoa now Lucius, hold on. He is not interested in any of your so called power and wealth."

Lucius looked surprised but no longer angry.

"And I cannot go and get Him for you. Please don't ask me why, just believe me when I say I cannot do this for you. You must go to Him yourself."

Although only one lamp lit the room, Joseph could still see Lucius' face turn ashen. "You are not an easy person to understand, my young friend," Lucius began slowly. Then he sighed deeply. "But for whatever reason, I trust you. You speak as if you are absolutely sure of what you are saying about this Jesus and how He can heal my friend. There is much for me to risk, going to Him. You know that, don't you? I must risk my past, everything."

"Yes, I know," responded Joseph softly. "I know. But your forgiveness and freedom are at stake here as well. Do not forget that."

Lucius shook his head impatiently. "I'm not worried about me getting something for myself right now. I am concerned about Isaac. I know I don't deserve to be forgiven."

"Lucius, focus on this for a moment, will you? No one deserves to be forgiven. No one. Compared to God, who can stand next to Him and say, 'I've never done anything wrong, never done any sin, nothing, never?' Who could dare say that? Who is righteous but God?" Joseph remembered something he'd read sometime in the past. "'For all have sinned and fall short of His glory.'" [1]

"Alright, I will think on that. But for now, do you know where this Jesus is?"

"I think He went into the village tonight. I guess that He would be there now."

"Then I will go now," replied Lucius as he stood and began putting on his outer clothes. "I know it's late, but the walk into town will give me a chance to think. I'll leave at once." Then he turned toward Joseph and Moondog and tried to smile. "I hope you are right, Joseph. I really hope you are right."

Joseph just nodded his head as he and Moon returned to the shed. They lay there until sunrise, listening to the sounds of the night, Joseph lost in prayer.

Chapter 25

It was a bit before daybreak, and Moon stirred when he heard the sound of hurried footsteps; the dog's alert reaction startled Joseph from his uneasy sleep. The two jumped up and peered out the door. Joseph saw John returning from town with the doctor and entering the house. Joseph followed to tell John why Lucius had left. He and Moon walked silently into the house and stopped outside Isaac's door. From there they could hear muffled words as the doctor examined Isaac.

John stood just inside the door, ready to report the doctor's findings to his commander in the next room. When he saw Joseph, he put up his hand to signal him to wait until the doctor had finished.

Joseph and Moon watched intently while the doctor examined Isaac. The precious man lay on his bed, fighting for every life-giving breath. When the doctor finished, he straightened up and walked outside the door with John close behind. The doctor looked at Joseph, then turned toward John and lifted an eyebrow.

"It's alright," John said, "you can speak before this one. He is a friend of the family. How is Isaac?"

The doctor shook his head and began to speak quietly so no one else in the house could hear. "He is dying. There is nothing I can do."

John took a deep breath. "Is there not something, anything... cost is of no importance. Can't you do something?"

The doctor put his hand on John's shoulder. "I know how much he means to Lucius, John. I know. Isaac is a good man. And you know if I could do anything, I would. But I've seen this sickness before. There is nothing I can do to help him. No one can. I've never seen anyone recover once it gets this bad. It won't be long now. I'm sorry."

Just then the door to the outside opened and footsteps came from around the corner. John, not knowing that Lucius had left the house, instinctively put his hand on the hilt of his sword as he whirled around to see who might come in at this hour. Joseph drew a sharp breath, and his eyes grew wide.

Lucius hurried in. Alone.

Joseph let out his breath, partly in relief, but mostly in disappointment. Moon walked over to Lucius, who stood wide-eyed

147

looking at the three men and a dog staring at him in the hallway of his own home. John spoke first.

"Lucius, where have you been? I had no idea you were gone. I should have been with you..."

Lucius interrupted. "It's alright, John, don't worry." Then he turned to the doctor. "How is Isaac?"

The doctor shook his head. "I'm sorry, Lucius. He is as comfortable as I know how to make him. You may want to be with him. He does not have long now." With that the doctor made his way out of the house and started back toward town.

John looked at the floor and bit his bottom lip.

Joseph looked at Lucius, who fidgeted and stared at his feet.

"Did you find Him?" asked Joseph softly. "Did you find Him?"

Lucius let out an uneasy sigh. "Yes, or at least I found where He is staying. I went to the door and tried to knock, but I could not move my hand to do so. I..." Lucius paused. "My hand, I tried, but I couldn't lift it." Lucius sighed again and looked at Joseph with hollow eyes.

"I went to the new synagogue and woke the elders of the church. They have given me their word that they will go straight to Jesus and ask Him to come. I made them vow to me to do this. They were on their way as I started for home. If He is coming, He may be here soon." At his own words, a look of terror seemed to pass across Lucius' face.

"Jesus!" John exclaimed as he studied Lucius. "You have asked for this Holy Man to come here, to your house?"

Lucius tried to respond but no words came. He turned away from John and walked back outside the house, to face Capernaum.

John looked at Joseph as the young man tried to swallow. "Here we go," Joseph said softly.

Lucius stood outside the house gazing toward town; John and Joseph were close by on either side. Moon remained next to Joseph, his nose tipped toward the sky and on full alert.

The rising sun began to paint long streaks of orange and yellow over the hills. Only Joseph and Moon noticed the start of a brilliantly clear day, and they noticed for only a moment.

Workers began to stir inside the house and two of the laborers arrived for work. They saw Lucius, John, Joseph, and his dog standing in front of the house, staring intently toward town. They looked at each other and held their questions, at least for the moment. And Joseph and Moon only needed a moment more. Both of them now saw a slight lifting of dust from over the far hillside, ever so slight.

Joseph's breath caught, and a broad smile spread across his face. Moon began to high step with his front feet, tail wagging wildly. Then the others saw too. For there, still a long ways off, came a throng of people over the hill. Too many people for so early in the morning on an ordinary day in Capernaum, far too many. But there was nothing ordinary about this day and this crowd, nothing ordinary at all. At the front of the multitude walked Jesus, and He came straight toward Lucius' house!

Standing behind Lucius, Joseph noticed the Roman centurion wobble. The mighty military man's chest rose and fell so quickly Joseph thought the centurion might hyperventilate. Joseph knew a little of the man's vile past, and he also knew Lucius' best friend lay dying a few yards away. Joseph continued to pray.

One of the inside workers came out to see what was going on as the crowd from town slowly drew closer.

Suddenly Lucius turned toward three of his workers. "Listen to me. Listen to me carefully."

The three jolted to attention as Lucius' eyes burned with intensity.

"In that crowd there is the One named Jesus. You go to Him straightaway and tell Him this. Tell Him – "Lord, do not trouble Yourself, for I am not worthy that You should enter under my roof. Therefore I did not even think myself worthy to come to You. But say the word, and my servant will be healed. For I also am a man placed under authority, having soldiers under me. And I say to one, 'Go,' and he goes; and to another, 'Come,' and he comes; and to my servant, 'Do this,' and he does it.[1]

"Now go, the three of you. Go quickly."

Joseph couldn't believe his ears, but he had no time to react. The three men ran toward the crowd as Joseph watched closely and struggled not to interfere. Moon looked quizzically at Joseph and then back at the multitude. He moved closer to Joseph, who instinctively reached down and stroked the top of Moon's head without ever shifting his gaze.

After what seemed like forever, the three workers reached the crowd and everyone stopped. From where he stood, Joseph could barely make out Lucius' three men. People seemed to push in on them from all sides. Moments passed. Finally, the large group of people slowly began moving back to town as the three messengers started their long run back toward the house.

Lucius stared at them for a few seconds. Then he began walking toward them, slowly at first, then quickening his pace until he too ran as fast as he could, with John, Joseph, and Moondog right behind him.

Joseph kept watch on Moon as he knew his big dog wanted to outrun them all, to run into the crowd and get close to the Creator of the universe. Moon loped easily alongside the men who were running as fast as they could toward the returning workers. When they met, Lucius spoke haltingly through his panting.

"What did He say? What did He say?" he pleaded.

The man who worked inside the house spoke first. "He said that He has not found such faith, not such great faith, not even in all of Israel!" the worker nearly shouted between breaths.

"And He said that it would be just as you believed, so let it be done for you. Just as you believed," chimed in another straining for breath.

Just then a cry came from the house. All the men, along with Moondog, turned and looked to see Isaac jumping about in front of the house, hands outstretched, arms reaching skyward.

"Hey, HEY!" he screamed. "HEEEEYYYYYY." A group of nearby workers tried to him to calm him down, for they knew of his sickness. But Isaac jumped far too high to be restrained.

Lucius sucked in his breath and held it. Then he and Joseph took a quick glance behind them as the crowd disappeared over the hill.

"Such…great…faith…" Lucius looked at Joseph, his eyes wide.

Joseph slowly nodded his head as he pointed at Lucius. "Not in all Israel. You, Lucius, you. Don't ever doubt your forgiveness, Lucius, never doubt it." A wide smile crept across Joseph's face.

Lucius seemed to be trying to hold back his own smile but he couldn't do it. Then he looked toward the house where Isaac had finally spotted Lucius. The two men raced toward each other as the others watched in amazement.

Joseph jumped up and pumped his fist into the air. "Yes!" he shouted, and then gave John a quick shot to the arm. "Come on, man. Don't just stand there with your mouth open catching flies, come on."

Joseph took one last look as the crowd disappeared over the hill toward town. He felt sure Jesus would be there for at least another day. Moondog did a perfect 360 turnaround as he leaped and spun in front of Joseph.

"I saw Isaac myself," John mumbled. "Paralyzed. He could hardly breathe. And the doctor told me. I heard him. He said Isaac was as good as dead. He told me himself not more than a few minutes ago. No one ever recovers when he's in Isaac's condition. The doc's seen it himself; no one ever gets well when it's this bad."

Lucius and Isaac hugged each other and pounded each other on the back. By now, most all of the workers had arrived and were gathered around the two men. Shouts of excitement and praise filled the air.

Joseph and Moon walked a little beyond the small crowd. The hoopla continued, but Joseph's attention was drawn elsewhere. Over their heads, he could see a small boat tethered to the dock with gentle waves lapping against its side. Beyond that he could see the large sea, dark water topped with glittering jewels in the morning sun. Far beyond the water Joseph could make out the shadowed mountains of a distant shore, and beyond them, the yellow sun climbing into the heavens. Over the din of the workers, even above Isaac's shouts of excitement, Joseph could hear Lucius' voice. A strong voice brimming with pure joy and relief, the voice of a man who finally knew forgiveness. Marcus Lucius had risked all, and had been granted, his pardon.

After seeing Jesus by the sea last night, there was never a doubt in Joseph's mind.

Never a doubt.

Chapter 26

Lucius declared a holiday. Some of the workers prepared a fatted calf for supper while others spent the day talking and joking with Isaac and Lucius.

It seemed to Joseph that Lucius looked several years younger. Joseph heard the name Jesus spoken time and again. Often he saw Lucius staring out toward the sea, and then shaking his head as if he didn't understand why he should be granted such a wonderful thing as this.

Isaac, for his part, told over and over again what had happened to him to anyone who would listen. "I couldn't move and could barely breathe. Then all of a sudden I felt this tremendous warmth, starting from inside and going throughout my whole body. A tingling sensation. At first I thought I was dying. Yet I felt so much peace. Then, the next thing I knew, I got up and started running around like when I was just a boy." Isaac often shook with excitement as he recounted his story.

The three workers who had been sent to talk to Jesus also repeated their story so many times that Joseph had every word memorized. He and Moon sat a little apart from the others as they ate, listening to stories others had heard about this Jesus. Some seemed so outrageous that a few of the workers didn't believe. Someone asked Lucius if he believed that Jesus could heal a man born blind, with not even any eyes in his head.

Lucius sat staring at the fire for such a long time that Joseph wondered if he'd heard the question. Finally Lucius spoke quietly, so that those sitting far away had to strain to hear.

"Yes, I do believe it. I believe it with my whole heart. I have seen firsthand how He healed my servant, Isaac." Then Lucius added in almost a whisper. "And how He has forgiven me."

This last statement caught everyone by surprise. Silence followed since no one dared to ask the centurion what he meant. A few of those out of earshot whispered to each other about what Lucius had said. Suddenly Lucius seemed aware of the awkwardness of the situation. "Eat more, eat; there is plenty of food here," he said loudly.

Soon the hum of conversation began again. Lucius looked over his shoulder and saw Joseph and Moon sitting off to the side, away from the crowd. He got up and refilled his plate, then made his way over to the young man and his dog. Moon lifted his head and thumped his tail against the ground as he watched Lucius approach and sit on the ground beside Joseph.

"You know," Lucius began in a voice only audible to Joseph and Moon, "I couldn't find it in me to allow this Holy Man to enter into my house. To put Him under my roof, under my authority – I felt so unworthy."

"I know, I know," said Joseph softly.

Lucius shook his head. "I am so overwhelmed by all this. Isaac is healed and I feel I've been given a whole new life, like I am just now starting to live. Almost like I've been born clean and new again. Does that make any sense to you, Joseph?"

"It makes more sense than you know," said Joseph. "Don't ever forget this day, Lucius. Never forget it."

Lucius laughed out loud. "I don't see how I ever could. And you know what?" Lucius smiled. "I don't think I've ever known anyone so young who feels so at ease telling a Roman centurion what to do. I don't know where you and your golden dog came from, Joseph, but I am grateful that you are here. There is much I wish to speak to you of. You seem to have wisdom far beyond your years."

Joseph looked out over the sea and sighed deeply. Then he looked at Lucius. "We cannot stay, Lucius. We must be leaving soon. Tonight."

Lucius nearly choked on his mouthful of food. "Leaving? Who said anything about leaving? You can stay as long as you like, and your salary will be increased greatly. I'll see to that myself. And you can sleep inside the house, in a real bed."

"Lucius, please. We cannot stay any longer. I have –" Joseph looked at his Moondog, who thumped his tail at his master's glance. "We have grown to consider you and your friends Isaac and John, as our friends as well. Please don't make this any more difficult than it already is. I appreciate your offer, but we cannot stay."

"But where will you go?" asked Lucius. "I feel I owe you so much, and you are still very much a mystery to me."

Joseph looked at Lucius as a huge smile spread across his face. "We will follow the One you call the Holy Man. We will follow Jesus." Joseph recalled the words spoken to him by Ruben and Simon of the coming Messiah. "For He is the One the prophets of old wrote about long ago."

Joseph studied Lucius' face in the fading light of the sunset. "You have spent some time with those from the synagogue. Do you know of Whom I am speaking, Lucius?"

Lucius narrowed his eyes as he studied Joseph. "You mean – but they told me the One written of long ago would be a King. A new King. Surely

One dressed as Jesus and living a lifestyle like the common people is not a King!"

Joseph nodded slowly. "Yes, Lucius, a King, The King. And at the same time, the most humble, the most obedient of Servants. Can you understand this, Lucius?"

Lucius looked at the ground then back at Joseph, shaking his head. "How can this be, a King and also a Servant? This does not make any sense at all to me, Joseph." The centurion's eyes pleaded for some explanation.

Joseph continued, "Not only The King and obedient Servant, but much more than that. Besides being the Creator, He is to be the Savior sent to take away the sins of this world. For any and all who will believe on Him and trust Him with everything they are, and who are willing to obey Him. I don't know how He is going to do this, so don't ask me. But Jesus came here not just to heal Isaac this day, but to heal you as well. Can you believe all this, Lucius? Can you believe it?"

Lucius squirmed and turned away from Joseph's eyes and looked up at Isaac. The man who had been virtually dead walked about, talking to others like he had never been sick a day in his entire life. Lucius trembled and stared at his feet. Joseph could see tears brim up in his eyes. For a few moments his breathing came in short bursts as he tried to regain his composure. Finally he did so. Then he sighed deeply and stared at the ground.

Lucius spoke softly. "I do not understand all of this, my friend, and I am not sure I know all of what you mean," started Lucius. "But the part about Jesus being sent here to take away my sins, yes I do believe it, for I am now a free man. Free from my past. I don't deserve it, and I don't understand it, but I believe on Him, and I am free. I don't even know how I know this, but I know it. All I feel now is gratitude beyond words. Beyond words."

Joseph looked at his Moondog and smiled. "Don't ever waver from this belief in Jesus, Lucius, regardless of the circumstances ahead. Always remember this. And with that I'll try my best not to give you any more orders." Joseph laughed.

Moon thumped his tail while he looked at Joseph and listened to his laughter.

Lucius chuckled softly as he collected himself. "I understand your desire to follow Him. If it were not for my responsibilities and ties here, I would have half a mind to do the very same thing myself. I guess there is no purpose in arguing with you to stay. Plus it looks like two against one again and I know when I'm beaten.

"I will miss you, Joseph. So much has happened in such a short time. I'm grateful you were here when you were. Isaac will miss you too; he has spoken highly of you. And John will probably miss you too, though he would never say it. It's the Roman way, you know." Joseph and Lucius laughed as one.

Moon got up and put his head on Lucius' knee. Lucius reached up and rubbed the big dog's ears.

"Yes, I'll miss you too, Moon. Thanks for your comfort when I had those awful dreams. I don't imagine I'll have any more of those."

Lucius thought a while longer. "I really don't want to tell Isaac you are leaving tonight. Would you consider staying until morning? Then at least you two could have a little time together. I think the poor man must be near exhaustion right now. People are still poking and prodding him to hear his story and make sure he's not a ghost."

Joseph looked toward the town, then at Isaac. "Alright, we'll stay until daybreak. Then we must be going. Who knows, we may see each other often if Jesus stays around these parts."

"That sounds great, Joseph, thank you. And tonight the two of you will stay in the big house, in the guest bedroom." Joseph began to protest, but Lucius insisted.

"For once, my young friend, just this once, let *me* give an order, alright?"

Chapter 27

The celebration wore on long into the night before the last of the workers left. They would soon spread the news of Isaac's healing.

Joseph and Moon retired late to the guest bedroom. Moon took up his usual post between Joseph and the door to protect his master from possible intruders.

The curtains over the window and the thickness of the walls blocked much of the early morning light and sounds as Joseph slept unusually late. Though Lucius and Isaac woke early, they kept quiet so as not to disturb him. Soon, however, Moon heard the morning noises and woke Joseph.

Opening the door, Joseph squinted at the bright sunshine coming in the windows along the hall. He and Moon joined Lucius and Isaac in the dining room where they were conversing quietly.

"Well hello and good morning, you two," greeted Isaac. "Lucius tells me that you are leaving us. I am sorry to see you go, Joseph. If you stayed I think you could soon be moving up in rank around here. I've been so out of it lately that I don't even know what's been going on outside. Are you sure you won't stay for at least a few more weeks and help me get back into the swing of things around here?"

Joseph smiled and shook his head. "We appreciate the offer, but I'm sure you'll do fine. The workers respect you as a supervisor, and they are good men. They have really worked hard to keep up while you were ill. I'm sure you'll be pleased with what they've done. But as for us, we must be going. Perhaps we will see each other again. I want to thank you for hiring me in the first place. I really didn't know why we came here, but I am glad we got to know you both."

Isaac looked at Lucius, who nodded his head once. "I told you – his mind is made up. And I can't really say that I blame him."

Lucius looked toward Joseph and Moon. "I do hope you two will find the time to stop by and see us. I am interested in what is going on with Jesus as well. We both are. And you've always got a place to stay when you stop in, don't forget that, Joseph. Now sit down while I have the cook get you something to eat."

157

Joseph shook his head. "I appreciate the offer of stopping back sometime. We will try and do that if we can. But we really don't need any breakfast. It's later than I realized when I woke. We need to be going."

Lucius and Isaac rose from the table and walked Joseph and Moon out the front door. Joseph took up his staff, his only earthly possession besides the clothes he wore, and, of course, his beloved Moondog. At the front door they all shook hands – even Moondog – much to the delight of the centurion and his friend. Lucius stuffed some money in Joseph's shirt pocket. When Joseph began to protest, Lucius held up his hand.

"Now Joseph," Lucius began with his serious tone, "this is not a gift. These are wages you earned while working here. You never know when you will need the money."

Lucius began to grin. "I've never known anyone quite like you before, in many ways. You don't even care about money, do you?" Lucius didn't give Joseph a chance to respond. "No matter. Take this money; it is yours to do with as you wish."

Then Lucius grew serious again. "I would like to go with you, Joseph, if you think it would be alright." Lucius' statement surprised Joseph. "I still do not feel worthy to meet this Jesus face to face, but I must thank Him for healing Isaac. And me. Besides, we still have much to discuss. Perhaps we can talk on the way to town."

Joseph smiled and nodded as he stuck the money deeper in his pocket. The two, along with a grinning Moondog, started off toward town. Joseph got only a few steps from the house before he looked down toward the sea and stopped.

"What is it, Joseph?" Lucius furrowed his brow.

Joseph turned back toward the house where Isaac still stood. "Isaac," said Joseph, his voice distressed, "who did you send to get water this morning?"

"Well, I'm feeling so good that I went myself, just before sunrise. Why do you ask?"

"Did you see a boat tied to the pier when you went down to the water? A small fishing boat with a sail. Did you see it?"

Isaac thought a moment. "Not that I can remember, Joseph. There were a few boats out fishing, but none tied to the pier. Why does that matter?"

Joseph knew he had allowed this to happen by his own carelessness. "It was the boat Jesus was in. And some of his friends I guess. We saw them come in two nights ago. They must have gone sometime last night."

"Oh no, Joseph, it can't be," said Lucius. "But if He did leave, perhaps He will be back soon. He may be back this evening, don't you think?"

"I'm not sure, Lucius. I have a feeling that's not going to happen. I don't know why, but that's what I think. I can't believe I let this happen."

"It was not you, Joseph, but me. I'm the one who insisted that you stay, that you sleep inside. If you had left last night like you wanted to, this would not have happened. Or perhaps if you had been out in the shed, you or Moon would have heard them as they left."

Joseph thought a moment. "It's alright, Lucius. I tell you the truth. I am greatly disappointed, but I think it may be alright, though I can't understand why right now. I'm beginning to learn that for those who will follow Jesus, all things which happen along the way happen for good, even if we don't think so at the time. After meeting Liam when we first got here, the last thing I wanted to do was to stay. But we did, and things turned out pretty good for everyone, wouldn't you say?"

Neither Isaac nor Lucius attempted to hide their smiles.

Joseph continued, "So don't be upset, it's not your fault any more than mine. But Moon and I will find Him, don't worry about that. We will. Now tell me, which way does the wind usually blow at night this time of year? It usually comes across the sea, toward the south and slightly to the east, doesn't it?"

"Yes," answered Lucius. "Pretty much toward the south, though it's usually not very strong this time of year. We can get some pretty bad storms though."

"And which is the quickest way to go to the opposite side from here, around to the north or the south?"

Isaac spoke. "Well, the south route is the shortest, but either way it would take someone a long time to walk from here. Perhaps days, Joseph, depending on the weather. And the country is none too friendly, either. You can't be serious about this. Perhaps Jesus will be back soon. Maybe you should just wait here for Him."

Joseph shook his head. "You may be right, but I feel we have waited too long already. We will go to the south."

"There is something else," said Lucius. "I planned on telling you this as we walked to town together. Liam will not forget what happened here. His kind never do. I doubt he will do anything out in the open for others to see, but if he gets the chance out in the wilds..."

"Or is drunk enough," interrupted Isaac.

Lucius nodded, "Yes, or is drunk enough. I have little doubt he will try to do either you or your Moon some serious harm. If you stayed around here you would pretty much be protected from that."

Joseph thought about this for a moment. "I appreciate your concern, but we'll be alright. Me and Moon sort of look out for each other that way. And the Good Lord looks out for us all."

"Well, if you're determined to go, and think you'll not be around town for a while, you'll need something to take with you," stated Isaac as he disappeared into the house. Joseph looked at Lucius, who returned Joseph's puzzled look. Soon Isaac reappeared carrying a rolled-up blanket similar to the one the keeper of the inn had given Joseph years ago.

"You'll need that to keep warm, wherever you are going," said Isaac as he tossed the bundle to Joseph. "It'll serve as a coat if you need it during the day, and a cover at night. It should be just big enough to wrap you both in if need be and light and small enough so it won't be much to carry."

Joseph smiled. "Thank you. We'll take it. And we'll remember you both when we use it. Now we must be going."

And with that, Joseph gave a short wave and smiled again. "Peace to you, my friends." The two men smiled back and nodded as Joseph and Moon started toward town.

"You take care of yourself, Joseph. And you take care of him, Moondog," shouted Lucius as the two departed. At the sound of his name, Moondog turned and grinned at the two. Then he turned back and stepped next to his master, eyes and ears alert, tail up and waving behind him like a big yellow feather in the breeze.

Joseph and Moon reached the crest of the hill which looked down on the town. Then they looked back one last time at the farm where so much had happened in such a short time. From there they could barely make out Lucius standing alone. Lucius saw them turn and raised his right hand in farewell.

Joseph raised the rolled blanket over his head and swung it back and forth.

"They *are* Romans, Moondoggie," Joseph said quietly. "But Marcus Lucius is now a free man."

Chapter 28

Joseph asked around to find out if Jesus might still be in town. He discovered that so many people had pressed in on Him that Jesus and his companions had left in the very early hours of the morning to escape the crush.

Joseph and Moon journeyed unnoticed out the other side of town, roughly following the water's edge when possible. All the while they kept a look out for Jesus or His boat tied along shore.

Near the water Joseph heard the coarse talk of the fishermen and merchants as they sold their wares. Once in a while someone would make a comment about the strange looking dog and call out to Moon. Moon and Joseph ignored them as best they could and continued their trek by the sea.

Bits and pieces of the fishermen's conversations floated in the air. Joseph's thoughts were on other things until, at one point, he heard Lucius' name mentioned. He stopped altogether to listen when he discovered the men were talking about one of Lucius' workers being healed of a dread disease. Some spoke about how Jesus had healed the man just by speaking a word to Lucius' three servants. Others said that wasn't possible, but that it sure seemed Lucius had all the luck. Joseph shook his head and walked on.

Finally they saw what looked like the boat tied to shore with no one around. Moon sniffed it long and hard with his tail up and flying, while Joseph studied the nearby tracks. The trail led away from the sea, to the south and slightly west.

They set out at once with renewed enthusiasm, Moon inhaling great quantities of air, then blowing it out quickly and repeating the process. Joseph smiled to himself as he watched his faithful companion. "From the looks of these tracks, we're not too many hours behind them, buddy." Moondog wagged his tail in agreement.

Soon they came upon several places where the trail branched off in different directions. Joseph struggled to find the right tracks with all the foot traffic that had crisscrossed the trails. Without Moon, each crossing would have taken him much longer to decipher. Even with his companion, every major crossing became a puzzle of tracks, and they needed all their skills to stay the correct course. Just when they seemed to gain a little ground, the two would come to another crossing. They continued following the trail which was leading farther away from the sea.

Joseph and Moon traveled about fifteen miles from the water before they came to a small village. There they saw a large crowd gathered in the streets, near the gates of the city. Joseph decided to climb a side hill to the west so they would have the sun behind them. He and Moon began circling the crowd, being careful not to draw attention to themselves.

From the hillside Joseph and Moon saw not one, but two good sized groups of people coming together along the road below, going in opposite directions. One group of people surrounded Jesus and pressed in on Him. The other group belonged to a funeral procession.

Joseph and Moon positioned themselves above where the two groups would meet. They managed to get close enough to see things transpire right before their eyes but far enough away that no one noticed them.

Moving slowly from left to right below them, they saw six men carrying the open casket of a young man. Behind the casket, leaning heavily on her friends, staggered a woman tortured with grief.

Although they stood several yards above the coffin, Joseph saw Moon's sensitive nose wrinkle at death's vile stench that lingered around the body.

The woman swayed behind the casket of her beloved. The men carried their load slowly as it looked like she could travel no faster. Her bent form and twisted face looked spent with anguish. Behind her came several others, wailing and weeping. Joseph couldn't remember witnessing a more pitiful scene. Moon's golden ears drooped and his tail sagged toward the ground as the two groups came together.

When the men carrying the casket came near to Jesus, He stopped talking to those around Him and turned to take in the scene. Those with Him fell silent. Only the mournful sobs and wails of the funeral party, especially of the woman, could be heard.

Jesus looked at the mother who had lost her only son, and His countenance changed. "Do not weep."[1]

The woman looked into His eyes and straightened up a little. Did she recognize Him? Did she sense in any way *Who* had just spoken to her? Joseph couldn't tell.

Jesus walked over to the coffin and touched it while those carrying it stood still. Joseph and Moon could sense some hostility growing in the group of people behind the woman. They seemed indignant that someone would cause this mother even more grief by disrupting the funeral procession.

Jesus looked directly at the man in the coffin. "Young man, I say to you, arise!"[2]

Immediately, the young man in the coffin sat up and began to speak. Those carrying the casket wavered and staggered at the sight. In awe and fear they quickly set the casket on the ground and stepped back. Audible gasps could be heard from most everyone, including Joseph.

Jesus took the young man's hand and helped him out of the casket. Then He turned and presented him – alive, whole, and healthy – to his mother.

The mother stared for a long moment in disbelief. Then she gave a great cry of joy and clung to her son, weeping uncontrollably. Some of those closest to the mother and son took a few steps back. Eyes grew wide and many seemed to forget how to breathe.

Joseph tried to steady himself with his staff as he swayed where he stood. He sat back on the hill, mouth agape. Moon leaned against Joseph, his tail slowly starting to rise and swing gently back and forth. His ears went up as the stench of death miraculously vanished from the air.

Everyone in both groups stared at the young man who moments before had been dead, but now stood very much alive before them all.

"There's no doubt in my mind that man was flat out D-dead," Joseph heard someone in the crowd say. "He was dead I tell you!" Those in the crowd looked at Jesus, then back at the man, and then they became afraid.

Joseph had seen this happen before, especially in large gatherings. Fear of something unknown rippled through the crowd. But then some began to shout praises to God. Jesus seemed pleased that at least some who had seen the work which He had done were giving glory to God.

News of this event spread quickly and Jesus soon left the area.

Joseph and Moon followed Jesus at a distance. Because the crowds trailed Jesus every step of the way, they had trouble finding a private place to put their bedroll. But at the same time, the crowds helped them remain unnoticed.

They slipped away from the road and into a small hollow among the hills. There, in the tall grass and brush, they found a shelter large enough to lie down.

Joseph began clearing a space on the ground for them to make their bed, all the while going over in his head what they had witnessed at the small village. One crowd, powerless to change things, had been following a dead man to his grave. And the other crowd, some dancing, some praising God out loud, following Jesus. Full of life and joy. No doubt some of the people following Him were ones He'd healed and set free from evil spirits. They followed Life itself, while those in the other group followed death. But when they met head to head, Jesus conquered death and brought life to even this hopeless situation. Joseph felt lightheaded, almost giddy, as he prepared their campsite.

Moon watched Joseph stomp down their evening bed in the tall grass. The big dog walked a large circle around the area, scanning with his sharp eyes and nose for any unknown hazards nearby.

Joseph unrolled the blanket on the ground and saw a small note inside. In the fading light he could barely make out Isaac's handwriting: "Farewell, my friends. You are always welcome here. I am so grateful. And if you see Jesus before I do, tell Him thanks for saving my life."

Joseph stretched out on his back and watched the stars begin to show themselves. Moondog curled up beside him and plopped down with a grunt. Joseph reached over and gently kneaded the fur behind Moon's ears as the big dog gave a sigh and stretched out his tired paws.

"I'll tell Him, Isaac, if I get a chance. But I don't have to. He already knows," said Joseph softly. A smile of contentment passed across his face. "He already knows."

And with that the two weary travelers fell asleep.

Chapter 29

Joseph and Moon woke about thirty minutes before sunrise. Moon stretched and yawned, his tail making lazy loops in the cool morning air. Then he sat next to Joseph with his eyes sparkling and reflecting the orange and yellow glow of the sky.

Joseph sat up and put his right arm around Moon and felt the welcome warmth of his companion against his side. "Well, buddy, looks like another big day for us."

Moon thumped his tail as he looked at his master.

"Moondog, I can't stop thinking about that night when we first saw Jesus by the sea. There is something more happening here than we can see. I just sense it somehow. Something different and difficult to perceive, but of such great value that I can't even comprehend it. I don't have a clue what it is, but the significance to everyone will be priceless. It's got something to do with Jesus taking on the sins of the world, but it's way beyond what I can imagine. Of course, Jesus raising that man from his coffin yesterday was way beyond what I could imagine too."

Joseph rolled up the blanket as Moon shook off the morning dampness and began prancing about. They emerged from the brush in the dim light of dawn and saw Jesus and His followers already up and moving. Many in the crowd began to stir, and soon they swarmed around Jesus, listening to His teaching and crying out for healing.

They moved closer; Joseph knew Moon was having trouble seeing with so many people to contend with. He did his best to maneuver them uphill, and finally they reached a spot where both could sit and see a little, although people kept jostling to get closer to Jesus.

"Moon, is this about perfect or what?" Joseph asked his companion softly. "Out here under a blue sky, even the warm breeze seems to be carrying a song. I can praise God so easily out here, maybe that's the real reason I'd rather live outside than in any man-made building."

Joseph paused for a moment as he stood up to observe. "Whoa, Moondog," Joseph whispered under his breath as he looked on. "Jesus just healed a blind man. He seemed completely blind a moment ago. Then Jesus just reached out His hand and touched him; and now, apparently, the man can see!"

Moon looked up at Joseph and tried to wag his tail at the sound of reverence in his master's voice, but too many people pressing in blocked his attempt.

Joseph crouched down next to Moon. "If that guy was blind from birth, then the very first thing he saw was the face of Jesus! The very first thing!" Joseph spoke as much to himself as to his companion. "I've heard that He also heals the deaf. The very first sound those folks may have ever heard was the sound of the voice of Jesus. The very first sound ever!"

Joseph's hands trembled as he hugged Moon close. "I can't believe we're getting to see this. This is awesome!"

People continued to crush in around Joseph and Moon. Joseph considered moving farther away, lest the masses trample them. He stood up to look for a better place from which to observe when suddenly a large disturbance began to take place in the crowd below. They could hear people yelling and shouting.

Joseph could see people scrambling to get away from someone. Below Joseph and Moon, the sea of humanity parted as if cut with a knife. Joseph could see people falling away to either side as some climbed over others to keep from being touched.

"Get away, get away!" cried people in the crowd. "You must not come near us, you cursed fool."

Joseph caught a glimpse of the man. He had ugly sores all over his body. His face was horribly disfigured and he had dirty bandages tied around his hands. He didn't look like he heard anyone screaming at him. He seemed determined to reach Jesus or die in the process.

Joseph watched the man approach as the people screamed and struggled to get away. When he finally reached Jesus, he fell at His feet. The crowd became so quiet that even Joseph and Moon could hear.

"Lord, if You are willing, You can make me clean,"[1] stated the desperate man hoarsely. He lay there in the dust, trembling. Joseph and Moon could smell his reeking flesh. The man appeared to be bleeding from his battle to get up the mountainside.

Jesus, seeing the man's faith and condition, paused for a moment, filled with compassion. "I am willing; be cleansed,"[2] He said, and reached down and TOUCHED him! Even some close friends of Jesus gasped at seeing Jesus' hand reach down and touch the leper.

The moment Jesus touched the man, the leprosy left him. The man slowly got up and looked at Jesus, seemingly afraid to believe what he had just heard. Then he untied the bandages and looked at his arms and hands, then down at his legs and feet. His fingers and toes looked normal. He held his hands up against the sky, looking first at one and then the other. His skin looked as clean and clear as a child's. Tears of joy began running down his face.

"Thank You, thank You," he said softly to Jesus as the Son of Man smiled back at him.

Jesus said to him, "See that you tell no one; but go your way, show yourself to the priest, and offer the gift that Moses commanded, as a testimony to them."[3]

The man turned slowly and walked back through the crowd, still staring at his hands while tears flowed freely from his eyes. The people around him did their best to move out of his way, but this time not out of terror. An undercurrent of wonder ran through the crowd.

Joseph smiled down at Moon and gave him a playful thump on the shoulder. Although Moon couldn't see the event, he returned the grin and again wagged his tail the best he could, brushing up against those standing beside them. No one seemed to mind.

The day passed quickly as Jesus healed many and people shouted praises to God. Toward the end of the day, Jesus looked on the huge multitude of people who had come out to see Him, some journeying long distances. He told his friends to get them all seated on the grass, thousands of them. Joseph and Moon sat down with the rest, all eyes fixed on the Master of the universe.

Jesus then told his friends to give all these people something to eat, so they could have strength for their journey home. Joseph saw this start a bit of a panic amongst His closest friends. They had no food and no money to go and buy the amount of food it would take to feed this many people. After a discussion amongst themselves, they turned back to Jesus and said so.

A boy offered a few loaves of bread and a couple of fish. But what could that do for a crowd this large?

Jesus' friends gave what little they themselves could come up with; Jesus took it, blessed it, and gave it back to them. Then they started passing the food out to the people. Joseph, with his eye for detail, studied the proceedings closely. The men with the baskets of food went from one group to the next. People reached in and pulled out bread and fish, as much as they wanted. Scores of people.

People continued passing the baskets around. And still they kept reaching inside and pulling out more and more food. Even though he had positioned himself above the action and watched closely, Joseph didn't even see where all the baskets had come from. He knew the original amount of food wouldn't get past the first two or three people. From where they sat, Joseph and Moon watched as the baskets went from group to group, until they couldn't see them anymore. Then a basket came by and

Joseph looked in. He reached in and pulled out some bread and a fish. He studied them both, then looked down at Moon and smiled.

"Bread," said Joseph softly to his friend. "And fish. *Ichthys*," he said as he looked at the scar on Moon's snoot.

Joseph watched as that basket went from his group all the way up the hillside and down around to more people who continued to pull out more fish and bread. Joseph turned back to look at Jesus, who sat peacefully with His eyes closed, apparently in prayer. After everyone had eaten, His helpers collected several baskets of leftover food.

Jesus' friends couldn't succeed by their own ability, thought Joseph. *But, at the urging of the Master, they didn't quit. They took what little they had and gave it to Jesus. He in turn blessed it and gave it back to them. And they stepped out in faith and served the people. And what a serving! Above and beyond everyone's needs or even wants.*

Joseph sat with his hand on the side of his head in deep thought while Moondog lay contented at his side. Around them people ate their fill and spoke of the remarkable things they had seen this day. Then Jesus sent the people home.

Slowly, reluctantly, most of the crowd began to disperse. Jesus and His friends moved back, closer to the sea, and tried to find refuge for the night away from the crowd.

Joseph and Moon got up and followed at a distance. They found a sheltered area in which to sleep, Joseph's head spinning with what he had witnessed. "Moondog, this crowd is wearing me out." Joseph said quietly as he unrolled their sleeping blanket. "But I wouldn't miss this for the world."

Moon gently swirled his tail in agreement. Then he circled the area checking for danger. Finally he stretched out next to his master and the two fell into a deep sleep.

Chapter 30

The next morning, crowds once again descended on Jesus and His friends. They made their way back to the boat and pushed off, much to the disappointment of the people. Many turned away, but some ran up or down the shoreline in search of boats so that they could follow.

Joseph and Moon observed the scene from a small hilltop a little distance away. "Buddy," Joseph said quietly to Moon, "these people are acting just like lost children. Kind of gives me the creeps."

Joseph and Moon watched the boat tack toward the horizon as the sun rose. Joseph knew he could stay and wait to see if Jesus would return, or he could try to anticipate where Jesus might go next. He checked the wind, then looked down at his companion. Moon looked up with a big grin and swung his tail from side to side.

"Come on, buddy," Joseph prodded as he started off along the shoreline to the southeast. Moon reared up slightly and made a great bound past Joseph, barely grazing his leg as he shot past. The two would much rather go exploring together than wait in one place just to see what might happen.

They trekked a good part of the day, circling the south side of the sea. Ever since the night near the pier, Joseph had noticed something fascinating. While he and Moon walked along they began to see things in greater detail than ever before. The water lapping the shoreline sounded like it was right next to their ears. When they moved away from the water to get around some obstacle, they now saw the trees, grass and birds with more clarity. It seemed that every aspect of life flowing from the earth gave glory to God, each thing in its own way. To Joseph and Moon, the birdsong now seemed to be in praise, not just random notes sounding in the air. The two walked on with light hearts as they covered the miles around the sea, once in a while passing through a small village along the way.

Soon Moon, and then Joseph, began to hear the sound of the Jordan River, emptying out of the sea and flowing toward the south. The river came into view. Joseph could tell by the speed of the water flowing by that they'd have to cross with caution. He decided to hike downstream to make sure they wouldn't be carried into any dangerous waters as they swam across. As they walked, both he and Moon noticed a trail which became more and more worn. Soon they came to a creative device for crossing the river.

A heavy sisal rope tied about waist high was tightly stretched from one bank of the river to the other. On the near side, a couple of small logs floated in the river, lashed together with rope, forming a crude raft. Two wooden pulleys, one on each end of the raft, had the heavy rope running through them. Joseph noticed two lighter ropes attached to the raft. The one on their side of the river was tied to a small tree on one end with the rest of it coiled up on the raft. Another small rope stretched from the other side of the river and was tied tightly to the raft itself.

Joseph surveyed the set up and looked down at Moon. He lifted one eyebrow in mock amazement at their good fortune. Moon grinned back and fanned the air with his tail. As Joseph stepped on the raft, he didn't need to coax his dog on board.

Joseph began pulling on the lighter rope, and the wooden pulleys creaked under the pressure of the raft and its occupants bucking the river's current. As Joseph pulled more rope and coiled it at his feet, the raft moved further into the river. At the same time, the top coils of rope at the back of the raft began to unwind behind them. Soon the current caught this rope and pulled the majority of it into the river. No matter, each end remained securely fastened, one to the raft, the other to the shore.

Joseph continued pulling and coiling the rope and soon the two travelers bobbed and floated on the current to the midway point in the river. Joseph stopped pulling for a moment and looked about. The murky river rushed past, swooshing and spraying water over both him and Moon as the power of the water rocked the small raft. Joseph looked down at Moon, who stood braced on the logs with all his toenails dug in as deeply as they could go. Moon looked intently at the logs and the water rolling rapidly past. Part of the adventurous streak in Joseph wanted to remain and take in the exhilaration of the moment, but he could tell Moon felt stressed with the entire situation.

"It's okay, Moon; it's alright!" Joseph shouted to his companion over the roar of the river as he turned and began pulling on the rope once again. Soon they reached the other shore.

Moondog finally took his eyes off the moving logs and the rushing river to see the eastern shore only a few feet away. Joseph felt his dog press up against him as they completed the river crossing. He knew Moon would have never tried crossing the river alone.

Joseph secured the raft as he looked behind him to the far shore where they had been. "Ingenious, Moon buddy," Joseph said as he stored all the information in his mind. "Nothing to worry about." They jumped off the raft and began hiking back toward the sea.

Near midday they passed through several small communities. Joseph counted nine in all, ten if he included the one just on the other side of the river. He heard no talk of Jesus as they walked.

The terrain grew steeper and Joseph and Moon could no longer walk along the water's edge. They cut back away from the shore and followed a footpath along the steep hillside. From here they could see a few people out tending to their animals, but more importantly, they could keep a watchful eye on the shoreline.

A short while after leaving the last of the ten towns, Joseph noticed a small boat coming in from the sea. It appeared that, if it continued on its course, it would reach the shore a couple of miles ahead of them.

Joseph signaled to Moon, and then he too saw the boat and began sniffing the air as it swirled toward them on the water below. It took him a few moments to catch the scent, and then Moon began to prance around Joseph much like he'd done the night on the pier. Joseph grinned at Moon's reaction and the two took off along the path at good pace, Moon running ahead and looking over his shoulder, urging Joseph to run faster.

Joseph and Moon were within a half mile of the boat when it landed. Between them and the boat they saw some old trees; beneath the trees, there seemed to be something like a very old graveyard of sorts. It appeared rundown and dark, even in the middle of the day. Below it, they saw Jesus with a small group of people gathered around Him.

As they approached the group, Joseph didn't know exactly what to do. He knew not to interfere, yet he wanted to get close enough to observe all he could. Only a dozen or so people stood about the boat, so he and Moon would surely draw attention to themselves if they just walked up to them.

He could make Moon stay put, then silently approach without being seen, but that might take a long time. Plus, Joseph suspected Moon might not hold his place. He dismissed the idea, however, as it dawned on him that he could not possibly sneak up on the Creator of the universe.

Joseph slowed Moon down and they began to descend the hill, walking under the trees and among the tombs, trying to get close enough to hear. Moon could hardly contain himself, but he obediently stayed alongside his master.

A violent jolt rocked them, stopping Joseph and Moon in their tracks and knocking them back against the hillside. They watched in stunned amazement as demon after demon tore out of a wild-looking fellow near Jesus, throwing the huge man down like a rag doll. So many demons flew by so fast that Joseph couldn't count them all.

Then they saw the hideous creatures rush, screaming and cursing, into a nearby herd of swine. Their combined, overwhelming power was crushed in only a moment by a single word from Jesus.

The swine ran down the hill, thrashing into the sea. Joseph looked from the churning sea back to the group of men. His eyes were wide open, his mouth agape, and his heart was pounding. He put his arm around Moon and held him tight. Then he saw Jesus reach down and gently lift the big man to his feet.

One of Jesus' companions took off his outer wrap and put it around the man who stood before them. He looked stunned. He stared at Jesus, then at his own hands which were no longer shaking.

He staggered and sat down. The small crowd stood by and shifted their weight from one foot to the other, as if they didn't know what to do or say. Some gazed at the swine floating in the sea. Others looked from the man to Jesus, and then back to the man again.

As Jesus spoke to the man and to His followers, those tending the swine ran into town and soon returned with more people. They hurried past Joseph and Moon, appearing not to notice them, and made their way to the small group standing on the shore.

Joseph sensed that great fear had overtaken all the swineherds and the townspeople. He watched them do what he'd seen others do when afraid. Instead of taking a risk and trying to understand, they tried to eliminate the cause of their fears. In part because of the watching crowd, they didn't want to risk appearing cowardly.

Joseph heard them beg Jesus to leave them, not to ever come back, just to leave right away. They begged the Son of the Most High God to go away from them and not return. Fear, pride, cowardice. Joseph realized that these evils, either by themselves or along with other things, could force a person to turn his back on the One Who could save his very soul.

Jesus turned to get back in the boat. The big man got up and asked to follow Him, but Jesus would not allow it. The man appeared greatly saddened by Jesus' words, but Jesus reached out and put His hand on the man's shoulder and smiled at him. He told him to go and tell all those in the surrounding towns of what great things God had done for him. He told him to go back to his family.

The man looked into Jesus' eyes, and a tremendous smile spread slowly across his face. Then he nodded as he touched Jesus' arm with his hand. Jesus and his followers got back in the boat and pushed off from shore.

Joseph wanted desperately to follow but knew he and Moon couldn't slip unnoticed into the boat. For now they would stay.

The crowd went back to town, shaking their heads and murmuring to themselves, leaving the once mad man standing alone on shore.

Joseph and Moon got up and silently approached the man as he watched Jesus and his followers sail farther from land. Moon walked up and nuzzled the man's hand. The startled man looked down, surprised to see a big golden snoot under his palm. Then he looked back at Joseph.

Tears of joy cut clean paths through the grime on the man's face as he fought for control. He wiped his eyes with the back of a huge paw of a hand and said softly, "I'm free. I'm completely clean. I know I look filthy. On the outside, I mean. But I've never felt so clean. Never in all my life."

Moondog looked up at the man and grinned while his tail looped behind him.

"I know," replied Joseph gently. "We saw, and I know."

Chapter 31

They stood and watched as the boat carrying Jesus faded into the horizon. No one spoke for a long time. Eventually the man turned back to Joseph. Tears continued streaking fresh paths down his filthy face. His tangled and matted hair stuck out in multiple directions. Joseph noted how burly the man was.

"Do you know who I am?" he asked in a deep voice.

Joseph shook his head.

The man looked out at the hillside beyond Joseph. "This is where I've lived for I don't know how long. Right now I can't even remember living anywhere else."

Joseph turned around. He could only see the hillside with tombs scattered about it. He turned back with an eyebrow raised.

"That's right," said the man. "This is my home. The tombs. This is where I have been for a long time, out of my head, racked with pain from those things that lived inside me." The man looked back over his shoulder. The last of the swine floated down the shoreline as the current swept them away.

"What I had inside of me is too horrible to describe. Come with me. I want to show you something." With that the man ran past Joseph and started up the hill into the tombs.

Joseph looked at Moon and shrugged his shoulders. The two followed the man to a cavern in the hillside. In front of it, Joseph saw that the ground was all torn up, like some terrific struggle had taken place on the spot not long ago.

"See these?" said the man pointing at the broken chains hanging on a beam of wood at the front of the cavern. "These are mine, or they were meant for me, I should say. Sometimes when I slept, a group of those townspeople that you saw would sneak up and jump me. They'd tie me up to this place with those chains 'cause they knew I was crazy. I guess they didn't want me running into town killing no one. They hated me."

The man picked up one of the heavy chains and rolled it around in his hand. Pain twisted across the man's face. Yet Joseph sensed no anger, no bitterness toward the people of the nearby towns. Moon walked up and

175

sniffed one of the chains covered with sweat and blood. He quickly trotted back to Joseph's side.

"You must have had at least one friend," said Joseph quietly. "Otherwise you would have died here. Who unlocked you from these chains?"

The man shook his head. "No one helped me. The chains, they couldn't hold me. I broke them with my own hands." The man showed Joseph his wrists, scarred from the shackles. The man's wrists looked bigger than Joseph's ankles. Joseph stared at them and back at the heavy chains in disbelief.

"You broke these with your own strength?"

"No, not my strength. Those things, those things living in me. Their strength. No one could control me. They tormented me constantly. I terrified everyone and everyone terrified me. I wanted to die, but those things wouldn't let me die. They just wanted to torment me. They enjoyed it thoroughly. Sometimes they'd take turns. Other times they'd all join in at once. I had no power against them. I was helpless and they knew it. So they continued on, never letting up, never."

Joseph looked at the chains and swallowed. Even if he had had a saw or a hammer and chisel, it probably would have taken him a long time to get through chains this heavy, if ever.

The man looked at his wrists again. "I tore my wrists up again today. Now look. They're healing up already. They're not even sore anymore."

The man smiled to himself as he threw the chain to the ground with a loud thump. "Come on, let's go into town. I must tell them what's happened to me. I must show them that I am healed. For God has truly healed me today." Then the big man burst into laughter that filled the hillsides, the same hillsides that had just earlier that day been filled with his screams of terror.

Joseph smiled at the sound of his laughter. "Well, now don't be angry at me or anything, but I think first you ought to go down to the water and wash off a bit."

The man looked at his arms and legs covered with mud and dried sweat and blood. Then he threw his head back and burst into laughter again. He gave Joseph a playful slap on the shoulder which almost knocked him down, and then ran back down the hill to the sea. At the shore he laid his outer garments on the bank and jumped into the cool water, laughing and shouting praises to God the whole while.

Joseph smiled at Moon. Moondog reared back and ripped a quick circle around his master, ending up in front of him with his rump in the air and his head down on his outstretched front paws. Joseph laughed as he looked away from Moon and at the hillside above.

The gloominess of the tombs that he and Moon had noticed when they first walked through them had lifted. It seemed that the more the man's praises echoed off the hillsides, the brighter the place became. Even the trees and the grass seemed to be reaching up to the heavens, giving glory to the Creator who had been so near, expelling the wicked darkness. Joseph heard birdsong from the hillside nearby for the first time as he looked back at Moon, who stared bright-eyed at him from his playful position.

"Come on," Joseph said as he sprinted around his dog toward the sea. Then he smiled as Moon whirled about and raced past him to the shore. From there Moondog bounded out into the water toward the big man, swimming around him and returning to shore where Joseph stood laughing. Moon trotted up close to Joseph and shook, spraying his master with sea water.

The man of the tombs threw back his dripping head and burst into laughter again. Joseph lay down his shepherd's staff and bedroll and chased his dog down the shore. There they wrestled playfully in the sand until Joseph jumped up and ran part of the way back. Moon then pounced in front of him and caused them both to tumble to the ground and wrestle some more. Finally they both lay on the shore facing each other, panting in the warm sun.

The man of the tombs smiled as he scrubbed the last of the dirt from his face and dipped himself once more in the clear water. Then he walked out of the water and shook with a great motion, flinging water off his hair almost as well as Moon. He put on his outer garments and walked down the shore to Joseph and Moon.

Moon lay upside down on the sand with his feet spread out in every direction. He swished his tail when the man walked toward them.

The man sat down and looked at Moon. His whole body shook as he chuckled at the sight. Joseph sat up straight and put out his hand.

"We haven't really met. My name is Joseph." Joseph watched as the man smiled and put out a paw of a hand that totally engulfed his. Joseph hoped he'd get his hand back before he heard bones crack.

"Hello, hello," the man said happily. "My name is...my ...." The man's voice left him as he got a puzzled look. Then he looked at Joseph. "I can't remember what my name is right now. I – Mott. Mott is all I can recall right now, but that's not right."

"Mott?"

"Mott," the man repeated. "That's all I can remember right now. It's what the townsfolk called me. Man of The Tombs. Mott for short I guess. I've been here for so long." The man gazed back over his shoulder at the tombs. Then he smiled as he looked back at Joseph.

"But it will come to me; I have no doubt it will. Besides, Mott is good for now. I want everyone I talk to around here to know it's me, not someone they think might just look like me. I want them to know what God did for me through this Jesus."

At the sound of Jesus' name, Moon righted himself, stood up and shook, sending sand flying everywhere. He then stepped over to Mott, who reached out and ruffled the fur behind Moon's ears. The man's immense hand nearly covered the top of Moon's head.

Moon wagged his approval, then stretched out on his stomach, front feet out in front of him, head up and eyes bright as he studied Mott smiling back at him.

"This one," smiled Joseph, "is named Moon. Except when he wears me out, then I call him all kinds of things."

Mott threw his head back again as he laughed. He had the face of a grown man, and yet his eyes sparkled like those of an excited child. A very big, excited child.

"This Jesus, do you know Him? Who is He? What can you tell me about Him? I didn't get to spend much time with Him. But oh, the time I did get to spend with Him." The man stopped as he reflected back a few moments to when his life was changed forever.

Joseph hesitated to speak as Mott recalled the moments he spent in the presence of Jesus. Joseph saw such peace in the man's eyes. Even if he hadn't seen Jesus talking to Mott, Joseph would have known that he had been in the presence of Jesus. So much peace, so much healing and hope shone from Mott's face.

"Are you a friend of His?" Mott repeated. "What can you tell me about Him?"

"Well," Joseph began, "yes, we are friends of His. Anyone who does the will of God, anyone who believes in the One whom He sent as the Savior is a friend of Jesus."

Then Joseph remembered once again the things he had learned from Ruben and Simon about the writings of the prophets of long ago. Joseph began to explain how the prophets had predicted centuries before that the Messiah would be born in Bethlehem, of a virgin, and how His name was to be called Immanuel, God with us. And how the wicked ruler of that time would call his soldiers out to slaughter Jesus, because He was a King. How there would be weeping and mourning in Bethlehem for the children who were killed.

Joseph stopped and looked out to sea as he remembered this. If he himself knew of these children who had been slaughtered, then Jesus surely knew as well. Yet another burden that He had to carry. Joseph shook his head and looked down to where the water gently lapped on the shore. Mott interrupted his thoughts as he asked Joseph to continue.

"He looked at me once, or looked right into me. I think that is a better way to put it," Joseph said softly. "It seems so many deep truths hit me at that instant. One of them is – and don't ask me to explain it – but it's that He is the Son of God."

Joseph smiled at the man who had been healed of so much. "It is written," continued Joseph, "that Jesus was born to be a King. And a Servant. And, perhaps the best of all for you and me, a Savior of the world. He is to take all of our sins upon Himself, to bring salvation to the lost, comfort to the poor, healing to the sick, freedom to those who are captive. He is to save any and all who will believe on Him. How He will accomplish all of this, for the whole world I mean, is something I don't know yet." Joseph paused as the disturbing feeling about coming events haunted him again. He looked back at Mott, who stared at him with wide-eyed, childlike wonder.

"If all of this is true – and I have no reason to doubt you, Joseph, for I know I am healed from the evil that lived in me – then why?"

"I'm not sure I understand your question."

"Why would the One, the Savior and Creator of the entire world, come and see me? Me, Joseph!" The man looked at his feet as tears came again. "Me. You don't understand, Joseph. I had to be the scum of this entire earth. Everything – and I mean *everything* – about me was vile and filthy, wicked, completely wicked. If ever there was a man on this earth who God would reject, it would be me. And now you're telling me that this Jesus is God with us, Immanuel! The Son of God! And He came to see me...." The man closed his eyes as he put his hands to his head. His big shoulders shook.

Moon looked at Joseph and started to get up, but Joseph gave him a hand signal to stay put for the moment. Finally Mott regained his composure and sighed deeply while wiping his eyes once again with the backs of his hands. He studied the horizon and then looked at Joseph and smiled.

"Jesus told me to do one thing before He left. He told me to go and tell others about what happened, about the healing that God gave me today. I think, if it were up to me, I might move away and hide. I mean go someplace where no one knows me. I used to run through this place naked, screaming and cursing day and night. I am embarrassed and ashamed of myself, and I'm sure everyone in these parts knows about me. But with all these things you just told me, and especially what Jesus asked me to do, I intend to do just what He said. And continue to tell folks for as long as I have breath in my body. Will you come with me?"

Joseph looked out at the sea, then back to his new friend. "We will, for today anyway. And then we will continue to follow Jesus as He travels about."

Mott jumped up so fast that it startled Moon. The big dog jumped up almost as quickly and let out an instinctive bark.

Joseph playfully thumped his Moondog on the chest. "Come on, Moon. We're all going into town for a while."

Moon shook himself again, and more sand flew from his coat. Then he started out in front, tail and head up.

Joseph picked up all his worldly possessions, and they walked back up the hillside.

"Tell me more about Jesus," Mott asked.

Joseph explained how Jesus had thus far fit all the prophecies exactly. Then he told Mott about the healing of Isaac and the raising of the dead man in the funeral procession and the other healings he'd seen Jesus perform.

They talked all the way back to the first small town while Moon kept watch for any danger, being especially alert as they walked back through the tombs.

As they approached the first town, a few of the townspeople looked out their window openings. Joseph wondered what Mott had in mind to do next.

Mott stopped for a moment and surveyed the area. The few children playing in the dirt street scattered and scurried inside their homes at the sight of the once crazy man. All knew about him and some had actually heard his terrifying screams in the night. Mott spotted the town's local tavern.

"Rumors ought to be flying wild in that place. Along with a lot of drink. Follow me," Mott said as he strode past Joseph and Moon.

Joseph started to protest but caught himself. He looked down at Moon. "Watch yourself, buddy," Joseph said quietly, then caught up with Mott.

Moon stepped in beside Joseph. They followed the big man up the steps and into the darkened room.

Mott caught everyone inside by surprise as he swung the door open, his huge silhouette outlined by the sunlight behind him. Instantly the place grew silent. Mott didn't wait for an introduction.

"Now you people listen to me," Mott's voice boomed out into the silence as his eyes adjusted to the darkness. "I got something to tell you, and I don't want anyone leaving until I finish."

Mott took another step inside and Joseph and Moon followed, the stench from the place repulsing them both. Still, Moondog stood by Joseph's side, trying to see into the dinginess, his hackles slightly raised.

"We ain't got no fight with you, Mott," came a man's voice from a dark corner. "You just leave us alone and go back to where you came from or there'll be trouble like you've never known."

Although the voice from the corner tried to sound tough, Joseph detected a trace of terror in it.

At the man's words, Mott threw back his big head in tremendous laughter. "Trouble like I've never known? Let me tell you about trouble like *you've* never known. Let me tell you about the evil one of this world who loved to torment me in my very heart and soul and mind. I have lived my very own hell on earth."

No one moved.

Joseph gripped his staff tightly as he and Moon sensed the tension in the air. Moondog moved closer to Joseph so that he touched the side of Joseph's leg with his shoulder. The big dog stood ready.

"First of all, I ain't got nothin' against none of you, so don't go getting all excited. Just listen to me a minute."

Silence.

"I was filled with evil. I couldn't help it and I terrified you folks and I'm sorry about that. I never meant to hurt no one or nobody, or scare you none, either. But this evil that had me," continued Mott, "that was before now, before this day, before the One called Jesus spoke to me. This Jesus, He has power over all this evil. They were strong, so strong that those chains you put me in couldn't hold them."

Mott looked down at his hands and wrists again. They no longer showed any signs of injury. "You people know about the strength of these things inside me."

Some people shifted about nervously.

"But this Jesus – this Jesus, He cast them all out with just a word. As powerful as they were, they had no power against *Him*. They shook and trembled and quaked at His very command. They begged Him again and again. All them wicked things, and only Jesus against them, and they begged Him again and again. They're terrified of Him. This Jesus, He cast them all out of me. Every single one, they're all gone.

"I was once as good as dead, but now I'm alive again. I'm alive! This Jesus –" Mott threw his head back and laughed so loudly that the walls shook. It seemed to Joseph that each time Mott mentioned the name of Jesus, people in the place began to be more curious than afraid. More interested in the Truth than in being scared. Some seemed to be actually listening to Mott with the desire to learn what had happened rather than seeing Mott as some horrible problem for them to deal with. Moondog began to let his hackles down.

"This Jesus," Mott said again, "He healed me. I'm free. I'm healed. Do you folks hear what I'm saying? I'm healed. Completely, from the inside out. Even the scars from the chains are fading."

Mott smiled as he looked at his hands and wrists again and held up his massive arms and showed them to the people. Then his face grew solemn. "He is the One the Jewish prophets wrote about years ago, centuries ago. He's got all the power there is, 'cause He's the Son of God Himself."

Mott startled Joseph as he quickly turned to him. "You tell them, Joseph, you tell them about all this prophecy stuff that you told me about."

It took Joseph a moment to respond. "Well, ah..." Mott's excitement made him grow impatient.

"This Jesus is God's own Son," interrupted Mott as he turned back to the crowd. "Those evil things shook at His very presence and His word. They are absolutely terrified of Him." Then Mott's eyes burned into the crowd as he boomed out, "And you people sent Him away!"

Just then an elderly woman appeared in the doorway. Joseph and Moon saw her bent profile as she shuffled past them to stand in front of Mott. She looked up at him, and Joseph could see in her face the eyes of hope struggling to emerge after years of despair. Mott looked down at the frail woman and studied her. Joseph saw him draw in a breath and hold it. The woman reached up and touched his face with a shaking hand.

"Silas?" she whispered. "My Silas?"

The big man grabbed her hand. "Mother? *Mother!*" he exclaimed as he embraced her and lifted her off the ground. The old woman clung to his neck and wept uncontrollably. Tears filled Mott's eyes for at least the third time that day.

A man in the back of the room put his hands on top of his head and rocked back in his chair. Many looked down at the floor. Some rose up and slowly gathered around the two.

Joseph and Moon stepped back to get out of the way. Joseph looked down and winked. Even in the dim light Joseph could see Moon loop his tail in a big circle.

The voice from the back corner, the voice of the man who had threatened Silas when he first came in, began to speak again. Joseph now sensed no fear in his words.

"Maybe He will – "the man's voice broke as he looked upon Silas and his mother as they continued to cling to each other, weeping. "Maybe," he started again, "this Jesus will come by here again."

Silas, still hugging his mother, looked up with love toward the man. "Perhaps," smiled Silas, "perhaps. And if He does, I plan to have already told everyone in each of these ten towns about what great things He has done for me this day. Next time, there will be no sending Him away."

At that, Silas, the man of the tombs no more, gave another tremendous laugh. Many in the room began to clap.

Joseph looked out the open doorway and saw the sun falling toward the western hills. He put his hand on Silas' huge shoulder as he caught the big man's eye. Silas nodded and gave Moon a scratch on the head with one free hand, still cradling his mother with a giant arm. The woman looked twenty years younger than when she had entered the room. Joseph nodded back as he and Moon made their exit.

They walked out into a magnificent evening where the air smelled twice as sweet as in the stuffy tavern. Joseph looked down at Moon and smiled.

"Let's get a little ways out of this town and find a place to sleep for the night, fella." Joseph grinned as he ruffled the fur on Moon's neck.

Moondog grinned back, and the two walked out of the town away from the tombs. They found a resting spot just as the sun disappeared into the horizon.

Chapter 32

A little after dawn Joseph and Moon set out northeast along the sea, leaving behind the tombs and the ten cities. The shoreline turned straight north as they trekked into the afternoon. The dark, overcast day pressed into Joseph, and he thought it might rain soon. The grey clouds hung low over the water and Joseph bent himself into the northwest wind. They journeyed until they stood almost directly across the water from the town of Capernaum.

Joseph began to think they might have gone the wrong way, but for now they continued on. He believed that if Jesus and His followers had sailed, the wind should probably be pushing them toward him and Moon. Finally they stopped and Joseph scanned the shoreline being pounded by the murky waves.

Although only mid-afternoon, darkness from the fast approaching storm made the grey skies look like late evening. Moon scanned the sea's horizon. His ears sometimes stood straight out to the sides when caught with a sudden gust of wind. The big dog had to squint his eyes into tight slits to keep the swirling breeze from blowing too hard against them. The wind picked up its pace. Joseph and Moon couldn't get too close to the shoreline, lest the driven spray from the waves soak them. It felt like the rain would begin at any moment.

Joseph gave one last glance at the vacant shore and horizon and turned his back to the wind. He knew it would be a cold night for them both if they got wet. He decided to retreat a short way from the water's edge and try to locate some kind of shelter before they lost what daylight they had left. Moon barely heard his shouted command from only a few yards away as the wind whistled past them. After walking a distance from the water's edge, Joseph looked to the left and behind them. He froze as he sucked in his breath. There, less than one hundred yards away, Joseph saw Him.

Jesus!

The Lord had sent his friends away in the boat and had gone off by Himself to pray to His heavenly Father. Joseph quickly scrambled for shelter from the wind behind some rocks. There he found a small cave that they could take refuge in if need be. He sat down and studied the Master.

185

The direction of the wind prevented Moon's sensitive snoot from realizing the Lord was near. Once out of the wind, Moon saw Him and wanted nothing more than to run to Him. Joseph had to firmly command his dog to sit down and behave.

Moon sat down grudgingly, studying the Lord from afar and quivering every once in a while, though not from the cold wind.

Joseph too ached to approach and speak, but he knew Jesus needed this solitary time with His Father. Joseph also knew he had given his word not to interfere in any way. Besides, if Jesus wanted to speak to him, Joseph knew He would do so. Part of Joseph wanted Jesus to turn and motion them over for a talk. Joseph felt his stomach twist up at the thought of talking with the Creator of the world, one on One. What would Joseph say?

"Hello, how are You?" He knew he could do better than that. "Hi, good to see You, my name's Joseph." No, that wouldn't work. Jesus already knew everything about everyone – He already knew Joseph's name. How about, "Pretty windy today, huh?" Joseph closed his eyes and shook his head. "Think Joseph, you twit, what are you going to say? Think!"

For now Joseph felt honored to see Him alone, praying and communicating with His heavenly Father. Darkness came early due to the heavy cloud cover. Still, just enough light shone around Jesus that both Joseph and Moon could see Him long into the night.

Neither of the two observers grew tired. Once in a while Moon would grow so excited that he would stand up and walk a tight circle. Then he would sit back down beside Joseph, leaning against him, still quivering every so often. Both he and his master sat at rigid attention as they watched Jesus. It seemed to them that this opportunity might never come again.

Late in the night, Jesus stood up. Although Joseph and Moon had been watching for hours, it seemed to them that this happened abruptly. At once they jumped to their feet, hearts pounding. Joseph trembled as much as Moon.

Jesus turned and walked down to the water's edge. From there He could see His friends' boat out on the horizon, buffeted by the wind and waves. Joseph and Moon followed at a distance.

Jesus then did an amazing thing. He stepped out onto the water and began walking toward the boat, His robe flapping as the wind swirled around Him!

Although Joseph had already witnessed Jesus' healing people of dreaded diseases, raising a man from the dead, and driving out demons, the sight of Him walking on the water still shocked him. His mouth dropped open and his eyes grew wide. As Joseph watched, his mind had trouble catching up to what he was seeing.

Moondog pranced with high steps and pushed into Joseph, urging him to follow down to the water. Joseph walked slowly down to the edge of the sea, all the while keeping his eyes glued on Jesus as He walked on top of the water away from shore.

The wind carried shrieks of terror from the men in the boat, stopping Joseph and Moon in their tracks. Then they heard Jesus' calm voice assuring the men that they need not fear. Abruptly, one of the men shouted to Jesus that he, too, wanted to climb out of the boat and walk on the water. Jesus told him to do so, and the man stepped out of the boat and started walking on top of the windblown sea!

Joseph's mind raced. He himself had witnessed hundreds, perhaps thousands, of happenings in the outdoors which no one else ever saw or noticed. Joseph knew he could trust himself on this one. He was actually watching the two men walk on water!

Joseph's eyes stung from the wind. He blinked a few times and then had a thought. An unthinkable, incredible, and stupid thought.

Joseph sat on a rock and hurriedly untied his boots. Moon looked from the sea and back to Joseph and let out a soft whine.

"Don't worry, Moon," Joseph said as he set his boots on the rock next to his blanket and staff. "In case this doesn't work, they won't be all wet."

Moon let out another low whine. Joseph ignored it as he stood at the shore and looked out at the sight before him. He put his foot out over the water, but then he heard the man from the boat crying out in panic. He saw the man was sinking. Jesus reached out and caught him. Just as Joseph shifted his weight from his foot on shore to the one over the water, he heard the Lord ask the man from the boat why he had doubted. Joseph immediately thought of why he had taken off his boots.

Too late.

Joseph tried to stop but couldn't. He stepped off shore and into a deep hole along the water's edge. In an instant the cold, dark sea swallowed him completely. The icy water made Joseph suck in his breath, and with it, what felt like several gallons of water. Joseph felt his feet touch the bottom, and he pushed up with all his might while gagging and choking. He thrashed wildly with his arms and legs, struggling to reach the surface.

Moon let out a low whine and crouched down, muscles tight. Just then the sound of Joseph's sputtering and coughing erupted from the frothy black water several feet away.

Joseph fought to get back to shore, the waves pummeling him against the rocks. After what seemed like forever, Joseph reached out his hand in desperation. He felt Moon's thick mane and clung to it.

Moon leaned backward, toenails scraping across the wet rocks, his feet churning in reverse. Moon slipped and fell, got his feet back under him and strained some more.

Joseph finally lay on the shore panting for breath and gathering his wits. He felt the scratches and bruises from the rocks as he shivered in the wind, soaked from head to toe. Still coughing up water, Joseph slowly got to his feet and took one last look at the horizon as Jesus and the man stepped into the boat and disappeared into the night.

Joseph looked down at his dog, who gazed back at him with ears blowing straight out from the wind and head tilted to the side. Moon's tail swung slowly, happy to see his master safe once again. Joseph had learned more than one lesson tonight. He'd witnessed genuine communion with a real living, caring Father, not just "Someone out there." And he'd learned that he needed to quit being so amazed at what God could do. And he'd also learned a valuable lesson in faith.

Although soaking wet and chilled to the bone by the wind, Joseph shook his head and smiled as he muttered to himself. He gathered his boots, staff and blanket.

So much to learn, Joseph, you goofball. So much. If you don't kill yourself in the process.

He and Moon walked back to the cave and spent the rest of the soggy night there out of the storm.

Chapter 33

The wind blew and the cold rain fell all that night and well into the next day as Joseph struggled to keep warm. He took off his wet clothes and huddled under the dry blanket while Moon curled up at his feet. Still, the soggy ground along with the unrelenting rain kept Joseph damp and chilled. He and Moon stayed inside their small shelter most of the morning while the rain poured down outside the cave's entrance.

Joseph could not see any indication of the sun's whereabouts in the rain-filled skies. He guessed it to be about mid-morning when Moon's hackles came up and a deep growl rose from within his chest. Joseph sat up abruptly and looked outside the entrance of the cave. He saw no one as the wind blew the rain sideways in front of him, but he knew better than to disregard Moon's warning.

Joseph wrapped himself in the blanket, poked his head out of the cave, and looked around. He saw no people or boats, only low clouds hanging down to the water not far from shore. Then Joseph got an uneasy feeling. He took one last look around and felt satisfied; but before he ducked back into the cave, something caught his eye from above.

He squinched up his eyes as he looked skyward into the driving rain and saw the black tips of a creature's wings poking through the charcoal clouds. They glistened in the rain for only a moment, then slipped back into the grey mist. Joseph ducked back into the cave. He knew the wings didn't belong to Krog, as neither had been clipped off, though this did little to comfort him. As best Joseph could tell from the brief sighting, the evil creature flew toward the southeast.

Joseph slid as far back in the shallow cave as he could. Moon leaned against him, facing the cave entrance, hackles up and a low rumble still coming from his chest.

"It's okay, Moon, it's okay," Joseph whispered as he stroked Moon's thick mane with one hand and kept a tight grip on his staff with the other.

As Moon finally began to relax, Joseph did too. The rains continued, and after a few hours Moon once again raised his hackles and began the low, chilling growl. He stood poised to attack whatever might come into the small cave.

The hair on the back of Joseph's neck rose as he sensed the evil nearby. This time he did not venture out, knowing the evil creatures now moved during the daytime. *If only Jesus would appear once again on the shoreline with His friends in the boat.* Joseph's mind raced as he gripped his staff. *And where is Tysius? It sure would be good to see him right about now.* Joseph listened intently but he and Moon only heard the heavy rains continue to fall throughout the day and night.

Dawn seemed to arrive slowly. Low clouds colored the sky a pale grey which held little cheer for Joseph and his dog. The rain had stopped for the time being, though it looked as if it might begin again at any time. Emerging cautiously from the cave, they looked around. The sea pounded the shoreline nearby, sending spray high into the air and causing poor visibility as Joseph and Moon scanned the horizon for any activity.

Moon clawed his way to the top of a wet rock and scented the air with his snoot pointed up as high as he could reach. His liver-colored nose twitched as he sought to pick up any scent that might tell him news of the area.

Joseph looked at the forbidding sky and then back at the empty sea as he weighed their options. He didn't like the thought of waiting around to see if Jesus would return. The countryside looked barren toward the north; and although he and Moondog usually preferred solitude, they now wanted to be near Jesus above all else. The longing to be near Him, even in the midst of large crowds, overpowered Joseph's usual desire for solitude. This thought surprised Joseph so much that he let out an involuntary "hmm" at the revelation. Then he looked around to see his Moondog looking curiously back at him, head tilted with ears up, tail swaying gently back and forth, a big grin covering his face.

Joseph put on his damp clothes and smiled back at his dog. "Come on, buddy," said Joseph as he started off toward the south. "Let's go see if Silas has been spreading the word like he said he would."

Moon scrambled down from his perch and joined Joseph as he took one last look at the grey sky hanging low overhead. "Let's keep an eye out for what's going on around here, too, okay?" Joseph said as much to himself as to Moon.

Joseph kept the sea within view whenever he could, but saw no sign of a boat of any kind. Even using his staff for support, the slick, wet rocks slowed their progress. Finally Joseph and Moon came back to the tombs outside the ten cities. Though now overcast, Joseph noticed that the tombs remained brighter than on that sunny day when they first saw the demon-possessed Silas.

Few people stirred outside the first town they came to. Joseph wanted to see his big friend Silas, but the tavern appeared empty, deserted. This struck Joseph as a bit odd, since he thought places like that stayed open all the time, and the gloomier the weather, the more people they tended to draw. Joseph considered asking about Silas, but decided against it. He didn't know the whereabouts of Krog, and really didn't want others to know his and Moon's location.

The low, grey clouds and imminent rain did little to relieve Joseph's uneasiness at being away from the open countryside by the sea. He felt apprehensive about staying here for the night, and he and Moon began a silent trek onward, slipping past one town after another. They seldom saw anyone, and no one up close. The sky looked like it would open up at any minute, and Joseph hoped that if it did, the only thing they would see coming out of it would be rain.

Finally they came to the small raft on the Jordan River. The dreariness made it seem late and the recent rains had raised the river to flood stage. As Joseph and Moon approached the raft, they realized that they'd have to wade out several feet into the water just to reach it. The raft itself bobbed peacefully in a protected back-eddy along the eastern side of the river. However, the murky water beyond it raced wildly in its mad rush to get to the sea.

The river rolled dark and brown, swirling and cascading toward the south, carrying small bushes and tree limbs along with it. It hardly looked like the same river that they had crossed only days before. The heavy, high rope, the one which connected the raft to the pulleys, remained only a few inches above the water as it stretched across to the other side. The small tree holding the light rope stood a few feet from shore and bent downstream under the pull of the rope and water.

The resounding roar of the river as it ripped past made the scene even more frightening to Joseph and Moondog. The ground seemed to shake at the strength of the racing water. As they stood looking on, a cold rain began to fall.

Joseph reevaluated their options. They could go back toward the north, walk all the way around the towns and the sea and perhaps find the boat with Jesus and His friends. Or they could cross over the in-flowing river at the north end of the sea and come back down the other side to Capernaum and see their friends Lucius and Isaac again. But Joseph didn't know just how long all that would take, and, he didn't know for sure that they could cross the river at the north end anyway.

Just then Moon looked up toward the northern sky and let out a low rumble. Joseph looked skyward into the darkened clouds. He shielded his eyes from the rain and thought he caught a glimpse of two creatures flying low, just barely visible, at least a half mile away. They flew toward the southeast.

The fur on Moon's back stood up from his neck all the way to his tail. Joseph's dog remained motionless, squinting his eyes into the rain and testing the air for any scent of the evil creatures. Joseph took a quick look around and saw nowhere to take shelter for the night. Except for a few trees nearby, they were exposed to anything which might happen upon them. To find any kind of refuge, they would either have to hike back up into the last town they had passed or chance crossing the river.

They couldn't make it back to the cave before dark. The thought of more creatures passing overhead while they remained in the open, or in one of these towns, did not appeal to Joseph. If the creatures looked for and found them in one of the towns, it would probably bring disaster on the town's inhabitants. The memory of what these creatures from hell had induced men to do to the children of Bethlehem remained fresh in his mind. Joseph had no desire to cause others that sort of pain, even if it meant that he and Moon would have to face these evil things alone.

He looked again at the river. It appeared to have risen slightly even in the past few minutes. Joseph made his decision. He secured the blanket and staff around his waist. Bone-chilling water surrounded his feet as he stepped in.

"Come on, buddy," he called over the roar of the river as he began to wade out to the raft. This time Joseph didn't bother to take off his boots.

Moon stood still and let out a soft whine barely audible to Joseph, who stopped and looked back at his companion. It had only been two days since Moon had seen Joseph disappear into the sea. Moon's wet ears and tail hung down as he looked toward Joseph. The big dog trembled. The river surged on just beyond the frightened pair.

Joseph smiled weakly and tried to sound confident. "Come on, Moon buddy. I won't leave you, fella. We've got to get to the other side and find some shelter soon. Come on, Moon."

Moon looked again into the northern sky and then back at his master. He stepped into the chilly water and waded out beside him.

Joseph waited for his companion to join him and gave him a soft stroke on top of his wet head. Moon half stepped and half swam out to the old raft. Joseph bent down and lifted his soaked dog up onto the rough wood, then tested the pulleys and ropes in the fading light. Joseph noticed that someone else had used the raft since their last trip.

After checking the ropes, he climbed on board and began a slow approach into the raging river. As they reached the end of the slack water Joseph looked to the other side. Even with the river nearing flood stage it did not seem all that far across. Joseph realized that he could possibly put his feet up on the rope and go hand over hand along the big rope and make it to the far shore, providing a large branch didn't float down and hit him as he went. But Moon would have no chance at swimming across this current without being swept away.

Joseph took one last look at the northern skies which seemed to be closing in on them as the clouds dropped lower. Then he looked again at Moon, who already crouched low on the raft, eyes looking up with faith at his master.

"Hold on, Moondog, hold on!" Joseph shouted to his companion over the roar of the river as he pulled on the small rope connected to the other bank.

As the raft left the calm of the back eddy, the fury of the current seized it and slammed it violently into the middle of the river. The swift current stretched the big rope into a giant "V" shape, the raft dangling precariously against the torrent at the bottom of the V. The hand-hewn pulleys sang as the big rope flew through them faster than ever before.

Joseph barely got his left hand clear of the pulleys as the rope burned a line into his palm. He instinctively dropped to his stomach to lower his center of gravity as the raft shot out from under him. When he hit the deck he grabbed a handful of Moon's mane in his left hand and the upstream edge of the raft with his right.

As the raft reached the middle of the river, it jolted to a violent stop just as abruptly as it had started. Joseph's momentum on top of the small logs nearly tossed him overboard. Moondog was not as fortunate. He left deep toenail marks across the weathered wood as he slid over the edge of the raft and into the raging river.

Joseph fought with all his strength to hold on both to the raft's edge with one hand and to his rapidly disappearing dog with the other. If he lost his grip on his dog, he might never see him again. The big rope held, and for a moment it seemed to Joseph that he might be able to inch his way over to Moon and haul him back onboard. But unexpectedly the front of the raft began to dip under the current.

Moon struggled in a wild attempt to keep his head above water as the front of the raft plowed into the river and plunged below the surface. The water's weight shredded the big rope which was already stretched to its limit. Just as Joseph realized he must let go of the raft to survive, a sound like a rifle shot rang out as the big rope broke, free at last of its heavy burden.

The raft immediately shot to the surface, and Joseph struggled to maintain a hold on the wet wood without losing his desperate grip on his dog. He and Moon were helpless against the strong current as the raft shot rapidly downstream and spun wildly in the swirling and treacherous water.

Still sprawled out on his stomach, Joseph lunged over the side to grab Moon with both hands. He locked his feet around one of the logs and pulled at his dog's mane with all his strength. Moon scrambled and clawed his way up onto the raft, lying down next to his master, toenails digging deeply into the soaked wood.

Joseph wrapped one arm around Moon and held on to the edge of the raft with the other. Both he and his dog lay on the raft sputtering and panting, exhausted from the adrenaline rush of nearly being sucked into and under the river.

The raft spun and bucked uncontrollably in the current as Joseph struggled to clear his head. Moon lay as close as he could to his master, frantically clinging to the small mass of bucking wood under him.

By the time Joseph's mind began to clear, they had traveled a great stretch of river, and darkness had closed in around them. Joseph began to hear the sound of rapids or perhaps even a waterfall below them. He knew they needed to get off the water and get to shore. Without warning, branches from a tree raked across them. Joseph tried to grab on, causing the raft to swing around hard and crash into some rocks. It spun out of control, tearing the tree from his hand.

Joseph didn't even know which bank of the river they were closest to, but it didn't matter. If a waterfall was below them, they had to get off the water now. The raft spiraled against more boulders and began to spin back into the strong current.

Joseph scrambled to his feet and jumped into the water, pulling the startled Moon with him. When Joseph's feet didn't touch bottom, his heart sank. He tried to cling to his dog with one hand and paddle with the other while he prayed. Moon fought to keep his head above water and his master next to him.

The current pushed them into one large bolder, then another. When they hit the second rock, Joseph planted his feet against it. He pushed Moon away from the strong current and hopefully toward land of some kind. He tried to push himself that way as well, as the two struggled to stay afloat. Joseph strained to see Moon, his eyes stinging from the cold, muddy water. "It's okay, Moon," Joseph called between coughs, "it's going to be okay. Stay with me, Moon!"

After being bashed against several more boulders, Joseph's feet touched bottom and he instinctively began walking toward shallow water. "Moon, come here buddy, where are you, Moon?" he called out as he panted for breath.

Relief nearly overwhelmed Joseph when he felt his wet dog swim up against him. Dirty water blurred his vision as he continued toward shore. Eventually Moon's feet also touched bottom and the two battered and fatigued explorers dragged themselves to the bank. Moon tried to shake water from his saturated fur but fell awkwardly on his side with the effort.

He lay there a moment, then staggered over to Joseph as the young man steadied himself on all fours. They leaned on each other, panting for several moments. Then Moon lay down next to his master on the rocky shore, and put his muddy head on Joseph's hands.

After a few more minutes Joseph managed to lift his eyes and look around in the last of the day's light. He blinked his burning eyes and saw some of the wildest country he'd ever experienced. He tried to stand up but felt something poking him in the back. He reached around behind him and found his blanket and staff miraculously still tied to his waist. With cut and swollen fingers, Joseph painstakingly loosed the staff. He and Moon gingerly rose to their feet and stumbled out of the wind and into some nearby brush.

Joseph wrung out the woolen blanket as best he could with his torn hands. He painfully broke branches to make a sort of bed, covering it with some leaves. Moon sniffed the air and staggered as he shook himself again.

After Joseph finished their makeshift nest, the battered dog curled up into a tight ball on top of the leaves and Joseph flopped down next to him. He covered them both with the woolen blanket and more leaves and branches.

"Thank You, God, for saving our lives today," Joseph prayed softly. Then he reached over, gently touching the top of Moon's head with the back of his sore hand. "See, Moondog," Joseph managed to say in a hoarse whisper to his friend, "I told you I wouldn't leave you."

Moon let out an uneasy sigh and a shudder as the two sought to warm up in their cocoon. From their make-shift bed they could hear the Jordan River rushing past. Totally exhausted, both fell into a deep sleep.

Chapter 34

The two worn travelers began to stir. Joseph couldn't decide if they had slept through one night or several. His eyes stung and were caked with dried mud. Raising his hands to his face he felt the sting of scrapes and bruises from the wild ride on the raft. His hands throbbed from gripping the corners of the raft. Joseph felt as if his whole body had been pummeled by someone with a very large stick. He lay still for a moment assessing the damage. Then he began to slowly remove the branches covering his head. The rustling sounds startled Moondog awake.

Moon arched his back and gingerly gave a big stretch with all four sore paws and legs.

Joseph removed the remaining branches and gazed up through small bushes at the sky. It looked like rain again today.

Moon lifted his head and scented the air, nose twitching. After a few moments he stood up and shook from head to tail. Then he took a step and put his head directly over Joseph's. He peered down at his master so that his ears protruded out to the sides and his jowls hung loose, his tail swaying slowly.

For a moment it seemed to Joseph that he looked up into the dark beady eyes of a big yellow pig. He momentarily forgot his sore body and began to laugh, silently at first, and then out loud.

At the sound, Moon's tail spun around, his ears shook, and his jowls jiggled. Joseph caught his breath as the pain from laughing cut his side like a knife. Moon laid the left side of his face on Joseph's shoulder and stood for a moment with his rear end up in the air. Then he flopped down with an audible "whomp", most of his weight landing on Joseph's side and stomach, pushing the air out of him.

"Ohh," Joseph grimaced as he gently pushed Moon away from him. "Take it easy, Bud. Take – oh – take it easy."

Moon flopped over and squirmed around on his back, seeing the world upside down once again. Finally he came to rest. His big golden head lay about ten inches from Joseph's, and he looked at his master with bright eyes that reflected the morning sky.

Joseph could hear the sound of leaves moving as Moon's tail swept back and forth while the two stared at each other. "Moondog, Moondog," Joseph said softly, "what would I do without you?"

The speed of Moon's tail increased at the sound of his name. Joseph looked around as he sat up and gave a loud sigh. "I wonder where we are, buddy."

Moon leapt to his feet, albeit a little unsteadily, and shook himself again, sending a shower of leaves and twigs all around them. He then looked at Joseph with tail swinging and a big grin on his face.

Joseph stood slowly and stretched. In spite of his aching muscles, he thought they'd be able to travel, as long as they took their time. After rolling up his blanket, he picked up his staff and took another look around. At least they had crossed over and were now on the west side of the river. Taking one last look at the wilderness surrounding them, the two began the long journey upriver.

Thick underbrush, bent toward them by past floods, continually poked and repelled them as they tried to move north. Joseph was slowed by his bruises and leaned on his staff as they went. They had covered little ground when the rains began again, but they pressed on well into the afternoon. By early evening they found limited shelter among some boulders. Weariness gripped them both and they welcomed an early end to the day. They huddled together, wet and cold, and soon fell into an uneasy sleep.

Over the next few days, the two made painfully slow progress as they continued upriver toward the sea. But by the third day Joseph began to feel stronger and could make a faster stride without pain. Moon too appeared more like his old self and urged Joseph to pick up the pace. They saw no one and sensed no more creatures flying overhead, though they remained cautious and stayed close to cover whenever possible. Finally the two reached the old raft crossing. The ropes dangled from the trees in the fast water, free from their wooden load. Joseph looked the area over and kept heading north. He hoped they would never have to cross this river again. Until someone rebuilt the raft, it seemed all but impossible anyway.

Joseph and Moon soon made their way to the only one of the ten towns on the west side of the Jordan. After a few minutes of scanning the grey skies for any more low-flying creatures, Joseph noticed Moon catching a familiar scent.

Lifting his head high, Moon looked toward town. Joseph followed Moon's gaze and saw out in the distance the silhouette of a large man lumbering toward them.

Moon reared up on his hind feet and looked up at Joseph. Silas had not yet seen the two of them as he trudged up the street, singing to himself and looking at the ground in front of him. Joseph smiled down at Moon and gave the simple command – go.

Moon took off like a shot and streaked toward the big man. Silas, however, remained so preoccupied with his thoughts that he didn't see Moon racing toward him until the big golden dog was almost on top of him. Joseph didn't realize that Silas hadn't seen Moon until too late.

Silas let out an involuntary "yeaohh" as Moon leaped squarely onto his chest with all four paws. They toppled to the ground and lay looking at each other. Silas' eyes were wide and his heart was pounding from the surprise as he tried to comprehend all that had just occurred. Moon, oblivious to Silas' shock, remained happily upon the big man's chest. The yellow dog was the picture of joy with his head down on his front paws, his rear end up in the air, and his tail waving crazily.

Joseph ran up to his two fallen friends. "Gee, Silas, I'm sorry about that. I had no idea Moon would greet you exactly like that. We've been through a lot lately and I guess he's really glad to see you."

Silas looked up. A huge grin spread over his face. Then he roared with laughter. "Well I'll be. I ain't never had something like that happen to me before, not ever." Silas laughed some more as Moon straightened up and grinned at Joseph. The big man rolled off his backside and got his feet under him as he stood. He grabbed Joseph's sore hand and about crushed it in his excitement.

"It's so good to see you again, my friends. It's good to see you. I wish you had been with me. He came here! Jesus came here! All the people in these parts haven't talked about anything else since. They welcomed Him too, welcomed Him right in. A bunch of us are His followers now. My mother too."

Silas shook his head in amazement and awe. Once again it seemed to Joseph that he now looked into the eyes of a child peering out from the body of a very big man.

"This has been the most incredible time in my life. After all the torment in the tombs, it's like I've been given a whole new life, like I've been born again or made into a new creation or something." Silas, realizing how huge he was and how strange that concept sounded, looked at Joseph and shrugged his shoulders. "I guess that sounds pretty stupid, doesn't it? But that's just how I feel. That's the best words I know to describe it."

Joseph smiled at the big man. "I think you've said it well. Things of old are gone forever for you. Forever, Silas, never to come back. Your whole life is now your own, to do with as you see fit."

A huge smile overtook Silas' face as he considered the wonderful truth of Joseph's words. His playful slug on Joseph's shoulder nearly knocked him down. "And I know just what I aim to do with my life too."

Silas failed to notice Joseph staggering at the shot to his arm. "I'll tell everyone and anyone I can about Jesus as long as I have breath in me to speak. I don't see how I can ever stop, do you? Not after what I've been through." Silas' eyes sparkled with excitement.

"Ah, no, Silas, I don't see how you can, or that you'd ever want to," stated Joseph as he fought back the urge to rub his shoulder. "I think that would be about the best thing you could do, in fact."

The big man smiled again, and then his expression changed to one of slight shock. "Say, what happened to you, Joseph. It looks like you've been dragged from one end of the sea across to the other. Are you alright?"

Silas looked down at Moon and the big dog grinned back.

"Looks like Moon went through it too, though it seems he's in better shape than you. Where have you two been?"

Joseph thought of the time they'd had on the other side of the river, seeing Jesus praying and walking on water. Then he thought of the rains and seeing the evil creatures flying low during the day. And then the crossing of the river.

"It's a long story, Silas, and I'm not sure I have time to tell you all about it right now. But I can tell you that the raft that goes across the river is out. Hope you didn't plan on using it today."

"Hmm, no, I didn't plan on it. The river is way too high to try to take it across right now. In fact, I've been here for a while waiting for it to go down so I could cross back over."

Silas squinted and studied Joseph and Moon for a moment. Then he closed his eyes and scratched his forehead. "You two wouldn't have tried to use that raft in this high water, would you?"

Joseph pawed at the ground with his foot. "Well, um, I thought we needed to get across, and so..."

"Joseph, you could have been killed, both of you." Silas shook his head. "What were you thinking?"

"I know, I know," said Joseph softly as he remembered all the demons which had been in this mountain of a man not long ago. "Silas, there are other things to consider, dark things, things which I don't think you know about, and perhaps should not, at least not right now. Anyway, the raft is gone and I'm responsible for it. I hope it will not take a lot to replace it. Normally we'd be glad to stay and help build a new one. But for some reason I feel an urgency to find Jesus, to see Him soon. I don't want to stay here unless He's still in this area."

Silas sighed. "Don't worry about the raft. I can rebuild it. And no, Jesus is not here right now; though I hope He will come back someday. But what things are you talking about, these 'dark things'?"

Joseph looked down at Moon who continued to scan the overcast skies for the hideous creatures. Talking to Silas about them would probably fall into Tysius' interpretation of interfering, especially after all Silas had been through recently. Joseph looked back at his big friend.

"I can't tell you right now, but just trust me on this one. Perhaps someday I will tell you, but not right now. But maybe you can tell *me* something. Do you know where Jesus is now?"

Silas studied Joseph for a moment. "Well, I do trust you. But no, I'm not sure where He is right now, Joseph. He may have gone to Jerusalem where many of His people go at this time of year. To a feast they call the Passover. I don't know much about it, most of their customs are strange to me."

"Which way is Jerusalem from here?"

Silas waved a huge arm behind him to the right. "That way, toward the south."

Joseph felt his stomach tighten as he noted the direction Silas pointed, the same course that they had seen the evil creatures flying. Almost exactly the same.

"How far is Jerusalem from here?" Joseph asked with a sense of urgency that he couldn't hide.

"Well, I've never been there myself, Joseph, but it is a long walk. Normally it would take you at least two days, probably three, and that's if you moved quickly with clear paths. At this time of year, during this feast, the roads will be crowded with people. It will take you several days I'm afraid. Perhaps you should stay here and rest until you are completely fit. Then maybe our friend Jesus will return again and you can see Him here."

Joseph shook his head. "No, we can't remain here right now, but thanks for your concern. We'll be alright, but we must go." Joseph began to stride away from Silas, and Moon fell in alongside. After traveling a few yards Joseph stopped and turned around. There stood the big man, a look of confusion and hurt on his face.

Joseph suddenly wondered if he would ever see Silas again. He shook his head at his own rudeness. Joseph quickly walked back to Silas. "Forgive me, Silas, my friend," said Joseph as he put out his aching right hand in friendship. "I don't know what's gotten into me lately, except that I know I must find Jesus, and soon."

Silas accepted his hand of friendship by engulfing Joseph's hand with his huge paw. He smiled, and Joseph wondered if he too felt that this would be the last time they would ever see each other.

"I understand. I want to be near Him as well. But He asked me to stay around here and tell others about Him, and I will be obedient to His request. But I too hope to spend time with Him again soon."

Joseph couldn't help but smile at this man who had come so far in such a short time. "One thing I have learned, Silas – if you will be obedient to Him, though you may not be able to see Him with your eyes, you will see Him with your heart. He is much nearer to you than you may think."

Joseph surprised himself by getting choked up as he somehow sensed that he indeed would not see Silas again. "You just keep telling people about Jesus, the Truth, Silas, and you won't ever go wrong. You may have trouble, and people may make fun of you, but don't give up. Don't ever give up. Hearing about Jesus is their only hope."

Silas smiled and nodded his huge head. Moon watched as the two locked eyes. Though different in so many ways, they remained united in the most important thing in the world, the One Hope of the world. Silas gave Joseph a slight reaffirming grip as he gently shook his hand. Joseph tried his hardest to match it with his own strength. Then Silas squatted down and ruffled the fur on Moon's neck as he looked him in the eyes.

"You take care of this fella for me, okay Moondog?" Moon swung his tail and rubbed the top of his head against Silas' forearm.

"You take care, too," said Joseph softly. He turned and started walking down the path which led along the sea. He stopped after a few moments and looked back one last time. The big man's hand was raised toward them in blessing.

"Until we meet again, my friends," Silas called, a catch in his voice. "You two are special to me. Please come back someday. You were the first to see me whole after Jesus touched my life. And next time, I hope to be ready for Moon's greeting."

"Until then," Joseph managed to say.

Chapter 35

Keeping up a good pace, Joseph and Moon traveled along the seashore until they reached the crossroad running north and south. Here many people, seemingly in no hurry, journeyed south, taking up the entire road. After studying the surrounding terrain, Joseph felt they could mostly avoid the mass of people, alternating with either a higher or lower route than the main roadway. But he could see some places so steep on either side where everyone would have to travel the same path. Joseph looked up at the clearing sky, then back down at his companion.

"Well, Moon, it looks like we'll just have to do the best we can about getting there. At least most everyone is going the same direction as we are, more or less, so that should help a little."

Joseph and Moon started off, dodging people and animals as they tried to speed along the road. They found a less populated path below the main one and thus were able to bypass the larger crowds, but only for a short while. Joseph began to realize the truth of Silas' words; at this rate, it would take them quite a while to get to Jerusalem.

The crowds began to thin out toward dusk as people made their camps for the night. Joseph decided that they would travel on for a while longer as a nearly full moon rose on their left, giving ample light for hiking. Long shadows crossed the road as they picked up their pace.

Normally Joseph and his dog enjoyed walks at night under a big moon. If they went slowly, they often saw more wildlife than they ever could in the daytime. But as this night started, they began seeing many dark creatures flying in the skies, first a few, than dozens of them. Though it gave both Joseph and Moondog chills to see them, none flew very close and none seemed concerned with anything other than swiftly moving toward the south.

Joseph gripped his staff tightly, and Moondog remained on full alert as they traveled the lonely moonlit road. Joseph perceived something different about the moon's appearance. Something strange. He couldn't comprehend what, but he and Moondog both felt a heaviness, almost like a sadness in the air. It felt very strange to them, like nature itself was mourning. Joseph couldn't put his finger on it; he had never experienced anything like it before. "What a total difference from the night the angels came to announce Jesus' birth. Or the night we saw Him by the sea," Joseph said softly to his traveling companion. "Then I felt vibrant life saturating the very air we breathed. Right now I can almost smell the dank tombs where we first met Silas."

Moondog seemed uneasy as well. Joseph correctly figured that Moon was wondering why he chose to head in the same direction the creatures flew.

The evening wore on and the moon had almost completed its trek across the sky when a large creature flew in from the northeast, on its way to join the others. As it passed overhead it made a sudden detour toward Joseph and Moon.

They both saw the beast change direction. The two travelers darted into a small clump of bushes along a shallow ditch near the road. Joseph squinted to see into the darkness as he held his staff solidly in front of him with both hands. He crouched down next to Moon. Moon's hackles were up and teeth bared, a low rumble coming from his chest.

The creature slowly circled, then looked away to the south, seemingly torn as to what to do. Joseph's breathing became shallow and his heart hammered in his chest as the thing hovered over them for a long time. It flew too high for Joseph to make out any details. Had it flown to the west, in front of the moon, Joseph would have been able to see its silhouette. For now, Joseph could barely make the thing out against the dark sky as it began to circle higher.

Suddenly, the wicked thing bent up its wings and plummeted straight toward them. Joseph prayed to God for protection as he lifted his staff above his head while gripping it as hard as he could. Moon crouched low. His muscles were as hard as a rock as he readied himself to leap at the huge thing before it reached his master.

At the last moment the thing turned and dove behind a hill further down the road. It stayed there a few moments before rising again. Then it circled once and spit out something from its mouth.

Joseph barely had time to grab Moon and jump aside before the object hit the ground. The vile smelling mass of filth burned into the earth, choking Joseph and Moon in the process.

The creature flew off toward the south, laughing.

As Joseph and Moon watched the thing fly off, they moved back to the road and away from the stench. They stood for a moment catching their breath. Joseph silently scolded himself for trying so hard to observe but failing to pray until the creature dove toward them. He vowed to pray as they continued, and although it took a lot of effort, he prayed for protection with such intensity that he surprised himself. Little did Joseph realize that their very lives depended on it.

Three men whom Krog had just infused with his poison lay in wait for any unsuspecting person who would foolishly travel this road at night. They each held razor sharp knives, ready to slay and rob the next person to walk past.

Because a slight breeze blew from behind Joseph and Moon, the big dog's sensitive nose had no opportunity to warn them. They walked around the next bend in the road and straight into the trap set for them. Joseph prayed fervently as they went. Suddenly they stopped in their tracks as brilliant streaks of light came from several directions above. Huge, powerful men, or at least they looked like men, surrounded them. Joseph and Moon saw that these men were dressed very much like Tysius, yet Joseph somehow knew right away that Tysius was not among them.

Neither of the two weary travelers felt afraid. The very light and presence of these angels so refreshed Joseph and Moon that they felt their tired bodies spring back to life. They began walking again as the powerful men marched alongside without speaking.

Even though nothing but moonlight illuminated the road, the three crouching bandits began to tremble at the sight of this band of mighty warriors. One of those walking next to Joseph, a being of incredible power, looked directly at the three men lying in wait. Then *all* of the powerful beings looked straight at the three thieves.

The robbers leaped up from their ambush and raced into the wilds, bruising and scraping themselves on rocks and brambles. The cries of the bandits startled Joseph and Moon, who caught only a glimpse of the three villains as they ran away, shrieking in panic.

Just as quickly, the mighty warriors of light who had escorted Joseph and Moon disappeared into the sky, leaving the two travelers bewildered and shaking. As Joseph began to realize the trap and certain tragedy that they had escaped, he knelt down and held Moondog close and began to thank God. Moon let out a quick trembling breath. No one else came along the road, and they remained there for a long time.

When Joseph finally looked up, the moon had set behind the hills and a hint of a sunrise painted the sky to the east. He took a deep breath and studied their surroundings. "Looks like we're alone again, Moon buddy," he said softly.

"And alive. Thank You God, we're alive."

Chapter 36

As the sun rose into the sky, crowds began to gather once again, walking along the road. But attempting to go cross-country proved slower than traveling amongst the hordes of people. Joseph felt his stomach curl into a knot as he and Moon got separated trying to pass through the crowd too quickly. From then on Joseph slowed their pace to be sure they wouldn't lose sight of each other.

On the morning of the third day since leaving Silas, Joseph and Moon drew near to Jerusalem. At this point, the crowds almost clogged the road, slowing travel to a crawl. To make matters worse, vendors lined the way selling their wares. Joseph felt his stomach twist again with all the hollering and shoving going on around them. Moon appeared nervous as well.

Joseph located a small animal trail above the main road which allowed them to stretch out their legs and walk at a good clip. Although they'd had little sleep for several days now, Joseph felt a burning desire to push on. Moon loped easily as they hurried along the hillside. Suddenly Moon put his head down and cut directly in front of Joseph, tripping his master and flipping him over on his back with a resounding whomp.

Joseph lay for a moment staring at the sky, trying to catch his breath and gather his wits about him. When he could breathe again, he rolled gingerly over on his stomach and looked at his dog. Moon excitedly worked a 'Z' pattern around him, nose to the ground and inhaling deeply.

'Hafoof." In his excitement, Moon seemed oblivious to knocking his master flat on his back.

As Joseph opened his mouth to scold his dog, he glanced down and saw a human footprint. The track of the left foot looked almost normal, but the heel of the right foot cut into the ground and dragged forward. As Joseph studied the track, his eyes grew wide. Bigger than he remembered, but an imprint he could never forget. Joseph crawled to the next footprint and studied it. As best as Joseph could tell, this track could only belong to one person.

Daniel!

Chapter 37

"Wwwsssnnnfffcchhh." Moondog, who had inhaled some dirt and grass in his excitement, sneezed explosively.

"Hafoof!"

Joseph knelt on the ground and continued to study the tracks. They looked only a day old to him, two at the very most. He also noted tracks from a flock of sheep. A big grin spread over his face.

"Good dog, Moon, good boy," praised Joseph as he roughed up the fur around Moon's neck. The big yellow dog thumped his tail on the dry grass as he looked into his master's eyes.

"Daniel shouldn't be hard to find," continued Joseph. "There is so much to talk about, so much has happened. I don't even know where to begin. Thirty years have gone by. This is going to be a great day." Joseph grabbed Moon and flopped him over on top of his own chest, Moondog wrestling playfully to get away.

The two tussled a while and then Joseph stood to study the direction of the footprints. He had taken only three paces when a voice from behind made them both jump. They whirled around.

"And just where do you think you're going?" asked Tysius.

Joseph's eyes flew open wide as Moon made a quick bound over to Tysius. The angel reached down and patted the top of Moon's head, causing tiny blue sparks to fly from Moon's fur. Everything behind Moon's nose seemed to wag.

"Tysius, where have you been? I was starting to think we'd never see you again! You won't believe all the things that have happened since we've last seen you."

Tysius looked up at Joseph. "Yes, I will, because I know all about it, or about most of it, anyway. As to where I've been, this is a demanding time for all like me, Joseph. A time that has never before been and will never again be. It is the most critical time in the history of your world. Now I ask you my question once again, where do you think you're going?"

Joseph noted the tone in Tysius' voice. It was not unfriendly, but precise – exact. He sensed that Tysius didn't have a lot of time for talk. But Joseph hadn't seen him in so long, he didn't want him to vanish again before he had a chance to ask some questions.

209

"Well, I'm sure you know that our old friend Daniel is not far from here. We intend to find him and his family, if they're still alive. We've got a lot of catching up to do."

"Joseph, look at yourself."

Joseph paused, with a puzzled look on his face. But he could tell Tysius was serious; Joseph obliged. He looked at himself from head to toe as best he could without a mirror. He looked a little ragged, but he knew Daniel wouldn't care, or even notice for that matter. Joseph shrugged and looked back at Tysius.

"Okay, so I've looked at myself. Now what?"

Tysius sighed. "Joseph, when did you last see Daniel?"

"I don't know, thirty years ago or so, according to what you told me the last time we talked. It's been a long time."

"Exactly. And what do you think has happened to Daniel in all this time?"

"I don't know, gotten older I guess. I don't have a clue, what's your point, Tysius?"

"You said it – he's gotten older. And what's happened to *you*?"

Joseph scratched his head and looked at Daniel's tracks. Then he looked at his own feet. Then back at Moon.

"Oh – I guess Moon and I haven't gotten any older at all, have we?"

"Well, yes, both of you have, but only slightly. And you can't possibly explain that without interfering, Joseph. Knowing you two and your ability to track people and animals, you will have no trouble locating Daniel. But you must not allow him to see you or talk to you. The risk is far too great at such a vital time as this. And you gave me your word that you would not interfere; although you have come close already. Most of that occurred without you knowing it. This time you do know, and you must not do it. It is forbidden. What must take place very soon is too critical, much, much too important. Everything depends on what is about to happen within the next few days. Everything."

Joseph had never heard Tysius speak in this tone of voice. The seriousness of the situation was plain, even if Joseph didn't understand it. He resigned himself to obedience, although he still had hope of somehow seeing Daniel again.

"Alright, I believe you. I give you my word I will do my best to not let him see us, nor will I talk to him. But please tell me, how is he?"

"Daniel is well; he and Simon have taken over their father's business. They have both married. Daniel has a son. And Ruben lives in town now. And although he is over 70 years old, he still gets into the hills once in a while. His sons have taken good care of him, and Daniel's son, his grandson, is a tremendous joy in his life.

"You should know that they have all believed in Jesus as the One spoken of many years ago by the prophets. They have given their lives and hearts to Him. They have to keep their beliefs to themselves mostly, since many in the synagogue wouldn't let them in if they knew. In fact, they are barely allowed in now, since they are viewed as lowly people by the ones in charge there. But the three of them share what they know to be true with close friends whom they can trust. They are doing a good work, Joseph. You needn't worry about them.

"Now I must go, and *you* must keep your word not to interfere with anything that you are about to see. Remember that, Joseph, and you also will do well, if you can remain steadfast to the end. There is untold danger for all involved just ahead of us now.

"As for your concern for Daniel – you told him a long time ago that you would pray for him, that God would heal his leg. If you persist in prayer and are observant, you now may have the opportunity to help make that possible. Moon can assist there too. Just continue to observe and learn, but *do not* interfere. There is not much time left now and I must go."

"What do you mean? Wait, you can't go yet. What do you mean I can still help? How can I do that if he can't even see me? And why don't people in the synagogues know what's going on? And what do you mean if I remain steadfast to the end, the end of what? What are you talking about? And what about Sarah –?"

Joseph blinked and Tysius vanished.

Joseph grimaced and scowled at Moon. The golden dog looked at Joseph and wagged his tail.

"He did it again, Moon buddy, he did it again. I sure wish you could tell me what the heck he just said, because I don't have a clue."

Moon walked over and put his head under Joseph's right hand. The big dog's tail looped behind him as he looked up at his master.

Joseph looked at his companion. "I wish I had as much confidence in me as you do."

Chapter 38

Joseph and Moon sat down and looked over the crowds below. Joseph thought about what Tysius had said and prayed for God to give him wisdom for the times to come. He then sighed and looked up the rolling hills behind him where he believed Daniel now stood tending to his flock.

When Joseph stood, Moon jumped to his feet and shook the grass from his coat. He looked up at Joseph with a big grin.

The two started toward Jerusalem and made their way to the outskirts of town. They heard the sounds of excitement in the streets as people shouted back and forth, jostling and calling out to one another.

As they stood at the edge of the multitude, Joseph caught sight of a small boy struggling to sell his wares. No one seemed to notice the lad. Joseph gave Moon a hand signal and they moved toward the boy who had only a few crudely made knives to sell. He looked so thin and ragged that it seemed to Joseph that the boy was almost starving.

The boy saw Joseph looking at him. He looked up hopefully at Joseph, holding out a knife in his two small hands.

Joseph looked down at the boy's pitiful offering and tried to smile. "I'm sorry," Joseph said softly, "I don't have any money."

At this, the boy's face fell, but only for a moment as he saw Moon standing at Joseph's side. "Is that your dog, mister?" the young one said. "Can I pet him?"

Joseph smiled as he'd never been called 'mister' before. Moon's tail swung as he studied the boy.

"Sure, you can pet him. His name's Moon."

The boy put the crude knives down, wrapped both arms around the big dog's neck and hugged him tightly. Moon grinned up at Joseph, tail waving in the air.

"I sure wish I could have a dog like him," the boy said softly as he continued to rub Moon's thick mane. "I used to have a dog. Before my father died. Now my mother says we don't have money for a dog. We don't have enough money for anything anymore. But someday I'm gonna have me a big dog just like this one. Don't worry, just you wait. I'll have a great dog, just like this one here."

All the while the boy talked, he looked into Moon's eyes. He didn't seem to be talking to anyone in particular, but rather to himself.

Moondog gazed back at the boy; the big dog's head was actually rocking back and forth from the force of his wagging tail.

Joseph looked from the boy to the crowd. He realized he could do nothing to help the boy and sighed. "Do you know if the One called Jesus is here?"

"Oh yes, He's here alright. A couple of days ago He rode into the city on a young colt. There was a real big uproar when He came in. Then He went into the temple and threw out all the thieves that sell their stuff there. I thought it was great. People have been talking about Him a lot, but I haven't heard anyone say exactly where He's staying. He comes into the city about the same time every day and teaches. I heard Him once and I like Him. But a lot of people from the temple are mad I guess."

"Do you know the way He comes and goes in and out of the city? Do you know the road that He travels on and about what time He travels back and forth?"

"Oh sure, I know about all those things. I've watched Him. I like to see Him; it makes me feel good inside." The boy thought about that for a moment. "I guess that sounds kind of silly, doesn't it?"

Joseph smiled. "No, no it makes more sense than you know. I think I understand." Suddenly Joseph had an idea. Not one without risks or the potential for disaster, but an idea nonetheless. Joseph considered all Tysius had said. This idea would, Joseph thought, be within the boundaries that Tysius set. It might just work.

"What's your name?" asked Joseph. He smiled at the boy.

The boy never stopped petting Moon nor took his eyes off the big dog. "Can't tell ya," came the response. "Mother says I shouldn't talk to strangers and tell them my name. Just sell my knives and bring back the money so we can buy food. I gave her my word."

"Good for you, we should all be so obedient to our parents. But can you tell me this – do you live around here?"

The boy thought about that for a moment. "My mother never gave me any instructions about that question, so I guess I can tell you. Yup, I grew up here."

"Do you know these hills around the city?"

"Sure, I've been over them all a thousand times with my father. I know every one of them. Why do you want to know?"

"Well, I'm not sure how to…" Just then Joseph remembered the money that Isaac had given him. He reached into his pocket. Some of it had made it through the rafting adventure.

Joseph pulled out one of the coins and the boy's eyes grew large. "I haven't made that much money selling my knives in a month. In fact, I've never made that much money. Just think of the food I could buy with that! My mother would be sooo happy."

"I wonder," continued Joseph, "if I gave you this —"

The boy quickly reached down and grabbed up all the dull knives and shoved them at Joseph.

Joseph held up his empty hand to stop him. "No, no, you don't understand. You can keep the knives. You may need to sell them another day. What I need you to do is give a message to someone for me, but you must follow my directions exactly. You must do precisely what I say, and you must give me your word that you'll say only what I tell you to."

The boy considered the proposal. Finally he nodded. He put the knives back down and returned his hands to Moon's soft mane. "If it's not anything bad, then I'll do it. It isn't anything bad, is it? I sure hope not 'cause I've never seen that much money before."

Joseph smiled again. "You are very wise for your young age. What I ask of you is not a bad thing. No harm will come to you. The one I want you to deliver the message to is a kind person. He will not hurt you. In fact, once he hears, he will be very happy. But you must say only what I tell you to, and nothing else, no matter how many questions he asks you. And believe me; he is going to ask you a lot of questions. Will you promise me that you'll only say what I tell you to?"

"If it is for good, then, yes. I promise you I will only say what you tell me to, and that will be all." Then the boy picked up the knives again. He looked at them and then back at Joseph. "Don't you like my knives?"

Joseph grinned as he took the smallest knife. He tied it on his staff so that it would be out of the way. Then he gave the boy the coin. "Let's get away from all these people. We need to find a place where I can think and pray about what you should say. This must be just right, so that everyone will be happy." Joseph glanced up toward the heavens.

They made their way up the hillside. The boy had one hand around his knives and the other on Moon's neck. The big dog obliged by slowing his gait and walking patiently next to his new friend. They found a relatively quiet place to sit and pray. After a little while, Joseph told the boy his plan.

Chapter 39

It took longer for Joseph to locate Daniel than he had hoped. Actually, he could have found him much sooner had he not needed to be sure that Daniel never saw them. Joseph found the task to be a challenge since the hillsides held very little cover. Still, even with their slow progress, the young boy grew fascinated with Joseph's ability to stalk and track so well.

When they came to a place where the tracks confused the boy, Joseph explained that this place held signs that Daniel had stopped to rest or eat a meal. Soon the young boy was captivated.

Finally, Joseph spotted a shepherd silhouetted against the sky, peacefully watching over his flock. Even at a distance, Joseph recognized Daniel. Moon saw him a moment later.

Moon began to groan softly as he looked up at Joseph for the signal to bolt across the fields and greet their long lost friend. The signal never came as Joseph instructed Moon to remain by his side. Moon looked back at Daniel, holding his snoot high to catch a scent of their friend on the evening breeze.

A dull, persistent ache grew in Joseph's gut at being so close to his dear friend and yet not being able to go and greet him. He remembered again some of the times that they had shared together and how Daniel had played such an important part in saving Moon's life so long ago.

Daniel took a few paces to his left, and immediately Joseph recognized his limp, except that it had grown more severe over the years. Joseph, overwhelmed at finding his old friend, spun and turned his back on Daniel. He squatted down next to Moon, taking hold of the big dog's mane to steady himself.

Taking a deep breath, Joseph composed himself. He turned back and continued to study Daniel and his surroundings. Moon stood alert beside him. The flock was much larger than it had been thirty years ago. Finally Joseph spoke. His voice was weak and inaudible at first, so much so that the young boy had to ask him to repeat himself. Joseph cleared his throat.

"That is the boy – I mean that is the man I told you about." Joseph turned to the boy, who stood about the same height as Joseph did as he squatted down, and looked him straight in the eyes.

"You remember what you are to say, just exactly what you are to say and do? You must not give in to any of his questions. Do you remember?" asked Joseph in a solemn voice.

The boy nodded. "I remember."

Joseph looked at the sky. He had so hoped to find Daniel sooner, so that he and Moon would have more time to move off and hide their tracks. But now there was no time for that. He looked back at the boy.

"Is this about the time Jesus usually travels out of the city?"

The boy glanced skyward and nodded.

Joseph took another look toward Daniel and gave a quick sigh. "Go then. Go quickly, and may you be true to your word."

The young boy took off in a full run toward Daniel, who stood several hundred yards away. Joseph took in the scene for a moment, then quickly turned and ran down the hill and across a deserted road, signaling Moon to follow. He knew that he and Moon needed to get out of sight before the boy reached Daniel.

Moon, with a last, quick sniff of the air, turned and galloped after Joseph. He caught up with his master as Joseph reached the deserted road, trotting next to him as they entered the ravine on the other side.

Joseph and Moon ran up the small canyon. Their goal was to get away from the road and Daniel and find some heavy cover. From here, the ravine continued on in the same direction, dropping back down out of sight from the road below. They could remain here and see a portion of the road as it came around a bend from the city. Joseph and Moon could also see Daniel from here. He was still a distance away, but they could clearly see him as the young boy drew near.

Joseph hastily broke off some dried bushes and made sure he and Moon remained concealed. Then they sat and watched as the boy reached Daniel. Joseph could feel himself holding his breath as he recited in his mind what the boy would be saying to Daniel at that moment. Although a long ways away, it appeared to Joseph that Daniel looked around, searching the hillsides where the boy had just approached from. This Joseph expected.

Then Daniel turned in a complete circle, looking all around, searching the surrounding fields for a sign of his boyhood friend who had mysteriously disappeared so long ago. No doubt Daniel had thought Joseph and Moondog long dead. Now Daniel squatted down so as to look the young boy straight in the eyes.

Joseph sucked in his breath. He knew the boy must keep his word and not yield to Daniel's questioning. He must tell Daniel only what Joseph had instructed. Joseph bit his lip as Daniel's interrogation of the young boy continued. Finally, Daniel stood up, took another long look around, and then began to walk straight toward them, the young boy leading the way.

Joseph let out his breath. Moon started to quiver at the sight of their old friend beginning to limp toward them. Joseph steadied his companion with an arm around his neck, whispering soft instructions. "Be still, Moon buddy, be still." Joseph then continued to pray.

It took a little while for Daniel and the boy to reach the road. By the time they did, several men had appeared on it, leaving the city as dusk began to settle in. As Daniel and the boy approached, Joseph and Moon clearly recognized their old friend. Joseph noted that other than being a full grown man, Daniel hadn't changed much. But that limp had indeed grown worse over the years. It hurt Joseph to see him this way, but he continued to pray that today would be the last day Daniel would have to suffer this pain. Soon Daniel and the boy stood almost directly across the road from where Joseph and Moon sat hidden in the brush. Daniel and the boy looked down at the few people passing below.

Then Joseph saw Daniel look to his left, toward the hillside that Joseph and Moon had run down before crossing the road. Suddenly Daniel stopped and stared. He took a step as if to investigate something he saw on the ground. Joseph and Moon's tracks!

Joseph's heart skipped a beat. *"Come on kid. We talked about this. You've got to come through now—c'mon, kid."*

Suddenly from around the bend in the road, some men Joseph recognized as being close followers of Jesus walked into view. From where Daniel and the young boy stood, they could see further around the bend toward the city than could Joseph and Moon.

Joseph watched as the boy took Daniel by the sleeve and pointed down below them to the road. Daniel's focus on the hillside tracks disappeared. The boy continued to point and tug at Daniel's sleeve. Joseph could see Daniel straighten up and slowly, reluctantly, shake his head no.

Now Joseph and Moon could see on the road below them the One the boy pointed at. The Lord, surrounded by some of His close followers, walked down the road. Moon trembled all over, hardly able to contain himself.

"Moon!" Joseph gave the stern command as he tried to keep his voice down, "Be still. You've got to stay with me now, buddy, you've just got to." Joseph looked at Jesus and then back at his old friend up on top of the opposite hillside facing them. Daniel continued to slowly shake his head no as the boy kept tugging on his arm and pleading.

Suddenly something the boy said jolted Daniel from his gaze at Jesus, and he looked at the boy intently. Joseph could only hope that the boy had spoken the exact words which Joseph had told him to say. Daniel shuddered, dropped his shepherd's staff, and turned to gaze at Jesus, Who walked below them on the road. He was now almost directly between them and Joseph. Joseph held his breath again and prayed.

Finally Daniel, seemingly in slow motion, took a staggering step down toward the road, leaving the boy to stand alone. Daniel became so transfixed on watching Jesus that he stumbled and fell. His body crashed to the ground in an awkward heap as he slid down the hill toward the group of men below.

The sound of his fall startled some of them and caused a few on the road to jump in surprise. Daniel struggled to his feet and pressed on, his bad leg dragging bits of brush and weeds with him.

The men on the road stopped their progress and stared at this man stumbling toward them. Although Joseph could not see their faces, he knew that the Lord looked with love at this broken man approaching Him.

As Daniel reached Jesus, he fell at his feet weeping. Jesus reached down, lifted Daniel up, and with His hands on the young man's shoulders gazed directly into Daniel's eyes. Instinctively, Daniel clung to the Lord's arms. Daniel seemed to reluctantly lift his head and search the eyes of Jesus. After a pause, Jesus spoke a few words which Joseph could not hear. Then He smiled at Daniel, turned and began His slow trek up the road with His friends.

For just a fleeting moment Joseph sensed a great sorrow come over Jesus, but it had nothing to do with Daniel. The power of His sorrow rocked Joseph for a moment; he could not understand it.

As Jesus and His followers walked farther up the road and out of sight, Daniel stood gazing at them. He stood a long time after they disappeared from sight. Then Daniel looked down at his feet.

He began to move his feet around inside his sandals. Then Daniel reached down and touched his right foot. He stuck his right foot straight out in front of him, then he moved it from left to right. Then he put it back on the ground and started jumping about and running up and down the road, jumping and yelling at the top of his lungs. The words he yelled didn't make any sense, but they didn't have to.

Daniel saw a wide-eyed young boy standing on the road a few yards above him, his mouth open. Daniel ran up the hill and grabbed the boy and swung him around in a circle, yelling and hollering all the while.

Joseph wanted with all his heart to raise his arms and shout and come running down the hill to his old friend. Fortunately for all, he controlled himself and remained hidden, holding on to Moon, who seemed about to jump out of his fur in his excitement.

"Whooooooeeeeeeeee, whooooooeeeeeeee, whooooooeeeeeeee!" Daniel hollered. He continued to twirl the boy around in circles while spinning around on his two good feet. Finally, he put the boy down.

The lad staggered and wobbled about the hillside. He then sat down, apparently trying to keep from tumbling over the embankment to the road below.

"Whooooooeeeeeeeee, whooooooeeeeeeee," Daniel continued, not seeming to notice the boy's condition. Suddenly Daniel became quiet and looked up to the sky. He then knelt down, put his face to the ground and covered his head with his hands.

From where Joseph and Moon sat, they could see their old friend sobbing as full realization of what had happened appeared to sink in. Joseph knew that Daniel understood in a new way the reality of Jesus' love. As much as the physical healing meant to Daniel, it remained only a piece of the whole. His comprehension of true forgiveness for all the wrong he had ever done, and all he'd falsely held against himself for so long about his own mother's death, began to blossom in his heart.

Joseph too felt the incredible, overwhelming presence of God. Seeing his friend healed of so much, Joseph's vision became clouded with tears. Moon sat next to Joseph, resting his head on his master's shoulder.

Daniel sat up and called the young boy. He spoke briefly to him. Then he got up, picked up his staff, and turned back to the flock.

Joseph breathed a sigh of relief that Daniel did not pursue their tracks. He watched as Daniel first began to walk, then trot, then run. For the first time in decades, he could actually *run* back to his flock. Daniel lifted his arms up to the heavens and shouted. His gratitude and praise resounded off the hillsides.

Joseph wrapped his arms around Moon and squeezed him so hard that Moon let out an involuntary grunt as he looked at his master. Joseph smiled and ruffled the fur on Moon's neck; the big dog buried the top of his head in Joseph's chest and bowled him over. Then he flopped down, stared into Joseph's face, and swished his tail gently on the dry ground. Joseph sat up to watch as Daniel herded the flock over the next hill, out of sight and away from them.

When Joseph felt certain of Daniel's departure, he and Moon emerged from their hiding place and descended to the road below the boy.

"Did you see that?" the boy almost shouted. "Did you see Daniel's foot get healed by Jesus? Did you see?"

"Yes, we saw. We saw it all. What did you tell Daniel?"

"I told him just what you said, honest, just what you said, and nothing more. I didn't tell him nothing about your dog. And he told me to tell you, if I ever saw you again, that he didn't understand why you couldn't see him. But to tell you that he trusted you. He said he hoped that he could see you sometime soon. He said he trusted you enough that he wouldn't try to find you or track you, though he sure wanted to. He also told me to tell you that your prayers from long ago are answered. That Jesus healed him, though he figured you already knew that."

Joseph smiled at the report. "You have done well, my little friend. You have done very, very well. Thank you. And don't forget what you saw here today, how Jesus healed that man. Don't ever forget about Jesus. And now it's probably time you got home. It's getting late. Do you think you can make it okay, or do you want us to walk you home?"

"Oh, I can make it okay. I don't live very far from here. And don't worry, I won't ever forget what happened to me today. I won't ever forget." The boy fingered the coin in his pocket. "And thank you too. I can't wait to tell my mother about all this."

Joseph watched the boy disappear over a hill, then he and Moon looked down at Daniel's tracks. They saw where he'd come down the embankment and dragged his twisted foot behind. Then they looked at his tracks as he ran back up the hill, both feet and legs carrying him effortlessly along. Joseph knelt and held Moon close, then he turned his gaze to the heavens as tears clouded his vision once again. "This has been a tremendous day. Thank You, dear God. Thank You, Jesus."

Joseph took a deep breath as he gathered himself together. He and Moon followed the footprints of Jesus a short distance out of Jerusalem to a town called Bethany. Here Joseph felt they could safely bed down for the night close to Jesus so they'd be alert to His whereabouts. Recalling the events of the day, Joseph couldn't stop smiling as the two curled up on the blanket, drowsiness overtaking them. But Joseph suddenly jerked awake as he remembered Jesus' sorrow as he walked away from Daniel. Moon let out a grunt and Joseph closed his eyes again, trying to put the thought out of his mind.

<h1 style="text-align:center">Chapter 40</h1>

Toward evening of the next day, Jesus and His followers went into Jerusalem. Joseph watched as they came to a small home and entered into an upper room.

Although the evening seemed pleasant enough, Joseph felt apprehensive. He also noticed Moon prancing about far more than normal. Joseph decided to stay awake and watch while Moondog sat next to him.

As the night wore on, Jesus and his companions left the house and walked to a nearby winepress. Joseph and Moon followed a safe distance behind, hiding themselves from view. Jesus told most of His friends to stay in one place while He took three of them a short distance away. Jesus left the three together while He went on a little farther. He then fell down and prayed like Joseph had never seen anyone pray before. Jesus looked as if He were desperate, in agony. After a while Jesus got up and went back to His three friends, who had fallen asleep. He woke them, then went off by Himself and fell to the ground in prayer once again.

This happened three times. Joseph could not understand what he was seeing. Jesus appeared to be experiencing deep, heartbreaking torment and grief. He seemed crushed by some terrible, horrific thing, but Joseph couldn't imagine what.

How could this be? Joseph's mind raced. *This is Jesus, God's Son. What could possibly do this to Him?* Joseph felt his stomach begin to twist.

Moon began to whine softly as the fur rose on his back. "Shhhh," Joseph attempted to calm his dog and himself at the same time.

A brilliant angel streaked down from the heavens and appeared to Jesus. The radiance of the angel illumined Jesus' anguished face. The Lord's face was stained with red, like sweat that was blood. Joseph's stomach tightened, and he suddenly felt very ill.

A strange clamor from the direction of town rocked the quiet hillside. Joseph and Moon instinctively turned toward it. Moon's fur now rose from his neck all the way down his back, a low rumble coming from his chest. Joseph, with his arm already around Moon, tightened his grasp and told him to take it easy, but his words were empty and hollow.

Men with torches marched out from the city. Angry men came, shouting and cursing, pushing up the worn path, directly toward them.

Although neither Joseph nor Moon could see them because of the darkness of the night, they both sensed that the wicked creatures came as well. The evil permeating the group began to overwhelm them, coming straight at them in the black night. Surely Jesus would wipe them all out with just a word.

One look at Jesus revealed a horrifying truth to Joseph: Jesus was not going to wipe them out at all! Joseph's breath left him and his heart chilled. He would allow them to take Him! Didn't He know them? He should fight – Joseph knew He could fight this evil and destroy it. Why didn't He destroy them? Why did He just wait for these men and this overwhelming evil to come to Him? He *must* destroy it!

Joseph shot a glance at the fast approaching torches and men, then at Jesus. Jesus must get away, they must all get away! Joseph began to shake and tremble uncontrollably. He couldn't think straight and didn't know if he trembled due to the approaching evil or to the voluntary helplessness of Jesus.

Joseph crouched behind the cover of the trees in a daze. The mob had arrived. They surrounded Jesus as His three friends ran to Him. One in the crowd stepped forward and embraced Jesus. Jesus spoke to him briefly and then the man looked away and stepped back. Everyone seemed to fall back from Him.

Perhaps now, Joseph thought, *now Jesus will take them out.*

Joseph saw one of Jesus' friends draw his sword and cut off the ear of one of the men. He heard Jesus tell him to put his sword away, that He could call on countless angels to rescue Him if He wanted to. Then Joseph watched in astonishment as Jesus healed the man's ear!

Surely this will show these men who Jesus is, thought Joseph. But then someone yelled a command, and the guards stepped forward and arrested Jesus. Shoving Him roughly, they took Him away.

Joseph shook. Beneath his sweaty hands, Joseph felt Moon tremble as well.

The guards began trying to grab anyone else around. Joseph heard shouting and cursing as Jesus' friends ran off. Pandemonium broke out. Joseph took one last look, feeling the wickedness engulfing them all.

Joseph turned and ran blindly into the night, heart pounding. Moondog ran next to him, terror in his eyes. They ran until Joseph could run no farther, branches and rocks tearing and tripping him. He collapsed upon the damp ground. The world was spinning as his insides twisted. His mind was reeling like a drunkard's. For so long they had yearned to be close to Jesus. Now the terror of this dark and evil power had made them abandon Him. Joseph wept, shaking uncontrollably as he held Moondog close. Cold darkness pressed in around them.

Chapter 41

The morning sun brought no joy or excitement of a new day to Joseph. He could hear no birds singing nor see any signs of animals moving. Even the plants and trees around them seemed to be in some kind of shock. The entire earth had apparently ceased living and existed only to mourn.

Joseph held on to Moon long into the morning. For the first time since he could remember, he had no idea where to go or what to do. Joseph felt shaken to his core, and he knew Moondog sensed it as well. Neither could draw strength from the other as they had done so often in the past.

Joseph tried to gather his wits. *Surely,* he finally convinced himself, *Jesus has gone with these men to their leader, and once there, will show them Who He really is. They will have to believe Him, how could they resist? He is the Son of God, how could they not see that? But how did they not see it already? Surely everything will be alright soon.*

Joseph tried to reassure himself and gain enough confidence to at least get up and move, to see what had happened. But as hard as he tried, the scene that he'd witnessed the night before kept him paralyzed with dread. He could not forget the terror that he'd felt. But he sensed something else also, something being poured out of Jesus. *Think, Joseph, think. What did you see?* Finally Joseph mustered the strength to stand.

He looked at Moon. His dog looked as pitiful as Joseph had ever seen him. He looked terrified. "It's okay, Moon – it's okay," But Joseph's words were empty, and he knew Moon realized it as well.

As Joseph took one step, Moondog took one. Joseph felt an overwhelming sense of terror. If things didn't change soon, he knew that they would probably die. Perhaps death would be better than living with this type of dread. He remembered that Tysius had said something about *if* they survived. Had he been speaking about last night, or would there be more yet to come?

Slowly, Joseph and Moon picked their way to the spot where they had hidden last night. There they found the shepherd's staff and blanket. Joseph gathered them up, and they walked slowly, side by side, until they came to the city wall.

The stench of evil filled the air and grew even stronger the closer they got to town. All the evil of the universe seemed to be here. Joseph felt weaker than he ever remembered. He saw Moondog look up at him for some reassurance, but he could give him none.

The gate to the city opened and a crowd of people began to emerge, including Roman soldiers. On their backs rode some of the hideous, evil creatures, but no one seemed to be able to see them except Joseph and Moon.

Crowds began to jostle them. The soldiers, with the vile creatures screaming hatred into their ears, proceeded to clear the streets and push away those in front of them. Joseph and Moon saw more evil creatures gathering overhead. With the confusion of the mob and people yelling and cursing and wailing, Joseph had difficulty seeing. He felt Moon, surrounded by the throng, lean hard against his legs so as not to be separated in the crowd.

Joseph considered running away as he saw the wicked men and horrible creatures approaching, but he couldn't move his feet. The noise of the crowd became deafening, and confusion and turmoil swirled about them. The soldiers, with the evil creatures on them, drew near. Joseph knelt on one knee next to Moon in hopes that the creatures would not see them.

From this vantage point, Joseph and Moon could catch glimpses of the passersby at close to ground level. Suddenly Someone in the midst of the people fell to the ground, a rough wooden beam that He carried on His shoulders crushing Him to the stone street. Joseph and Moon looked on in horror and disbelief. Jesus, the Savior. He was beaten nearly beyond recognition. He no longer looked like a person.

The soldiers grabbed Him and yanked Him back to His feet; and in that split second, Jesus looked into Joseph's eyes. Joseph could not believe what he saw. Eyes of love that he had seen once before, that night by the pier. That same love that Jesus had then for him, He still had now. Love for him and for all of mankind. Love for those who were torturing Him. Love so strong, so powerful, yet so vulnerable that it defied description. Love to conquer the entire world, more powerful than any weapon or evil ever imagined. Yet Love being despised and crushed before his eyes. By the very people Jesus had created. This split-second glance into His eyes told Joseph that Jesus was carrying the sins of the world on His shoulders.

Joseph felt his own heart nearly ripped out of him – for Jesus carried *his* sins as well. All Joseph had ever done against God was now crushing the life out of Jesus in the most horrific way imaginable. Jesus had allowed Himself to become the sacrifice for everyone. He was becoming sin Himself.

The emotion was palpable: the soldiers and crowd spewed insults and hatred, yet some were weeping. The scene was one Joseph would never forget. He crawled back away from everyone, among some large rocks off the road, and began to retch.

Joseph, on all fours and reeling from what he had just witnessed, saw Moon's front right paw next to his hand. Moon was trembling. While still staring at the ground under him, Joseph reached out and grabbed hold of Moon's shaking leg.

"Stay here," panted Joseph as he tried to regain control. "Stay here, Moon. Stay with me. Whether we're going to live or die, we're going to do it together."

Joseph continued to whisper to his dog as he tried to think. "Right now dying seems a lot better than living to me, but we'll go together, buddy. We need to stay together. We'll go out together."

At the touch of Joseph's hand and the sound of his voice, Moon leaned against his master and his trembling subsided a little.

It took Joseph a long time to be able to sit upright. Moon sat leaning against him, and the two looked out into the street. No people were there now. Joseph could see Jesus' blood still staining the ground. Evil permeated the air around them. The slimy creatures continued flying overhead, drunk with glee. For the moment they didn't seem to notice Joseph or Moon.

Joseph tried to stand but felt so ill that he had to sit down. His insides were spun into a tight ball. Finally he and Moon stood and walked the path toward the people. There they saw the Lord nailed to a cross between two thieves.

Joseph and Moon seemed to be moving in slow motion. Joseph couldn't sense his feet touching the ground, and his legs and arms felt numb. They collapsed on a hill some distance away. Moondog leaned against his master and whined softly; both were paralyzed and unable to go farther.

All about the cross flew the demons from hell, joyful in their captured prey. High above, more and more creatures flew, screaming their profanities at God and man. All different sizes gathered, some huge, some small, all hideous and repulsive. They argued and cursed amongst themselves, jockeying for position, vying to take credit for the events below.

Somewhere Joseph thought he saw Krog, although he couldn't be sure since the skies had now grown so dark. The middle of the day, and the sky grew dark. Although Joseph and Moon noticed it, they didn't care. Joseph didn't care if Krog flew over them now. It didn't matter. In fact he wished

Krog would fly down so he and Moon could try to do battle and die quickly.

Rough talk of soldiers, laughing and mocking of various onlookers, and pitiful weeping of women filled the air around Joseph and Moon. Joseph watched for only a moment, and then had to look away in despair. Had they been torturing an animal, Joseph would have felt totally repulsed by the wickedness of these men. But three *people* hung there. One of them the Son of God, and yet men stood about jeering at their agony. Joseph's anger rose and his breath grow short. If he and Moon survived this, they would move so far away from any man that no one would ever find them again, not ever.

Joseph stared down at his feet and hands. He took the small knife from his staff and began to cut into the wood, below the carving of the lamb. Joseph tried to focus and tune out their surroundings. He couldn't bend his mind to the task. But slowly and meticulously, he carved the image of three crosses. The one in the middle, the highest one on the hill, the cross of the Lord.

As he finished, they heard a commotion from above. It seemed that some of the more powerful demons had now made their delayed, pompous arrival. Fear came from the south – a huge creature that made the others appear small, even those like Krog. Many of the demons backed away in terror, but a few foolish ones tried to stand their ground.

Fear flew up to them, and as they crumbled and melted in his presence, the rest of the creatures laughed and mocked. But they quickly quieted down when Fear whirled about, snarling and glaring. Fear swooped down on some of the men around the cross and filled them with his ugly self. Soon he flew back up with glee, and Joseph could hear the uproar from the men. Rage, Jealousy and Pride soon swooped in and dug their talons deep into the men. Joseph heard the increased cursing and mocking from those beneath the cross. The slimy Fear soon took the best place and began ordering the others around, commanding certain ones to continue their course of destruction on those below.

Then slowly, from far away, came the most evil, vile-looking creature Joseph and Moon had ever seen. He took his time, and the other demons quickly fled well out of his way. Even the monstrous Fear grudgingly backed off from the best place. Joseph sensed that within this creature resided all the powers of hell combined.

Death finally arrived, strutting about in front for all the demons to see and to pay homage. The vile monster laughed its putrid wickedness.

Suddenly Joseph and his dog heard Jesus cry out in a loud voice, "It is finished!"

Joseph and Moon struggled to their feet and watched His body go limp, finally free of the unspeakable agony of the last hours.

Death shouted a victory cry. Then most of the demons became eerily silent. Even as Death himself tried to act confident, Fear and Doubt shot the wicked thing a word, from a safe distance away.

"He took others from you, remember?" Fear hissed at his rival, Death.

"Remember? What about the widow's son? You had him, and that Man snatched him from you. And what about Lazarus? Remember him? You had him too, but He took him back. Aren't you just a little bit afraid that you can't hold this One?"

"That's right," added Doubt, a hideous demon. "Aren't you just a little too sure of yourself with this One? Remember, He said He would rise again!"

The sky above Joseph rocked with mocking and laughter as the demons tormented each other in a frightful frenzy of heckling and hatred and derision.

"Shut up!" raged Death, grabbing the nearest demon and crushing the life out of him. "Shut up, all of you, or I'll kill you all, just like I did to that Man down there." Death screamed and cursed as he pointed a slimy wing at Jesus.

Joseph glared at the demons. He noticed that not once in all these wicked creatures' coarse conversations did any of the demons actually say the name 'Jesus.' They seemed to deliberately avoid saying His Name. Even after Jesus hung lifeless on the cross. Even then, Death himself avoided saying His Name.

Joseph turned his attention back to the crosses. All three men were now dead. The soldiers tore down the lifeless remains of the three men; and darkness strengthened its grip on the land. Joseph and Moon slowly made their way to the bottom of the hill and followed those carrying the body of Jesus. They watched as a few men and women took Jesus to a new grave, a cave carved out of the rocks. Here they placed Him inside. Then they emerged, the men rolling a huge rock in front of and down against the entrance so that no one could go in.

Joseph and Moon remained far enough away that no one noticed them. Moon stood close to Joseph, still trembling. Joseph stood still, staring at the grave and shaking his head slowly back and forth. The men and women walked away, bent in grief, back toward a village a few miles from Jerusalem. They soon disappeared from view.

In the dim light Joseph saw a shallow indentation up the side of a hill, across a small clearing. From there he and Moon could stay out of the weather and still see the gravesite below.

When they reached the spot, Joseph stared silently. There was no birdsong; and even in the deepening gloom he could discern a strange sadness in even the plants about him. The leaves of the trees, the grass, the shrubs – all drooping and wilted and lifeless as if from pain. The demonic party above his head, however, was raging on as the beasts circled and laughed and cursed in celebration of their great victory.

Joseph sat down with his back against the hillside. He put down his belongings and wrapped his arms around his stomach. He had not stopped feeling sick since he had seen Jesus fall in the street, under the weight of the cross. Moon sat next to Joseph, his back also to the hill. He pressed his shoulder into his master's. And in stony silence, they mourned over the scene of the most devastating day of their lives.

Joseph's mind had been filled with the excitement of trying to get close and observe Jesus for as long as he could remember. Now Jesus lay dead, inside the grave before them. What could Joseph do now? Even when he thought about how they might go away somewhere – away from people – what good would that do? Together they had experienced incredible and magnificent things in creation. But nothing they had ever found in this world had even come close to seeking and finding Jesus.

Joseph and Moon lost all track of time. When the muted daylight came the next morning, they looked about. The branches and leaves on the trees still drooped toward the ground. Joseph noticed hundreds, perhaps thousands of large orange flowers on the hillside. They should have been vibrant and beautiful, but they were bent with faces turned downward. Apparently they'd had their life extinguished from the roots. The air remained motionless. It lay heavy against Joseph's and Moon's skin, and both labored to draw any into their lungs. The demons continued flying about, some celebrating and some passing the time by fighting amongst themselves. Their vile stench poisoned the already oppressive air.

It seemed to Joseph that the sun had lost its brilliance as it labored across the sky into the western horizon. Joseph tried to think what they should do or where they should go, but his mind went blank when he tried to concentrate.

Sometime, Joseph didn't know when, he started to go over in his mind all he could remember about himself and Moon. It started with him and Moon speaking to Tysius and running to catch up to a couple walking along the crowded, dusty road to Bethlehem.

Joseph couldn't remember anything before that, how he and Moon had ever gotten together or anything. So he started at this point and went slowly, meticulously, through all he could remember.

He remembered the sky filled with the angels singing. *Why didn't they show up when Jesus seemed to need them the most?*

Joseph remembered how he and Daniel, Ruben, and Simon had met, and the glorious feeling of being near the Christ child. Joseph smiled as he relived in his mind the times with the three shepherds, and the friendship they had shared. And he remembered Sarah.

Joseph put his arm around Moondog. The big dog was curled up by Joseph's side; he looked up at his master and even in his sorrow managed to pat his tail in response.

Joseph remembered how fiercely Moon had protected the three lambs from the wolves, and how he'd rescued Joseph from the king's guard. And, how Moon had risked his own life for Joseph when they did battle with Krog. He remembered their time with Lucius and Isaac, and with Silas in the tombs, and the near fatal river crossing on the raft. Slowly, painstakingly, Joseph went over each and every detail that he could recall.

Although Joseph and Moon remained awake, Joseph didn't take much notice of the passing of the hours or days as time went by. But all of a sudden, Joseph became aware of several soldiers standing near the tomb, as if guarding it. If they noticed Joseph and Moon, they gave no sign of it. Joseph saw them, but he still bent his mind to focus on sorting out his past. He fought his thoughts in a battle to find something he might have missed. Surely there was something to help him figure out what to do next. In his mind he relived all they had been through. As he had so long ago taught himself, he could picture things and see them in his mind almost as clearly as at the very moment that the events had taken place.

He thought of the times they had been near Jesus, and Joseph smiled as he recalled all the details of each meeting. He remembered the night by the pier. Then he looked at the grave below them, and his heart sank once again.

How could this have happened, how, and why? Joseph asked himself over and over, but could find no answers. Then he would force himself to pick up where he'd left off, pondering the details of the days and progressing toward the present time.

He remembered his joy in seeing his dear friend Daniel healed. And then, finally, he came to the most recent past. Joseph looked at the ground, then at the grave. He didn't know if he could stand to relive this next segment of his life. He kneaded Moon's fur nervously with his hand and steeled himself.

Joseph began to replay in his mind the scene in the garden and beyond. When Joseph got to the time when he realized that Jesus was suffering and dying for his sins, he shuddered. He had always known that to sin is wrong, but he had never realized the seriousness of it until now. Joseph had never realized the enormous cost, the tremendous price that must be paid for his sins. How ugly his own sin seemed to Joseph at this moment. Although extremely painful, he held the thought for a long time, so that he would never, never forget it. And never forget the love that Jesus had for him as He suffered, the love that it took to get rid of these sins.

Then Joseph sighed and said softly to himself, so that only he and Moon heard, "But if He's dead – if He's dead – then what are we supposed to do now? What is anyone supposed to do? I don't have any power of myself. And nobody can fight these demons on their own, we'll all be wiped out. Or worse, live in fear and terror all our lives. If He's dead, what are we going to do now?"

Moondog whined softly and laid his head on Joseph's lap as he shut his eyes.

Joseph looked down at his companion as he gently stroked the top of his head. Then Joseph closed his own eyes and leaned back until his head rested against the hill behind him. It had been a few days and nights now. They couldn't just sit here the rest of their lives, could they? He had to think, but when he tried, his head hurt. Still, he pressed on and relived in his mind the last events leading up to the present. Never had Joseph felt so utterly hopeless.

Chapter 42

Joseph had his eyes closed when the light flashed and the sound thundered and the earth shook beneath them. The light shone brighter than the sun; pure and clear and beautiful. When Joseph first opened his eyes, he couldn't see anything but the light.

As the earth beneath them trembled, Joseph's heart beat with such fervor that he shuddered. Quickly and powerfully, the sound came and went, but the earth continued to shake. The brilliant light continued even longer.

Moon jumped to his feet and stood at attention next to Joseph. Joseph sat stone still, seeing Moon's head out of the corner of his right eye. The dazzling light radiated from the direction of the tomb; it illuminated everything. In its brilliance, Moon appeared white. Joseph's hands and feet looked white also, yet it didn't hurt their eyes to look at the light.

Joseph forgot to breathe. He stared wide-eyed. His mouth hung open. He looked into the light, but he couldn't see anything – anything except Moon's big head next to his. Yet, Joseph did not fear any of this, and he could sense that Moon didn't either.

Even as he closed his eyes tight, Joseph could still see the light. *Am I dreaming? Have we died? Am I imagining this?* He opened his eyes again and the light remained. Joseph gathered his wits and began to struggle with all his senses to understand. He worked methodically as he'd trained himself to do, sorting through his jumbled thoughts, trying to find some explanation. His eyes told him there was a dazzling, brilliant light; both he and Moon were in it. His ears seemed to be playing tricks; for when he concentrated on the faint, far off ringing sound he was sure he'd heard, it seemed to fade away. Was the thunderous sound still reverberating around the air and bouncing off the hilltops? Joseph couldn't tell, and he was hesitant to focus on that piece of the puzzle lest he miss anything else about to happen.

Finally, Joseph did let his mind race back to the sound that he'd heard. What had caused it? He'd never heard anything like it before. It seemed as if the trees and the flowers and the entire earth had shouted one glorious exclamation of joy for an instant in time. Joseph also noticed that he no longer heard any poisonous laughter or any noise at all from the vile demons.

And Joseph smelled something new as well. It smelled pure, slightly sweet, and somehow perfect, although Joseph didn't know how something could smell perfect. But it did, and Joseph felt grateful for the peace it brought. He took a deep breath and the wonderful fragrance filled his lungs.

Moondog's gaze remained locked on the light before them as he lifted his nose slightly and scented the air.

The two remained still, concentrating on their surroundings. After having their eyes closed for so long, the intense light seemed like lightning cutting across a black night. Joseph couldn't tell if the light had gone and left its imprint on his eyes, or if it still shone in front of them. He closed his eyes again and the light remained. Neither Joseph nor Moon knew what to expect next. They had been so blanketed in despair that neither wanted to move for fear of losing the peace that now enveloped them.

After a while the light slowly faded, but the two remained motionless, with Joseph's hand resting on Moon's back. As the dazzling light subsided and the light of dawn began to break the sky in the east, they noticed some women walking toward the tomb. Suddenly there appeared an angel from heaven sitting on the stone by the tomb. Joseph and Moon could see the open mouth of the tomb. The huge stone had been rolled away! Then the angel spoke to the women. Joseph strained to hear what he said. Although he couldn't hear everything, what he did hear made his heart pound once again.

"Why do you seek the living among the dead? He is not here, but is risen!"[1]

The two women turned and ran away, but soon two people Joseph recognized as being close friends of Jesus came running up. One raced ahead of the other as they approached the tomb. The first man stopped at the entrance and looked in. The other caught up to him and went inside where Joseph couldn't see. Then the first man entered the tomb as well.

By now, the women had returned and stood beside the entrance. The men came out, spoke a few words to them that Joseph couldn't hear, and then walked slowly back the way they had come. The women seemed greatly disturbed, and Joseph thought for a moment that he should do something to help, though he didn't know what. Tysius had made him give his word not to interfere with anything, but since he had seen Jesus die, what difference could it make now?

Unexpectedly, Someone appeared behind the women, and one of them turned and saw Him. The Man asked one of the women why she was crying and who she was looking for. She said something to Him, and then the Man removed his head covering. Joseph sucked in his breath and Moon began trembling and prancing under his hand.

Jesus!

Joseph jumped up so fast that he clobbered his head on the overhanging cliff. Stars blinded him and his unsteady legs wobbled dangerously; only a quick drop onto one knee saved Joseph from tumbling down the hillside.

Moondog's feet pranced about unceasingly, but the faithful dog remained close by his master.

Joseph reached up and grabbed his dog by the mane to steady himself. By the time Joseph's head cleared, no one else remained in the area.

Joseph slowly stood. He and Moon began walking, then running, down to the tomb. They looked inside, but found nothing there but the grave clothes the men had wrapped Jesus in three days earlier. They walked over to where the women had been, and Joseph began to look at the tracks. He found tracks from the soldiers' boots, tracks from the women, and tracks from the two men who had been there earlier and had left.

Then he saw them. A set of footprints in the dust. They appeared from nowhere and vanished into the air. Joseph knelt down and studied them closely. He put his head down next to them. With his trained eyes only inches away, he ran his hands gently along their outline. Joseph's breath caught. His heart pounded. He could not only feel it, he could hear it.

There, inside the print, Joseph saw an amazing thing – a particular disturbance in the dust. Marks of the nails that had been driven through innocent, precious feet had left tell-tale signs behind.

Jesus! Jesus had made these tracks!

Of the thousands of tracks that Joseph had ever looked at, he had never seen any more beautiful, more perfect, and more precious than these. Joseph's hands started to shake and he drew them back so as not to disturb the prints in any way. He sucked in his breath and looked up at Moon, who stood directly in front of him, tail swinging so fast that his whole body moved.

Joseph lifted both hands and grabbed his dog behind the ears and looked into his eyes from about six inches away. Moon grinned back.

"He's alive. He's alive! HE'S ALIVE!"

Joseph jumped up and looked to the heavens. He saw no signs of demons anywhere. He looked at the trees around him. They lifted their branches to the sky as if they'd just been washed with a sweet summer rain. For the first time in days, all of the birds were singing their hearts out, perhaps as they did on that first day of creation.

Joseph pumped his fists up to the heavens and shouted at the top of his lungs, "He's alive! He's alive!" over and over again. He began jumping around. Moon commenced running in huge circles around him, racing recklessly to and fro, running over the grass and leaping over massive bushes like they were small pebbles on a beach.

Joseph started laughing and took off running up the hill, past where they had spent the last three days, and into a field beyond. His whole body felt brand new, his mind new, his heart new. Clean and perfect and new.

Moon caught up to him. The big dog bowled Joseph over and the two tumbled joyfully onto the soft grass. All the flowers around them had opened up and burst forth with color as they swayed gently in the sweet breeze. Moon leaped to his feet, flew fifty yards across the field, and sprinted back to Joseph.

Joseph laughed hysterically. He sat up in time to see Moon running straight at him from only a few yards away. Joseph felt sure Moon would run into him at breakneck speed, so he instinctively fell backwards just as Moon reached him. The golden missile flew up and over the top of Joseph, landing and tumbling and getting up again.

As Joseph lay on his back, he saw Moon standing, his head down on his front feet and rear end up in the air, ready to pounce. From Joseph's perspective, Moon looked upside down. Joseph couldn't stop laughing.

Moon straightened up and cocked his head sideways, ears up as he listened to his master laugh. He took two bounds and stood staring down at Joseph's face.

Moon's eyes were dark and his jowls and ears were hanging loose. Joseph grabbed his big dog and wrestled him to the ground. The two lay in the morning sunshine for a long time, Joseph softly laughing and Moon resting his head on his master's chest. Finally Joseph's laughter died down and he began to grasp a tiny bit of what had just happened. He couldn't make sense of it, other than to feel overwhelming gratitude for Jesus dying for his sins and taking the punishment that belonged to him.

After a long think Joseph sat up, disturbing Moon who had fallen into a peaceful sleep for the first time in days. Moon jumped up, sneezed, and tilted his head to the side. With a big grin on his face he looked at his master.

Joseph stood and took in their surroundings. Of all the mornings he had ever observed, he could not recall a more perfect one. He breathed in deeply and the air itself seemed so sweet and pure that it gave energy to his very being.

Joseph walked back to pick up his belongings as Moon trotted beside him, tail flying. When Joseph reached for the staff, he noticed that the lamb which Daniel and Sarah had carved so long ago had turned a brilliant white. Joseph pondered this for a while but couldn't understand. Then he looked around and smiled.

"Well Moondog, I'm not sure where we're going from here, but if we can get a clue where Jesus is, we'll go looking. For now I think we might want to see if we can find out where His friends are staying. Then we'll go from there."

"Good thinking."

Joseph and Moon whirled around to see their old friend Tysius. Moon trotted over to be petted as Joseph, getting over his fright, felt his heart begin to slow down in his chest.

"Can't you figure out another way to come up on us?" Joseph grinned. "I may be young, but my heart can't take this kind of stuff forever you know."

Tysius nodded his apology. "Perhaps not, but perhaps you won't need to worry about it much more. Although you never know. Anyway, as I was saying, that was a good idea that you mentioned to your Moondog. However, it won't work this time. You see, there is not enough time for that right now."

"What do you mean there's not enough time right now?" asked Joseph. "We've just seen the most incredible thing that ever happened. We've got all the time in the world. At least I think we do. There's still a lot I don't understand though. But all we want to do now is find Jesus. I really want to see Him again; more than anything else, I want to see Him. But whether I get to or not, I know everything is going to be okay, no matter what happens next. Does that make any sense to you?"

"Yes, it does," answered Tysius. "It does. Come, we will walk together for a while to a place you'll want to see. This request of yours will be granted. I'll take you to where you can see Jesus again. And, you'll be glad to know, I will answer some of your questions as we walk."

Chapter 43

"It's been too long now. I'm going out to look." His voice, although strong and trying to sound confident, couldn't mask his concern.

"How are you going to get through, and how will you know where to look?" Joseph's mother asked her husband. "There are trees down everywhere. It's dark and the snow is already deep, and it's still coming down like crazy."

"I'll take Cap. He's good in the snow, and he has a good head about him. I think the wind has slowed some. Open every shutter you can and keep candles burning in all the windows until the power comes back on. If it does, turn on every light we've got. Maybe he'll be able to see..." He turned quickly and dressed in his winter clothes.

"We'll be back," he said as he looked at his wife wringing her hands. He walked over to her and they embraced.

"I don't want to lose both my men in this storm. Please be careful. I won't stop praying," she managed to say.

"We'll be back," he repeated softly. He turned and left the house to fight his way to the barn through the veil of snow. He grunted as he struggled to open the door against the snow's weight. With a flashlight, he found Cap standing in his stall. Silently he saddled him up and put on his bridle.

Tightening the cinches in the dark, he stepped up gingerly into the saddle. He gave a command and rode out of the barn into the icy blast. Guiding the horse down the long winding driveway in front of the house and next to the big pines laden with snow, they made their way across the road and into the timber.

"Joseph! Moon! Joseph!" he yelled into the twisting wind. He looked in vain with his flashlight for any sign of his son and dog as the darkness and swirling snow swallowed up the beam.

Cap plowed through the heavy snow, weaving a path through the dense timber. The flashlight on the trees made eerie shadows that danced alongside them in the black woods. Often they had to stop while Joseph's father scanned the area. Then they would travel a short distance and stop again and search some more. He did not want to miss Joseph by going too fast. He knew he had a lot of ground to cover. If he missed his son, he would not be back in this area at all tonight. By the time he could get back, it might be too late. He grew hoarse as he shouted the names of Joseph and Moon, listening hopefully for any sound from them. Instead he heard only the whistling wind coming through nearly leafless trees.

After several long, slow hours, the hopelessness of his task began to take its toll. In places, deep snow touched the brave horse's chest. Cap now began to stumble over unseen logs and into snow-covered holes. He knew his horse could not hold out forever.

Joseph's father pulled Cap to a stop very near where Joseph and Moon had sat just before the storm hit. His father knew Joseph loved to watch for wildlife in this place. He scanned the area with his fading flashlight, blinded by the snow and tangle of fallen timber.

"Dear God," he prayed, "I know I don't talk to You much, but I'm asking You to listen now if You will. From what I understand, You know what it's like to have a Son that's in a bad way. Please, please help me to find my son."

Chapter 44

"This is critical, so try to understand. What I'm saying to you is this, Joseph," Tysius continued as the three of them hurried along. "Anyone who believes on Jesus and calls out to Him in faith will have everlasting life. A person needs to humble himself and confess that he or she is a sinner. From the heart, ask for forgiveness of those sins; believe that Jesus died for his sins, and that God raised Him from the dead. Then ask Jesus to come and live in his heart, to be Lord and Savior. Surrender to Him, complete surrender to live his or her life for Him. That's the only life worth living. Then that person will spend eternity in heaven with Jesus.

"But anyone who rejects Jesus will spend eternity in hell with satan and all his demons. Forever in the lake of fire, in torment. Do you understand all I've been telling you, about the necessity of the blood sacrifice for sins, about the spotless Lamb being slain for the sins of the world? And Jesus being this sacrifice, that all who believe on Him will be saved?"

"I think I see what you're saying," replied Joseph. "But how could anyone who knows this truth reject Jesus? I mean, I've seen Him and heard Him. He's pure love. Once someone knows this, how could anyone reject Him?"

Tysius stopped for a moment and looked at Joseph. "Did you not see what wicked men did to Him? They saw Him, same as you."

Joseph looked at the ground. Slowly he nodded as he remembered.

"And the wicked will continue in their own way, some of them. They will teach others to follow the wrong path as well. They will teach hatred to their children, if things go as they have in the past.

"But you can be of good cheer, my inquisitive friend. Each individual must make his or her own decision. No one can make it for anyone else. And every individual is vitally important to God. That is why Jesus suffered so much, because of how much He loves each person.

"Everyone has been given gifts that only he or she can use at this particular point in history to further the Kingdom. Of course without faith in Jesus, all the good works in the world are of no value. But with *Him*, the work takes on real meaning, both now and for eternity. And it's not about success in man's eyes. Some may be called to go before many and serve.

Some may be called to help others with only a few ever knowing about it. Or maybe even *no one* else knowing. But good works done in service of the one true God, whether they are made known to man or not, will be recognized and rewarded by Him. Be assured of that. This means you too, Joseph. The potential is tremendous. But it all begins with faith in Jesus. Without that, the rest is worthless.

"You won't need that staff and blanket anymore. Trust me on this one."

Joseph cut his eyes toward Tysius as the angel changed the subject so quickly. Just then the young boy who had helped Joseph find Daniel came around a bend in the path.

"Hello, how are you?" The boy couldn't hide his excitement at seeing his two new friends again. He gave Moon a big hug around his thick mane as he grinned from ear to ear.

Joseph struggled to shift gears. "Oh, hello – we're fine – just fine. This is my friend, Tysius." As soon as he said it, Joseph knew he'd messed up. The boy looked around quizzically, shrugged and looked at Moon while petting his big golden head. Moon returned the greeting with his own big grin and swinging tail.

"Whatever you say," the boy replied.

Joseph looked at Tysius, who smiled innocently and shrugged his shoulders. Then he pointed at the staff and blanket. Joseph gave him a puzzled look for a moment, and then understood what Tysius meant.

"Do you think you could do me another favor?" Joseph asked as he turned back to the boy. "Do you think you could find my friend Daniel again?"

"Sure, I could find him. What do you want me to tell him this time?"

"Well, I'd like you to give him this staff for me. And tell him – tell him that if I don't see him soon, I will see him again. I give him my absolute word on that. Just tell him that he needs to keep believing on Jesus, no matter what. He needs to tell his family this too. Can you remember that? And can you use this blanket? I don't think we'll need it anymore."

The young boy's eyes lit up. "Sure, I can remember what to tell him, and my family could really use that blanket. I'll tell him just exactly as you said it, too."

Joseph unfolded the blanket and took one last look at it as he remembered his friends Lucius and Isaac. He rolled it back up and handed it to the boy. "You take good care of that now. It has served us well; a couple of dear friends gave it to us."

Then Joseph studied his staff one last time as he remembered the battle with Krog and how the image of the lamb had cut the evil creature when neither he nor Moon had the power to fight. The lamb on the staff now appeared pure white, almost glowing. Joseph smiled as he ran his hand across it and remembered when Daniel and Sarah had carved it for him as a gift. He handed the staff to the boy. Then he reached into his pocket and pulled out all the money he had. He looked at Tysius, who nodded his agreement.

"Here," said Joseph as he handed it all to the boy. "Please just give the staff to Daniel. Tell him I could have never, ever, gotten along without it, but I won't need it anymore. He should take good care of it, or pass it on to someone else if he feels led to. *You* keep the money. I thank you for all your help. And you'll do well to believe on Jesus too, and tell your family about Him, okay?"

The boy's mouth dropped open as he saw all the money. Then he looked up at Joseph.

"Yes sir, I'll tell them alright. I'll tell them everything you said. Yes sir."

"Good," Joseph laughed. "Now you take care. And don't be forgetting this big dog either, okay?"

The boy patted Moon one last time with his free hand, then waved goodbye to Joseph and his dog. "Wait till Mother hears about this!"

"You catch on rather quickly now, Joseph," stated Tysius.

Joseph looked at him with mock indignation. "That's because I had a teacher who would never tell me anything. Moondog and I had to figure everything out on our own since you wouldn't answer any of my questions."

"Come now, Joseph," said Tysius. "Never answer anything? Never?"

"Well, not much anyway. Had to learn most of it ourselves."

"Exactly," smiled Tysius.

"Oh brother." Joseph rolled his eyes. "You think it was fun trying to figure everything out when you could've answered my questions right away? It wasn't a lot of fun, you know?"

"Yes, I believe I do know. But tell me, Joseph, do you think you'll ever forget the things you learned the hard way?"

Joseph mumbled as he smiled down at Moon and rubbed the top of his companion's head. Moon returned the grin.

"I didn't hear you, Joseph," said Tysius, "but I'll take that as an agreement with my statement. Regardless, let me help you to understand a few more things. Sin came into the human race long ago, with Adam and Eve. Sin is tremendously serious. It is deadly. There are huge consequences to it, as I believe you have recently learned firsthand. There needed to be a blood sacrifice for sin, because of how serious it is, in that it separates people from God. For years the Jews offered animal sacrifices to God for covering of their sin. They did it year after year because the sacrifice was incomplete, not sufficient to wash away their sins. Now, however, there has been the ultimate sacrifice for the sins of all people. God sent His only Son to this world to be the ultimate sacrifice. By believing on Him, by being obedient to Him, you can be set forever free from the curse of death. Forever free, Joseph.

"You will be tempted. You may even stumble and fall. But if you go straight to Him and confess your sin, He is faithful. He will forgive you your sin. He will also cleanse you from all unrighteousness. Sin is no longer just covered over, as with the past sacrifices of animals. Now it is taken away. The difference is tremendous. As you will soon read for yourself, 'He made Him Who knew no sin to be sin for us that we might become the righteousness of God in Him.'[1] This is not just some good idea or something to be taken lightly. Jesus paid a terrible price for you. Do you understand what I'm saying?"

"I think I'm beginning to."

"There isn't much time, Joseph, and I'm sure you still have many questions."

Joseph felt his stomach tighten and he took a deep breath. "Alright, tell me what happened to Sarah. I suppose she's married with a family of her own?"

"She was married but only for a few days. Her husband died in an accident."

Joseph stood stunned. "That must have been very painful for her."

"Actually, her husband was unfaithful to her both before and after the wedding. She found out about it soon after he died. So in reality she was spared some very deep pain in her future. She conceived during her short time with him and bore a son."

"What a jerk he must have been. So did she ever marry again?"

"No, she never did. And she is in her forties now, quite old for a woman in this culture to get married. She became a follower of Jesus and is in His close circle of friends. Marriage no longer enters her mind. If it is of any value for you to know, she was extremely fond of you. In fact she named her son Joseph."

"Really?"

"Really."

"To know that is of great value to me, Tysius. Thank you for telling me."

Tysius stopped walking and looked around. "Now we're almost where we need to be. Close your eyes."

"What?"

"Close your eyes. Trust me. You said the one desire in your heart is to see Jesus again, isn't it? Now close your eyes."

Joseph looked at Tysius, and then looked up to the heavens, then back at Tysius. Then he closed his eyes.

"Alright, you can open them now," replied Tysius in an instant.

Joseph opened his eyes. He stood in the exact same place. Moondog and Tysius also stood in the same place. A good distance away, on the other side of a valley, a small crowd of people now stood who weren't there a moment ago. Also something about their surroundings seemed different to Joseph, though he couldn't quite put his finger on it. Puzzled, he looked all around.

"What's the matter, Joseph?" asked Tysius.

"I – I don't know. There is something different here, even besides that group of people over there. There is something special about right where we are standing, but I can't quite figure out what it is. I don't think I've ever seen anything like this before. There's something unique about these plants around us, the flowers and the grass..."

Tysius shook his head in amazement. "I should have known you are too observant to have missed it, Joseph. Sometimes you impress me, I have to say. We're in the same place, but forty of your days have passed. You remember me telling you that we didn't have much time a while ago, don't you? Well, we don't. We have even less time now. Follow me."

"What are you talking about..." began Joseph, but Tysius spun around and walked toward the group of people, leaving Joseph and Moon behind. Joseph looked down at Moon and motioned for him to come along. They had to trot to catch up to Tysius.

Chapter 45

Joseph's father tied Cap to a tree and walked to the edge of the ridge overlooking the creek below. Hollering once more for his son, he slipped on a snow covered log. He tumbled through deep snow and slid into the icy creek, soaking his feet and lower legs. He scrambled up the bank out of the cold water. His shoulders slumped as he trudged back up the slope and untied Cap. He knew he couldn't last much longer now without getting back to the warmth of home.

He turned Cap back toward the south and continued his search. After a short while the horse stumbled over a fallen tree. This time, exhaustion prevented Cap from getting his feet back under him and he fell heavily into the snow. The man tumbled off, and snow found its way down his back. The shock and the icy chill sapped what little strength he had left.

Both man and horse struggled to their feet. Joseph's father held Cap's head next to his own and spoke softly to the frightened and weary horse. "We're going to be okay, boy, it's going to be okay. You'll be alright. We've just got to find them soon." Then he shook most of the snow from his coat and looked around.

The snow fell as hard as ever and he felt cold and wet and bone-weary, but he would not give up. He knelt back down and searched with icy hands in the snow until he found his flashlight. He could now just barely work its switch with his numb fingers. He shined the light up to the skies as if to get God's attention for his desperate prayers.

Snowflakes filled the shaft of light, but he thought he saw some type of movement at the end of the beam. It came from up in the trees, yet it didn't look like snow. It vanished and re-appeared almost as soon as he looked at it. He whispered, "Am I starting to hallucinate?"

He stumbled and squinted as he looked upward. He studied the movement, but couldn't make out anything for sure. He turned off the light to conserve the dying batteries and reached for Cap's reins. Joseph's father struggled and pushed through the deep snow leading Cap toward the movement he had just discerned. The tired horse stepped obediently behind, relieved to have a broken trail to follow.

After going a little distance, Joseph's father turned on the flashlight again, shining it up into the trees. He saw nothing at first, then thought he

247

caught a glimpse of the movement again. "What *is* that?" he said to himself and Cap.

He tapped the flashlight with its fading batteries against his hand and shone it skyward once more, straining to see the area up in the trees. Then he saw it. Smoke! Light smoke wafting slowly upward through the falling snow. Perhaps Joseph had started a fire to keep warm! Feeling a glimmer of hope for the first time that night, he let go of the reins and stumbled forward, tripping and falling into the heavy snow. He struggled to his feet, his breathing labored. Cap stayed put as Joseph's father staggered up to the big hollow tree. He shone the light up inside and his heart sank.

"It's smoking alright," he said softly to himself, "but not from any fire Joseph started. This thing got hit by lightning. It must have been the strike I saw from the house when the storm hit."

Joseph's father slumped against the big tree. The snow drift reached waist high, and his feet were numb; the cold, cruel night was rapidly sapping his dwindling strength. He turned off the weakening flashlight, closed his eyes, and tried to regain his composure.

<h1 style="text-align:center">Chapter 46</h1>

Joseph and Moon hurried to catch up with Tysius. They reached him just as he came to the bottom of a small valley. Though they still traveled toward the group of people, they couldn't see them due to the depression of the ground around them.

Tysius began to speak almost before Joseph got close enough to hear. Joseph knew his rapid words meant he had no time to repeat anything, so Joseph tried to focus as they rushed across the field, Moon trotting contentedly alongside.

"It is unusual for me to know specifics of some of the events I have spoken to you about, and some of those to come," Tysius stated. "But I think it is so you will remember later when I may not be able to speak to you. When Jesus comes again, it will be the most amazing thing this world of yours has ever known. The heavens will roll up like a scroll. The stars will be swept from the skies."

Joseph had never seen Tysius so animated.

"You remember how the magos brought Him the best gifts that they could?" Tysius gave Joseph no chance to answer as he strode up the hill. "Well this time, it will be He who brings the gifts. To those who are wicked, who have rejected the Son of God, He will bring everlasting judgment. But to those who have believed in Him, who have held on until the end, He will bring gifts beyond belief, Joseph.

"You may think that you have seen wondrous things in creation in your life so far, but none of it will compare to the incredible glory you will see then. All you've seen so far will not compare with what is to come for those who will hold on and obey Him, regardless of the cost.

"You came on this journey for a reason. This is just the beginning of your, what you call, adventures, Joseph, if you will believe it. But beware, there are many in this world who would have you stray from His way if you are not on guard. That may sound unthinkable to you right now, but the time will come, and the draw of the world and of the ways of men will be very strong. Do not forget this, lest you stumble.

"Be strong in the Lord, and in the power of His might. Put on the whole armor of God that you may stand against the wiles of the devil.[1] You do not need to be afraid of the likes of Krog."

Just then they reached the crest of the hill. From here, Joseph and Moon could clearly see the crowd of people.

"Oh wow!" exclaimed Joseph as they drew near. Moon saw Him too and began prancing about. They approached the edge of the crowd just as Jesus began rising into heaven. Joseph forgot all about Tysius for the moment.

Joseph stood still, his eyes wide and mouth open. Next to Joseph stood the faithful Moondog; the dog's tail was up, but motionless. All eyes remained on the Lord as He ascended into the sky. As He disappeared, Joseph, with the same wide-eyed expression on his face, turned slowly toward Tysius.

The angel stood in perfect posture. His hands were raised in honor and homage to the Lord, and his face was shining – glowing – as if it were reflecting the sun.

Joseph dared not say a word. Looking back into the seemingly empty sky, Joseph heard Tysius speak again. This time the words sounded much farther away than the angel next to him.

"You may not remember me, Joseph, but that won't matter. Do not be troubled by this. There is only One worthy of worship. I am just a servant of His, the same as you. Never worship His servants. Do you remember me telling you that you should be mindful to be whom God made you to be and not concern yourself with what others think or say about you? If you will heed this advice, events far greater than you can imagine await you. Peer pressure will tempt you to turn away from the Truth. Do not give in to it. Stay focused on the One Who died for you. Be who He created you to be. Farewell."

Unexpectedly another heavenly being was now standing next to Tysius; one of them spoke, but not to Joseph.

"Men of Galilee, why do you stand gazing up into heaven? This same Jesus, Who was taken up from you into heaven, will so come in like manner as you saw Him go into heaven."[2]

Joseph took a step back and knelt down beside Moon. He buried his head in Moon's thick mane, closed his eyes, and said a prayer of thanksgiving as the revelation of what he had experienced swirled in his thoughts. As he did so, he put his left arm under Moon's front legs and his right arm over Moon's back, hands joined, forming a complete circle with his arms.

Chapter 47

The disappointment of not finding Joseph beside a warm fire was too much. Joseph's father was crushed, and exhaustion won. He looked up to the heavens. His eyes misted over, and he cried out to God for help once more.

"Please, please tell me which way to go. I don't have a clue and the snow is deep. I can't go on without some direction." He held his breath and listened for some kind of answer but heard only the labored sound of his horse's breathing and the heavy snow landing on his hat. The man was panting now from exhaustion and desperation, and there was no strength left to even get back on Cap. He leaned numbly against the tree and waited.

Although a sturdy horse, even Cap had limits. Joseph's father knew the horse could not go much farther this night. Perhaps they could get back home and he could take one of the other horses out again. But how much longer could he himself hold out, even if he and Cap made it back? Perhaps Joseph had gotten home already. His mind began to reel from the thought of what might have happened to his only son.

Chapter 48

She had kept the candles burning in each of the windows for several hours, so that the house could be seen from any direction. Every so often Joseph's mother would rise from her knees to tend to them, making her rounds throughout the house, replacing candles that had burned down. But even as she left her knees she never stopped praying for her husband and son. She even found herself praying for Moondog too, that perhaps the Lord would give him strength to somehow find a way to help.

She looked at her watch: 4:00 am. Her husband had been gone for over seven hours now, Joseph and Moondog many more than that. She put two more logs on the fire and adjusted the draft on the woodstove. Then she returned to her place at the front window and knelt down.

As she had already done hundreds of times over the last seven hours, she shone her flashlight through the window, down the long winding driveway where she had watched her husband and Cap disappear into the night. Snow filled the beam of light as it pierced the darkness. She could barely make out the tall pines which lined the right side of the drive. The snow was already deep by the time Cap and her husband had left. But now because of all the new snow, she could scarcely make out the path they had taken. She turned off the flashlight and folded her hands on the windowsill, resting her head on them with her eyes closed.

Suddenly a log collapsed in the stove, startling her for a moment. She opened her eyes. The fire burned more fiercely, filling the room with the sounds of crackling sparks and embers. She closed her eyes again. Then she heard a faint noise, something that didn't sound quite right.

Joseph's mother lifted her head and stared out into the darkness. She turned on the flashlight and tried, by sheer will, to force the light to cut deeper through the falling snow. She was about to turn it off again when she thought she caught a slight movement at the end of the beam. She strained her eyes along the shaft of light, pressing her head against the window. Then she heard the sound again, only this time she heard it clearly enough – the sound that a horse makes when he's 'stretching out his lips.'

She leapt to her feet and ran to the front door. The eave had not stopped nearly three feet of snow drifting up against the door, but this proved no hindrance to a desperate mother. She shoved the door wide open. Standing in the nearly waist deep snow, she shone the flashlight down the drive and frantically called out to her husband. She heard no reply but could make out some motion – Cap, laboring through the deep snow, struggling to make it home.

Joseph's mother spun around and yanked on her boots and coat. In a matter of seconds, she was out the door, through the snow, and over the downed branches that covered the front yard and driveway.

Cap stood still. His sides were heaving, and blasts of steam puffed from his nostrils. The beam from the flashlight spiraled through the air while snow churned up in the whirlwind. Had the big horse been anything but dead-tired he would have bolted. But now he simply stood, wobbling under his load, his legs about to give out, but not his will to carry his precious cargo.

When Joseph's mother reached Cap, she involuntarily sucked in her breath. In spite of the biting cold, Cap was lathered and soaked. Sweat dripped from his belly as steam rolled off him like fog rising from a warm lake on a frosty morning. The reins lay on the snow on either side of him, balls of ice frozen to the ends. Over his wide back lay her son, face down, and limp as a wet rag. Behind him lay the golden Moondog, motionless and covered with snow. Her husband's ice-covered form bent over the two passengers. His hands appeared almost frozen around Cap's neck.

Her husband's head remained down and his eyes closed. He urged his horse on in a barely audible voice: "Home, Cap, take us home."

Joseph's mother took the reins and led the exhausted horse to the front porch. Then she pulled her husband off of Cap's back and with strength she didn't know she had, dragged him into the living room next to the stove. She threw a blanket over him and returned to retrieve Joseph, towing him into the room and covering him with quilts. Only then did she dare check for a pulse.

She whispered her gratitude as she stroked her son's face. "Thank God." Then she hurried back to bring Moondog in. She lay him gently next to Joseph and put a thick blanket over him. She returned to the faithful Cap. He stood on three legs with eyes nearly closed, snow changing to water as it landed on his steaming back.

Joseph's mother broke a path to the barn as she led Cap to his stall. She pulled off his saddle and toweled him down. Then she threw in some extra straw and hay and gave the animal a big hug around his warm neck.

As she made her way back to the house, a small shaft of dazzling, glowing light broke through the eastern sky. It undercut the grey snow-clouds overhead and enveloped her home. She opened the door and found her husband fast asleep but Joseph up and leaning on his elbows. Next to him sat his big golden Moondog, still covered with his blanket.

At the sight of his mother, Joseph smiled widely, too tired to get up, and almost too tired to speak. Moon flopped his tail twice under the blanket, and then lay down next to Joseph, resting his weary head on his master's lap.

As his mother approached, tears filled her eyes. She held her son close. "Joseph, my dear Joseph," she said over and over. Finally she sat next to him as Joseph lay down flat on his back.

"Oh, Mom," he whispered, "you won't believe what happened! We were there. We were there! We saw Jesus, Mom. We *saw* Him! And Mary and Joseph. And Daniel and Sarah and Ruben and Simon. And Lucius and Silas. We saw them, Mom. Me and Moon. We saw them."

"Now, now, Joseph," said his mother as she gently put her loving hand on the side of his face. "Just rest, my son. You're home now. You're home. We can talk later. Just try to sleep now. You're home."

"But, Mom," protested Joseph. He tried to sit up, but exhaustion pulled him back down. "We saw Jesus, Mom. We saw Him! The self-sacrifice of the King for His Kingdom. He's alive. We *saw* Him!"

"It's alright, Joseph. It's alright. You're home now, and so is your father. And so are Moondog and Cap. Everything is going to be alright. Just rest now; we'll talk later."

Joseph tried to explain, but weariness won out. Before sleep overwhelmed him, Joseph laid his left hand on Moon's snout as his companion's head rested on his chest. The big dog let out a long and exhausted sigh as he and his young master fell into a deep, deep sleep.

Chapter 49

Of the many who walk this earth, only a handful are blessed with the ability to observe outdoor life to the extent of Joseph and Moon. But even a casual observer would have had trouble missing the scar when the weary travelers awakened later that day. For under Joseph's left hand, on Moon's snout, a mark remained which had not existed before they took this particular walk in the woods. An old scar, from a long, long time ago, and well healed over. Anyone who took the time to look could now see it. Not surprisingly, Joseph had noticed it first, then Ruben and Sarah, soon after the wolf attack.

The mark remained in perfect form. The mark of the *ichthys*.

~~~

The End of Book One
~~~

End Notes

Chapter 7. [1]Luke 2:14
Chapter 15 [1]Micah 5:2
Chapter 24. [1]Romans 3:23
Chapter 25. [1]Luke 7:6-8
Chapter 28. [1]Luke 7:13   [2]Luke 7:14
Chapter 29. [1]Matthew 8:2   [2]Matthew 8:3   [3]Matthew 8:4
Chapter 42. [1]Luke 24:5-6
Chapter 44 [1] 2 Corinthians 5:21
Chapter 46 [1] Ephesians 6:10-11   [2]Acts 1:11

About the Author

Thomas Trock is a career biologist with the Fish and Wildlife Service. He enjoys hiking "where no man has gone before," armed with a backpack, fly rod, and one of the goofiest dogs on the planet. When not reveling in the solitude of the mountains, he likes to visit nursing homes with Star the Wonderdog and serenade the residents with his acoustic guitar.

Thomas has lived in Africa, and he and his beloved wife have worked with some remarkable folks in several third-world countries. He describes himself as a simple man who has found a remarkable Truth.

Some of his favorite movies are *The Secrets of Jonathan Sperry*, *The Chronicles of Narnia* series, and *Babe*.

Theodor Geisel is a favorite author, as Thomas claims Dr. Seuss is one of the few writers he can understand. Usually. Well – sometimes anyway.

~~~

To read about the real Moondog who helped inspire this book, or find out about other books by Thomas, please visit:
Thomastrock.com

~~~

Thank YOU for reading my book. If you enjoyed it, please take a moment to leave a review at your favorite book retailer.

Hafoof!

www.ingramcontent.com/pod-product-compliance
Lightning Source LLC
Chambersburg PA
CBHW031231120726
47905CB00002B/550